Main Street (1920) was the first successful novel written by **Sinclair Lewis** (1885–1951), and his reputation was secured by the publication of *Babbitt* (1922). Lewis was awarded a Pulitzer Prize for *Arrowsmith* (1925) but refused to accept the honor. He did accept, however, when in 1930 he became the first American writer to receive the Nobel Prize for Literature. During the latter part of his life, he spent a great deal of time in Europe and continued to write both novels and plays.

Sally E. Parry is the Director of Undergraduate Studies for the English Department of Illinois State University. She is currently the Executive Director of the Sinclair Lewis Society and editor of the *Sinclair Lewis Society Newsletter.* Her articles have appeared in numerous journals, and in such books as the *Encyclopedia of the Midwest, War and American Popular Culture,* and *Encyclopedia of Urban America.* She has also contributed chapters to books such as *Grant Wood's Main Street: Art, Literature, and the American Midwest; Sinclair Lewis: New Critical Essays; Nancy Drew and Company: Culture, Gender, and Girls' Series;* and *Sinclair Lewis at 100.*

GO EAST, YOUNG MAN

SINCLAIR LEWIS
ON CLASS IN AMERICA

Edited and with an Introduction by
Sally E. Parry

SIGNET CLASSICS

SIGNET CLASSICS
Published by New American Library, a division of
Penguin Group (USA) Inc., 375 Hudson Street,
New York, New York 10014, USA
Penguin Group (Canada), 10 Alcorn Avenue, Toronto,
Ontario M4V 3B2, Canada (a division of Pearson Penguin Canada Inc.)
Penguin Books Ltd., 80 Strand, London WC2R 0RL, England
Penguin Ireland, 25 St. Stephen's Green, Dublin 2,
Ireland (a division of Penguin Books Ltd.)
Penguin Group (Australia), 250 Camberwell Road, Camberwell, Victoria 3124,
Australia (a division of Pearson Australia Group Pty. Ltd.)
Penguin Books India Pvt. Ltd., 11 Community Centre, Panchsheel Park,
New Delhi - 110 017, India
Penguin Group (NZ), cnr Airborne and Rosedale Roads, Albany,
Auckland 1310, New Zealand (a division of Pearson New Zealand Ltd.)
Penguin Books (South Africa) (Pty.) Ltd., 24 Sturdee Avenue,
Rosebank, Johannesburg 2196, South Africa

Penguin Books Ltd., Registered Offices:
80 Strand, London WC2R 0RL, England

Published by Signet Classics, an imprint of New American Library,
a division of Penguin Group (USA) Inc.

First Signet Classics Printing, March 2005
10 9 8 7 6 5 4 3 2 1

Library of Congress Catalog Card Number: 2004025036

Printed in the United States of America

Contents

Introduction

Sinclair Lewis was ambivalent about the American Dream. He was well aware that American culture celebrates the acquisition of money and rise in social position that comes with it. However he was uneasy about this as a central value and usually presented it ironically in his writings. He was awarded the Pulitzer Prize in 1926 for his novel *Arrowsmith,* but refused it, contending that such prizes are "dangerous." He felt not only that competition among writers was wrong, but that a prize such as this confirmed the status quo. The Pulitzer's terms are that the chosen novel should represent "the wholesome atmosphere of American life," a phrase that had nothing to do with "literary merit," Lewis noted, other than "whatever code of Good Form may chance to be popular at the moment." The controversy that he aroused by his refusal drew attention to his concerns about the limited value of fame and money.

His goals for his fiction were not modest. He wanted to shake up American society. Although he knew that his country would never be perfect, he tried to expose its flaws in the hope that Americans would take heed and do better, rather than just be satisfied with things as they are. The Nobel Prize Committee respected this and in 1930 awarded Sinclair Lewis the Nobel Prize for Literature, the first American to be so honored. Many people thought Lewis hypocritical for accepting this award after refusing the Pulitzer. But Lewis felt that the Nobel Prize honored his vision and the body of his work and was quite different from the competition occasioned by the Pulitzer. Some critics, especially proponents of what Malcolm Cowley called the "safe genteel literary tradition" (Cowley, p. 6), expressed concern that Europeans were confirming their prejudices against overly materialistic Americans by choosing Lewis (Anderson, pp. 84–90). But the award should be seen as positive, proving that American literature had truly come into its own. Erik Axel Karfeldt, one of the Nobel jurors, especially praised *Main Street* and *Babbitt* for their characters and saw Lewis's criticism of the United States as "a sign of health" of the nation (Karfeldt, p. 82). Karfeldt said of Lewis, "He asks us to consider that this nation is not finished yet or melted down; that it is still in the turbulent years of adolescence" (Karfeldt, p. 82). In a tribute following his death, Lewis's second wife, journalist Dorothy Thompson, echoed this, writing that he had rebelled all his life against "mediocrity—enthroned as the God of Democracy" (Thompson, p. 1).

In Lewis's fiction, there are many characters who fall prey to the American Dream, never being satisfied with what they have and always wanting more. Lewis describes the culture in such a way that it's evident his characters are not bad people, but feel pressured by society's expectations. There is a sense of ambivalence in his portrayal. He shows sympathy for people who cannot figure out what is truly important in life but rely on what they've been told by the media, politicians, and other authority figures. A good example of how society has enculturated its citizens with this desire occurs in Lewis's bestselling novel *Babbitt* (1922). George F. Babbitt is a real estate salesman whose name has become synonymous with the striving but secretly discontented businessman. Early in the novel Babbitt tries to convince his son, Theodore Roosevelt Babbitt, that he needs to go to college so that he can get a good job and go on to law school, a plan that will move him up in class both socially and economically. Ted, however, is interested in cars, airplanes, and new technology and doesn't see the connection between getting ahead in the world and an education.

"I don't see what's the use of law-school—or even finishing high school. I don't want to go to college 'specially. Honest, there's lot of fellows that have graduated from colleges that don't begin to make as much money as fellows that went to work early. Old Shimmy Peters, that teaches Latin in the High, he's a what-is-it from Columbia and he sits up all night reading a lot of greasy books and he's always spieling about the 'value of languages,' and the poor soak doesn't make but eighteen hundred a year, and no traveling salesman would think of working for that." (Lewis, *Babbitt*, pp. 73–74)

Although Babbitt is sympathetic to his son's enthusiastic desire to make money, he argues that education is important not just for monetary reasons. He tells Ted, "Trouble with a lot of folks is: they're so blame material; they don't see the spiritual and mental side of American supremacy; . . . they think these mechanical improvements are all that we stand for; whereas to a real thinker, he sees that spiritual and, uh, dominating movements like Efficiency, and Rotarianism, and Prohibition, and Democracy are what compose our deepest and truest wealth" (Lewis, *Babbitt*, p. 82). Babbitt tries his best to present what he believes are higher-class ideas about education, but because he can't articulate any thoughts beyond the superficial, deep down life really does seem to be about the money.

Lewis was nevertheless sympathetic to the dreamer in both Babbitt and Ted, although his father, Dr. E. J. Lewis, was firmly convinced that the way to get ahead in the world was by joining a profession and making money. Dr. Lewis encouraged all three of his sons, Fred, Claude, and Harry (Sinclair), to become professionals. The oldest, Fred, ran a flour mill rather than becoming the dentist that he started out to be; Claude became what his father wanted, a successful doctor and surgeon, one whom young Harry looked up to and to whom he always felt a little inferior. Harry was imaginative and smart, and wanted to be a writer, not a practical choice according to his father. Dr. Lewis once said to Fred and Claude, "You boys will always be able to make a living. But poor Harry, there's nothing he can do" (Lingeman, p. 7). At the end of his life Dr. Lewis seemed astonished that his son was not only able to make money by something as nebulous as writing, but that the world would celebrate him for it.

Sauk Centre, Minnesota, where Lewis was born in 1885, was a practical pioneer town that Lewis would alternately flee from and return to, at least in spirit. As one can see from his 1927 "Self-Portrait," the adventurous, romantic Lewis alternates with the practical, self-aware Midwesterner who is skeptical of pomposity, pretentiousness, and self-aggrandizement. This sketch provides a good introduction to Lewis the man and to those things about which he is passionate. It also discloses one of Lewis's working methods—that of trying out the language of his characters in social situations. He was a man with a highly sensitive ear for the way that people, particularly middle-class people, spoke in ordinary conversation. In many of his stories, what stands out is how his characters reveal themselves in their speech. This is especially true as they try to impress one another with their social standing or at least with how they want others to perceive it. Their language usually gives them away.

In an unpublished introduction to *Babbitt*, Lewis discusses the great mass of business people who have made the United States a complacent and standardized nation. Although America ranks high in terms of creature comforts, its citizens in general seem to value intellectual accomplishments or the arts only as a way to gain status in the eyes of others. To Lewis the arts seem to serve many people as "obvious symbols of prosperity [that] give social prestige. To attend a concert is almost as valuable a certificate of wealth as to be seen riding in a Pierce-Arrow car."

The short story "Things" (1919) is an excellent example of this need for acquisition as a way to prove one's rise in social class. Lyman Duke makes a fortune from iron mines in northern Minnesota and transforms himself from an average person into one who must buy and furnish a mansion in order to announce to the world how rich he is. Like William Randolph Hearst or the fictional Charles Foster Kane, Duke brings home "a carload of treasures" to furnish the mansion, and although he becomes "exceedingly weary" of all the things he is accumulating, as a "celebrated collector one must keep on collecting and showing the collections." This acquisitiveness isolates him from the rest of the community and even his family. But because of Lewis's optimism that there is a level of self-reflection in all good people, Duke is finally able to confront his possessions and recognize them for the prison they are.

The desire for money and the ill effects it can bring are even more dramatically illustrated in "The Willow Walk" (1918). This is a creepy tale of Jasper Holt, a trusted bank teller by day and a gifted actor in community theater by night. He puts his talents to work by creating a spurious twin brother, who is a religious fanatic and recluse, someone he can become after he takes advantage of his position and embezzles money. Unlike Duke, he becomes so caught up in his other life that he is unable to make an escape.

Sidney Dow of "Land" (1931) also leads a double life. He is a respectable dentist, but he has always had a deep desire to become a farmer, as his grandparents were. However, he "was named Sidney, for the sake of elegance," and every time he tried to throw off the upward mobility that his parents thrust upon him, he was rebuffed. His father, much like George Babbitt or Dr. E. J. Lewis, told him "he should go to college, he should be a doctor or a preacher or a lawyer, he should travel in Europe, he should live in a three-story graystone house in the Forties in Manhattan. . . ." Although he grudgingly studies to be a dentist, he keeps hoping to return to his grandfather's farm, but his wife, echoing his parents, insists that farming is not a job for someone who wants to amount to anything.

In many of his short stories Lewis toned down the social criticism that was prominent in his novels. Most of these stories were published in popular magazines, such as the *Saturday Evening Post, Redbook,* and *Cosmopolitan,* and were expected to adhere to primarily positive presentations of American culture. "Young Man Axelbrod" (1917), for example, contains a critique of education, but the focus is on the personal—Knute Axelbrod, a sixty-four-year-old man who decides to go to college. He is a farmer, the sort of dull, plain man that Sidney Dow wanted to be. "All his life he had wanted to. Why not do it?" He studies Latin, German, history, and English literature, and like Lewis, gets accepted at Yale University. Unfortunately the Yale that Axelbrod attends is full of people who are there to get ahead rather than to acquire knowledge for its own sake. Like Ted Babbitt, most of them scorn knowledge unless it gets them something. One magical day Axelbrod meets a fellow scholar, and they read poetry, attend a concert, and stay up all night talking of "great men and heroic ideals." For Axelbrod, this night is the one he "had lived almost seventy years and traveled fifteen hundred miles" to experience. But he also comes to the realization that the scholarly life he has romanticized does not really exist.

The opposite dream is evident in "Go East, Young Man" (1930). Whitney Dibble lives in Zenith, the same city as Babbitt, and like Sidney Dow, his father wants Whitney to be what he could never be himself. Whit's father, T. Jefferson Dibble, is a successful businessman with a yen for the arts, the chairman of a lecture committee and a member of the Opera Festival Committee. Because T. Jefferson, like his father before him, has to spend his life in an office, he wants his son to do something better. "I hope I shall live to see you one of the world's great pictorial artists, exhibiting in London, Rome, Zenith, and elsewhere . . . making a bigger and better—no, no, I mean a bigger and—a bigger—I mean a better world!" He, like Babbitt, confuses achievement with an elevated place in society. But Whit is more like his father and grandfather than anyone cares to admit; his art is the art of the salesman.

Whit Dibble and George Babbitt see adventure and romance in aspects of business, and Lewis was able to adopt that perspective sympathetically. Lewis was familiar with many different types of jobs. While in college, he was a janitor for Upton Sinclair's Helicon Hall and worked on a cattleboat, and after graduation from Yale, he was a reporter, a secretary for a pair of writers, a translator, and an editor and publicist for a publishing house. In short stories as well as novels such as *The Job, Babbitt,* and *Work of Art* he portrays the drama of life in the office, a place where people spend many of their waking hours, but which is infrequently portrayed in literature. Although many writers have considered the business world an uninspiring place in which to set a novel, Lewis felt that the heart of the American character was there and struck a chord with his readers. An example of this business drama is "Moths in the Arc Light" (1919), which shows the hierarchy in offices and the situation of women who must work for a living in a time when "nice" women didn't work. Bates, a successful executive, and "glad that he was a business man," romanticizes a young secretary in the building across the street from his office. Over a number of months, they develop a relationship solely based on observation, occasional waves, gestures, and pantomimes. He develops a fantasy about her family and her life, one that eventually is shattered when she turns out to be an ordi-

nary young woman who has to make her way in the
world. He becomes her Prince Charming who wants
to take her away from her lonely life, although he
values the work that she does.

Another tale of an upper-class man romancing a
woman from straitened economic circumstances is
found in the charming story "Speed" (1919). Lewis
often contrasted the experiences of small-town and
urban America, aware that the country was undergo-
ing a major shift in population. His novel *Main Street*
(1920) criticized small towns for having an inflated
sense of self-importance and a narrow-mindedness
that is often antithetical to new people and new ideas.
But he was aware that the small town "was still con-
ventionally viewed—as by Sinclair Lewis himself in
other moods—as the best place after all, the real
America, America at its roots, America at its kindest,
its friendliest, its human best" (Schorer, p. 271). Lewis's ambivalence is muted in this tale of professional
driver J. T. Buffum, whose car breaks down in a small
Iowa town. There he meets a young female school-
teacher who seems to him reminiscent of old New
England villages and a simpler way of life. She consid-
ers him an "aristocrat" because he is adventurous,
doing "things that other people don't dare to." Because he finds her refreshingly old-fashioned, he decides to gain her favor by bringing her back something
from her ancestral hometown in Massachusetts, where
her family had a mansion. Ironically he finds out that
her father made up this romanticized past, complete
with phony pictures of houses and ancestors, and that
her grandfather was a drunken Portuguese fisherman.
Rather than making him feel sorry for her, this knowledge gives him the courage to convince her to break
away from this falsely constructed past and come away
with him to start a new life, not defined by past social standing.

Lewis's ambivalence about small towns is more evident in "The Hack Driver" (1923), a humorous tale
about another urban man coming to a small town,

but this time receiving his comeuppance rather than a fiancée. A young lawyer with aspirations to "houses and motors and expensive wives" dreams of being famous so that he can "dine at large houses with men who shuddered at the Common People who don't dress for dinner." However, the reality is that he is fifteenth assistant clerk at a large law firm and is sent to serve a summons in a small village. The man he's seeking always seems to be one step ahead of him, despite all the help that the local taxi driver and every other inhabitant in town can provide. This story is one that the author of *Main Street* must have found amusing to write since he presents the small-town inhabitant and his native creativity with fondness.

In "He Had a Brother" (1929), one of Lewis's most serious and autobiographical short stories, the small town becomes a place of escape—from stress, competition, and alcohol. Ostensibly the story of Charles Haddon, successful attorney and alcoholic, its descriptions of the hangovers, guilt, and the difficulty of quitting drinking come very close to Lewis's well-known problems with alcohol. Haddon visits his brother in a small town in order to escape from his drinking friends, much as Lewis visited his own brother Claude and later traveled with him in order to have his support and guidance. But Haddon finds drinking buddies in his brother's town, as Lewis did when he returned to Sauk Centre. Although Haddon seems to reform his ways in the face of a crisis, his permanent recovery is left ambiguous.

The search for a better life is part of the American Dream, but all too often people don't exactly know what it is they want. Doctor Selig, in the bittersweet "Letter from the Queen" (1929), hopes to become a famous historian and chooses to vacation near the home of a retired senator, eager to interview him in connection with his partially completed manuscript on European history. The story becomes a commentary on fame in America. As Selig notes, "we honor our great men in America—sometimes for as much as two months after the particular act of greatness that tickles us. . . . We mustn't let anyone suppose that because we have given him an (undesired) parade up Broadway and a (furiously resented) soaking of publicity on March first, he may expect to be taken seriously on May second." And unfortunately for the ninety-two-year-old Senator Ryder, who welcomed the renewed attention, Selig proves to be a "true" American, whose interest in the senator flags when he meets an attractive young woman.

"I'm a Stranger Here Myself" (1916) and "Ring Around a Rosy" (1931) reflect, albeit humorously, the peripatetic nature, not just of Americans, but human beings in general, who assume that happiness can always be found somewhere other than where they are. In the first of these stories, the Johnsons travel around the country, hoping they can impress the folks back home and improve their social status, even though every place they go they invariably compare unfavorably to their hometown. The second story focuses on four couples, each in a different country, who want to move to another country because they perceive that the next place they go will be better—more historic, more civilized, more open to ideas, more up-to-date. But this is a story of the grass being always greener elsewhere—the attributes of a country that make it appealing to one couple make it very unappealing to the next.

Sinclair Lewis was a good storyteller with an ear for the way that people spoke. When we read these stories, we can hear the voices of men and women of the past, their hopes and aspirations and disappointments, and travel with them to the towns and cities where their fates are played out. Lewis holds a unique place in American letters for being able to combine popular success with social criticism. Paradoxically his criticisms were a mixture of love and disgust: love of his country and the people within it, and disgust at the way in which the greedy and ignorant are threatening to pervert the democratic ideals on which this nation was founded. For his incisive depiction of the many facets of the American character, Sinclair Lewis merits continuing study as a critical voice for the American people.

—Sally E. Parry

Works Cited

Anderson, Carl L. *The Swedish Acceptance of American Literature*. Philadelphia: University of Pennsylvania Press, 1957.

Cowley, Malcolm. "Foreword: The Revolt Against Gentility." *After the Genteel Tradition*. 1937. Carbondale: Southern Illinois University Press, 1964.

Karfeldt, Erik Axel. "Why Sinclair Lewis Got the Nobel Prize." *Why Sinclair Lewis Got the Nobel Prize and Address by Sinclair Lewis Before the Swedish Academy*. Trans. Naboth Hedin. New York: Harcourt Brace, 1930. Rpt. in *Twentieth Century Interpretations of* Arrowsmith*: A Collection of Critical Essays*. Ed. Robert J. Griffin. Englewood Cliffs: Prentice Hall, 1968.

Lewis, Sinclair. *Babbitt*, 1922. New York: Signet, 1998.

Lingeman, Richard. *Sinclair Lewis: Rebel from Main Street*. New York: Random House, 2002.

Schorer, Mark. *Sinclair Lewis: An American Life*. New York: McGraw-Hill, 1961.

Thompson, Dorothy. "On the Record: Another Peak Falls." Column written for Bell Syndicate, 15 January 1951. Dorothy Thompson Papers. George Arents Library, Syracuse University.

GO EAST,
YOUNG MAN

Letter to the Pulitzer Prize Committee

Sirs:—I wish to acknowledge your choice of my novel *Arrowsmith* for the Pulitzer Prize. That prize I must refuse, and my refusal would be meaningless unless I explained the reasons.

All prizes, like all titles, are dangerous. The seekers for prizes tend to labor not for inherent excellence but for alien rewards: they tend to write this, or timorously to avoid writing that, in order to tickle the prejudices of a haphazard committee. And the Pulitzer Prize for novels is peculiarly objectionable because the terms of it have been constantly and grievously misrepresented.

Those terms are that the prize shall be given "for the American novel published during the year which shall best present the wholesome atmosphere of American life, and the highest standard of American manners and manhood." This phrase, if it means anything whatever, would appear to mean that the appraisal of the novels shall be made not according to their actual literary merit but in obedience to whatever code of Good Form may chance to be popular at the moment.

That there is such a limitation of the award is little understood. Because of the condensed manner in which the announcement is usually reported, and be-

cause certain publishers have trumpeted that any
novel which has received the Pulitzer Prize has thus
been established without qualification as *the best*
novel, the public has come to believe that the prize is
the highest honor which an American novelist can
receive.

The Pulitzer Prize for novels signifies, already, much
more than a convenient thousand dollars to be accepted even by such writers as smile secretly at the
actual wording of the terms. It is tending to become
a sanctified tradition. There is a general belief that the
administrators of the prize are a pontifical body with
the discernment and power to grant the prize as the
ultimate proof of merit. It is believed that they are
always guided by a committee of responsible critics,
though in the case both of this and other Pulitzer
Prizes, the administrators can, and sometimes do,
quite arbitrarily reject the recommendations of their
supposed advisers.

If already the Pulitzer Prize is so important, it is
not absurd to suggest that in another generation it
may, with the actual terms of the award ignored, become the one thing for which any ambitious novelist
will strive; and the administrators of the prize may
become a supreme court, a college of cardinals, so
rooted and so sacred that to challenge them will be
to commit blasphemy. Such is the French Academy,
and we have had the spectacle of even an Anatole
France intriguing for election.

Only by regularly refusing the Pulitzer Prize can
novelists keep such a power from being permanently
set up over them.

Between the Pulitzer Prizes, the American Academy of Arts and Letters and its training-school, the
National Institute of Arts and Letters, amateur boards
of censorship, and the inquisition of earnest literary
ladies, every compulsion is put upon writers to become
safe, polite, obedient, and sterile. In protest, I declined
election to the National Institute of Arts and Letters

some years ago, and now I must decline the Pulitzer Prize.

I invite other writers to consider the fact that by accepting the prizes and approval of these vague institutions we are admitting their authority, publicly confirming them as the final judges of literary excellence, and I inquire whether any prize is worth that subservience.

> I am, Sirs,
> Yours sincerely,
> (Signed) Sinclair Lewis

Self-Portrait
(Berlin, August 1927)

Mr. Joseph Hergesheimer, an American author whom I peculiarly recommend to Europe because he is free of that sociological itch which afflicts so many writers like myself, said once in a brief autobiography that there was really nothing to recount of Hergesheimer the man which had not already been exhibited in the characters of his novels. And that is true of every novelist who, whether he be capable or lacking, is a serious workman.

It is not true of the hack writer. In private life the hack is often a charming fellow, a seer and a companion to his children, tolerable to his wife, an excellent poker-player, and a great camp cook, despite the sapless virgin heroines and the pompously patriotic heroes whom he has created.

Mr. Hergesheimer's contention I may claim for myself. Whether or no there is any merit in my books, I do not know and I do not vastly care, since I have had the somewhat exhausting excitement of writing them. But, good or not, they have in them everything I have been able to get from life or to give to life.

There is really no Sinclair Lewis about whom even that diligent scribbler himself could write, outside of what appears in his characters. All his respect for learning, for integrity, for accuracy, and for the possibilities of human achievement are to be found not in the rather hectic and exaggerative man as his intimates see him, but in his portrait of Professor Max Gottlieb, in *Arrowsmith.* Most of the fellow's capacity for loyalty to love and friendship has gone into Leora in that same novel, and into the account of George F. Babbitt's affection for his son and for his friend Paul— most, but thank Heaven, not quite all, since it is one of the few virtues of Lewis, in *propria persona,* that he remains fond and almost childishly admiring of a few friends, men and women. And whatever potentialities for hard, lean, Lindbergh-courage this Lewis, this product of the pioneer forests and wheatfields of Minnesota, may once have had, it has seemingly all gone into the depiction of such characters as "Hawk" Ericson (that aviator so curiously like Lindbergh, though created a dozen years ago) in the *Trail of the Hawk* or the resolute country doctor, Will Kennicott, in *Main Street,* or Frank Shallard, quakingly but unyieldingly facing the bloody Fundamentalist fanatics in *Elmer Gantry.* In his private life, the fellow himself has no drop of such courage. He trembles on the funiculars of the Swiss mountains, in automobiles speeding on wet pavements, on ships moaning terror in the mid-sea fog.

I am assuredly not indulging in that pretended modesty which is a reversed and irritating egotism—that "see me, I'm so noble that I can even admit that I am not noble." Nor am I hinting that here is a case interesting in its peculiarity. It's very common. I know a novelist who, in that real and uninhibited portion of him which is his novels, depicts with authentic impressiveness a high, free, passionate, winged love between men and women, but who in private life is always creeping and peeping around corners as pitifully as any clerk starving for romance in his boarding-house. I know another who is all strength and soaring beauty in his books, yet privately sits by his fireside, puffy, pudgy, fussing over little bibelots. And I know a good many writers who find that the best inspiration for their accounts of austere self-rule is to be had in a bottle of whisky.

No! If the ordinary lay-reader were wise, he would flee desperately from meeting most of his favorite authors. And this ecclesiastical secret which I am so unprofessionally giving away explains why the biographies of authors would be achingly dull if they were but written honestly.

Take the subject of this particular biography—Sinclair Lewis.

There was never in private life a less attractive or admirable fellow—except to a few people who like him from perversity or because they find his conversation amusing. Of that one thing, talk, he is a master, in certain of its minor and more flippant and hysterical phases. He imitates an American Babbitt boasting about his motor car, a Swede or a Yankee speaking German, a college professor lecturing ponderously on nothing in particular.

An occasional auditor is delighted and exclaims, "This Lewis is giving us the very soul of a character, and through him of a civilization."

But they overpraise the fellow. When they know him well enough, they find him repeating these parlor tricks over and over, as childishly as the village clowns described in his own *Main Street*. And anyway, he is really only practicing, only making a sketch, for the next character he is to paint. When he is in such almost vaudeville-like moods, he is intolerably inconsiderate of the fact that others in the company might now and then like to talk. He rides them down, bewilders them and buries them in the flood of his boisterous comedy. Only thus, apparently, can he impress them. In the profundities of scientific conferences, in the delicate give and take of well-bred worldly chatter, in really earnest and scholarly consideration of the arts—even of his own novel-writing—the fellow is as dumb as a fish.

Besides a certain amount of lasting affection for his friends and this pyrotechnical conversation, the man

seems to me to have no virtues whatever save a real,
fiery, almost reckless hatred of hypocrisy—of what the
Americans call "bunk," from the older word "bun-
combe," and this may not be a virtue at all, but only
an envy-inspired way of annoying people by ignoring
their many excellent qualities and picking out the few
vices into which they have been betrayed by custom
and economic necessity.

He hates, equally, politicians who lie and bully and
steal under cover of windy and banal eloquence, and
doctors who unnecessarily and most lucratively convince their patients that they are ill; merchants who
misrepresent their wares, and manufacturers who pose
as philanthropists while underpaying their workmen;
professors who in wartime try to prove that the enemy
are all fiends, and novelists who are afraid to say what
seems to them the truth. Why, this man, still so near
to being an out and out Methodist or Lutheran that
he would far rather chant the hymns of his boyhood
evangelicism than the best drinking song in the world,
is so infuriated by ministers who tell silly little jokes
in the pulpit and keep from ever admitting publicly
their confusing doubts that he risks losing all the good
friends he once had among the ministers by the de-
nunciations in *Elmer Gantry*.

But aside from these three virtues—if they be
such—the man is a most dingy and unstimulating recluse. Tall, awkward, rusty of hair, long-nosed, dressed
neither handsomely nor with picturesque disarray, a
Yorkshire yeoman farmer with none of the farmer's
strength and horsey dash, he is a figure altogether unromantic. He has no hobbies save rather unimaginative travel to obvious and uninterestingly safe tourist
centers. And he has no games. He has never in his
life played bridge, golf, mah jong, or billiards; he plays
tennis like an eight-year-old boy—quite definitely and
literally so; his swimming is confined to a timorous
paddling near shore; and even in motoring, though he
comes from a land in which there must be at least
60,000,000 proficient drivers, he has as much dash and

speed as an archdeacon of eighty, with false teeth and rheumatism.

He detests polite dinner parties. As he listens to the amiable purring of nice matrons, he is afflicted with ennui as with disease. And years in Europe, even in Paris, have given him none of the charming tastes of the gourmet. He is (yet without any of the barbarian's virility) a barbarian in the arts of the table. He prefers whisky and soda to the most delicate vintage; he is often known to commit that least excusable of American atrocities—smoking cigarettes between courses at a perfect dinner. And he boasts. He may seem modest enough in writing, but when he is gabbling and off his guard, he tells at tedious length what fools are all the critics who criticize him.

The man is now forty-two. He looks, when he hasn't stayed up too late (as he is likely to do, talking, forever talking), slightly younger, because of his thinness. He was born, son and grandson of country doctors, in the sort of shambling prairie village which he has described in *Main Street*; a village of low wooden shops, of cottages each set in its little garden, of rather fine trees, with the wheat a golden sea for miles about.

His boyhood was utterly commonplace—lessons in school, swimming in summer, hunting ducks in the autumn, skating in winter, with such household tasks as sawing stove-wood and cleaning from the sidewalk the deep snow of the far-northern land. It was a boyhood commonplace except for a love of reading not very usual in that raw new town. He reveled in Dickens, Walter Scott, Washington Irving.

Doubtless this habit of reading led to his writing. He began as a wild romanticist. His first efforts were entirely in verse—banal and imitative verse, all about troubadours and castles as sagely viewed from the eminence of a Minnesota prairie village. It is ironical that later in regions where castles and the memory of troubadours really did exist—in Kent and Cornwall, Fontainebleau and London and Rome—he should sit writing of Minnesota prairie villages!

Lewis had a singularly easy youth. No picturesque chronicle of gallant fighting against poverty and inappreciation was his. His father sent him to Yale University; afterward he became a newspaper reporter, a magazine editor, and literary adviser to publishers. In between there were a few adventures and a few lean years but they were only amusing incidents of youth. He went to a radical co-operative colony as a janitor, and was titanically a failure at the job. He ventured to Panama, during the time when the great canal was being excavated, in the hope of a job in that picturesque jungle. He sailed to Panama in the steerage and came back stowaway—without the job! For a year and a half he lived in California; partly in a cottage near the beach of the Pacific, existing on borrowed money and trying to write short stories, in company with the American poet, William Rose Benét; partly doing (and doing very badly) newspaper work in San Francisco.

But from 1910 to December, 1915, he was a very prosaic and unenterprising editor in New York, acquiring a wife, and a conviction that he never would, never could, learn to compose anything more imaginative than advertisements for bad novels—though in America such advertisements can be very imaginative indeed. He did, with difficulty, manage to write two novels, *Our Mr. Wrenn* and *The Trail of the Hawk*, during evenings after days of editorial work, but they were financial failures and at first critically unnoticed.

A humorous story, written as a lark and without expectation that it would ever be published, opened for him the doors of the *Saturday Evening Post*, and in a few months he had enough money saved to be able to leave his position and start free lancing.

That was in December, 1915, and ever since then he has wandered, by train, motor, steamer, on foot. Naturally he is always being congratulated for thus scouring the world for information, and naturally he travels for no such estimable reason but only because he is afflicted with Wanderlust, which is one of the most devouring of diseases. In these eleven and a half years, the longest time he has spent in any one place was nine months in London. He has motored through nearly every state in America. He has seen Europe from Berlin down to Seville and Athens. He has spent weeks in Northern Canada, two hundred miles from any railroad or even wagon road. He has drifted through the West Indies to Venezuela and Colombia. But meantime he has written eleven books and some scores of short stories and articles, because he is able to settle down in a strange room in a strange city, and be serenely at work within three hours. During his hours of writing, he is indifferent as to whether his typewriter is beside a window looking on Fifth Avenue, a London fog, or a silent mountain.

He is vaguely thinking now of the Orient—of India, Java, Japan—from which it is to be judged that his Wanderlust is incorrigible.

A dull fellow, and probably unimaginative. Otherwise he would stay home and be inspired by his own vision instead of having to be aroused by new streets, new hills, new faces.

A dull fellow whose virtue—if there be any—is to be found only in his books.

Unpublished Introduction
to *Babbitt*

This is the story of the ruler of America.

The story of the Tired Business Man, the man with toothbrush mustache and harsh voice who talks about motors and prohibition in the smoking compartment of the Pullman car, the man who plays third-rate golf and first-rate poker at a second-rate country club near an energetic American city.

Our conqueror, dictator over our commerce, education, labor, art, politics, morals, and lack of conversation.

There are thirty millions of him, male and female, and his autocracy is unparalleled. No czar controlled the neckware and dice-throwing of his serfs; no general in the most perilous climax of war has codified his soldiers' humor or demanded that while they engaged the enemy they admire narratives about cowpunchers and optimistic little girls. But this completeness our ruler has attained.

Though English morals and French politics and German industry have been determined by the Sound Middle-Class, the Bourgeoisie, the Pumphreysie, have never dared also to announce standards in sculpture and table-manners. For in those lands there are outcasts and aristocrats who smile at the impertinence of the unimaginative. But in America we have created the superman complete, and the mellifluous name of the archangelic monster is Pumphrey, good old G. T. Pumphrey, the plain citizen and omnipotent power.

Note: Above too much hints of another Main St. Most of this and all of "pos. part of Intro." cd be used, say, as Chapter [word indistinct] in Part III or IV.

Though this is the individual romance of one G. T. Pumphrey and not the breviary of his community, that community enters his every moment, for it is himself, created in his varnished image. Monarch City is every "progressive, go-ahead, forward-looking, live, up-to-date" city of more than eighty thousand in the United States and Western Canada, with 8 or 10 venerable exceptions.

These exceptional cities Pumphrey visits with frequency, and stirs their theaters, hotels, books, and wholesalers to emulate the perfection of Monarch City, that even we who faint may win at the last to purity, efficiency, and ice water.

Distinctly, however, Pumphrey is not a satiric figure, nor a Type.

He is too tragic a tyrant for the puerilities of deliberate satire. And he is an individual, very eager and well-intentioned, credulous of pioneering myths, doubtful in his secret hours, affectionate toward his rebellious daughter and those lunch-mates who pass for friends—a god self-slain on his modern improved altar—the most grievous victim of his own militant dullness—crying in restless dreams for the arms of Phryne, the shirt of Jurgen and the twilight sea that knows not purity nor efficiency nor 34 x 4 casings.

As a PART OF INTRODUCTION, or in the story, or just implied in the story, or in an appendix *on Main Street vs. the Boulevard vs. Fifth Ave.*

———

They are complex phenomena, these American cities of from 80,000 to 1,000,000. They are industrially magnificent. They supply half the world with motor cars, machine tools, flour, locomotives, rails, electric equipment—with necessities miraculous and admirable. They are provided with houses more elaborate than any palaces, with hotels and office buildings as vast as and more usable than any cathedral. Their citizens are not unaccustomed to Fifth Avenue, to Piccadilly, to the Champs Élysées. Hither comes Galsworthy to lecture, Caruso to sing, Kreisler to play (even though they do beg him always to play the Humoresque), and here, in a Little Theater, a Schnitzler play may have a hearing as soon as Vienna, long before London. Yet they are villages, these titanic huddles. They import Kreisler as they import silks—not because they passionately love music or silks, but because those obvious symbols of prosperity give social prestige. To attend a concert is almost as valuable a certificate of wealth as to be seen riding in a Pierce-Arrow car. It is not an elegant and decorous listening to a great violinist which attests musical understanding; it is a passionate playing of one's own music—though the playing may be very bad indeed; may be nothing but the agitated scratching of four old cellists in a beery cellar. Since there is—as yet—no instrument which measures ergs of spiritual energy, the matter cannot be neatly and statistically proven, but one suspects that there is not one of these cities with a million, or half a million, people which has one tenth of the joyous mental activity of little Weimar, with its 35,000— among whom once moved no Crackajack Salesmen, perhaps, but only Goethe and Schiller.

And those glorious Little Theaters—those radiant and eager Little Theaters—indeed they do revel in Glaspell and Eugene O'Neill and Ervine—for one season or two; and then the players who have gone into this new sport for social prestige grow weary; the professional producer grows yet wearier of begging for funds, and of seeing newspapers which give a column to a road-company in a musical comedy, and two columns to a wedding between patent medicines and steel, present a brilliant performance of Shaw in two paragraphs with four solecisms; he goes his ways, and the Little Theater is not.

Villages—overgrown towns—three-quarters of a million people still dressing, eating, building houses, attending church, to make an impression on their neighbors, quite as they did back on Main Street, in villages of two thousand. And yet not villages at all, the observer uneasily sees, as he beholds factories with ten thousand workmen, with machines more miraculous than the loaves and fishes, with twice the power and ten times the skill of a romantic grand duchy. They are transitional metropolises—but that transition will take a few hundred years, if the custom persists of making it a heresy punishable by hanging or even by ostracism to venture to say that Cleveland or Minneapolis or Baltimore or Buffalo is not the wisest, gayest, kindliest, usefullest city in all the world. So long as every teacher and journalist and workman admits that John J. Jones, the hustling sales-manager for the pickle factory is the standard in beauty and courtesy and justice—well, so long will they be sore stricken with a pest of J. J. Joneses.

It is not quite a new thought to submit that though admittedly Mr. Jones somewhat lacks in the luxuries of artistic taste and agreeable manners, yet he is so solid a worker, so true a friend, and so near to genius in the development of this astounding and adventurously new industrial system, that he is worthier, he is really more beautiful, than any Anatole France or [word omitted]. Are his pickle machines with their power and ingenuity a new art, comparable to vers libre, and is there not in his noisiest advertising, his billboards smeared across tranquil fields, a passion for achievement which is, to the unprejudiced discernment, a religious fervor, an esthetic passion, a genius such as inspired the crusader and explorer and poet? Is not his assailant a blind and reactionary fellow who demands in this rough glorious pioneer outworn standards and beauties dead and dry?

Only it happens that these generous inquirers who seek to make themselves comfortable by justifying their inescapable neighbor, Mr. Jones, give him somewhat too much credit. Mr. Jones, the sales-manager, Mr. Brown, the general manager, Mr. Robinson, the president—all the persons in the pickle hierarchy most to be accredited with passion and daring and new beauties—are nothing in the world but salesmen, commercial demagogues, industrial charlatans, creators of a demand which they wistfully desire to supply. Those miraculous, those admittedly noble machines—they were planned and built and improved and run by very common workmen, who get no credit whatever for pioneering. Those astounding pickle formulae, they were made by chemists, unknown and unglorified. Even those farflung billboards, the banners of Mr. Jones's gallant crusade—their text was written by forty-a-week copy-writers, their pictures—their very terrible pictures—painted by patient hacks, and the basic idea, of having billboards, came not from the passionate brain of Mr. Jones but was cautiously worked out, on quite routine and unromantic lines, by hesitating persons in an advertising agency.

And it is these workmen, chemists, hacks, who are likely to be eager about beauty, courageous in politics—Moon-Calves—children of the new world. Mr. Jones himself—ah, that rare and daring and shining-new creator of industrial poetry, he votes the Republican ticket straight, he hates all labor unionism, he belongs to the Masons and the Presbyterian Church, his favorite author is Zane Grey, and in other particulars noted in this story, his private life seems scarce to mark him as the rough, ready, aspiring, iconoclastic, creative, courageous innovator his admirers paint him. He is a bagman. He is a pedlar. He is a shopkeeper. He is a camp-follower. He is a bag of aggressive wind.

America has taken to itself the credit of being the one pioneering nation of the world; it has thereby (these three hundred years now) excused all flabbiness of culture and harshness of manner and frantic oppres-

sion of critics. And, strangely, Europe has granted that
assertion. Never an English author descends upon
these palpitating and grateful shores without informing us that from our literature one expects only
the burly power and clumsiness of ditch-diggers. We
listen to him, and are made proud of the clumsiness
and burliness—without quite going so far as to add
also the power.

It is a national myth.

England has, in India, Africa, Canada, Australia,
had quite as many new frontiers, done quite as much
pioneering—and done it as bravely and as cruelly and
as unscrupulously—as have we in pushing the western
border from the Alleghenies to Honolulu. Thus
France in Africa, Holland in the West Indies, Germany all over the world. And England has quite as
many Rough Fellows as America. Lord Fisher criticiz-
ing the British navy in the tones of a tobacco-chewing
trapper—is he so much less of a Rough Fellow and
Pioneer and Innovator than the Harvard instructor
reading Austin Dobson by candle-light? The silk salesman, crossing the Arizona desert—in a Pullman—is
he so much bolder a ditch-digger than Ole Bill, the
English Tommy?

A myth! America is no longer an isolated race of
gallant Indian-slayers. It is a part of the world. Like
every other nation, it is made up of both daring inno-
vators and crusted crabs. Its literature and its J. J.
Joneses are subject to the same rules as the literature
and the bustling innumerous J. J. Joneses of England
or Spain or Norway. Mr. Henry van Dyke is no newer
or more pioneering than Mr. H. G. Wells—and subject
to no more lenient rules or more provincial judgments.

Of this contradiction between pioneering myth and
actual slackness, these Monarchs, these cities of
300,000 or so, are the best examples. Unfortunately
American literature has discerned as types of commu-
nities only the larger or older cities—as New York,
San Francisco, Richmond—and the villages, with nothing between. Yet there is a sort of community in be-

tween, an enormously important type—the city of a few hundred thousand, the metropolis that yet is a village, the world-center that yet is ruled by cautious villagers. Only Booth Tarkington, with his novels flavored by Indianapolis, and a few local celebrities eager to present the opulence of their several Monarchs, have dealt with these cities which, more than any New York, produce our wares and elect our presidents— and buy our books. Yet they are important enough to quarrel over—they are great enough to deserve the compliment of being told one's perception of the truth about them.

Just use "city man & country girl" How dif from N. Y.

To say that they are subject to the same rules as Munich or Florence does not at all mean that they are like Munich or Florence. They have grown so rapidly, they have been so innocent and so Republican and so Presbyterian and so altogether boosting and innocent, that they have produced a type of existence a little different from any other in the world. It may not continue to be so different—it some time may be subject also to fine tradition and the vision of quiet and honest work as against noisy selling of needless things—but this fineness it will not attain without self-study, and an admission that twenty-story buildings are not necessarily nobler than Notre Dame, and that the production of 19,000 motor cars a day does not of itself prove those cars to be better built than cars produced at one a day.

This foreshadowing of a future adoption of richer traditions does not, of course, mean at all that in the future these Monarchs are to be spiritually or physically like Munich or Florence. It is a paradox of psychology that it is precisely the richest philosophies, with the largest common fund of wisdom from all ages, which produce the most diverse and lovely products, while it is the thinner and hastier philosophies which produce the most standardized and boresomely similar products.

German Munich and Italian Florence are vastly and entertainingly different in all that counts—in passions, wines, aspirations, and furniture—for the reason that they have both digested and held and brilliantly changed a common wisdom of Plato and Shakespeare and Karl Marx. But German Milwaukee and Italian Hartford are uncomfortably alike because they have cast off all the hard-earned longings of mankind and joined in a common aspiration to be rich, notorious, and One Hundred Per Cent American.

It is this fact which is the second great feature of the American cities of 300,000—and as important as their other feature of unconquerable villageness. It is this fact which makes a novel that chanced to be local and concrete and true in regard to Omaha equally local and concrete and true regarding twenty other cities. Naturally, they are not all precisely alike. There is a difference resulting from situation—from a background of hills or plain, of river or seacoast; a difference from the products of the back-country—iron, wheat, cotton; a distinct difference from the various ages—the difference between Seattle and Charleston.

But these differences have for a long time now tended to decrease, so powerful is our faith in standardization. When a new hotel, factory, house, garage, motion-picture theater, row of shops, church, or synagogue is erected in gray Charleston, rambling New Orleans, or San Francisco of the '49ers, that structure is precisely, to the last column of reinforced concrete and the last decorative tile, the same as a parallel structure in the new cities of Portland or Kansas City. And the souls of those structures—the hospitality of the hotels, the mechanical methods in the garages, the minutest wording of the sermons in the churches—are increasingly as standardized as the shells.

It would not be possible to write a novel which would in every line be equally true to Munich and Florence. Despite the fundamental hungers equally true to all human beings, despite the similarity of manners and conversation in the layer of society which contentedly travels all over the world, despite the like interest of kissing at Fiesole and at Gansedorf, so vastly and subtly are the differences in every outward aspect, every detail of artistic aspiration and national pride and hope, that the two cities seem to belong to two different planets.

But Hartford and Milwaukee—the citizens of those two distant cities go to the same offices, speak the same patois on the same telephones, go to the same lunch and the same athletic clubs, etc., etc., etc.

Novel unlike M. St. cf Carol [Kennicott] on standardized life in U.S.

The test of the sameness is in the people. If you were by magic taken instantly to any city of over 80,000 in the United States and set down in the business center, in a block, say, with a new hotel, a new motion-picture theater, and a line of newish shops, not three hours of the intensest study of the passing people—men on business errands, messenger boys, women shopping, pool-room idlers—would indicate in what city, indeed in what part of the country, you were. Only by traveling to the outskirts and discovering mountains or ocean or wheat fields, and perhaps Negro shanties, Mexican adobes, or German breweries, would you begin to get a clue—and these diverse clues lessen each year. They know it not but all these bright women and pompous men are in uniforms, under the discipline of a belligerent service, as firmly as any soldier in khaki. For those that like it— that is what they like; but there are those of us who hesitated about being drafted into the army of complacency.

Things

This is not the story of Theodora Duke and Stacy Lindstrom, but of a traveling bag with silver fittings, a collection of cloisonné, a pile of ratty school-books, and a fireless cooker that did not cook.

Long before these things were acquired, when Theo was a girl and her father, Lyman Duke, was a so-so dealer in cut-over lands, there was a feeling of adventure in the family. They lived in a small brown house which predicated children and rabbits in the back yard, and a father invariably home for supper. But Mr. Duke was always catching trains to look at pine tracts in northern Minnesota. Often his wife went along and, in the wilds, way and beyond Grand Marais and the steely shore of Lake Superior, she heard wolves howl and was unafraid. The Dukes laughed much those years, and were eager to see mountains and new kinds of shade trees.

Theo found her own freedom in exploring jungles of five-foot mullein weeds with Stacy Lindstrom. That pale, stolid little Norwegian she chose from her playmates because he was always ready to try new games.

The city of Vernon was newer then—in 1900. There were no country clubs, no fixed sets. The pioneers from Maine and York State who had appropriated lumber and flour were richer than the newly come

25

Buckeyes and Hoosiers and Scandinavians, but they were friendly. As they drove their smart trotters the leading citizens shouted "Hello, Heinie," or "Evenin', Knute," without a feeling of condescension. In preferring Stacy Lindstrom to Eddie Barnes, who had a hundred-dollar bicycle and had spent a year in a private school, Theo did not consider herself virtuously democratic. Neither did Stacy!

The brown-haired, bright-legged, dark-cheeked, glowing girl was a gorgeous colt, while he was a fuzzy lamb. Theo's father had an office, Stacy's father a job in a planing mill. Yet Stacy was the leader. He read books, and he could do things with his hands. He invented Privateers, which is a much better game than Pirates. For his gallant company of one privateers he rigged a forsaken dump cart, in the shaggy woods on the Mississippi bluffs, with sackcloth sails, barrel-hoop cutlasses, and a plank for victims to walk. Upon the request of the victims, who were Theo, he added to the plank a convenient handrail.

But anyone could play Ship—even Eddie Barnes. From a territorial pioneer Stacy learned of the Red River carts which, with the earthquaking squawk of ungreased wheels and the glare of scarlet sashes on the buckskin-shirted drivers, used to come plodding all the redskin-haunted way from the outposts of the Free Trappers, bearing marten and silver fox for the throats of princesses. Stacy changed the privateers' brigantine into a Red River cart. Sometimes it was seven or ten carts, and a barricade. Behind it Stacy and Theo kept off hordes of Dakotas.

After voyaging with Stacy, Theo merely ya-ah'd at Eddie Barnes when he wanted her to go skating. Eddie considered a figure eight, performed on the ice of a safe creek, the final accomplishment of imaginative sport, while Stacy could from immemorial caverns call the Wizard Merlin as servitor to a little playing girl. Besides, he could jump on ski! And mend a bike! Eddie had to take even a dirty sprocket to the repair shop.

The city, and Theo, had grown less simple-hearted when she went to Central High School. Twenty-five hundred boys and girls gathered in those tall gloomy rooms, which smelled of water pails and chalk and worn floors. There was a glee club, a school paper, a debating society and dress-up parties. The school was brisk and sensible, but it was too large for the intimacy of the grade buildings. Eddie Barnes was conspicuous now, with his energy in managing the athletic association, his beautifully combed hair and his real gold watch. Stacy Lindstrom was lost in the mass.

It was Eddie who saw Theo home from parties. He was a man of the world. He went to Chicago as calmly as you or I would go out to the St. Croix River to spear pickerel.

Stacy rarely went to parties. Theo invited him to her own, and the girls were polite to him. Actually he danced rather better than Eddie. But he couldn't talk about Chicago. He couldn't talk at all. Nor did he sing or go out for sports. His father was dead. He worked Saturdays and three nights a week in an upholstery shop—a dingy, lint-blurred loft, where two old Swedes kept up as a permanent institution a debate on the Lutheran Church versus the Swedish Adventist.

"Why don't you get a good live job?" Eddie patronizingly asked Stacy at recess, and Theo echoed the question; but neither of them had any suggestions about specific good live jobs.

Stacy stood from first to fifth in every class. But what, Eddie demanded, was the use of studying unless you were going to be a school teacher? Which he certainly was not! He was going to college. He was eloquent and frequent on this topic. It wasn't the darned old books, but the association with the fellows, that educated you, he pointed out. Friendships. Fraternities. Helped a fellow like the dickens, both in society and business, when he got out of college.

"Yes, I suppose so," sighed Theo.

Eddie said that Stacy was a longitudinal, latitudinous, isothermic, geologic, catawampaboid Scandahoofian. Everybody admired the way Eddie could make up long words. Theo's older sister, Janet, who had cold, level eyes, said that Theo was a fool to let a shabby, drabby nobody like that Stacy Lindstrom carry her books home from school. Theo defended Stacy whenever he was mentioned. There is nothing which so cools young affection as having to defend people.

After high school Eddie went East to college, Stacy was a clerk in the tax commissioner's department of the railroad—and the Dukes became rich, and immediately ceased to be adventurous.

Iron had been found under Mr. Duke's holdings in northern Minnesota. He refused to sell. He leased the land to the iron-mining company, and every time a scoop brought up a mass of brown earth in the open pit the company ran very fast and dropped twenty-five cents in Mr. Duke's pocket. He felt heavy with silver and importance; he bought the P. J. Broom mansion and became the abject servant of possessions.

The Broom mansion had four drawing rooms, a heraldic limestone fireplace and a tower and a half. The half tower was merely an octagonal shingle structure with a bulbous Moorish top; but the full tower, which was of stone on a base of brick, had cathedral windows, a weather vane, and a metal roof down which dripped decorative blobs like copper tears. While the mansion was being redecorated the Duke senior took the grand tour from Miami to Port Said, and brought home a carload of treasures. There was a ready-made collection of cloisonné, which an English baron had spent five years in gathering in Japan and five hours in losing at Monte Carlo. There was a London traveling bag, real seal, too crammed with silver fittings to admit much of anything else, and too heavy for anyone save a piano mover to lift. There were rugs, and books, and hand-painted pictures, and a glass window from Nuremberg, and ushabti figures from Egypt, and a pierced brass lamp in the shape of a mosque.

All these symbols of respectability the Dukes installed in the renovated Broom mansion, and settled down to watch them.

Lyman Duke was a kindly man, and shrewd, but the pride of ownership was a germ, and he was a sick man. Who, he meditated, had such a lamp? Could even the Honorable Gerard Randall point to such glowing rods of book backs?

Mrs. Duke organized personally conducted excursions to view the Axminster rug in the library. Janet forgot that she had ever stood brushing her hair before a pine bureau. Now she sat before a dressing table displaying candlesticks, an eyelash pencil, and a powder-puff box of gold lace over old rose. Janet moved graciously, and invited little sister Theo to be cordially unpleasant to their grubby friends of grammar-school days.

The accumulation of things to make other people envious is nothing beside their accumulation because it's the thing to do. Janet discovered that life would be unendurable without an evening cloak. At least three evening cloaks were known to exist within a block of the Broom mansion. True, nobody wore them. There aren't any balls or plays except in winter, and during a Vernon winter you don't wear a satin cloak—you wear a fur coat and a muffler and a sweater and arctics, and you brush the frozen breath from your collar, and dig out of your wraps like a rabbit emerging from a brush pile. But if everybody had them Janet wasn't going to be marked for life as one ignorant of the niceties. She used the word "niceties" frequently and without quailing.

She got an evening cloak. Also a pair of fifteen-dollar pumps, which she discarded for patent leathers as soon as she found that everybody wore those—everybody being a girl in the next block, whose house wasn't anywhere near as nice as "ours."

II

Theo was only half glad of their grandeur. Oh, undoubtedly she was excited about the house at first,

and mentioned it to other girls rather often, and rang
for maids she didn't need. But she had a little pain in
the conscience. She felt that she hadn't kept up defending Stacy Lindstrom very pluckily.

She was never allowed to forget Stacy's first call at
the mansion. The family were settled in the house.
They were anxious for witnesses of their nobility. The
bell rang at eight one Saturday evening when they
were finishing dinner. It was hard to be finishing dinner at eight. They had been used to starting at six-
thirty-one and ending the last lap, neck and neck, at
six-fifty-two. But by starting at seven, and having a
salad, and letting Father smoke his cigar at the table,
they had stretched out the ceremony to a reasonably
decent length.

At the sound of the buzz in the butler's pantry Janet
squeaked: "Oh, maybe it's the Garlands! Or even the
Randalls!" She ran into the hall.

"Janet! Jan-et! The maid will open the door!" Mrs.
Duke wailed.

"I know, but I want to see who it is!"

Janet returned snapping: "Good heavens, it's only
that Stacy Lindstrom! Coming at this early hour! And
he's bought a new suit, just to go calling. It looks like
sheet iron."

Theo pretended she had not heard. She fled to the
distant library. She was in a panic. She was ashamed
of herself, but she didn't trust Stacy to make enough
impression. So it was Mr. Duke who had the first
chance at the audience:

"Ah, Stacy, glad to see you, my boy. The girls are
round some place. Theo!"

"Lyman! Don't shout so! I'll send a maid to find
her," remonstrated Mrs. Duke.

"Oh, she'll come a-running. Trust these girls to
know when a boy's round!" boomed Mr. Duke.

Janet had joined Theo in the library. She veritably
hissed as she protested: "Boys-s-s-s-s! We come running for a commonplace railway clerk!"

Theo made her handkerchief into a damp, tight little

ball in her lap, smoothed it out, and very carefully began to tear off its border.

Afar Mr. Duke was shouting: "Come see my new collection while we're waiting."

"I hate you!" Theo snarled at Janet, and ran into the last of the series of drawing rooms. From its darkness she could see her father and Stacy. She felt that she was protecting this, her brother, from danger; from the greatest of dangers—being awkward in the presence of the stranger, Janet. She was aware of Janet slithering in beside her.

"Now what do you think of that, eh?" Mr. Duke was demanding. He had unlocked a walnut cabinet, taken out an enameled plate.

Stacy was radiant. "Oh, yes. I know what that stuff is. I've read about it. It's cloysoan." He had pronounced it to rime with moan.

"Well, not precisely! Cloysonnay, most folks would call it. Culwasonnay, if you want to be real highbrow. But cloysoan, that's pretty good! Mamma! Janet! The lad says this is cloysoan! Ha, ha! Well, never mind, my boy. Better folks than you and I have made that kind of a mistake."

Janet was tittering. The poisonous stream of it trickled through all the rooms. Stacy must have heard. He looked about uneasily.

Suddenly Theo saw him as a lout, in his new suit that hung like wood. He was twisting a button and trying to smile back at Mr. Duke.

The cloisonné plate was given to Stacy to admire. What he saw was a flare of many-colored enamels in tiny compartments. In the center a dragon writhed its tongue in a field of stars, and on the rim were buds on clouds of snow, a flying bird, and amusing symbols among willow leaves.

But Mr. Duke was lecturing on what he ought to have seen:

"This is a *sara,* and a very fine specimen. Authorities differ, but it belonged either to the *Shi sinwo* or the *Monzeki*—princely monks, in the monastery of

Nin-na-ji. Note the extreme thinness of the cloisons, and the pastes are very evenly vitrified. The colors are remarkable. You'll notice there's slate blue, sage green, chrome yellow, and—uh—well, there's several other colors. You see the ground shows the *kara kusa.* That bird there is a *ho-ho* in flight above the branches of the *kiri* tree."

Stacy had a healthy suspicion that a few months before Mr. Duke had known no more about Oriental art than Stacy Lindstrom. But he had no Japanese words for repartee, and he could only rest his weight on the other foot and croak "Well, well!"

Mr. Duke was beatifically going on: "Now this *chat-subo,* you'll notice, is not cloisonné at all, but champlevé. Very important point in studying *shippo* ware. Note the unusually fine *kiku* crest on this *chawan.*"

"I see. Uh—I see," said Stacy.

"Just a goat, that's all he is, just a giddy goat," Janet whispered to Theo in the dark room beyond, and pranced away.

It was five minutes before Theo got up courage to rescue Stacy. When she edged into the room he was sitting in a large leather chair and fidgeting. He was fidgeting in twenty different but equally irritating ways. He kept recrossing his legs, and every time he crossed them the stiff trousers bagged out in more hideous folds. Between times he tapped his feet. His fingers drummed on the chair. He looked up at the ceiling, licking his lips, and hastily looked down, with an artificial smile in acknowledgment of Mr. Duke's reminiscences of travel.

Theo swooped on Stacy with hands clapping in welcome, with a flutter of white muslin skirts about young ankles.

"Isn't the house comfy? When we get a pig we can keep him under that piano! Come on, I'll show you all the hidey holes," she crowed.

She skipped off, dragging him by the hand—but she realized that she was doing altogether too much dragging. Stacy, who had always been too intent on their games to be self-conscious, was self-conscious enough now. What could she say to him?

She besought: "I hope you'll come often. We'll have lots of fun out of——"

"Oh, you won't know me any more, with a swell place like this," he mumbled.

As women do she tried to bandage this raw, bruised moment. She snapped on the lights in the third drawing room, and called his attention to the late Mr. P. J. Broom's coat of arms carved on the hulking stone fireplace. "I got the decorator to puzzle it out for me, and as far as he could make out, if Pat Broom was right he was descended from an English duke, a German general and a Serbian undertaker. He didn't miss a trick except——"

"Well, it's a pretty fine fireplace," Stacy interrupted. He looked away, his eyes roving but dull, and dully he added: "Too fine for me, I guess."

Not once could she get him to share her joy in the house. He seemed proud of the virtue of being poor. Like a boast sounded his repeated "Too darned fine for me—don't belong in with all these doo-dads." She worked hard. She showed him not only the company rooms but the delightful secret passage of the clothes chute which led from an upstairs bedroom to the laundry; the closet drawers which moved on rollers and could be drawn out by the little finger; the built-in clock with both Trinity and Westminster chimes; the mysterious spaces of the basement, with the gas drier for wet wash, and the wine cellar which—as it so far contained only a case of beer and seven bottles of ginger ale—was chiefly interesting to the sense of make-believe.

Obediently he looked where she pointed; politely he repeated that everything was "pretty fine"; and not once was he her comrade. The spirit of divine trust was dead, horribly mangled and dead, she panted, while she caroled in the best nice-young-woman tone she could summon: "See, Stace. Isn't this cun-ning?"

It is fabled that sometimes the most malignant ghosts

are souls that in life have been the most kindly and
beloved. Dead though this ancient friendship seemed, it
had yet one phase of horror to manifest. After having
implied that he was a plain honest fellow and glad of it,
Stacy descended to actual boasting. They sat uneasily in
the smallest of the drawing rooms, their eyes fencing.
Theo warned herself that he was merely embarrassed.
She wanted to be sorry for him. But she was tired—
tired of defending him to others, tired of fighting to hold
his affection.

"I certainly am eating the work in the tax commissioner's office. I'm studying accounting systems and banking
methods evenings, and you want to watch your Uncle
Stacy. I'll make some of these rich fellows sit up! I know
the cashier at the Lumber National pretty well now, and
he as much as said I could have a job there, at better
money, any time I wanted to."

He did not say what he wished to put into the railroad
and the bank—only what he wished to get out of them.
He had no plans, apparently, to build up great institutions for Vernon, but he did have plans to build up a
large salary for Stacy Lindstrom.

And one by one, as flustered youth does, he dragged
in the names of all the important men he had met. The
conversation had to be bent distressingly, to get them
all in.

He took half an hour in trying to make an impressive exit.

"I hate him! He expects me to be snobbish! He made
it so hard for me to apologize for being rich. He——
Oh, I hate him!" Theo sobbed by her bed.

III

Not for a week did she want to see the boy again;
and not for a month did he call. By that time she was
used to doing without him. Before long she was used
to doing without most people. She was left lonely.
Janet had gone East to a college that wasn't a college
at all, but a manicurist's buffer of a school, all cham-

ois, celluloid, and pink powder—a school all roses and
purring and saddle horses and pleasant reading of little manuals about art. Theo had admired her older
sister. She had been eager when Janet had let her
wash gloves and run ribbons. She missed the joy of
service. She missed too the conveniences of the old
brown house—the straw-smelling dog house in the
back yard, with the filthy, agreeable, gentlemanly old
setter who had resided there; and the tree up which
a young woman with secret sorrows could shin
resentfully.

Not only Janet and Eddie Barnes but most of
Theo's friends had escaped domestic bliss and gone
off to school. Theo wanted to follow them, but Mrs.
Duke objected: "I wouldn't like to have both my little
daughters desert me at once." At the age halfway between child and independent woman Theo was alone.
She missed playing; she missed the achievements of
housework.

In the old days, on the hired girl's night out, Theo
had not minded splashing in rainbow-bubbled suds
and polishing the water glasses to shininess. But now
there was no hired girl's night out, and no hired girls.
There were maids instead, three of them, with a man
who took care of the furnace and garden and put on
storm windows. The eldest of the maids was the
housekeeper-cook, and she was a straight-mouthed,
carp-eyed person named Lizzie. Lizzie had been in the
Best Houses. She saw to it that neither the other servants nor the Dukes grew slack. She would have
fainted at the sight of Sunday supper in the kitchen
or of Theo washing dishes.

Mr. Duke pretended to be glad that they had a
furnace man; that he no longer had to put on overalls
and black leather gloves to tend the furnace and sift
the ashes. That had been his before-supper game at
the shabby brown house. As a real-estate man, he had
been mediocre. As a furnace man, he had been a surgeon, an artist. He had operated on the furnace delicately, giving lectures on his technic to a clinic of

admiring young. You mustn't, he had exhorted, shake for one second after the slivers of hot coal tumble through the grate. You must turn off the draft at exactly the moment when the rose-and-saffron flames quiver above the sullen mound of coal.

His wife now maintained that he had been dreadfully bored and put upon by chores. He didn't contradict. He was proud that he no longer had to perch on a ladder holding a storm window or mightily whirling the screw driver as the screws sunk unerringly home. But with nothing to do but look at the furnace man, and gaze at his collection of jugs and bugs and rugs, he became slow of step and foggy of eye, and sometimes, about nothing in particular, he sighed.

Whenever they had guests for dinner he solemnly showed the cloisonné and solemnly the guests said, "Oh," and "Really?" and "Is it?" They didn't want to see the cloisonné, and Mr. Duke didn't want to show it, and of his half-dozen words of Japanese he was exceedingly weary. But if one is a celebrated collector one must keep on collecting and showing the collections.

These dinners and private exhibits were part of a social system in which the Dukes were entangled. It wasn't an easy-fitting system. It was too new. If we ever have professional gentlemen in this country we may learn to do nothing and do it beautifully. But so far we want to do things. Vernon society went out for businesslike activities. There was much motoring, golf and the discussion of golf, and country-club dances at which the men's costumes ran from full evening dress through dinner coats to gray suits with tan shoes.

Most of the men enjoyed these activities honestly. They danced and motored and golfed because they liked to; because it rested them after the day in the office. But there was a small exclusive set in Vernon that had to spend all its time in getting recognized as a small exclusive set. It was social solitaire. By living in a district composed of a particular three blocks on the Boulevard of the Lakes Mr. Duke had been pushed into that exclusive set—Mrs. Duke giving a hand in the pushing.

Sometimes he rebelled. He wanted to be back at work. He had engaged a dismayingly competent manager for his real-estate office, and even by the most ingenious efforts to find something wrong with the books or the correspondence he couldn't keep occupied at the office for more than two hours a day. He longed to discharge the manager, but Mrs. Duke would not have it. She enjoyed the ownership of a leisure-class husband.

For rich women the social system in Vernon does provide more games than for men. The poor we have always with us, and the purpose of the Lord in providing the poor is to enable us of the better classes to amuse ourselves by investigating them and uplifting them and at dinners telling how charitable we are. The poor don't like it much. They have no gratitude. They would rather be uplifters themselves. But if they are taken firmly in hand they can be kept reasonably dependent and interesting for years.

The remnants of the energy that had once taken Mrs. Duke into the woods beyond the end of steel now drove her into poor-baiting. She was a committeewoman five deep. She had pigeonholes of mysteriously important correspondence, and she hustled about in the limousine. When her husband wanted to go back and do real work she was oratorical:

"That's the trouble with the American man. He really likes his sordid office. No, dearie, you just enjoy your leisure for a while yet. As soon as we finish the campaign for censoring music you and I will run away and take a good trip—San Francisco and Honolulu."

But whenever she actually was almost ready to go even he saw objections. How ridiculous to desert their adorable house, the beds soft as whipped cream, the mushrooms and wild rice that only Lizzie could cook, for the discomforts of trains and hotels! And was it safe to leave the priceless collections? There had been a burglar scare—there always has just been a burglar

scare in all cities. The Dukes didn't explain how their
presence would keep burglars away, but they gallantly
gave up their lives to guarding the cloisonné while
they talked about getting a caretaker, and never tried
to get him.

Thus at last was Lyman Duke become a prison
guard shackled to the things he owned, and the longest
journey of the man who had once desired new peaks
and softer air was a slow walk down to the Commercial Club for lunch.

IV

When Janet and Eddie Barnes and the rest of Theo's
friends came back from college; when the sons went
into their fathers' wholesale offices and clubs, and the
daughters joined their mothers' lecture courses and
societies, and there was an inheriting Younger Set and
many family plans for marriages—then Theo ceased to
be lonely, and remembered how to play. She had gone
to desultory dances during their absence, but only with
people too old or too young. Now she had a group of
her own. She danced with a hot passion for music and
movement; her questioning about life disappeared in
laughter as she rose to the rushing of people and the
flashing of gowns.

Stacy Lindstrom was out of existence in this colored
world. Stacy was now chief clerk in the railroad tax
commissioner's office, and spoken of as future assistant cashier in the Lumber National Bank. But he was
quite insignificant. He was thin—not slim. He was
silent—not reserved. His clothes were plain—not clev-
erly inconspicuous. He wore eyeglasses with a gold
chain attached to a hoop over one ear; and he totally
failed to insist that he was bored by the vaudeville
which everybody attended and everybody sneered at.
Oh, he was ordinary, through and through.

Thus with boarding-school wisdom Janet dissected
the unfortunate social problem known as Stacy Lindstrom. Theo didn't protest much. It was not possible

for youth to keep on for five years very ardently defending anybody who changed as little as Stacy. And Theo was busy.

Not only to dances did Janet lead her, but into the delights of being artistic. Janet had been gapingly impressed by the Broom mansion when the family had acquired it, but now, after vacation visits to Eastern friends, she saw that the large brown velvet chairs were stuffy, and the table with the inlaid chessboard of mother-of-pearl a horror. What Janet saw she also expressed.

In one of the manuals the girls had been tenderly encouraged to glance through at Janet's college it was courageously stated that simplicity was the keynote in decoration. At breakfast, dinner, and even at suppers personally abstracted from the ice box at two A.M., Janet clamored that their ratty old palace ought to be refurnished. Her parents paid no attention. That was just as well.

Otherwise Janet would have lost the chance to get into her portable pulpit and admonish: "When I have a house it will be absolutely simple. Just a few exquisite vases, and not one chair that doesn't melt into the environment. Things—things—things—they are so dreadful! I shan't have a thing I can't use. Use is the test of beauty."

Theo knew that the admirable Janet expressed something which she had been feeling like a dull, unplaced pain. She became a member of an informal art association consisting of herself, Janet, Eddie Barnes, and Harry McPherson, Janet's chief suitor. It is true that the art association gave most of its attention to sitting together in corners at dances and giggling at other people's clothes, but Janet did lead them to an exhibit at the Vernon Art Institute, and afterward they had tea and felt intellectual and peculiar and proud.

Eddie Barnes was showing new depths. He had attended a great seaboard university whose principal distinction, besides its athletics, was its skill in instructing select young gentlemen to discuss any topic in the world without having any knowledge of it whatever. During Janet's pogrom against the Dukes' mosque-shaped brass lamp Eddie was heard to say a number of terribly good things about the social value of knowing wall sconces.

When Janet and Harry McPherson were married Eddie was best man, Theo bridesmaid.

Janet had furnished her new house. When Theo had accompanied Janet on the first shopping flight she had wanted to know just what sort of chairs would perform the miracle of melting into the environment. She wondered whether they could be found in department stores or only in magic shops. But Janet led her to a place only too familiar—the Crafts League, where Mrs. Duke always bought candle shades and small almond dishes.

Janet instantly purchased a hand-tooled leather box for playing cards, and a desk set which included a locked diary in a morocco cover and an ingenious case containing scissors, magnifying glass, pencil sharpener, paper cutter, steel ink eraser, silver penknife. This tool kit was a delightful toy, and it cost thirty-seven dollars. The clerk explained that it was especially marked down from forty-five dollars, though he did not explain why it should be especially marked down.

Theo wailed: "But those aren't necessary! That last thingumajig has four different kinds of knives, where you only need one. It's at least as useless as Papa's cloisonné."

"I know, but it's so amusing. And it's entirely different from Papa's old stuff. It's the newest thing out!" Janet explained.

Before she had bought a single environment-melting chair Janet added to her simple and useful furnishings a collection of glass fruit for table centerpiece, a set of Venetian glass bottles, a traveling clock with a case of gold and platinum and works of tin. For her sensible desk she acquired a complicated engine consisting of a tiny marble pedestal, on which was an onyx ball, on which was a cerise and turquoise china parrot, from whose back, for no very clear anatomical reason, issued a candlestick. But not a stick for candles. It was wired for electricity.

As she accepted each treasure Janet rippled that it was so amusing. The clerk added "So quaint," as though it rimed with amusing. While Theo listened uncomfortably they two sang a chorus of disparagement of Mid-Victorian bric-a-brac and praise of modern clever bits.

When Janet got time for the miraculous chairs——

She had decided to furnish her dining room in friendly, graceful Sheraton, but the clerk spoke confidentially of French lacquer, and Theo watched Janet pledge her troth to a frail red-lacquered dining-room set of brazen angles. The clerk also spoke of distinguished entrance halls, and wished upon Janet an enormous Spanish chair of stamped leather upholstery and dropsical gilded legs, with a mirror that cost a hundred and twenty dollars, and a chest in which Janet didn't intend to keep anything.

Theo went home feeling that she was carrying on her shoulders a burden of gilded oak; that she would never again run free.

When Janet's house was done it looked like a sale in a seaside gift shop. Even her telephone was covered with a brocade and china doll. Theo saw Janet spending her days vaguely endeavoring to telephone to living life through brocade dolls.

After Janet's marriage Theo realized that she was tired of going to parties with the same group; of hearing the same Eddie tell the same stories about the cousin of the Vanderbilts who had almost invited him to go yachting. She was tired of Vernon's one rich middle-aged bachelor; of the bouncing girl twins who always rough-housed at dances. She was peculiarly weary of the same salads and ices which all Vernon hostesses always got from the same caterer. There was one kind of cake with rosettes of nuts which Theo met four times in two weeks—and expected to meet till the caterer passed beyond. She could tell beforehand how any given festivity would turn out. She knew at just what moment after a luncheon the conversation about babies would turn into uneasy yawns, and the hostess would, inevitably, propose bridge. Theo desired to assassinate the entire court of face cards.

Stacy Lindstrom had about once a year indicated a shy desire to have her meet his own set. He told her that they went skiing in winter and picnicking in summer; he hinted how simply and frankly they talked at dinners. Theo went gladly with him to several parties of young married people and a few unmarried sisters and cousins. For three times she enjoyed the change in personnel. As she saw the bright new flats, with the glassed-in porches, the wicker furniture, the colored prints and the davenports; as she heard the people chaff one another; as she accompanied them to a public skating rink and sang to the blaring band—she felt that she had come out of the stupidity of stilted social sets and returned to the naturalness of the old brown house.

But after three parties she knew all the jokes of the husbands about their wives, and with unnecessary thoroughness she knew the opinions of each person upon movies, Chicago, prohibition, the I. W. W., Mrs. Sam Jenkins' chronic party gown, and Stacy's new job in the Lumber National. She tried to enliven the parties. She worked harder than any of her hostesses. She proposed charades, music. She failed. She gave them one gorgeous dance, and disappeared from their group forever.

She did go with Stacy on a tramp through the snow, and enjoyed it—till he began to hint that he, too, might have a great house and many drawing rooms some day. He had very little to say about what he hoped to do for the Lumber National Bank in return.

Then did Theo feel utterly deserted. She blamed herself. Was something wrong with her that she alone found these amusements so agonizingly unamusing? And feeling thus why didn't she do something about it? She went on helping her mother in the gigantic task of asking Lizzie what orders Lizzie wanted them to give her. She went on planning that some day she would read large books and know all about world problems, and she went on forgetting to buy the books. She was twenty-six, and there was no man to marry except the chattering Eddie Barnes. Certainly she could not think romantically about that Stacy Lindstrom whose ambition seemed to be to get enough money to become an imitation chattering Eddie Barnes.

Then America entered the war.

V

Eddie Barnes went to the first officers' training camp, and presently was a highly decorative first lieutenant in a hundred-dollar uniform. Stacy Lindstrom made his savings over to his mother, and enlisted. While Eddie was still stationed at a cantonment as instructor Stacy was writing Theo ten-word messages from France. He had become a sergeant, and French agriculture was interesting, he wrote.

Stacy's farewell had been undistinguished. He called—a slight, commonplace figure in a badly fitting private's uniform. He sat on the piano stool and mouthed: "Well, I have a furlough. Then we get shipped across. Well—don't forget me, Theo."

At the door Stacy kissed her hand so sharply that his teeth bruised her skin, and ran down the steps, silent.

But Eddie, who came up from the cantonment at least once a month, at least that often gave a long, brave farewell to Theo. Handsome, slim, erect, he invariably paced the smallest drawing room, stopped, trembled, and said in a military tone, tenor but resolute: "Well, old honey, this may be the last time I see you. I may get overseas service any time now. Theo dear, do you know how much I care? I shall take a picture of you in my heart, and it may be the last thing I ever think of. I'm no hero, but I know I shall do my duty. And, Theo, if I don't come back——"

The first two times Theo flared into weeping at this point, and Eddie's arm was about her, and she kissed him. But the third, fourth and fifth times he said good-by forever she chuckled, "Cheer up, old boy." It was hard for her to feel tragic about Eddie's being in the service, because she was in the service herself.

At last there was work that needed her. She had started with three afternoons a week at Red Cross; chatty afternoons, with her mother beside her, and familiar neighbors stopping in the middle of surgical dressings to gurgle: "Oh, did you hear about how angry George Bangs was when Nellie bought a case of toilet soap at a dollar a cake? Think of it. A dollar! When you can get a very nice imported soap at twenty-five cents."

Theo felt that there was too much lint on the conversation and too little on their hands. She found herself one with a dozen girls who had been wrens and wanted to be eagles. Two of them learned motor repairing and got across to France. Theo wanted to go, but her mother refused. After a dignified protest from Mrs. Duke, Theo became telephone girl at Red Cross headquarters, till she had learned shorthand and typing, and was able to serve the head of the state Red Cross as secretary. She envied the motor-corps women in their uniforms, but she exulted in power—in being able to give quick, accurate information to the distressed women who came fluttering to headquarters.

Mrs. Duke felt that typing was low. Theo was protected by her father.

"Good thing for the girl to have business training," he kept insisting, till the commanding officer of the house impatiently consented.

It was the American Library Association collection which turned Theo from a dim uneasiness about the tyranny of possessions to active war. She bounced into the largest drawing room one dinner time, ten minutes late, crying: "Let's go over all our books tonight and weed out a dandy bunch for the soldiers!"

Mrs. Duke ruled: "Really, my dear, if you would only try to be on time for your meals! It's hard enough on Lizzie and myself to keep the house running——"

"Come, come, come! Get your hat off and comb your hair and get ready for dinner. I'm almost starved!" grumbled Mr. Duke.

Theo repeated the demand as soon as she was seated. The soldiers, she began, needed——

"We occasionally read the newspapers ourselves! Of course we shall be very glad to give what books we can spare. But there doesn't seem to be any necessity of going at things in this—this—hit-or-a-miss! Besides, I have some letters to write this evening," stated Mrs. Duke.

"Well, I'm going over them anyway!"

"I wish to see any books before you send them away!"

With Theo visualizing herself carrying off a carload of books, the Dukes ambled to the library after finishing dinner—and finishing coffee, a cigar and chocolate peppermints, and a discussion of the proper chintz for the shabby chairs in the guest room. Theo realized as she looked at the lofty, benign, and carefully locked bookcases that she hadn't touched one of the books for a year; that for six months she hadn't seen anyone enter the room for any purpose other than sweeping.

After fifteen minutes spent in studying every illustration in a three-volume history Mrs. Duke announced: "Here's something I think we might give away, Lym. Nobody has ever read it. A good many of the pages are uncut."

Mr. Duke protested: "Give that away? No, sir! I been meaning to get at that for a long time. Why, that's a valuable history. Tells all about modern Europe. Man ought to read it to get an idea of the sources of the war."

"But you never will read it, Papa," begged Theo.

"Now, Theo," her mother remonstrated in the D.A.R. manner, "if you father wishes to keep it that's all there is to be said, and we will make no more words about it." She returned the three volumes to the shelf.

"I'll turn it over to you just as soon as I've read it," her father obliged. Theo reflected that if any soldiers in the current conflict were to see the history they would have to prolong the war till 1950.

But she tried to look grateful while her father went on: "Tell you what I was thinking, though, Mother. Here's these two shelves of novels—none of 'em by standard authors—all just moonshine or blood and thunder. Let's clear out the whole bunch."

"But those books are just the thing for a rainy day—nice light reading. And for guests. But now this—this old book on saddlery. When we had horses you used to look at it, but now, with motors and all——"

"I know, but I still like to browse in it now and then."

"Very well."

Theo fled. She remembered piles of shabby books in the attic. While the Dukes were discovering that after all there wasn't one of the four hundred volumes in the library which they weren't going to read right away Theo heaped the dining-room table with attic waifs. She called her parents. The first thing Mrs. Duke spied was a Tennyson, printed in 1890 in a type doubtless suitable to ants, small sand-colored ants, but illegible to the human eye. Mrs. Duke shrieked: "Oh! You weren't thinking of giving that handsome Tennyson away! Why, it's a very handsome edition. Besides, it's one of the first books your father and I ever had. It was given to us by your Aunt Gracie!"

"But Moth-er dear! You haven't even seen the book for years!"

"Well, I've thought of it often."

"How about all these Christmas books?"

"Now, Theodora, if you wouldn't be so impatient, but kindly give your father and me time to look them over,——"

Two hours and seventeen minutes after dinner, Mr.

and Mrs. Duke had almost resignedly agreed to present the following literary treasures to the soldiers of these United States for their edification and entertainment:

One sixth-grade geography. One *Wild Flowers of Northern Wisconsin*. Two duplicate copies of *Little Women*. The *Congressional Record* for part of 1902. One black, depressed, religious volume entitled *The Dragon's Fight With the Woman for 1260 Prophetic Days,* from which the last seven hundred days were missing, leaving the issue of the combat in serious doubt. Four novels, all by women, severally called *Griselda of the Red Hand, Bramleigh of British Columbia, Lady Tip-Tippet,* and *Billikins' Lonely Christmas*.

Theo looked at them. She laughed. Then she was sitting by the table, her head down, sobbing. Her parents glanced at each other in hurt amazement.

"I can't understand the girl. After all the pains we took to try to help her!" sighed Mrs. Duke later, when they were undressing.

"O-o-o-oh," yawned Mr. Duke as he removed his collar from the back button—with the slight, invariable twinge in his rheumatic shoulder blades. "Oh, she's nervous and tired from her work down at that Red Cross place. I'm in favor of her having a little experience, but at the same time there's no need of overdoing. Plenty of other people to help out."

He intended to state this paternal wisdom to Theo at breakfast, but Theo at breakfast was not one to whom to state things paternally. Her normally broad shining lips were sucked in. She merely nodded to her parents, then attended with strictness to her oatmeal and departed—after privily instructing Lizzie to give the smaller pile of books in the dining room to the junk collector.

Three novels from the pile she did take to the public library for the A.L.A. To these she added twenty books, mostly trigonometries, bought with her own pocket money. Consequently she had no lunch save a glass of milk for twenty days. But as the Dukes didn't know that, everybody was happy.

The battle of the books led to other sanguinary skirmishes.

VI

There was the fireless cooker.

It was an early, homemade fireless cooker, constructed in the days when anything in the shape of one box inside another, with any spare scraps of sawdust between, was regarded as a valuable domestic machine. Aside from the fact that it didn't cook, the Dukes' cooker took up room in the kitchen, gathered a film of grease which caught a swamp of dust, and regularly banged Lizzie's shins. For six years the Dukes had talked about having it repaired. They had run through the historical, scientific, and financial aspects of cookers at least once a season.

"I've wondered sometimes if we couldn't just have the furnace man take out the sawdust and put in something else or—— Theo, wouldn't you like to run into Whaley & Baumgarten's one of these days, and price all of the new fireless cookers?" beamed Mrs. Duke.

"Too busy."

In a grieved, spacious manner Mrs. Duke reproved: "Well, my dear, I certainly am too busy, what with the party for the new rector and his bride——"

"Call up the store. Tell 'em to send up a good cooker on trial," said Theo.

"But these things have to be done with care and thought——"

Theo was stalking away as she retorted: "Not by me they don't!"

She was sorry for her rudeness afterward, and that evening she was gay and young as she played ballads for her father and did her mother's hair. After that, when she was going to bed, and very tired, and horribly confused in her thinking, she was sorry because she had been sorry because she had been rude.

The furnace went wrong, and its dissipations were discussed by Mr. Duke, Mrs. Duke, Mrs. Harry McPherson *née* Duke, Lizzie, the furnace man, and the plumber, till Theo ran up to her room and bit the pillow to keep from screaming. She begged her father to install a new furnace: "The old one will set the house afire—it's a terrible old animal."

"Nonsense. Take a chance on fire," said he. "House and everything well insured anyway. If the house did burn down there'd be one good thing—wouldn't have to worry any more about getting that twelve tons of coal we're still shy!"

When Mr. Duke was summoned to Duluth by the iron-mining company Mrs. Duke sobbingly called Theo home from the midst of tearing work.

Theo arrived in terror. "What is it? What's happened to Papa?"

"Happened? Why, nothing. But he didn't have a chance to take a single thing to Duluth, and he simply won't know what to do without his traveling bag—the one he got in London—all the fittings and everything that he's used to, so he could put his hand on a toothbrush right in the dark——"

"But, Mother dear, I'm sure bathrooms in Duluth have electric lights, so he won't need to put his hand on toothbrushes in the dark. And he can get nice new lovely brushes at almost any drug store and not have to fuss——"

"Fuss? Fuss? It's you who are doing the fussing. He just won't know what to do without his traveling bag."

While she helped her mother and Lizzie drag the ponderous bag down from the attic; while her mother, merely thinking aloud, discussed whether "your father" would want the madras pajamas or the flannelette; while, upon almost tearful maternal request, Theo hunted all through the house for the missing cut-glass soap case, she was holding herself in. She disliked herself for being so unsympathetic. She remembered how touched she had been by exactly the same domestic comedy two years before. But unsympathetic she was, even two days later, when her mother triumphantly showed Mr. Duke's note: "I can't tell you how glad I was to see good old bag showing up here at hotel; felt lost without it."

"Just the same, my absence that afternoon cost the Red Cross at least fifty dollars, and for a lot less than that he could have gone out and bought twice as good a bag—lighter, more convenient. Things! Poor Dad is the servant of that cursed pig-iron bag," she meditated.

She believed that she was being very subtle about her rebellion, but it must have been obvious, for after Mr. Duke's return, her mother suddenly attacked her at dinner.

"So far as I can make out from the way you're pouting and sulking and carrying on, you must have some sort of a socialistic idea that possessions are unimportant. Now you ought—"

"Anarchist, do you mean, Mother dear?"

"Kindly do not interrupt me! As I was saying: It's things that have made the world advance from barbarism. Motor cars, clothes you can wash, razors that enable a man to look neat, canned foods, printing presses, steamers, bathrooms—those are what have gotten men beyond living in skins in horrid damp caves."

"Of course. And that's why I object to people fussing so about certain things, and keeping themselves from getting full use of bigger things. If you're always so busy arranging the flowers in the vase in a limousine that you never have time to go riding, then the vase has spoiled the motor for——"

"I don't get your logic at all. I certainly pay very little attention to the flowers in our car. Lizzie arranges them for me!" triumphed Mrs. Duke.

Theo was charging on. She was trying to get her own ideas straight. "And if a man spends valuable time in tinkering with a worn-out razor when he could buy a new one, then he's keeping himself in the damp cave and the bearskin undies. That isn't thrift. It's waste."

"I fancy that people in caves, in prehistoric times, did not use razors at all, did they, Lyman?" her mother majestically corrected.

"Now you always worry about Papa's bag. It was nice once, and worth caring for, but it's just a bother now. On your principle a factory would stop running for half the year to patch up or lace up the belting, or whatever it is they do, instead of getting new belting and thus——Oh, can't you see? Buy things. Use 'em. But throw them away if they're more bother than good. If a bag keeps you from enjoying traveling—chuck it in the river! If a man makes a tennis court and finds he really doesn't like tennis, let the court get weedy rather than spend glorious free October afternoons in mowing and raking——"

"Well, I suppose you mean rolling it," said her mother domestically. "And I don't know what tennis has to do with the subject. I'm sure I haven't mentioned tennis. And I trust you'll admit that your knowledge of factories and belting is not authoritative. No. The trouble is, this Red Cross work is getting you so you can't think straight. Of course with this war and all, it may be permissible to waste a lot of good time and money making dressings and things for a lot of green nurses to waste, but you girls must learn the great principle of thrift."

"We have! I'm practicing it. It means—oh, so much, now. Thrift is doing without things you don't need, and taking care of things as long as they're useful. It distinctly isn't wasting time and spiritual devotion over things you can't use—just because you happen to be so unfortunate as to own 'em. Like our eternal fussing over that clock in the upper hall that no one ever looks at——"

Not listening, her mother was placidly rolling on: "You seem to think this house needs too much attention. You'd like it, wouldn't you, if we moved to a couple of rooms in the Dakota Lodging House!"

Theo gave it up.

Two days later she forgot it.

Creeping into her snug life, wailing for her help, came a yellow-faced apparition whose eyes were not for seeing but mere gashes to show the suffering within. It was—it had been—one Stacy Lindstrom, a sergeant of the A.E.F.

Stacy had lain with a shattered shoulder in a shell pit for three days. He had had pneumonia. Four distinct times all of him had died, quite definitely died—all but the desire to see Theo.

His little, timid, vehemently respectable mother sent for Theo on the night when he was brought home, and despite Mrs. Duke's panicky protest Theo went to him at eleven in the evening.

"Not going to die for little while. Terribly weak, but all here. Pull through—if you want me to. Not asking you to like me. All I want—want you to want me to live. Made 'em send me home. Was all right on the sea. But weak. Got touch of typhoid in New York. Didn't show up till on the train. But all right and cheerful——Oh! I hurt so. Just hurt, hurt, hurt, every inch of me. Never mind. Well, see you again. Can die now. Guess I will."

Thus in panting words he muttered, while she knelt by him and could not tell whether she loved him or hated him; whether she shrank from this skinny claw outstretched from the grave or was drawn to him by a longing to nurse his soul back to a desire for life. But this she knew: Even Red Cross efficiency was nothing in the presence of her first contact with raw living life—most rawly living when crawling out from the slime of death.

She overruled Mrs. Lindstrom; got a nurse and Doctor Rollin—Rollin, the interior medicine specialist.

"Boy's all right. Hasn't got strength enough to fight very hard. Better cheer him up," said Doctor Rollin. "Bill? My bill? He's a soldier, isn't he? Don't you suppose I wanted to go into the army too? Chance to see beautiful cases for once. Yes. Admit it. Like to have fool salutes too. Got to stay home, nurse lot of dam-fool women. Charge a soldier? Don't bother me," he grumbled, while he was folding up his stethoscope, and closing his bag, and trying to find his hat, which Mrs. Lindstrom had politely concealed.

Every day after her work Theo trudged to the Lindstrom house—a scrubbed and tidied cottage in whose living room was a bureau with a lace cover, a gilded shell, and two photographs of stiff relatives in Norway. She watched Stacy grow back into life. His hands, which had been yellow and drawn as the talons of a starved Chinaman, became pink and solid. The big knuckles, which had been lumpy under the crackly skin, were padded again.

She had been surprised into hot pity for him. She was saved equally by his amusement over his own weakness, and by his irritableness. Though he had called for her, during the first week he seemed to dislike her and all other human beings save his nurse. In the depths of lead-colored pain nothing mattered to him save his own comfort. The coolness of his glass of water was more to him than the war. Even when he became human again, and eager at her coming, there was nothing very personal in their talk. When he was able to do more than gasp out a few words she encouraged in him the ambition to pile up money which she detested.

Uncomfortably she looked at him, thin against a plump pillow, and her voice was artificially cheery as she declared: "You'll be back in the bank soon. I'm sure they'll raise you. No reason why you shouldn't be president of it some day."

He had closed his pale eyelids. She thought he was discouraged. Noisily she reassured, "Honestly! I'm sure you'll make money—lots of it."

His eyes were open, blazing. "Money! Yes! Wonderful thing!"

"Ye-es."

"Buy tanks and shells, and food for homeless babies. But for me—I just want a living. There isn't any

Stacy Lindstrom any more." He was absorbed in that bigger thing over there, in that Nirvana—a fighting Nirvana! "I've got ambitions, big 'uns, but not to see myself in a morning coat and new gloves on Sunday!"

He said nothing more. A week after, he was sitting up in bed, reading, in a Lindstromy nightgown of white cotton edged with red. She wondered at the book. It was *Colloquial French*.

"You aren't planning to go back?" she asked casually.

"Yes. I've got it straight now." He leaned back, pulled the bedclothes carefully up about his neck and said quietly, "I'm going back to fight. But not just for the duration of the war. Now I know what I was meant for. I can do things with my hands, and I get along with plain folks. I'm going back on reconstruction work. We're going to rebuild France. I'm studying— French, cottage architecture, cabbages. I'm a pretty good farmer—'member how I used to work on the farm, vacations?"

She saw that all self-consciousness was gone from him. He was again the Stacy Lindstrom who had been lord of the Red River carts. Her haunted years of nervousness about life disappeared, and suddenly she was again too fond of her boy companion to waste time considering whether she was fond of him. They were making plans, laughing the quick curt laughs of intimates.

A week later Mrs. Lindstrom took her aside.

Mrs. Lindstrom had always, after admitting Theo and nodding without the slightest expression in her anaemic face, vanished through the kitchen doorway. Tonight, as Theo was sailing out, Mrs. Lindstrom hastened after her through the living room.

"Miss! Miss Duke! Yoost a minute. Could you speak wit' me?"

"Why, yes."

"Dis—ay—da boy get along pretty gude, eh? He seem werry gude, today. Ay vish you should——" The little woman's face was hard. "Ay don't know how to say it elegant, but if you ever—— I know he ain't your fella, but he always got that picture of you, and maybe now he ban pretty brave soldier, maybe you could like him better, but—I know I yoost ban Old Country woman. If you and him marry—I keep away, not bother you. Your folks is rich and—— Oh, I gif, I gif him to you—if you vant him."

Mrs. Lindstrom's sulky eyes seemed to expand, grow misty. Her Puritanical chest was terribly heaving. She sobbed: "He always talk about you ever since he ban little fella. Please excuse me I spoke, if you don't vant him, but I vanted you should know, I do anyt'ing for him. And you."

She fled, and Theo could hear the scouring of a pot in the kitchen. Theo fled the other way.

It was that same evening, at dinner, that Mrs. Duke delicately attempted social homicide.

"My dear, aren't you going to see this Lindstrom boy rather oftener than you need to? From what you say he must be convalescing. I hope that your pity for him won't lead you into any foolish notions and sentiment about him."

Theo laughed. "No time to be sentimental about anything these days. I've canned the word——"

" 'Canned'! Oh, Theo!"

"—'sentiment' entirely. But if I hadn't, Stace wouldn't be a bad one to write little poems about. He used to be my buddy when——"

"Please—do—not—be—so—vulgar! And Theo, however you may regard Stacy, kindly do stop and think how Mrs. Lindstrom would look in this house!"

The cheerful, gustatory manner died in Theo. She rose. She said with an intense, a religious solemnity: "This house! Damn this house!"

The Lindstroms were not mentioned again. There was no need. Mrs. Duke's eyebrows adequately repeated her opinions when Theo came racing in at night, buoyant with work and walking and fighting over Stacy's plans.

Theo fancied that her father looked at her more

sympathetically. She ceased to take Mr. Duke as a
matter of course, as one more fixed than the radiators.
She realized that he spent these autumn evenings in
staring at the fire. When he looked up he smiled, but
his eyes were scary. Theo noticed that he had given
up making wistful suggestions to Mrs. Duke that he
be permitted to go back to real work, or that they get
a farm, or go traveling. Once they had a week's excur-
sion to New York, but Mrs. Duke had to hasten back
for her committees. She was ever firmer with her husband; more ready with reminders that it was hard to
get away from a big house like this; that men oughtn't
to be so selfish and just expect Lizzie and her——

Mr. Duke no longer argued. He rarely went to his
office. He was becoming a slippered old man.

VII

Eddie Barnes was back in Vernon on the sixth of his
positively last, final, ultimate farewells.

Theo yelled in joy when he called. She was positively blowzy with healthy vulgarity. She had won an
argument with Stacy about teaching the French to
plant corn, and had walked home almost at a trot.

"Fine to see you! Saying an eternal farewell again?"
she brutally asked Eddie.

For one of the young samurai Eddie was rather
sheepish. He stalked about the largest drawing room.
His puttees shone. Eddie really had very nice legs, the
modern young woman reflected.

"Gosh, I'm an awful fareweller. Nope, I'm not going
to do a single weep. Because this time—I've got my
orders. I'll be in France in three weeks. So I just
thought—I just thought—maybe—I'd ask you if you
could conveniently—— Ouch, that tooth still aches;
have to get this bridge finished tomorrow sure. Could
you marry me?"

"Ungh!" Theo flopped into a chair.

"You've queered all my poetic tactics by your rude
merry mirth. So just got to talk naturally."

"Glad you did. Now let me think. Do I want to marry you?"

"We get along bully. Listen—wait till I get back from France, and we'll have some celebration. Oh, boy! I'll stand for the cooties and the mud till the job's done, but when I get back and put the Croix de Guerre into the safe-deposit I'm going to have a drink of champagne four quarts deep! And you and I—we'll have one time! Guess you'll be pretty sick of Red Cross by——"

"No. And I know a man who thinks that when the war is over then the real work begins."

Eddie was grave, steady, more mature than he had ever seemed. "Yes. Stacy Lindstrom. See here, honey, he has big advantages over me. I'm not picturesque. I never had to work for my bread and butter, and I was brought up to try to be amusing, not noble. Nothing more touching than high ideals and poverty. But if I try to be touching, you laugh at me. I'm—— I may get killed, and I'll be just as dead in my expensible first lieut's pants as any self-sacrificing private."

"I hadn't thought of that. Of course. You have disadvantages. Comfort isn't dramatic. But still—— It's the champagne and the big time. I've——"

"See here, honey, you'd be dreadfully bored by poverty. You do like nice things."

"That's it. Things! That's what I'm afraid of. I'm interested in tractors for France, but not in the exact shade of hock glasses. And beauty—— It's the soul of things, but it's got to be inherent, not just painted on. Nice things! Ugh! And—— If I married you what would be your plans for me? How would I get through twenty-four hours a day?"

"Why—uh—why, how does anybody get through 'em? You'd have a good time—dances, and playin' round and maybe children, and we'd run down to Palm Beach——"

"Yes. You'd permit me to go on doing what I always did till the war came. Nope. It isn't good enough. I want to work. You wouldn't let me, even in the house. There'd be maids, nurses. It's not that I want a career. I don't want to be an actress or a congress-woman. Perfectly willing to be assistant to some man. Providing he can really use me in useful work. No. You pre-war boys are going to have a frightful time with us post-war women."

"But you'll get tired——"

"Oh, I know, I know! You and Father and Mother will wear me out. You-all may win. You and this house, this horrible sleek warm house that Mrs.—— that she isn't fit to come into! She that gave him——"

Her voice was rising, hysterical. She was bent in the big chair, curiously twisted, as though she had been wounded.

Eddie stroked her hair, then abruptly stalked out.

Theo sat marveling: "Did I really send Eddie away? Poor Eddie. Oh, I'll write him. He's right. Nice to think of brave maiden defiantly marrying poor hero. But they never do. Not in this house."

VIII

The deep courthouse bell awakening Theo to bewil-dered staring at the speckled darkness—a factory whistle fantastically tooting, then beating against her ears in long, steady waves of sound—the triumphant yelping of a small boy and the quacking of a toy horn—a motor starting next door, a cold motor that bucked and snorted before it began to sing, but at last roared away with the horn blaring—finally the distant "Extra! Extra!"

Her sleepy body protestingly curled tighter in a downy ball in her bed on the upper porch, but her mind was frantically awake as the clamor thickened. "Is it really peace this time? The armistice really signed?" she exulted.

In pleasant reasonable phrases the warm body ob-jected to the cold outside the silk comforter. "Remem-ber how you were fooled on Thursday. Oo-oo! Bed feels so luxurious!" it insisted.

She was a practical heroine. She threw off the covers. The indolent body had to awaken, in self-defense. She merely squeaked "Ouch!" as her feet groped for their slippers on the cold floor. She flung downstairs, into rubbers and a fur coat, and she was out on the walk in time to stop a bellowing newsboy.

Yes. It was true. Official report from Washington. War over.

"Hurray!" said the ragged newsboy, proud of being out adventuring by night; and "Hurray!" she answered him. She felt that she was one with awakening crowds all over the country, from the T Wharf to the Embarcadero. She wanted to make great noises.

The news had reached the almost-Western city of Vernon at three. It was only four, but as she stood on the porch a crush of motor cars swept by, headed for downtown. Bumping behind them they dragged lard cans, saucepans, frying pans. One man standing on a running board played Mr. Zip on a cornet. Another dashing for a trolley had on his chest a board with an insistent electric bell. He saw her on the porch and shouted, "Come on, sister! Downtown! All celebrate! Some carnival!"

She waved to him. She wanted to get out the electric and drive down. There would be noise—singing.

Four strange girls ran by and shrieked to her, "Come on and dance!"

Suddenly she was asking herself: "But do they know what it means? It isn't just a carnival. It's sacred." Sharply: "But do I know all it means, either? Worldwide. History, here, now!" Leaning against the door, cold but not conscious that she was cold, she found herself praying.

As she marched back upstairs she was startled. She fancied she saw a gray figure fleeing down the upper hall. She stopped. No sound.

"Heavens, I'm so wrought up! All jumpy. Shall I give Papa the paper? Oh, I'm too trembly to talk to anyone."

While the city went noise-mad it was a very solemn

white small figure that crawled into bed. The emotion that for four years had been gathering burst into sobbing. She snuggled close, but she did not sleep. Presently: "My Red Cross work will be over soon. What can I do then? Come back to packing Papa's bag?"

She noticed a glow on the windows of the room beside the sleeping porch. "They're lighting up the whole city. Wonder if I oughtn't to go down and see the fun? Wonder if Papa would like to go down? No, Mother wouldn't let him! I want the little old brown shack. Where Stacy could come and play. Mother used to give him cookies then.

"I wish I had the nerve to set the place afire. If I were a big fighting soul I would. But I'm a worm. Am I being bad to think this way? Guess so—committed mental arson, but hadn't the nerve—— My God, the house *is* afire!"

She was too frightened to move. She could smell smoke, hear a noise like the folding of stiff wrapping paper. Instantly, apparently without ever having got out of bed, she was running by a bedroom into which flames were licking from the clothes chute that led to the basement. "That dratted old furnace!" She was bursting into her parents' room, hysterically shaking her mother.

"Get up! Get up!"

With a drowsy dignity her mother was saying, "Yes—I know—peace—get paper morning—let me sleep."

"It's fire! Fire! This house is afire!"

Her mother sat up, a thick gray lock bobbing in front of one eye, and said indignantly, "How perfectly preposterous!"

Already Mr. Duke was out of bed, in smoke-prickly darkness, flapping his hands in the air. "Never could find that globe. Ought to have bedside light. Come, Mother, jump up! Theo, have you got a warm bathrobe?" He was cool. His voice trembled, but only with nervousness.

He charged down the back hall, Theo just behind.

Mrs. Duke remained at the head of the front stairs, lamenting, "Don't leave me!"

The flames were darting hissing heads into the hall. As Theo looked they caught a box couch and ran over an old chest of drawers. The heat seemed to slap her face.

"Can't do anything. Get out of this. Wake the servants. You take your mother down," grumbled Mr. Duke.

Theo had her mother into a loose gown, shoes, and a huge fleecy couch cover, and down on the front porch by the time Mr. Duke appeared driving the maids—Lizzie a gorgon in curl papers.

"Huh! Back stairs all afire," he grunted, rubbing his chin. His fingers, rubbing then stopping, showed that for a split second he was thinking, "I need a shave."

"Theo! Run down to the corner. Turn in alarm. I'll try to phone. Then save things," he commanded.

Moved by his coolness to a new passion of love Theo flung her arm, bare as the sleeve of her bathrobe fell from it, about his seamed neck, beseeching: "Don't save anything but the cloisonné. Let 'em burn. Won't have to go in there, risk your life for things. Here—let me phone!"

Unreasoning she slammed the front door, bolted him out. She shouted their address and "Fire—hustle alarm!" at the telephone operator. In the largest drawing room she snatched bit after bit of cloisonné from the cabinet and dumped them into a wastebasket. Now the lower hall, at her back, was boiling with flame-tortured smoke. The noise expanded from crackling to a roar.

The window on the porch was smashed. Her father's arm was reaching up to the catch, unlocking the window. He was crawling in. As the smoke encircled him he puffed like a man blowing out water after a dive.

Theo ran to him. "I didn't want you here! I have the cloisonné——"

As calmly as though he were arguing a point at cards he mumbled, "Yes, yes, yes! Don't bother me. You forgot the two big *saras* in the wall safe."

While the paint on the balusters in the hall bubbled and charred, and the heat was a pang in her lungs, he twirled the knob of the safe behind the big picture and drew out two cloisonné plates. Flames curled round the door jamb of the room like fingers closing on a stick.

"We're shut off!" Theo cried.

"Yep. Better get out. Here. Drop that basket!"

Mr. Duke snatched the cloisonné from her, dropped it, hurled away his two plates, shoved her to the window he had opened, helped her out on the porch. He himself was still in the burning room. She gripped his arm when he tried to dart back. The cloisonné was already hidden from them by puffs of smoke.

Mr. Duke glanced back. He eluded her; pulled his arm free; disappeared in the smoke. He came back with a cheap china vase that for a thing so small was monumentally ugly. As he swung out of the window he said, "Your mother always thought a lot of that vase." Theo saw through eyes stinging with smoke that his hair had been scorched.

Fire engines were importantly unloading at the corner, firemen running up. A neighbor came to herd the Dukes into her house, and into more clothes.

Alone, from the room given to her by the neighbor, Theo watched her home burn. The flames were leering out of all the windows on the ground floor. Her father would never read the three-volume history that was too valuable for soldiers. Now the attic was glaring. Gone the elephant of a London traveling bag. Woolly smoke curled out of the kitchen windows as a fireman smashed them. Gone the fireless cooker that would not cook. She laughed. "It's nicely cooked itself! Oh, I'm beastly. Poor Mother. All her beautiful marked linen——"

But she did not lose a sensation of running ungirdled, of breathing Maytime air.

Her father came in, dressed in the neighbor-host's corduroy hunting coat, a pair of black dress trousers and red slippers. His hair was conscientiously combed, but his fingers still querulously examined the state of his unshaven chin.

She begged: "Daddy dear, it's pretty bad, but don't worry. We have plenty of money. We'll make arrangements——"

He took her arms from about his neck, walked to the window. The broken skeleton of their home was tombed in darkness as the firemen controlled the flames. He looked at Theo in a puzzled way.

He said hesitatingly: "No, I won't worry. I guess it's all right. You see—I set the house afire."

She was silent, but her trembling fingers sought her lips as he went on: "Shoveled hot coals from the furnace into kindling bin in the basement. Huh! Yes. Used to be good furnace tender when I was a real man. Peace bells had woke me up. Wanted to be free. Hate destruction, but—no other way. Your mother wouldn't let me sell the house. I was going mad, sticking there, waiting—waiting for death. Now your mother will be willing to come. Get a farm. Travel. And I been watching you. You couldn't have had Stacy Lindstrom, long as that house bossed us. You almost caught me, in the hall, coming back from the basement. It was kind of hard, with house afire, to lie there in bed, quiet, so's your mother wouldn't ever know—waiting for you to come wake us up. You almost didn't, in time. Would have had to confess. Uh, let's go comfort your mother. She's crying."

Theo had moved away from him. "But it's criminal! We're stealing—robbing the insurance company."

The wrinkles beside his eyes opened with laughter.

"No. Watched out for that. I was careful to be careless, and let all the insurance run out last month. Huh! Maybe I won't catch it from your mother for that, though! Girl! Look! It's dawn!"

The Willow Walk

From the drawer of his table Jasper Holt took a pane of window glass. He laid a sheet of paper on the glass and wrote, "Now is the time for all good men to come to the aid of their party." He studied his round business-college script, and rewrote the sentence in a small finicky hand, that of a studious old man. Ten times he copied the words in that false pinched writing. He tore up the paper, burned the fragments in his large ash tray and washed the delicate ashes down his stationary washbowl. He replaced the pane of glass in the drawer, tapping it with satisfaction. A glass underlay does not retain an impression.

Jasper Holt was as nearly respectable as his room, which, with its frilled chairs and pansy-painted pincushion, was the best in the aristocratic boarding house of Mrs. Lyons. He was a wiry, slightly bald, black-haired man of thirty-eight, wearing an easy gray flannel suit and a white carnation. His hands were peculiarly compact and nimble. He gave the appearance of being a youngish lawyer or bond salesman. Actually he was senior paying teller in the Lumber National Bank in the city of Vernon.

He looked at a thin expensive gold watch. It was six-thirty, on Wednesday—toward dusk of a tranquil spring day. He picked up his hooked walking stick and his gray silk gloves and trudged downstairs. He met his landlady in the lower hall and inclined his head. She effusively commented on the weather.

"I shall not be there for dinner," he said amiably.

"Very well, Mr. Holt. My, but aren't you always going out with your swell friends though! I read in the *Herald* that you were going to be a star in another of those society plays in the Community Theater. I guess you'd be an actor if you wasn't a banker, Mr. Holt."

"No, I'm afraid I haven't much temperament." His voice was cordial, but his smile was a mere mechanical sidewise twist of the lip muscles. "You're the one that's got the stage presence. Bet you'd be a regular Ethel Barrymore if you didn't have to take care of us."

"My, but you're such a flatterer!"

He bowed his way out and walked sedately down the street to a public garage. Nodding to the night attendant, but saying nothing, he started his roadster and drove out of the garage, away from the center of Vernon, toward the suburb of Rosebank. He did not go directly to Rosebank. He went seven blocks out of his way, and halted on Fandall Avenue—one of those petty main thoroughfares which, with their motion-picture palaces, their groceries, laundries, undertakers' establishments and lunchrooms, serve as local centers for districts of mean residences. He got out of the car and pretended to look at the tires, kicking them to see how much air they had. While he did so he covertly looked up and down the street. He saw no one whom he knew. He went into the Parthenon Confectionery Store.

The Parthenon Store makes a specialty of those ingenious candy boxes that resemble bound books. The back of the box is of imitation leather, with a stamping simulating the title of a novel. The edges are apparently the edges of a number of pages. But these pages are hollowed out, and the inside is to be filled with candy.

Jasper gazed at the collection of book boxes and

chose the two whose titles had the nearest approach to dignity—Sweets to the Sweet and The Ladies' Delight. He asked the Greek clerk to fill these with the less expensive grade of mixed chocolates, and to wrap them.

From the candy shop he went to the drugstore that carried an assortment of reprinted novels, and from these picked out two of the same sentimental type as the titles on the booklike boxes. These also he had wrapped. He strolled out of the drugstore, slipped into a lunchroom, got a lettuce sandwich, doughnuts, and a cup of coffee at the greasy marble counter, took them to a chair with a table arm in the dim rear of the lunchroom and hastily devoured them. As he came out and returned to his car he again glanced along the street.

He fancied that he knew a man who was approaching. He could not be sure. From the breast up the man seemed familiar, as did the customers of the bank whom he viewed through the wicket of the teller's window. When he saw them in the street he could never be sure of them. It seemed extraordinary to find that these persons, who to him were nothing but faces with attached arms that held out checks and received money, could walk about, had legs and a gait and a manner of their own.

He walked to the curb and stared up at the cornice of one of the stores, puckering his lips, giving an impersonation of a man inspecting a building. With the corner of an eye he followed the approaching man. The man ducked his head as he neared, and greeted him, "Hello, Brother Teller." Jasper seemed startled; gave the "Oh! Oh, how are you!" of sudden recognition; and mumbled, "Looking after a little bank property."

The man passed on.

Jasper got into his car and drove back to the street that would take him out to the suburb of Rosebank. As he left Fandall Avenue he peered at his watch. It was five minutes to seven.

At a quarter past seven he passed through the main street of Rosebank and turned into a lane that was but little changed since the time when it had been a country road. A few jerry-built villas of freckled paint did shoulder upon it, but for the most part it ran through swamps spotted with willow groves, the spongy ground covered with scatterings of dry leaves and bark. Opening on this lane was a dim-rutted grassy private road which disappeared into one of the willow groves.

Jasper sharply swung his car between the crumbly gate posts and along on the bumpy private road. He made an abrupt turn, came in sight of an unpainted shed and shot the car into it without cutting down his speed, so that he almost hit the back of the shed with his front fenders. He shut off the engine, climbed out quickly and ran back toward the gate. From the shield of the bank of alder bushes he peered out. Two clattering women were going down the public road. They stared in through the gate and half halted.

"That's where that hermit lives," said one of them.

"Oh, you mean the one that's writing a religious book, and never comes out till evening? Some kind of a preacher?"

"Yes, that's the one. John Holt, I think his name is. I guess he's kind of crazy. He lives in the old Beaudette house. But you can't see it from here—it's clear through the block, on the next street."

"I heard he was crazy. But I just saw an automobile go in here."

"Oh, that's his cousin or brother or something— lives in the city. They say he's rich, and such a nice fellow."

The two women ambled on, their clatter blurring with distance. Standing behind the alders Jasper rubbed the palm of one hand with the fingers of the other. The palm was dry with nervousness. But he grinned.

He returned to the shed and entered a brick-paved walk almost a block long, walled and sheltered by overhanging willows. Once it had been a pleasant path; carved wooden benches were placed along it, and it widened to a court with a rock garden, a fountain and a stone bench. The rock garden had degenerated into a riot of creepers sprawling over the sharp stones; the paint had peeled from the fountain, leaving its iron cupids and naiads eaten with rust. The bricks of the wall were smeared with lichens and moss and were untidy with windrows of dry leaves and caked earth. Many of the bricks were broken; the walk was hilly in its unevenness. From willows and bricks and scuffled earth rose a damp chill. But Jasper did not seem to note the dampness. He hastened along the walk to the house—a structure of heavy stone which, for this newish Midwestern land, was very ancient. It had been built by a French fur trader in 1839. The Chippewas had scalped a man in its dooryard. The heavy back door was guarded by an unexpectedly expensive modern lock. Jasper opened it with a flat key and closed it behind him. It locked on a spring. He was in a crude kitchen, the shades of which were drawn. He passed through the kitchen and dining room into the living room. Dodging chairs and tables in the darkness as though he was used to them he went to each of the three windows of the living room and made sure that all the shades were down before he lighted the student lamp on the game-legged table. As the glow crept over the drab walls Jasper bobbed his head with satisfaction. Nothing had been touched since his last visit.

The room was musty with the smell of old green rep upholstery and leather books. It had not been dusted for months. Dust sheeted the stiff red velvet chairs, the uncomfortable settee, the chill white marble fireplace, the immense glass-fronted bookcase that filled one side of the room.

The atmosphere was unnatural to this capable business man, this Jasper Holt. But Jasper did not seem oppressed. He briskly removed the wrappers from the genuine books and from the candy-box imitations of

books. One of the two wrappers he laid on the table
and smoothed out. Upon this he poured the candy
from the two boxes. The other wrapper and the strings
he stuffed into the fireplace and immediately burned.
Crossing to the bookcase he unlocked one section on
the bottom shelf. There was a row of rather cheap-
looking novels on this shelf, and of these at least six
were actually such candy boxes as he had purchased
that evening.

Only one shelf of the bookcase was given over to
anything so frivolous as novels. The others were filled
with black-covered, speckle-leaved, dismal books of
history, theology, biography—the shabby-genteel sort
of books you find on the fifteen-cent table at a second-
hand bookshop. Over these Jasper pored for a moment as though he was memorizing their titles.

He took down *The Life of the Rev. Jeremiah Bodfish*
and read aloud: "In those intimate discourses with his
family that followed evening prayers I once heard Brother
Bodfish observe that Philo Judaeus—whose scholarly career always calls to my mind the adumbrations of Melanchthon upon the essence of rationalism—was a mere
sophist——"

Jasper slammed the book shut, remarking contentedly, "That'll do. Philo Judaeus—good name to spring."

He relocked the bookcase and went upstairs. In a
small bedroom at the right of the upper hall an electric
light was burning. Presumably the house had been deserted till Jasper's entrance, but a prowler in the yard
might have judged from this ever-burning light that
someone was in the residence. The bedroom was Spartan—an iron bed, one straight chair, a washstand, a
heavy oak bureau. Jasper scrambled to unlock the bottom drawer of the bureau, yank it open, take out a
wrinkled shiny suit of black, a pair of black shoes, a
small black bow tie, a Gladstone collar, a white shirt
with starched bosom, a speckly brown felt hat and
a wig—an expensive and excellent wig with artfully
unkempt hair of a faded brown.

He stripped off his attractive flannel suit, wing col-

lar, blue tie, custom-made silk shirt and cordovan
shoes, and speedily put on the wig and those gloomy
garments. As he donned them the corners of his
mouth began to droop. Leaving the light on and his
own clothes flung on the bed he descended the stairs.
He was obviously not the same Jasper, but less
healthy, less practical, less agreeable, and decidedly
more aware of the sorrow and long thoughts of the
dreamer. Indeed it must be understood that now he
was not Jasper Holt, but Jasper's twin bother, John
Holt, hermit and religious fanatic.

II

John Holt, twin brother of Jasper Holt, the bank
teller, rubbed his eyes as though he had for hours
been absorbed in study, and crawled through the living
room, through the tiny hall, to the front door. He
opened it, picked up a couple of circulars that the post-
man had dropped through the letter slot in the door,
went out and locked the door behind him. He was facing a narrow front yard, neater than the willow walk
at the back, on a suburban street more populous than
the straggly back lane.

A street arc illuminated the yard and showed that
a card was tacked on the door. John touched the card,
snapped it with a nail of his finger to make sure it
was securely tacked. In that light he could not read it,
but he knew that it was inscribed in a small finicky
hand: "Agents kindly do not disturb, bell will not be
answered, occupant of the house engaged in literary
work."

John stood on the doorstep until he made out his
neighbor on the right—a large stolid commuter, who
was walking before his house smoking an after-dinner
cigar. John poked to the fence and sniffed at a spray
of lilac blossoms till the neighbor called over, "Nice
evening."

"Yes, it seems to be pleasant."

John's voice was like Jasper's but it was more guttural, and his speech had less assurance.

"How's the story going?"

"It is—it is very difficult. So hard to comprehend all the inner meanings of the prophecies. Well, I must be hastening to Soul Hope Hall. I trust we shall see you there some Wednesday or Sunday evening. I bid you good-night, sir."

John wavered down the street to the drugstore. He purchased a bottle of ink. In a grocery that kept open evenings he got two pounds of cornmeal, two pounds of flour, a pound of bacon, a half pound of butter, six eggs and a can of condensed milk.

"Shall we deliver them?" asked the clerk.

John looked at him sharply. He realized that this was a new man, who did not know his customs. He said rebukingly: "No, I always carry my parcels. I am writing a book. I am never to be disturbed."

He paid for the provisions out of a postal money order for thirty-five dollars, and received the change. The cashier of the store was accustomed to cashing these money orders, which were always sent to John from South Vernon, by one R. J. Smith. John took the bundle of food and walked out of the store.

"That fellow's kind of a nut, isn't he?" asked the new clerk.

The cashier explained: "Yep. Doesn't even take fresh milk—uses condensed for everything! What do you think of that! And they say he burns up all his garbage—never has anything in the ashcan except ashes. If you knock at his door, he never answers it, fellow told me. All the time writing this book of his. Religious crank, I guess. Has a little income though—guess his folks were pretty well fixed. Comes out once in a while in the evening and pokes round town. We used to laugh about him, but we've kind of got used to him. Been here about a year, I guess it is."

John was serenely passing down the main street of Rosebank. At the dingier end of it he turned in at a hallway marked by a lighted sign announcing in crude housepainter's letters: "Soul Hope Fraternity Hall. Experience Meeting. All Welcome."

It was eight o'clock. The members of the Soul Hope cult had gathered in their hall above a bakery. Theirs was a tiny, tight-minded sect. They asserted that they alone obeyed the scriptural tenets; that they alone were certain to be saved, that all other denominations were damned by unapostolic luxury, that it was wicked to have organs or ministers or any meeting places save plain halls. The members themselves conducted the meetings, one after another rising to give an interpretation of the scriptures or to rejoice in gathering with the faithful, while the others commented with "Hallelujah!" and "Amen, brother, amen!" They were plainly dressed, not overfed, somewhat elderly, and a rather happy congregation. The most honored of them all was John Holt.

John had come to Rosebank only eleven months before. He had bought the Beaudette house with the library of the recent occupant, a retired clergyman, and had paid for them in new one-hundred-dollar bills. Already he had great credit in the Soul Hope cult. It appeared that he spent almost all his time at home, praying and reading and writing a book. The Soul Hope Fraternity were excited about the book. They had begged him to read it to them. So far he had only read a few pages, consisting mostly of quotations from ancient treatises on the Prophecies. Nearly every Sunday and Wednesday evening he appeared at the meeting and in a halting and scholarly way lectured on the world and the flesh.

Tonight he spoke polysyllabically of the fact that one Philo Judaeus had been a mere sophist. The cult were none too clear as to what either a Philo Judaeus or a sophist might be, but with heads all nodding in a row, they murmured: "You're right, brother! Hallelujah!"

John glided into a sad earnest discourse on his

worldly brother Jasper, and informed them of his struggles with Jasper's itch for money. By his request the fraternity prayed for Jasper.

The meeting was over at nine. John shook hands all round with the elders of the congregation, sighing: "Fine meeting tonight, wasn't it? Such a free outpouring of the Spirit!" He welcomed a new member, a servant girl just come from Seattle. Carrying his groceries and the bottle of ink he poked down the stairs from the hall at seven minutes after nine.

At sixteen minutes after nine John was stripping off his brown wig and the funereal clothes in his bedroom. At twenty-eight after, John Holt had become Jasper Holt, the capable teller of the Lumber National Bank.

Jasper Holt left the light burning in his brother's bedroom. He rushed downstairs, tried the fastening of the front door, bolted it, made sure that all the windows were fastened, picked up the bundle of groceries and the pile of candies that he had removed from the booklike candy boxes, blew out the light in the living room and ran down the willow walk to his car. He threw the groceries and candy into it, backed the car out as though he was accustomed to backing in this bough-scattered yard, and drove along the lonely road at the rear.

When he was passing a swamp he reached down, picked up the bundle of candies, and steering with one hand removed the wrapping paper with the other hand and hurled out the candies. They showered among the weeds beside the road. The paper which had contained the candies, and upon which was printed the name of the Parthenon Confectionery Store, Jasper tucked into his pocket. He took the groceries item by item from the labeled bag containing them, thrust that bag also into his pocket, and laid the groceries on the seat beside him.

On the way from Rosebank to the center of the city of Vernon, he again turned off the main avenue and halted at a goat-infested shack occupied by a crippled

Norwegian. He sounded the horn. The Norwegian's grandson ran out.

"Here's a little more grub for you," bawled Jasper.

"God bless you, sir. I don't know what we'd do if it wasn't for you!" cried the old Norwegian from the door.

But Jasper did not wait for gratitude. He merely shouted: "Bring you some more in a couple of days," as he started away.

At a quarter past ten he drove up to the hall that housed the latest interest in Vernon society—The Community Theater. The Boulevard Set, the "best people in town," belonged to the Community Theater Association, and the leader of it was the daughter of the general manager of the railroad. As a well-bred bachelor Jasper Holt was welcome among them, despite the fact that no one knew much about him except that he was a good bank teller and had been born in England. But as an actor he was not merely welcome: he was the best amateur actor in Vernon. His placid face could narrow with tragic emotion or puff out with comedy, his placid manner concealed a dynamo of emotion. Unlike most amateur actors he did not try to act—he became the thing itself. He forgot Jasper Holt, and turned into a vagrant or a judge, a Bernard Shaw thought, a Lord Dunsany symbol, a Noel Coward man-about-town.

The other one-act plays of the next program of the Community Theater had already been rehearsed. The cast of the play in which Jasper was to star were all waiting for him. So were the ladies responsible for the staging. They wanted his advice about the blue curtain for the stage window, about the baby-spot that was out of order, about the higher interpretation of the rôle of the page in the piece—a rôle consisting of only two lines, but to be played by one of the most popular girls in the younger set. After the discussions, and a most violent quarrel between two members of the play-reading committee, the rehearsal was called. Jasper Holt still wore his flannel suit and a wilting carnation; but he was not Jasper; he was the Duc de San Saba, a cynical, gracious, gorgeous old man, easy of gesture, tranquil of voice, shudderingly evil of desire.

"If I could get a few more actors like you!" cried the professional coach.

The rehearsal was over at half-past eleven. Jasper drove his car to the public garage in which he kept it, and walked home. There, he tore up and burned the wrapping paper bearing the name of the Parthenon Confectionery Store and the labeled bag that had contained the groceries.

The Community Theater plays were given on the following Wednesday. Jasper Holt was highly applauded, and at the party at the Lakeside Country Club, after the play, he danced with the prettiest girls in town. He hadn't much to say to them, but he danced fervently, and about him was a halo of artistic success.

That night his brother John did not appear at the meeting of the Soul Hope Fraternity out in Rosebank.

On Monday, five days later, while he was in conference with the president and the cashier of the Lumber National Bank, Jasper complained of a headache. The next day he telephoned to the president that he would not come down to work—he would stay home and rest his eyes, sleep and get rid of the persistent headache. That was unfortunate, for that very day his twin brother John made one of his frequent trips into Vernon and called at the bank.

The president had seen John only once before, and by a coincidence it had happened on this occasion also Jasper had been absent—had been out of town. The president invited John into his private office.

"Your brother is at home; poor fellow has a bad headache. Hope he gets over it. We think a great deal of him here. You ought to be proud of him. Will you have a smoke?"

As he spoke the president looked John over. Once or twice when Jasper and the president had been out at lunch Jasper had spoken of the remarkable resemblance between himself and his twin brother. But the president told himself that he didn't really see much resemblance. The features of the two were alike, but John's expression of chronic spiritual indigestion, his unfriendly manner, and his hair—unkempt and lifeless brown, where Jasper's was sleekly black about a shiny bald spot—made the president dislike John as much as he liked Jasper.

And now John was replying: "No, I do not smoke. I can't understand how a man can soil the temple with drugs. I suppose I ought to be glad to hear you praise poor Jasper, but I am more concerned with his lack of respect for the things of the spirit. He sometimes comes to see me, at Rosebank, and I argue with him, but somehow I can't make him see his errors. And his flippant ways——!"

"We don't think he's flippant. We think he's a pretty steady worker."

"But he's play-acting! And reading love stories! Well, I try to keep in mind the injunction, 'Judge not, that ye be not judged.' But I am pained to find my own brother giving up immortal promises for mortal amusements. Well, I'll go and call on him. I trust that some day we shall see you at Soul Hope Hall, in Rosebank. Good day, sir."

Turning back to his work, the president grumbled: "I am going to tell Jasper that the best compliment I can hand him is that he is not like his brother."

And on the following day, another Wednesday, when Jasper reappeared at the bank, the president did make this jesting comparison, and Jasper sighed, "Oh, John is really a good fellow, but he's always gone in for metaphysics and Oriental mysticism and Lord knows what all, till he's kind of lost in the fog. But he's a lot better than I am. When I murder my landlady—or say, when I rob the bank, Chief—you go get John, and I bet you the best lunch in town that he'll do his best to bring me to justice. That's how square he is!"

"Square, yes—corners just sticking out! Well, when you do rob us, Jasper, I'll look up John. But do try to keep from robbing us as long as you can. I'd hate to have to associate with a religious detective in a boiled shirt!"

Both men laughed, and Jasper went back to his cage. His head continued to hurt, he admitted. The president advised him to lay off for a week. He didn't want to, he said. With the new munition industries due to the war in Europe there was much increase in factory pay rolls, and Jasper took charge of them.

"Better take a week off than get ill," argued the president late that afternoon.

Jasper did let himself be persuaded to go away for at least a week-end. He would run up north, to Wakamin Lake, the coming Friday, he said; he would get some black-bass fishing, and be back on Monday or Tuesday. Before he went he would make up the pay rolls for the Saturday payments and turn them over to the other teller. The president thanked him for his faithfulness, and as was his not infrequent custom, invited Jasper to his house for the evening of the next day—Thursday.

That Wednesday evening Jasper's brother John appeared at the Soul Hope meeting in Rosebank. When he had gone home and magically turned back into Jasper this Jasper did not return the wig and garments of John to the bureau but packed them in a suitcase, took the suitcase to his room in Vernon and locked it in his wardrobe.

Jasper was amiable at dinner at the president's house on Thursday, but he was rather silent, and as his head still throbbed he left the house early—at nine-thirty. Sedately carrying his gray silk gloves in one hand and pompously swinging his stick with the other, he walked from the president's house on the fashionable boulevard back to the center of Vernon. He entered the public garage in which he stored his car. He commented to the night attendant, "Head aches. Guess I'll take the 'bus out and get some fresh air."

He drove away at not more than fifteen miles an hour. He headed south. When he had reached the outskirts of the city he speeded up to a consistent twenty-five miles an hour. He settled down in his seat with the unmoving steadiness of the long-distance driver; his body quiet except for the tiny subtle movements of his foot on the accelerator, of his hand on the steering wheel—his right hand across the wheel, holding it at the top, his left elbow resting easily on the cushioned edge of his seat and his left hand merely touching the wheel.

He drove down in that southern direction for fifteen miles—almost to the town of Wanagoochie. Then by a rather poor side road he turned sharply to the north and west, and making a huge circle about the city drove toward the town of St. Clair. The suburb of Rosebank, in which his brother John lived, is also north of Vernon. These directions were of some importance to him; Wanagoochie eighteen miles south of the mother city of Vernon; Rosebank, on the other hand, eight miles north of Vernon, and St. Clair twenty miles north—about as far north of Vernon as Wanagoochie is south.

On his way to St. Clair, at a point that was only two miles from Rosebank, Jasper ran the car off the main road into a grove of oaks and maples and stopped it on a long-unused woodland road. He stiffly got out and walked through the woods up a rise of ground to a cliff overlooking a swampy lake. The gravelly farther bank of the cliff rose perpendicularly from the edge of the water. In that wan light distilled by stars and the earth he made out the reedy expanse of the lake. It was so muddy, so tangled with sedge grass that it was never used for swimming, and as its inhabitants were only slimy bullheads few people ever tried to fish there. Jasper stood reflective. He was remembering the story of the farmer's team which had run away, dashed over this cliff and sunk out of sight in the mud bottom of the lake.

Swishing his stick he outlined an imaginary road from the top of the cliff back to the sheltered place where his car was standing. Once he hacked away with a large pocketknife a mass of knotted hazel bushes which blocked that projected road. When he had traced the road to his car he smiled. He walked to the edge of the woods and looked up and down the main highway. A car was approaching. He waited till it had passed, ran back to his own car, backed it out on the highway, and went on his northward course toward St. Clair, driving about thirty miles an hour.

On the edge of St. Clair he halted, took out his kit of tools, unscrewed a spark plug, and sharply tapping the plug on the engine block, deliberately cracked the porcelain jacket. He screwed the plug in again and started the car. It bucked and spit, missing on one cylinder, with the short-circuited plug.

"I guess there must be something wrong with the ignition," he said cheerfully.

He managed to run the car into a garage in St. Clair. There was no one in the garage save an old negro, the night washer, who was busy over a limousine with sponge and hose.

"Got a night repair man here?" asked Jasper.

"No, sir; guess you'll have to leave it till morning."

"Hang it! Something gone wrong with the carburetor or the ignition. Well, I'll have to leave it then. Tell him—— Say will you be here in the morning when the repair man comes on?"

"Yes, sir."

"Well, tell him I must have the car by tomorrow noon. No, say by tomorrow at nine. Now, don't forget. This will help your memory."

He gave a quarter to the negro, who grinned and shouted: "Yes, sir; that'll help my memory a lot!" As he tied a storage tag on the car the negro inquired: "Name?"

"Uh—my name? Oh, Hanson. Remember now, ready about nine tomorrow."

Jasper walked to the railroad station. It was ten minutes of one. Jasper did not ask the night operator about the next train into Vernon. Apparently he knew that there was a train stopping here at St. Clair at one-thirty-seven. He did not sit in the waiting room but in the darkness outside, on a truck behind the baggage room. When the train came in he slipped into the last seat of the last car, and with his soft hat over his eyes either slept or appeared to sleep. When he reached Vernon he got off and came to the garage in which he regularly kept his car. He stepped inside. The night attendant was drowsing in a large wooden chair tilted back against the wall in the narrow runway which formed the entrance to the garage.

Jasper jovially shouted to the attendant: "Certainly ran into some hard luck. Ignition went wrong—I guess it was the ignition. Had to leave the car down at Wanagoochie."

"Yuh, hard luck, all right," assented the attendant.

"Yump. So I left it at Wanagoochie," Jasper emphasized as he passed on.

He had been inexact in this statement. It was not at Wanagoochie, which is south, but at St. Clair, which is north, that he had left his car.

He had returned to his boarding house, slept beautifully, hummed in his morning shower bath. Yet at breakfast he complained of his continuous headache, and announced that he was going up north, to Wakamin, to get some bass fishing and rest his eyes. His landlady urged him to go.

"Anything I can do to help you get away?" she queried.

"No, thanks. I'm just taking a couple of suitcases, with some old clothes and some fishing tackle. Fact, I have 'em all packed already. I'll probably take the noon train north if I can get away from the bank. Pretty busy now, with these pay rolls for the factories that have war contracts for the Allies. What's it say in the paper this morning?"

Jasper arrived at the bank, carrying the two suit-cases and a neat, polite, rolled silk umbrella, the silver top of which was engraved with his name. The door-man, who was also the bank guard, helped him carry the suitcases inside.

"Careful of that bag. Got my fishing tackle in it," said Jasper, to the doorman, apropos of one of the suitcases which was heavy but apparently not packed full. "Well, I think I'll run up to Wakamin today and catch a few bass."

"Wish I could go along, sir. How is the head this morning? Does it still ache?" asked the doorman.

"Rather better, but my eyes still feel pretty rocky. Guess I've been using them too much. Say, Connors, I'll try to catch the train north at eleven-seven. Better have a taxicab here for me at eleven. Or no; I'll let you know a little before eleven. Try to catch the eleven-seven north, for Wakamin."

"Very well, sir."

The president, the cashier, the chief clerk—all asked Jasper how he felt; and to all of them he repeated the statement that he had been using his eyes too much, and that he would catch a few bass at Wakamin.

The other paying teller, from his cage next to that of Jasper, called heartily through the steel netting: "Pretty soft for some people! You wait! I'm going to have the hay fever this summer, and I'll go fishing for a month!"

Jasper placed the two suitcases and the umbrella in his cage, and leaving the other teller to pay out current money he himself made up the pay rolls for the next day—Saturday. He casually went into the vault—a narrow, unimpressive, unaired cell with a hard lino-leum floor, one unshaded electric bulb, and a back wall composed entirely of steel doors of safes, all painted a sickly blue, very unimpressive, but guarding several millions of dollars in cash and securities. The upper doors, hung on large steel arms and each provided with two dials, could be opened only by two officers of the bank, each knowing one of the two combinations. Below these were smaller doors, one of which Jasper could open, as teller. It was the door of an insignificant steel box, which contained one hundred and seventeen thousand dollars in bills and four thousand dollars in gold and silver.

Jasper passed back and forth, carrying bundles of currency. In his cage he was working less than three feet from the other teller, who was divided from him only by the bands of the steel netting.

While he worked he exchanged a few words with this other teller.

Once, as he counted out nineteen thousand dollars, he commented: "Big pay roll for the Henschel Wagon Works this week. They're making gun carriages and truck bodies for the Allies, I understand."

"Uh-huh!" said the other teller, not much interested.

Mechanically, unobtrusively going about his ordinary routine of business, Jasper counted out bills to amounts agreeing with the items on a typed schedule of the pay rolls. Apparently his eyes never lifted from his counting and from the typed schedule which lay before him. The bundles of bills he made into packages, fastening each with a paper band. Each bundle he seemed to drop into a small black leather bag which he held beside him. But he did not actually drop the money into these pay-roll bags.

Both the suitcases at his feet were closed and presumably fastened, but one was not fastened. And though it was heavy it contained nothing but a lump of pig iron. From time to time Jasper's hand, holding a bundle of bills, dropped to his side. With a slight movement of his foot he opened that suitcase and the bills slipped from his hand down into it.

The bottom part of the cage was a solid sheet of stamped steel, and from the front of the bank no one could see this suspicious gesture. The other teller could have seen it, but Jasper dropped the bills only when the other teller was busy talking to a customer or when his back was turned. In order to delay for such a favorable moment Jasper frequently counted packages of bills twice, rubbing his eyes as though they hurt him.

After each of these secret disposals of packages of bills Jasper made much of dropping into the pay-roll bags the rolls of coin for which the schedule called. It was while he was tossing these blue-wrapped cylinders of coin into the bags that he would chat with the other teller. Then he would lock up the bags and gravely place them at one side.

Jasper was so slow in making up the pay rolls that it was five minutes of eleven before he finished. He called the doorman to the cage and suggested, "Better call my taxi now."

He still had one bag to fill. He could plainly be seen dropping packages of money into it, while he instructed the assistant teller: "I'll stick all the bags in my safe and you can transfer them to yours. Be sure to lock my safe. Lord, I better hurry or I'll miss my train! Be back Tuesday morning, at latest. So long; take care of yourself."

He hastened to pile the pay-roll bags into his safe in the vault. The safe was almost filled with them. And except for the last one not one of the bags contained anything except a few rolls of coin. Though he had told the other teller to lock his safe, he himself twirled the combination—which was thoughtless of him, as the assistant teller would now have to wait and get the president to unlock it.

He picked up his umbrella and two suitcases, bending over one of the cases for not more than ten seconds. Waving good-by to the cashier at his desk down front and hurrying so fast that the doorman did not have a chance to help him carry the suitcases, he rushed through the bank, through the door, into the waiting taxicab, and loudly enough for the doorman to hear he cried to the driver, "M. & D. Station."

At the M. & D. R.R. Station, refusing offers of

redcaps to carry his bags, he bought a ticket for Wakamin, which is a lake-resort town one hundred and
forty miles northwest of Vernon, hence one hundred
and twenty beyond St. Clair. He had just time to get
aboard the eleven-seven train. He did not take a chair
car, but sat in a day coach near the rear door. He
unscrewed the silver top of his umbrella, on which was
engraved his name, and dropped it into his pocket.

When the train reached St. Clair, Jasper strolled out
to the vestibule, carrying the suitcases but leaving the
topless umbrella behind. His face was blank, uninter-
ested. As the train started he dropped down on the
station platform and gravely walked away. For a second the light of adventure crossed his face, and
vanished.

At the garage at which he had left his car on the
evening before he asked the foreman: "Did you get
my car fixed—Mercury roadster, ignition on the
bum?"

"Nope! Couple of jobs ahead of it. Haven't had
time to touch it yet. Ought to get at it early this
afternoon."

Jasper curled his tongue round his lips in startled
vexation. He dropped his suitcases on the floor of the
garage and stood thinking, his bent forefinger against
his lower lip.

Then: "Well, I guess I can get her to go—sorry—
can't wait—got to make the next town," he grumbled.

"Lot of you traveling salesmen making your territory by motor now, Mr. Hanson," said the foreman
civilly, glancing at the storage check on Jasper's car.

"Yep. I can make a good many more than I could
by train."

He paid for overnight storage without complaining,
though since his car had not been repaired this charge
was unjust. In fact, he was altogether prosaic and inconspicuous. He thrust the suitcases into the car and
drove away, the motor spitting. At another garage he
bought another spark plug and screwed it in. When
he went on, the motor had ceased spitting.

He drove out of St. Clair, back in the direction of Vernon—and of Rosebank where his brother lived. He ran the car into that thick grove of oaks and maples only two miles from Rosebank, where he had paced off an imaginary road to the cliff overhanging the reedy lake. He parked his car in a grassy space beside the abandoned woodland road. He laid a light robe over the suitcases. From beneath the seat he took a can of deviled chicken, a box of biscuits, a canister of tea, a folding cooking kit and a spirit lamp. These he spread on the grass—a picnic lunch.

He sat beside that lunch from seven minutes past one in the afternoon till dark. Once in a while he made a pretense of eating. He fetched water from the brook, made tea, opened the box of biscuits and the can of chicken. But mostly he sat still and smoked cigarette after cigarette.

Once, a Swede, taking this road as a short cut to his truck farm, passed by and mumbled, "Picnic, eh?"

"Yuh, takin' the day off," said Jasper dully.

The man went on without looking back.

At dusk Jasper finished a cigarette down to the tip, crushed out the light and made the cryptic remark:

"That's probably Jasper Holt's last smoke. I don't suppose you can smoke, John—damn you!"

He hid the two suitcases in the bushes, piled the remains of the lunch into the car, took down the top of the car, and crept down to the main road. No one was in sight. He returned. He snatched a hammer and a chisel from his tool kit, and with a few savage cracks he so defaced the number of the car stamped on the engine block that it could not be made out. He removed the license numbers from fore and aft, and placed them beside the suitcases. Then, when there was just enough light to see the bushes as cloudy masses, he started the car, drove through the woods and up the incline to the top of the cliff, and halted, leaving the engine running.

Between the car and the edge of the cliff which overhung the lake there was a space of about one

hundred and thirty feet, fairly level and covered with
straggly red clover. Jasper paced off this distance, returned to the car, took his seat in a nervous, tentative
way and put her into gear, starting on second speed
and slamming her into third. The car bolted toward
the edge of the cliff. He instantly swung out on the
running board. Standing there, headed directly toward
the sharp drop over the cliff, steering with his left
hand on the wheel, he shoved the hand throttle up—
up—up with his right. He safely leaped down from
the running board.

Of itself, the car rushed forward, roaring. It shot
over the edge of the cliff. It soared twenty feet out
into the air, as though it were a thick-bodied aeroplane. It turned over and over, with a sickening drop
toward the lake. The water splashed up in a tremendous noisy circle. Then silence. In the twilight the surface of the lake shone like milk. There was no sign of
the car on the surface. The concentric rings died away.
The lake was secret and sinister and still. "Lord!"
ejaculated Jasper, standing on the cliff; then: "Well,
they won't find that for a couple of years anyway."

He turned to the suitcases. Squatting beside them
he took from one the wig and black garments of John
Holt. He stripped, put on the clothes of John, and
packed those of Jasper in the bag. With the cases and
the motor-license plates he walked toward Rosebank,
keeping in various groves of maples and willows till
he was within half a mile of the town. He reached the
stone house at the end of the willow walk and sneaked
in the back way. He burned Jasper Holt's clothes in
the grate, melted down the license plates in the stove,
and between two rocks he smashed Jasper's expensive
watch and fountain pen into an unpleasant mass of
junk, which he dropped into the cistern for rain water.
The silver head of the umbrella he scratched with a
chisel till the engraved name was indistinguishable.

He unlocked a section of the bookcase and taking a
number of packages of bills in denominations of one,
five, ten and twenty dollars from one of the suitcases he

packed them into those empty candy boxes which, on the shelves, looked so much like books. As he stored them he counted the bills. They came to ninety-seven thousand five hundred and thirty-five dollars.

The two suitcases were new. There were no distinguishing marks on them. But taking them out to the kitchen he kicked them, rubbed them with lumps of blacking, raveled their edges and cut their sides, till they gave the appearance of having been long and badly used in traveling. He took them upstairs and tossed them up into the low attic.

In his bedroom he undressed calmly. Once he laughed: "I despise those pretentious fools—bank officers and cops. I'm beyond their fool law. No one can catch me—it would take me myself to do that!"

He got into bed. With a vexed "Hang it!" he mused, "I suppose John would pray, no matter how chilly the floor was."

He got out of bed and from the inscrutable Lord of the Universe he sought forgiveness—not for Jasper Holt, but for the denominations who lacked the true faith of Soul Hope Fraternity.

He returned to bed and slept till the middle of the morning, lying with his arms behind his head, a smile on his face.

Thus did Jasper Holt, without the mysterious pangs of death, yet cease to exist, and thus did John Holt come into being not merely as an apparition glimpsed on Sunday and Wednesday evenings but as a being living twenty-four hours a day, seven days a week.

III

The inhabitants of Rosebank were familiar with the occasional appearances of John Holt, the eccentric recluse, and they merely snickered about him when on the Saturday evening following the Friday that has been chronicled he was seen to come out of his gate and trudge down to a news and stationery shop on Main Street.

He purchased an evening paper and said to the clerk: "You can have the *Morning Herald* delivered at my house every morning—27 Humbert Avenue."

"Yuh, I know where it is. Thought you had kind of a grouch on newspapers," said the clerk pertly.

"Ah, did you indeed? The *Herald,* every morning, please. I will pay a month in advance," was all John Holt said, but he looked directly at the clerk, and the man cringed.

John attended the meeting of the Soul Hope Fraternity the next evening—Sunday—but he was not seen on the streets again for two and a half days.

There was no news of the disappearance of Jasper Holt till the following Wednesday, when the whole thing came out in a violent, small-city, front-page story, headed:

PAYING TELLER

SOCIAL FAVORITE—MAKES GET-AWAY

The paper stated that Jasper Holt had been missing for four days, and that the officers of the bank, after first denying that there was anything wrong with his accounts, had admitted that he was short one hundred thousand dollars—two hundred thousand, said one report. He had purchased a ticket for Wakamin, this state, on Friday and a trainman, a customer of the bank, had noticed him on the train, but he had apparently never arrived at Wakamin.

A woman asserted that on Friday afternoon she had seen Holt driving an automobile between Vernon and St. Clair. This appearance near St. Clair was supposed to be merely a blind, however. In fact, our able chief of police had proof that Holt was not headed north, in the direction of St. Clair, but south, beyond Wanagoochie—probably for Des Moines or St. Louis. It was definitely known that on the previous day Holt had left his car at Wanagoochie, and with their customary thoroughness and promptness the police were making search at Wanagoochie. The chief had already communicated with the police in cities to the south, and the capture of the man could confidently be expected at any moment. As long as the chief appointed by our popular mayor was in power, it went ill with those who gave even the appearance of wrongdoing.

When asked his opinion of the theory that the alleged fugitive had gone north the chief declared that of course Holt had started in that direction, with the vain hope of throwing pursuers off the scent, but that he had immediately turned south and picked up his car. Though he would not say so definitely the chief let it be known that he was ready to put his hands on the fellow who had hidden Holt's car at Wanagoochie.

When asked if he thought Holt was crazy the chief laughed and said: "Yes, he's crazy two hundred thousand dollars' worth. I'm not making any slams, but there's a lot of fellows among our political opponents who would go a whole lot crazier for a whole lot less!"

The president of the bank, however, was greatly distressed, and strongly declared his belief that Holt, who was a favorite in the most sumptuous residences on the Boulevard, besides being well known in local dramatic circles, and who bore the best of reputations in the bank, was temporarily out of his mind, as he had been distressed by pains in the head for some time past. Meantime the bonding company, which had fully covered the employees of the bank by a joint bond of two hundred thousand dollars, had its detectives working with the police on the case.

As soon as he had read the paper John took a trolley into Vernon and called on the president of the bank. John's face drooped with the sorrow of the disgrace. The president received him. John staggered into the room, groaning: "I have just learned in the newspaper of the terrible news about my brother. I have come——"

"We hope it's just a case of aphasia. We're sure he'll turn up all right," insisted the president.

"I wish I could believe it. But as I have told you,

Jasper is not a good man. He drinks and smokes and play-acts and makes a god of stylish clothes——"

"Good Lord, that's no reason for jumping to the conclusion that he's an embezzler!"

"I pray you may be right. But meanwhile I wish to give you any assistance I can. I shall make it my sole duty to see that my brother is brought to justice if it proves that he is guilty."

"Good o' you," mumbled the president. Despite this example of John's rigid honor he could not get himself to like the man. John was standing beside him, thrusting his stupid face into his.

The president pushed his chair a foot farther away and said disagreeably: "As a matter of fact, we were thinking of searching your house. If I remember, you live in Rosebank?"

"Yes. And of course I shall be glad to have you search every inch of it. Or anything else I can do. I feel that I share fully with my twin brother in this unspeakable sin. I'll turn over the key of my house to you at once. There is also a shed at the back where Jasper used to keep his automobile when he came to see me." He produced a large, rusty, old-fashioned door key and held it out, adding: "The address is 27 Humbert Avenue, Rosebank."

"Oh, it won't be necessary, I guess," said the president, somewhat shamed, irritably waving off the key.

"But I just want to help somehow! What can I do? Who is—in the language of the newspapers—who is the detective on the case? I'll give him any help——"

"Tell you what you do: Go see Mr. Scandling, of the Mercantile Trust and Bonding Company, and tell him all you know."

"I shall. I take my brother's crime on my shoulders—otherwise I'd be committing the sin of Cain. You are giving me a chance to try to expiate our joint sin, and, as Brother Jeremiah Bodfish was wont to say, it is a blessing to have an opportunity to expiate a sin, no matter how painful the punishment may seem to be to the mere physical being. As I may have told you

I am an accepted member of the Soul Hope Fraternity, and though we are free from cant and dogma it is our firm belief——"

Then for ten dreary minutes John Holt sermonized; quoted forgotten books and quaint, ungenerous elders; twisted bitter pride and clumsy mysticism into fanatical spider web. The president was a churchgoer, an ardent supporter of missionary funds, for forty years a pewholder at St. Simeon's Church, but he was alternately bored to a chill shiver and roused to wrath against this self-righteous zealot.

When he had rather rudely got rid of John Holt he complained to himself: "Curse it, I oughtn't to, but I must say I prefer Jasper the sinner to John the saint. Uff! What a smell of damp cellars the fellow has! He must spend all his time picking potatoes. Say! By thunder, I remember that Jasper had the infernal nerve to tell me once that if he ever robbed the bank I was to call John in. I know why, now! John is the kind of egotistical fool that would muddle up any kind of a systematic search. Well, Jasper, sorry, but I'm not going to have anything more to do with John than I can help!"

John had gone to the Mercantile Trust and Bonding Company, had called on Mr. Scandling, and was now wearying him by a detailed and useless account of Jasper's early years and recent vices. He was turned over to the detective employed by the bonding company to find Jasper. The detective was a hard, noisy man, who found John even more tedious. John insisted on his coming out to examine the house in Rosebank, and the detective did so—but sketchily, trying to escape. John spent at least five minutes in showing him the shed where Jasper had sometimes kept his car.

He also attempted to interest the detective in his precious but spotty books. He unlocked one section of the case, dragged down a four-volume set of sermons and started to read them aloud.

The detective interrupted: "Yuh, that's great stuff,

but I guess we aren't going to find your brother hiding behind those books!"

The detective got away as soon as possible, after insistently explaining to John that if they could use his assistance they would let him know.

"If I can only expiate——"

"Yuh, sure, that's all right!" wailed the detective, fairly running toward the gate.

John made one more visit to Vernon that day. He called on the chief of city police. He informed the chief that he had taken the bonding company's detective through his house, but wouldn't the police consent to search it also? He wanted to expiate—— The chief patted John on the back, advised him not to feel responsible for his brother's guilt and begged: "Skip along now—very busy."

As John walked to the Soul Hope meeting that evening, dozens of people murmured that it was his brother who had robbed the Lumber National Bank. His head was bowed with the shame. At the meeting he took Jasper's sin upon himself, and prayed that Jasper would be caught and receive the blessed healing of punishment. The others begged John not to feel that he was guilty—was he not one of the Soul Hope brethren who alone in this wicked and perverse generation were assured of salvation?

On Thursday, on Saturday morning, on Tuesday and on Friday, John went into the city to call on the president of the bank and the detective. Twice the president saw him, and was infinitely bored by his sermons. The third time he sent word that he was out. The fourth time he saw John, but curtly explained that if John wanted to help them the best thing he could do was to stay away.

The detective was out all four times.

John smiled meekly and ceased to try to help them. Dust began to gather on certain candy boxes on the lower shelf of his bookcase, save for one of them, which he took out now and then. Always after he had taken it out a man with faded brown hair and a wrin-

kled black suit, a man signing himself R. J. Smith,
would send a fair-sized money order from the post
office at South Vernon to John Holt, at Rosebank—
as he had been doing for more than six months. These
money orders could not have amounted to more than
twenty-five dollars a week, but that was even more
than an ascetic like John Holt needed. By day John
sometimes cashed these at the Rosebank post office,
but usually, as had been his custom, he cashed them at
his favorite grocery when he went out in the evening.

In conversation with the commuter neighbor, who
every evening walked about and smoked an after-
dinner cigar in the yard at the right, John was frank
about the whole lamentable business of his brother's
defalcation. He wondered, he said, if he had not shut
himself up with his studies too much, and neglected
his brother. The neighbor ponderously advised John
to get out more. John let himself be persuaded, at
least to the extent of taking a short walk every afternoon and of letting his literary solitude be disturbed
by the delivery of milk, meat, and groceries. He also
went to the public library, and in the reference room
glanced at books on Central and South America—as
though he was planning to go south some day.

But he continued his religious studies. It may be
doubted if previous to the embezzlement John had
worked very consistently on his book about Revelation. All that the world had ever seen of it was a
jumble of quotations from theological authorities. Presumably the crime of his brother shocked him into
more concentrated study, more patient writing. For
during the year after his brother's disappearance—a
year in which the bonding company gradually gave up
the search and came to believe that Jasper was dead—
John became fanatically absorbed in somewhat nebulous work. The days and nights drifted together in
meditation in which he lost sight of realities, and
seemed through the clouds of the flesh to see flashes
from the towered cities of the spirit.

It has been asserted that when Jasper Holt acted a

rôle he veritably lived it. No one can ever determine
how great an actor was lost in the smug bank teller.
To him were imperial triumphs denied, yet he was not
without material reward. For playing his most subtle
part he received ninety-seven thousand dollars. It may
be that he earned it. Certainly for the risk entailed it
was but a fair payment. Jasper had meddled with the
mystery of personality, and was in peril of losing all
consistent purpose, of becoming a Wandering Jew of
the spirit, a strangled body walking.

IV

The sharp-pointed willow leaves had twisted and
fallen, after the dreary rains of October. Bark had
peeled from the willow trunks, leaving gashes of bare
wood that was a wet and sickly yellow. Through the
denuded trees bulked the solid stone of John Holt's
house. The patches of earth were greasy between the
tawny knots of grass stems. The bricks of the walk
were always damp now. The world was hunched up
in this pervading chill.

As melancholy as the sick earth seemed the man
who in a slaty twilight paced the willow walk. His
step was slack, his lips moved with the intensity of his
meditation. Over his wrinkled black suit and bleak
shirt bosom was a worn overcoat, the velvet collar
turned green. He was considering.

"There's something to all this. I begin to see—I
don't know what it is I do see! But there's lights—
supernatural world that makes food and bed seem ridiculous. I am—I really am beyond the law! I make
my own law! Why shouldn't I go beyond the law of
vision and see the secrets of life? But I sinned, and I
must repent—some day. I need not return the money.
I see now that it was given me so that I could lead
this life of contemplation. But the ingratitude to the
president, to the people who trusted me! Am I but the
most miserable of sinners, and as the blind? Voices—I

hear conflicting voices—some praising me for my courage, some rebuking——"

He knelt on the slimy black surface of a wooden bench beneath the willows, and as dusk clothed him round about he prayed. It seemed to him that he prayed not in words but in vast confusing dreams—the words of a language larger than human tongues. When he had exhausted himself he slowly entered the house. He locked the door. There was nothing definite of which he was afraid, but he was never comfortable with the door unlocked.

By candle light he prepared his austere supper—dry toast, an egg, cheap green tea with thin milk. As always—as it had happened after every meal, now, for eighteen months—he wanted a cigarette when he had eaten, but did not take one. He paced into the living room and through the long still hours of the evening he read an ancient book, all footnotes and cross references, about The Numerology of the Prophetic Books, and the Number of the Beast. He tried to make notes for his own book on Revelation—that scant pile of sheets covered with writing in a small finicky hand. Thousands of other sheets he had covered; through whole nights he had written; but always he seemed with tardy pen to be racing after thoughts that he could never quite catch, and most of what he had written he had savagely burned.

But some day he would make a masterpiece! He was feeling toward the greatest discovery that mortal man had encountered. Everything, he had determined, was a symbol—not just this holy sign and that, but all physical manifestations. With frightened exultation he tried his new power of divination. The hanging lamp swung tinily. He ventured: "If the arc of that moving radiance touches the edge of the bookcase, then it will be a sign that I am to go to South America, under an entirely new disguise, and spend my money."

He shuddered. He watched the lamp's unbearably slow swing. The moving light almost touched the bookcase. He gasped. Then it receded.

It was a warning; he quaked. Would he never leave this place of brooding and of fear, which he had thought so clever a refuge? He suddenly saw it all.

"I ran away and hid in a prison! Man isn't caught by justice—he catches himself!"

Again he tried. He speculated as to whether the number of pencils on the table was greater or less than five. If greater, then he had sinned; if less, then he was veritably beyond the law. He began to lift books and papers, looking for pencils. He was coldly sweating with the suspense of the test.

Suddenly he cried, "Am I going crazy?"

He fled to his prosaic bedroom. He could not sleep. His brain was smoldering with confused inklings of mystic numbers and hidden warnings.

He woke from a half sleep more vision-haunted than any waking thought, and cried: "I must go back and confess! But I can't! I can't, when I was too clever for them! I can't go back and let them win. I won't let those fools just sit tight and still catch me!"

It was a year and a half since Jasper had disappeared. Sometimes it seemed a month and a half; sometimes gray centuries. John's will power had been shrouded with curious puttering studies; long, heavy-breathing sittings with the ouija board on his lap, midnight hours when he had fancied that tables had tapped and crackling coals had spoken. Now that the second autumn of his seclusion was creeping into winter he was conscious that he had not enough initiative to carry out his plans for going to South America. The summer before he had boasted to himself that he would come out of hiding and go South, leaving such a twisty trail as only he could make. But—oh, it was too much trouble. He hadn't the joy in play-acting which had carried his brother Jasper through his preparations for flight.

He had killed Jasper Holt, and for a miserable little pile of paper money he had become a moldy recluse!

He hated his loneliness, but still more did he hate his only companions, the members of the Soul Hope

Fraternity—that pious shrill seamstress, that surly carpenter, that tight-lipped housekeeper, that old shouting man with the unseemly frieze of whiskers. They were so unimaginative. Their meetings were all the same; the same persons rose in the same order and made the same intimate announcements to the Deity that they alone were his elect.

At first it had been an amusing triumph to be accepted as the most eloquent among them, but that had become commonplace, and he resented their daring to be familiar with him, who was, he felt, the only man of all men living who beyond the illusions of the world saw the strange beatitude of higher souls.

It was at the end of November, during a Wednesday meeting at which a red-faced man had for a half hour maintained that he couldn't possibly sin, that the cumulative ennui burst in John Holt's brain. He sprang up.

He snarled: "You make me sick, all of you! You think you're so certain of sanctification that you can't do wrong. So did I, once! Now I know that we are all miserable sinners—really are! You all say you are, but you don't believe it. I tell you that you there that have just been yammering, and you, Brother Judkins, with the long twitching nose, and I—I—I, most unhappy of men, we must repent, confess, expiate our sins! And I will confess right now. I st-stole——"

Terrified he darted out of the hall, and hatless, coatless, tumbled through the main street of Rosebank, nor ceased till he had locked himself in his house. He was frightened because he had almost betrayed his secret, yet agonized because he had not gone on, really confessed, and gained the only peace he could ever know now—the peace of punishment.

He never returned to Soul Hope Hall. Indeed for a week he did not leave his house save for midnight prowling in the willow walk. Quite suddenly he became desperate with the silence. He flung out of the house, not stopping to lock or even close the front door. He raced uptown, no topcoat over his rotting garments, only an old gardener's cap on his thick brown hair. People stared at him. He bore it with resigned fury.

He entered a lunchroom, hoping to sit inconspicuously and hear men talking normally about him. The attendant at the counter gaped. John heard a mutter from the cashier's desk: "There's that crazy hermit!"

All of the half-dozen young men loafing in the place were looking at him. He was so uncomfortable that he could not eat even the milk and sandwich he had ordered. He pushed them away and fled, a failure in the first attempt to dine out that he had made in eighteen months; a lamentable failure to revive that Jasper Holt whom he had coldly killed.

He entered a cigar store and bought a box of cigarettes. He took joy out of throwing away his asceticism. But when, on the street, he lighted a cigarette it made him so dizzy that he was afraid he was going to fall. He had to sit down on the curb. People gathered. He staggered to his feet and up an alley.

For hours he walked, making and discarding the most contradictory plans—to go to the bank and confess, to spend the money riotously and never confess.

It was midnight when he returned to his house.

Before it he gasped. The front door was open. He chuckled with relief as he remembered that he had not closed it. He sauntered in. He was passing the door of the living room, going directly up to his bedroom, when his foot struck an object the size of a book, but hollow sounding. He picked it up. It was one of the booklike candy boxes. And it was quite empty. Frightened, he listened. There was no sound. He crept into the living room and lighted the lamp.

The doors of the bookcase had been wrenched open. Every book had been pulled out on the floor. All of the candy boxes, which that evening had contained almost ninety-six thousand dollars, were in a pile, and all of them were empty. He searched for ten minutes, but the only money he found was one five-dollar bill, which had fluttered under the table. In his pocket he had one dollar and sixteen cents. John Holt had six dollars and sixteen cents, no job, no friends—and no identity.

V

When the president of the Lumber National Bank was informed that John Holt was waiting to see him he scowled.

"Lord, I'd forgotten that minor plague! Must be a year since he's been here. Oh, let him—— No, hanged if I will! Tell him I'm too busy to see him. That is, unless he's got some news about Jasper. Pump him, and find out."

The president's secretary sweetly confided to John:

"I'm so sorry, but the president is in conference just now. What was it you wanted to see him about? Is there any news about—uh—about your brother?"

"There is not, miss. I am here to see the president on the business of the Lord."

"Oh! If that's all I'm afraid I can't disturb him."

"I will wait."

Wait he did, through all the morning, through the lunch hour—when the president hastened out past him—then into the afternoon, till the president was unable to work with the thought of that scarecrow out there, and sent for him.

"Well, well! What is it this time, John? I'm pretty busy. No news about Jasper, eh?"

"No news, sir, but—Jasper himself! I am Jasper Holt! His sin is my sin."

"Yes, yes, I know all that stuff—twin brothers, twin souls, share responsibility——"

"You don't understand. There isn't any twin brother. There isn't any John Holt. I am Jasper. I invented an imaginary brother, and disguised myself—— Why, don't you recognize my voice?"

While John leaned over the desk, his two hands upon it, and smiled wistfully, the president shook his head and soothed: "No, I'm afraid I don't. Sounds like good old religious John to me! Jasper was a cheerful, efficient sort of crook. Why, his laugh——"

"But I can laugh!" The dreadful croak which John uttered was the cry of an evil bird of the swamps. The president shuddered. Under the edge of the desk his fingers crept toward the buzzer by which he summoned his secretary.

They stopped as John urged: "Look—this wig—it's a wig. See, I am Jasper!"

He had snatched off the brown thatch. He stood expectant, a little afraid.

The president was startled, but he shook his head and sighed.

"You poor devil! Wig, all right. But I wouldn't say that hair was much like Jasper's!"

He motioned toward the mirror in the corner of the room.

John wavered to it. And indeed he saw that his hair had turned from Jasper's thin sleek blackness to a straggle of damp gray locks writhing over a yellow skull.

He begged pitifully: "Oh, can't you see I am Jasper? I stole ninety-seven thousand dollars from the bank. I want to be punished! I want to do anything to prove—— Why, I've been at your house. Your wife's name is Evelyn. My salary here was——"

"My dear boy, don't you suppose that Jasper might have told you all these interesting facts? I'm afraid the worry of this has—pardon me if I'm frank, but I'm afraid it's turned your head a little, John."

"There isn't any John! There isn't! There isn't!"

"I'd believe that a little more easily if I hadn't met you before Jasper disappeared."

"Give me a piece of paper. You know my writing——"

With clutching claws John seized a sheet of bank stationery and tried to write in the round script of Jasper. During the past year and a half he had filled thousands of pages with the small finicky hand of John. Now, though he tried to prevent it, after he had traced two or three words in large but shaky letters the writing became smaller, more pinched, less legible.

Even while John wrote the president looked at the sheet and said easily: "Afraid it's no use. That isn't Jasper's fist. See here, I want you to get away from Rosebank—go to some farm—work outdoors—cut out this fuming and fussing—get some fresh air in your lungs." The president rose and purred: "Now, I'm afraid I have some work to do."

He paused, waiting for John to go.

John fiercely crumpled the sheet and hurled it away. Tears were in his weary eyes.

He wailed: "Is there nothing I can do to prove I am Jasper?"

"Why, certainly! You can produce what's left of the ninety-seven thousand!"

John took from his ragged waistcoat pocket a five-dollar bill and some change. "Here's all there is. Ninety-six thousand of it was stolen from my house last night."

Sorry though he was for the madman, the president could not help laughing. Then he tried to look sympathetic, and he comforted: "Well, that's hard luck, old man. Uh, let's see. You might produce some parents or relatives or somebody to prove that Jasper never did have a twin brother."

"My parents are dead, and I've lost track of their kin—I was born in England—Father came over when I was six. There might be some cousins or some old neighbors, but I don't know. Probably impossible to find out, in these wartimes, without going over there."

"Well, I guess we'll have to let it go, old man." The president was pressing the buzzer for his secretary and gently bidding her: "Show Mr. Holt out, please."

From the door John desperately tried to add: "You will find my car sunk——"

The door had closed behind him. The president had not listened.

The president gave orders that never, for any reason, was John Holt to be admitted to his office again.

He telephoned to the bonding company that John Holt had now gone crazy; that they would save trouble by refusing to admit him.

John did not try to see them. He went to the county jail. He entered the keeper's office and said quietly: "I have stolen a lot of money, but I can't prove it. Will you put me in jail?"

The keeper shouted: "Get out of here! You hoboes always spring that when you want a good warm lodging for the winter! Why the devil don't you go to work with a shovel in the sand pits? They're paying two-seventy-five a day."

"Yes, sir," said John timorously. "Where are they?"

Land

He was named Sidney, for the sake of elegance, just as his parents had for elegance in their Brooklyn parlor a golden-oak combination bookcase, desk, and shield-shaped mirror. But Sidney Dow was descended from generations of Georges and Johns, of Lorens and Lukes and Nathans.

He was little esteemed in the slick bustle of his city school. He seemed a loutish boy, tall and heavy and slow-spoken, and he was a worry to his father. For William Dow was an ambitious parent. Born on a Vermont farm, William felt joyously that he had done well in the great city of Brooklyn. He had, in 1885, when Sidney was born, a real bathroom with a fine tin tub, gas lights, and a handsome phaeton with red wheels, instead of the washtub in the kitchen for Saturday-night baths, the kerosene lamps, and the heavy old buggy which his father still used in Vermont. Instead of being up at 5:30, he could loll abed till a quarter of seven, and he almost never, he chuckled in gratification at his progress, was in his office before a quarter to eight.

But the luxury of a red-wheeled carriage and late lying did not indicate that William's Yankee shrewdness had been cozened by urban vice, or that he was any less solid and respectable than old George, his

105

own father. He was a deacon in the Universalist church, he still said grace before meals, and he went to the theater only when Ben-Hur was appearing.

For his son, Sidney, William Dow had even larger ambitions. William himself had never gone to high school, and his business was only a cautious real-estate and insurance agency, his home a squatting two-story brick house in a red, monotonous row. But Sidney— he should go to college, he should be a doctor or a preacher or a lawyer, he should travel in Europe, he should live in a three-story graystone house in the Forties in Manhattan, he should have a dress suit and wear it to respectable but expensive hops!

William had once worn dress clothes at an Odd Fellows' ball, but they had been rented.

To enable Sidney to attain all these graces, William toiled and sacrificed and prayed. American fathers have always been as extraordinary as Scotch fathers in their heroic ambitions for their sons—and sometimes as unscrupulous and as unwise. It bruised William and often it made him naggingly unkind to see that Sidney, the big slug, did not "appreciate how his parents were trying to do for him and give him every opportunity." When they had a celebrated Columbia Heights physician as guest for dinner, Sidney merely gawked at him and did not at all try to make an impression.

"Suffering cats! You might have been one of your uncles still puttering around with dirty pitchforks back on the farm! What are you going to do with yourself, anyway?" raged William.

"I guess maybe I'd like to be a truck driver," mumbled Sidney.

Yet, even so, William should not have whipped him. It only made him sulkier.

To Sidney Dow, at sixteen, his eagerest memories were of occasional weeks he had spent with his grandfather and uncles on the Vermont farm, and the last of these was seven years back now. He remembered

Vermont as an enchanted place, with curious and amusing animals—cows, horses, turkeys. He wanted to return, but his father seemed to hate the place. Of Brooklyn, Sidney liked nothing save livery stables and occasional agreeable gang fights, with stones inside iced snowballs. He hated school, where he had to cramp his big knees under trifling desks, where irritable lady teachers tried to make him see the importance of A's going more rapidly than B to the town of X, a town in which he was even less interested than in Brooklyn—school where hour on hour he looked over the top of his geography and stolidly hated the whiskers of Longfellow, Lowell, and Whittier. He hated the stiff, clean collar and the itchy, clean winter underwear connected with Sunday school. He hated hot evenings smelling of tarry pavements, and cold evenings when the pavements were slippery.

But he didn't know that he hated any of these things. He knew only that his father must be right in saying that he was a bad, disobedient, ungrateful young whelp, and in his heart he was as humble as in his speech he was sullen.

Then, at sixteen, he came to life suddenly, on an early June morning, on his grandfather's farm. His father had sent him up to Vermont for the summer, had indeed exiled him, saying grimly, "I guess after you live in that tumbledown big old shack and work in the fields and have to get up early, instead of lying abed till your majesty is good and ready to have the girl wait on you—I guess that next fall you'll appreciate your nice home and school and church here, young man!" So sure of himself was his father that Sidney was convinced he was going to encounter hardship on the farm, and all the way up, in the smarting air of the smoker on the slow train, he wanted to howl. The train arrived at ten in the evening, and he was met by his uncle Rob, a man rugged as a pine trunk and about as articulate.

"Well! Come for the summer!" said Uncle Rob; and after they had driven three miles: "Got new calf—yeh,

new calf"; and after a mile more: "Your pa all right?"
And that was all the conversation of Uncle Rob.

Seven years it was since Sidney had been in any
country wilder than Far Rockaway, and the silent hills
of night intimidated him. It was a roaring silence, a
silence full of stifled threats. The hills that cut the stars
so high up on either side of the road seemed walls
that would topple and crush him, as a man would
crush a mosquito between his two palms. And once
he cried out when, in the milky light from the lantern
swung beneath the wagon, he saw a porcupine lurch
into the road before them. It was dark, chill, unfriendly and, to the boy, reared to the lights and
cheery voices of the city, even though he hated them,
it was appallingly lonely.

His grandfather's house was dark when they arrived.
Uncle Rob drove into the barn, jerked his thumb at
a ladder up to the haymow and muttered, "Y'sleep
up there. Not allowed t' smoke. Take this lantern
when we've unharnessed. Sure to put it out. No smoking in the barn. Too tired to help?"

Too tired? Sidney would have been glad to work
till daylight if Uncle Rob would but stay with him. He
was in a panic at the thought of being left in the
ghostly barn where, behind the pawing of horses and
the nibble of awakened cows, there were the sounds
of anonymous wild animals—scratchings, squeaks, pat-
terings overhead. He made the task as slow as possible, though actually he was handy with horses, for the
livery stables of Brooklyn had been his favorite refuge
and he had often been permitted to help the hostlers,
quite free.

"Gee, Uncle Rob, I guess I'm kind of all thumbs
about unharnessing and like that. Seven years since I
been here on the farm."

"That so? G'night. Careful of that lantern now. And
no smoking!"

The barn was blank as a blind face. The lantern was
flickering, and in that witching light the stalls and the

heap of sleighs, plows, old harness, at the back wall of the barn were immense and terrifying. The barn was larger than his whole house in Brooklyn, and ten times as large it seemed in the dimness. He could not see clear to the back wall, and he imagined abominable monsters lurking there. He dashed at the ladder up to the haymow, the lantern handle in his teeth and his imitation-leather satchel in one hand.

And the haymow, rising to the darkness of its hand-hewn rafters, seemed vaster and more intimidating than the space below. In one corner a space had been cleared of hay for a cot, with a blanket and a pea-green comforter, and for a chair and a hinged box. Sidney dashed at the cot and crawled into it, waiting only to take off his shoes and jacket. Till the lantern flame died down to a red rim of charred wick, he kept it alight. Then utter darkness leaped upon him.

A rooster crowed, and he startled. Past him things scampered and chittered. The darkness seemed to swing in swift eddies under the rafters, the smell of dry hay choked him—and he awoke to light slipping in silver darts through cracks in the roof, and to jubilant barn swallows diving and twittering.

"Gee, I must have fell asleep!" he thought. He went down the ladder, and now, first, he saw the barn.

Like many people slow of thought and doubtful of speech, Sidney Dow had moments of revelation as complete as those of a prophet, when he beheld a scene or a person or a problem in its entirety, with none of the confusing thoughts of glibber and more clever people with their minds forever running off on many tracks. He saw the barn—really saw it, instead of merely glancing at it, like a normal city boy. He saw that the beams, hand-hewn, gray with sixty years, were beautiful; that the sides of the stalls, polished with rubbing by the shoulders of cattle dead these fifty years, were beautiful; that the harrow, with its trim spikes kept sharp and rustless, was beautiful; that most beautiful of all were the animals—cows and horses, chickens that walked with bobbing heads through the straw, and a calf tethered to the wall. The calf capered with alarm as he approached it; then stood considering him with great eyes, letting him stroke its head and at last licking his hand. He slouched to the door of the barn and looked down the valley. More radiant in that early morning light than even the mountain tops covered with maples and hemlock were the upland clearings with white houses and red barns.

"Gosh, it looks nice! It's—it's sort of—it looks nice! I didn't hardly get it when I was here before. But gee"—with all the scorn of sixteen—"I was just a kid then!"

With Uncle Rob he drove the cows to pasture; with Uncle Ben he plowed; with his grandfather, sourly philanthropic behind his beard, he split wood. He found an even greater menagerie than in the barn—turkeys, geese, ducks, pigs and, in the woods and mowings, an exciting remnant of woodchucks, chipmunks, rabbits, and infrequent deer. With all of them—uncles and grandfather, beasts, wild or tame—he felt at home. They did not expect him to chatter and show off, as had his gang in Brooklyn; they accepted him. That, perhaps, more than any ancestral stoutness, more than the beauty of the land, made a farmer of him. He was a natural hermit, and here he could be a hermit without seeming queer.

And a good farmer he was—slow but tireless, patient, unannoyed by the endless work, happy to go to bed early and be up at dawn. For a few days his back felt as though he were burning at the stake, but after that he could lift all day in the hayfield or swing the scythe or drive the frisky young team. He was a good farmer, and he slept at night. The noises which on his first night had fretted his city-tortured nerves were soporific now, and when he heard the sound of a distant train, the barking of a dog on the next farm, he inarticulately told himself that they were lovely.

"You're pretty fair at working," said Uncle Rob, and that was praise almost hysterical.

Indeed, in one aspect of labor, Sidney was better than any of them, even the pine-carved Uncle Rob. He could endure wet dawns, wild winds, all-day drenching. It seems to be true that farmers are more upset by bad weather than most outdoor workers—sailors, postmen, carpenters, brakemen, teamsters. Perhaps it is because they are less subject to higher authority; except for chores and getting in the hay, they can more nearly do things in their own time, and they build up a habit of taking shelter on nasty days. Whether or no, it was true that just the city crises that had vexed Sidney, from icy pavements to sudden fire alarms, had given him the ability to stand discomforts and the unexpected, like a little Cockney surprisingly stolid in the trenches.

He learned the silent humor of the authentic Yankee. Evenings he sat with neighbors on the bench before the general store. To a passing stranger they seemed to be saying nothing, but when the stranger had passed, Uncle Rob would drawl, "Well, if I had fly nets on my hosses, guess I'd look stuck-up too!" and the others would chuckle with contempt at the alien.

This, thought Sidney, was good talk—not like the smart gabble of the city. It was all beautiful, and he knew it, though in his vocabulary there was no such word as "beautiful," and when he saw the most flamboyant sunset he said only, "Guess going to be clear tomorrow."

And so he went back to Brooklyn, not as to his home but as to prison, and as a prison corridor he saw the narrow street with little houses like little cells.

Five minutes after he had entered the house, his father laughed. "Well, did you get enough of farming? I guess you'll appreciate your school now! I won't rub it in, but I swear, how Rob and Ben can stand it——"

"I kind of liked it, Dad. I think I'll be a farmer. I—kind of liked it."

His father had black side whiskers, and between them he had thin cheeks that seemed, after Uncle Rob and Uncle Ben, pallid as the under side of a toadstool. They flushed now, and William shouted:

"You're an idiot! What have I done to have a son who is an idiot? The way I've striven and worked and economized to give you a chance to get ahead, to do something worth while, and then you want to slip right back and be ordinary, like your uncles! So you think you'd like it! You're a fool! Sure you like it in summer, but if you knew it like I do—rousted out to do the chores five o'clock of a January morning, twenty below zero, and maybe have to dig through two feet of snow to get to the barn! Have to tramp down to the store, snowstorm so thick you can't see five feet in front of you!"

"I don't guess I'd mind it much."

"Oh, you don't! Don't be a fool! And no nice company like here—go to bed with the chickens, a winter night, and no nice lodge meeting or church supper or lectures like there is here!"

"Don't care so much for those things. Everybody talking all the while. I like it quiet, like in the country."

"Well, you will care so much for those things, or I'll care you, my fine young man! I'm not going to let you slump back into being a rube like Ben, and don't you forget it! I'll make you work at your books! I'll make you learn to appreciate good society and dressing proper and getting ahead in the world and amounting to something! Yes, sir, amounting to something! Do you think for one moment that after the struggle I've gone through to give you a chance—the way I studied in a country school and earned my way through business college and went to work at five dollars a week in a real-estate office and studied and economized and worked late, so I could give you this nice house and advantages and opportunity—— No, sir! You're going to be a lawyer or a doctor or somebody that amounts to something, and not a rube!"

It would have been too much to expect of Sidney's imagination that he should have seen anything fine and pathetic in William's fierce ambition. That did not move him, but rather fear. He could have broken his father in two, but the passion in this blenched filing-case of a man was such that it hypnotized him.

For days, miserably returned to high school, he longed for the farm. But his mother took him aside and begged: "You mustn't oppose your father so, dearie. He knows what's best for you, and it would just break his heart if he thought you were going to be a common person and not have something to show for all his efforts."

So Sidney came to feel that it was some wickedness in him that made him prefer trees and winds and meadows and the kind cattle to trolley cars and offices and people who made little, flat, worried jokes all day long.

He barely got through high school. His summer vacations he spent in warehouses, hoisting boxes. He failed to enter medical school, botched his examinations shockingly—feeling wicked at betraying his father's ambitions—and his father pushed him into a second-rate dental school with sketchy requirements, a school now blessedly out of existence.

"Maybe you'd be better as a dentist anyway. Requires a lot of manipulation, and I will say you're good with your hands," his father said, in relief that now Sidney was on the highway to fortune and respectability.

But Sidney's hands, deft with hammer and nails, with reins or hoe or spade, were too big, too awkward for the delicate operations of dentistry. And in school he hated the long-winded books with their queer names and shocking colored plates of man's inwards. The workings of a liver did not interest him. He had never seen a liver, save that of a slain chicken. He would turn from these mysteries to a catalogue of harvesting machinery or vegetable seed. So with difficulty he graduated from this doubtful school, and he was uneasy at the pit of his stomach, even when his father, much rejoicing now, bought for him a complete dental

outfit, and rented an office, on the new frontier of
the Bronx, in the back part of a three-story red-brick
apartment house.

His father and mother invited their friends over
from Brooklyn to admire the office, and served them
coffee and cake. Not many of them came, which was
well, for the office was not large. It was really a single
room, divided by a curtain to make a reception hall.
The operating room had pink-calcimined walls and,
for adornment, Sidney's diploma and a calendar from
a dental supply house which showed, with no apparent
appropriateness, a view of Pike's Peak.

When they had all gone, mouthing congratulations,
Sidney looked wistfully out on the old pasture land
which, fifteen years later, was to be filled solidly with
tall, cheap apartment houses and huge avenues with
delicatessen shops and movie palaces. Already these
pastures were doomed and abandoned. Cows no
longer grazed there. Gaunt billboards lined the roads
and behind their barricades were unkempt waste lands
of ashes and sodden newspapers. But they were open
grass, and they brought back the valleys and uplands
of Vermont. His great arms were hungry for the strain
of plowing, and he sighed and turned back to his shining new kit of tools.

The drill he picked up was absurd against his wide
red palm. All at once he was certain that he knew no
dentistry, and that he never would; that he would
botch every case; that dreadful things would happen—
suits for malpractice——

Actually, as a few and poorly paying neighborhood
patients began to come in, the dreadful things didn't
happen. Sidney was slow, but he was careful; if he did
no ingenious dental jeweling, he did nothing wrong.
He learned early what certain dentists and doctors
never learn—that nature has not yet been entirely sup-
planted by the professions. It was not his patients who
suffered; it was he.

All day long to have to remain indoors, to stand in
one place, bent over gaping mouths, to fiddle with tiny

instruments, to produce unctuous sounds of sympathy for cranks who complained of trivial aches, to try to give brisk and confident advice which was really selling talk—all this tortured him.

Then, within one single year, his mother died, his grandfather died on the Vermont farm, Uncle Rob and Uncle Ben moved West, and Sidney met the most wonderful girl in the world. The name of this particular most wonderful girl in the world, who unquestionably had more softness and enchantment and funny little ways of saying things than Helen of Troy, was Mabelle Ellen Pflugmann, and she was cultured; she loved the theater, but rarely attended it; loved also the piano, but hadn't time, she explained, to keep up her practice, because, her father's laundry being in a state of debility, for several years she had temporarily been cashier at the Kwiturwurry Lunch.

They furnished a four-room apartment and went to Vermont for their honeymoon. His grandfather's farm—Sidney wasn't quite sure just who had bought it—was rented out to what the neighborhood considered foreigners—that is, Vermonters from way over beyond the Ridge, fifteen miles away. They took in Sidney and Mabelle. She enjoyed it. She told how sick she had become of the smell and dish clatter of the ole lunch and the horrid customers who were always trying to make love to her. She squealed equally over mountains and ducklings, sunsets and wild strawberries, and as for certain inconveniences—washing with a pitcher and bowl, sleeping in a low room smelling of the chicken run, and having supper in the kitchen with the menfolks in shirt sleeves—she said it was just too darling for words—it was, in fact, sweet. But after ten days of the fortnight on which they had planned, she thought perhaps they had better get back to New York and make sure all the furniture had arrived.

They were happy in marriage. Mabelle saw him, and made him see himself, as a man strong and gallant but shy and blundering. He needed mothering, she said, and he got it and was convinced that he liked it.

He was less gruff with his patients, and he had many more of them, for Mabelle caused him to be known socially. Till marriage he had lived in a furnished room, and all evening he had prowled alone, or read dentistry journals and seed catalogues. Now Mabelle arranged jolly little parties—beer and Welsh rabbit and a game of five hundred. If at the Kwiturwurry Lunch she had met many light fellows, West Farms Lotharios, she had also met estimable but bohemian families of the neighborhood—big traveling men whose territory took them as far west as Denver, assistant buyers from the downtown department stores, and the office manager of a large insurance agency.

Mabelle, a chatelaine now, wanted to shine among them, and wanted Sidney to shine. And he, feeling a little cramped in a new double-breasted blue serge coat, solemnly served the beer, and sometimes a guest perceived that here was an honest and solid dentist upon whom to depend. And once they gave a theater party—six seats at a vaudeville house.

Yet Sidney was never, when he awoke mornings, excited about the adventure of standing with bent, aching shoulders over patients all this glorious coming day.

They had two children in three years and began to worry a little about the rent bill and the grocery bill, and Sidney was considerably less independent with grumbling patients than he had been. His broad shoulders had a small stoop, and he said quite humbly, "Well, I'll try my best to fix 'em to your satisfaction, Mrs. Smallberg," and sometimes his thick fingers tapped nervously on his chin as he talked. And he envied now, where once he had despised them, certain dental-school classmates who knew little of dentistry, but who were slick dressers and given to verbal chuckings under the chin, who had made money and opened three-room offices with chintz chairs in the waiting room. Sidney still had his old office, with no assistant, and the jerry-built tenement looked a little shabby now beside the six-story apartment houses of yellow brick trimmed with marble which had sprung up all about it.

Then their children, Rob and Willabette, were eight and six years old, and Mabelle began to nag Sidney over the children's lack of clothes as pretty as those of their lovely little friends at school.

And his dental engine—only a treadle affair at that—was worn out. And his elbows were always shiny. And in early autumn his father died.

His father died, muttering, "You've been a good boy, Sid, and done what I told you to. You can understand and appreciate now why I kept you from being just a farmer and gave you a chance to be a professional man. I don't think Mabelle comes from an awful good family, but she's a spunky little thing, and real bright, and she'll keep you up to snuff. Maybe some day your boy will be a great, rich banker or surgeon. Keep him away from his Vermont relations—no ambition, those folks. My chest feels so tight! Bless you, Sid!"

He was his father's sole heir. When the will was read in the shabby lawyer's office in Brooklyn, he was astonished to find that his father had still owned—that he himself now owned—the ancestral Vermont home. His slow-burning imagination lighted. He was touched by the belief that his father, for all his pretended hatred of the place, had cherished it and had wanted his son to own it. Not till afterward did he learn from Uncle Rob that William, when his own father had died, had, as eldest son, been given the choice of the farm or half the money in the estate, and had taken the farm to keep Sidney away from it. He had been afraid that if his brothers had it they would welcome Sidney as a partner before he became habituated as a dentist. But in his last days, apparently, William felt that Sidney was safely civilized now and caught. With the farm Sidney inherited some three thousand dollars—not more, for the Brooklyn home was mortgaged.

Instantly and ecstatically, while the lawyer droned senseless advice, Sidney decided to go home. The tenant on his farm—his!—had only two months more on his lease. He'd take it over. The three thousand dollars would buy eight cows—well, say ten—with a cream separator, a tractor, a light truck, and serve to put the old buildings into condition adequate for a few years. He'd do the repairing himself! He arched his hands with longing for the feel of a hammer or a crowbar.

In the hall outside the lawyer's office, Mabelle crowed: "Isn't it—oh, Sid, you do know how sorry I am your father's passed on, but won't it be just lovely! The farm must be worth four thousand dollars. We'll be just as sensible as can be—not blow it all in, like lots of people would. We'll invest the seven thousand, and that ought to give us three hundred and fifty dollars a year— Think of it, an extra dollar every day! You can get a dress suit now, and at last I'll have some decent dresses for the evening, and we'll get a new suit for Rob right away—how soon can you get the money? did he say?—and I saw some lovely little dresses for Willabette and the cutest slippers, and now we can get a decent bridge table instead of that rickety old thing, and——"

As she babbled, which she did, at length, on the stairs down from the office, Sidney realized wretchedly that it was going to take an eloquence far beyond him to convert her to farming and the joys of the land. He was afraid of her, as he had been of his father.

"There's a drug store over across. Let's go over and have an ice-cream soda," he said mildly. "Gosh, it's hot for September! Up on the farm now it would be cool, and the leaves are just beginning to turn. They're awful pretty—all red and yellow."

"Oh, you and your old farm!" But in her joy she was amiable.

They sat at the bright-colored little table in the drug store, with cheery colored drinks between them. But the scene should have been an ancient castle at midnight, terrible with wind and lightning, for suddenly they were not bright nor cheery, but black with tragedy.

There was no manner of use in trying to cajole her. She could never understand how he hated the confinement of his dental office; she would say, "Why, you get the chance of meeting all sorts of nice, interesting people, while I have to stay home," and not perceive that he did not want to meet nice, interesting people. He wanted silence and the smell of earth! And he was under her spell as he had been under his father's. Only violently could he break it. He spoke softly enough, looking at the giddy marble of the soda counter, but he spoke sternly:

"Look here, May. This is our chance. You bet your sweet life we're going to be sensible and not blow in our stake! And we're not going to blow it in on a lot of clothes and a lot of fool bridge parties for a lot of fool folks that don't care one red hoot about us except what they get out of us! For that matter, if we were going to stay on in New York——"

"Which we most certainly are, young man!"

"Will you listen to me? I inherited this dough, not you! Gee, I don't want to be mean, May, but you got to listen to reason, and as I'm saying, if we were going to stay in the city, the first thing I'd spend money for would be a new dental engine—an electric one.

"Need it like the mischief—lose patients when they see me pumping that old one and think I ain't up-to-date—which I ain't, but that's no skin off their nose!"

Even the volatile Mabelle was silent at the unprecedented length and vigor of his oration.

"But we're not going to stay. No, sir! We're going back to the old farm, and the kids will be brought up in the fresh air instead of a lot of alleys. Go back and farm it——"

She exploded then, and as she spoke she looked at him with eyes hot with hatred, the first hatred he had ever known in her:

"Are you crazy? Go back to that hole? Have my kids messing around a lot of manure and dirty animals and out working in the hayfield like a lot of cattle? And attend a little one-room school with a boob for a teacher? And play with a lot of nitwit brats? Not on your life they won't! I've got some ambition for 'em, even if you haven't!"

"Why, May, I thought you liked Vermont and the farm! You were crazy about it on our honeymoon, and you said——"

"I did not! I hated it even then. I just said I liked it to make you happy. That stifling little bedroom, and kerosene lamps, and bugs, and no bathroom, and those fools of farmers in their shirt sleeves—— Oh, it was fierce! If you go, you go without the kids and me! I guess I can still earn a living! And I guess there's still plenty of other men would like to marry me when I divorce you! And I mean it!"

She did, and Sidney knew she did. He collapsed as helplessly as he had with his father.

"Well, of course, if you can't stand it——" he muttered.

"Well, I'm glad you're beginning to come to your senses! Honest, I think you were just crazy with the heat! But listen, here's what I'll do: I won't kick about your getting the electric dental doodingus if it don't cost too much. Now how do you go about selling the farm?"

There began for this silent man a secret life of plotting and of lies. Somehow—he could not see how—he must persuade her to go to the farm. Perhaps she would die—— But he was shocked at this thought, for he loved her and believed her to be the best woman living, as conceivably she may have been. But he did not obey her and sell the farm. He lied. He told her that a Vermont real-estate dealer had written that just this autumn there was no market for farms, but next year would be excellent. And the next year he repeated the lie, and rented the farm to Uncle Rob, who had done well enough on Iowa cornland but was homesick for the hills and sugar groves and placid maples of Vermont. Himself, Sidney did not go to the farm. It was not permitted.

Mabelle was furious that he had not sold, that they had only the three thousand—which was never invested—for clothes and bridge prizes and payments on the car and, after a good deal of irritated talk, his electric dental engine.

If he had always been sullenly restless in his little office, now he was raging. He felt robbed. The little back room, the view—not even of waste land now, but of the center of a cheap block and the back of new tenements—the anguish of patients, which crucified his heavy, unspoken sympathy for them, and that horrible, unending series of wide-stretched mouths and bad molars and tongues—it was intolerable. He thought of meadows scattered with daisies and devil's-paintbrush, of dark, healing thundershowers pouring up the long valley. He must go home to the land!

From the landlord who owned his office he got, in the spring a year and a half after his father's death, the right to garden a tiny patch amid the litter and cement areaways in the center of the block. Mabelle laughed at him, but he stayed late every evening to cultivate each inch of his pocket paradise—a large man, with huge feet, setting them carefully down in a plot ten feet square.

The earth understood him, as it does such men, and before the Long Island market gardeners had anything to display, Sidney had a row of beautiful radish plants. A dozen radishes, wrapped in a tabloid newspaper, he took home one night, and he said vaingloriously to Mabelle, "You'll never get any radishes like these in the market! Right out of our own garden!"

She ate one absently. He braced himself to hear a jeering "You and your old garden!" What he did hear was, in its uncaring, still worse: "Yes, they're all right, I guess."

He'd show her! He'd make her see him as a great farmer! And with that ambition he lost every scruple. He plotted. And this was the way of that plotting:

Early in July he said, and casually, "Well, now we

got the darn car all paid for, we ought to use it. Maybe we might take the kids this summer and make a little tour for a couple weeks or so."

"Where?"

She sounded suspicious, and in his newborn guile he droned, "Oh, wherever you'd like. I hear it's nice up around Niagara Falls and the Great Lakes. Maybe come back by way of Pennsylvania, and see Valley Forge and all them famous historical sites."

"Well, yes, perhaps. The Golheims made a tour last summer and—they make me sick!—they never stop talking about it."

They went. And Mabelle enjoyed it. She was by no means always a nagger and an improver; she was so only when her interests or what she deemed the interests of her children were threatened. She made jokes about the towns through which they passed—any community of less than fifty thousand was to her New Yorkism a "hick hole"—and she even sang jazz and admired his driving, which was bad.

They had headed north, up the Hudson. At Glens Falls he took the highway to the right, instead of left toward the Great Lakes, and she, the city girl, the urban rustic, to whom the only directions that meant anything were East Side and West Side as applied to New York, did not notice, and she was still unsuspicious when he grumbled, "Looks to me like I'd taken the wrong road." Stopping at a filling station, he demanded, "How far is it to Lake George? We ought to be there now."

"Well, stranger, way you're headed, it'll be about twenty-five thousand miles. You're going plumb in the wrong direction."

"I'll be darned! Where are we? Didn't notice the name of the last town we went through."

"You're about a mile from Fair Haven."

"Vermont?"

"Yep."

"Well, I'll be darned! Just think of that! Can't even

be trusted to stay in one state and not skid across the border line!"

Mabelle was looking suspicious, and he said with desperate gayety, "Say, do you know what, May? We're only forty miles from our farm! Let's go have a look at it." Mabelle made a sound of protest, but he turned to the children, in the back seat amid a mess of suitcases and tools and a jack and spare inner tubes, and gloated, "Wouldn't you kids like to see the farm where I worked as a kid—where your grandfather and great-grandfather were born? And see your Granduncle Rob? And see all the little chicks, and so on?"

"Oh, yes!" they shrilled together.

With that enthusiasm from her beloved young, with the smart and uniformed young filling-station attendant listening, Mabelle's talent for being righteous and indignant was gagged. Appearances! She said lightly to the filling-station man, "The doctor just doesn't seem to be able to keep the road at all, does he? Well, Doctor, shall we get started?"

Even when they had gone on and were alone and ready for a little sound domestic quarreling, she merely croaked, "Just the same, it seems mighty queer to me!" And after another mile of brooding, while Sidney drove silently and prayed: "Awfully queer!"

But he scarcely heard her. He was speculating, without in the least putting it into words, "I wonder if in the early summer evenings the fireflies still dart above the meadows? I wonder if the full moon, before it rises behind the hemlocks and sugar maples along the Ridge, still casts up a prophetic glory? I wonder if sleepy dogs still bark across the valley? I wonder if the night breeze slips through the mowing? I, who have for fortress and self-respect only a stuffy office room—I wonder if there are still valleys and stars and the quiet night? Or was that all only the dream of youth?"

*   *   *

They slept at Rutland, Sidney all impatient of the citified hotel bedroom. It was at ten in the morning—he drove in twenty minutes the distance which thirty years ago had taken Uncle Rob an hour and a half—that he drove up to the white house where, since 1800, the Dows had been born.

He could see Uncle Rob with the hayrake in the south mowing, sedately driving the old team and ignoring the visitors.

"I guess he prob'ly thinks we're bootleggers," chuckled Sidney. "Come on, you kids! Here's where your old daddy worked all one summer! Let's go! . . . Thirsty? Say, I'll give you a drink of real spring water—not none of this chlorinated city stuff! And we'll see the menagerie."

Before he had finished, Rob and Willabette had slipped over the rear doors of the car and were looking down into the valley with little sounds of excitement. Sidney whisked out almost as quickly as they, while Mabelle climbed down with the dignity suitable to a dweller in the Bronx. He ignored her. He clucked his children round the house to the spring-fed well and pumped a bucket of water.

"Oh, it's so cold, Daddy. It's swell!" said Rob.

"You bet your life it's cold and swell. Say! Don't use words like 'swell'! They're common. But hell with that! Come on, you brats! I'll show you something!"

There were kittens, and two old, grave, courteous cats. There was a calf—heaven knows by how many generations it was descended from the calf that on a June morning, when Sidney was sixteen, had licked his fingers. There were ducklings, and young turkeys with feathers grotesquely scattered over their skins like palm trees in a desert, and unexpected more kittens, and an old, brown-and-white, tail-wagging dog, and a pen of excited little pigs.

The children squealed over all of them until Mabelle caught up, puffing a little.

"Well," she said, "the kits are kind of cute, ain't they?" Then, darkly: "Now that you've got me here, Sid, with your plans and all!"

Uncle Rob crept up, snarling, "What you folks want? . . . By gracious, if it ain't Sid! This your wife and children? Well, sir!"

It was, Sidney felt, the climax of his plot, and he cried to his son, "Rob! This is your granduncle, that you were named for. How'd you like to stay here on the farm instead of in New York?"

"Hot dog! I'd love it! Them kittens and the li'l' ducks! Oh, they're the berries! You bet I'd like to stay!"

"Oh, I'd love it!" gurgled his sister.

"You would not!" snapped Mabelle. "With no bathroom?"

"We could put one in," growled Sidney.

"On what? On all the money you'd make growing orchids and bananas here, I guess! You kids—how'd you like to walk two miles to school, through the snow, in winter?"

"Oh, that would be slick! Maybe we could kill a deer," said young Rob.

"Yes, and maybe a field mouse could kill you, you dumb-bell! Sure! Lovely! All evening with not a dog-gone thing to do after supper!"

"Why, we'd go to the movies! Do you go to the movies often, Granduncle Rob?"

"Well, afraid in winter you wouldn't get to go to the movies at all. Pretty far into town," hesitated Uncle Rob.

"Not—go—to—the—movies?" screamed the city children, incredulous. It was the most terrible thing they had ever heard of.

Rob, Jr., mourned, "Oh, gee, that wouldn't be so good! Say, how do the hicks learn anything if they don't go to the movies? But still, we could go in the summer, Ma, and in the winter it would be elegant, with sliding and hunting and everything. I'd love it!"

Mabelle cooked supper, banging the pans a good deal and emitting opinions of a house that had no porcelain sink, no water taps, no refrigerator, no gas or electricity. She was silent through supper, silent as

Sidney, silent as Uncle Rob. But Sidney was exultant. With the children for allies, he would win. And the children themselves, they were hysterical. Until Mabelle screamed for annoyance; they leaped up from the table, to come back with the most unspeakable and un-Bronxian objects—a cat affectionately carried by his hind leg, but squealing with misunderstanding of the affection, a dead mole, an unwiped oil can, a muck-covered spade.

"But, Mother," they protested, "in the city you never find anything, except maybe a dead lemon."

She shooed them off to bed at eight; herself, sniffily, she disappeared at nine, muttering to Sidney, "I hope you and your boy friend, Uncle Rob, chew the rag all night and get it out of your systems!"

He was startled, for indeed the next step of his plot did concern Uncle Rob and secret parleys.

For half an hour he walked the road, almost frightened by the intensity of stillness. He could fancy catamounts in the birch clumps. But between spasms of skittish city nerves he stretched out his arms, arched back his hands, breathed consciously. This was not just air, necessary meat for the lungs; it was a spirit that filled him.

He knew that he must not tarry after 9:30 for his intrigue with Uncle Rob. Uncle Rob was seventy-five, and in seventy-five times three hundred and sixty-five evenings he had doubtless stayed up later than 9:30 o'clock several times—dancing with the little French Canuck girls at Potsdam Forge as a young man, sitting up with a sick cow since then, or stuck in the mud on his way back from Sunday-evening meeting. But those few times were epochal. Uncle Rob did not hold with roistering and staying up till all hours just for the vanities of the flesh.

Sidney crept up the stairs to Uncle Rob's room.

Mabelle and Sidney had the best bedroom, on the ground floor; young Rob and Bette had Grampa's room, on the second; Uncle Rob lived in the attic.

City folks might have wondered why Uncle Rob,

tenant and controller of the place, should have hidden in the attic, with three good bedrooms below him. It was simple. Uncle Rob had always lived there since he was a boy.

Up the narrow stairs, steep as a rock face, Sidney crept, and knocked.

"Who's there!" A sharp voice, a bit uneasy. How many years was it since Uncle Rob had heard anyone knock at his bedroom door?

"It's me, Rob—Sid."

"Oh, well—well, guess you can come in. Wait 'll I unlock the door."

Sidney entered his uncle's room for the first time in his life. The hill people, anywhere in the world, do not intrude or encourage intrusion.

Perhaps to fastidious and alien persons Uncle Rob's room would have seemed unlovely. It was lighted by a kerosene lamp, smoking a little, with the wick burned down on one side. There was, for furniture, only a camp cot, with a kitchen chair, a washstand and a bureau. But to make up for this paucity, the room was rather littered. On the washstand, beside a pitcher dry from long disuse, there were a mail-order catalogue, a few packets of seed, a lone overshoe, a ball of twine, a bottle of applejack, and a Spanish War veteran's medal. The walls and ceiling were of plaster so old that they showed in black lines the edges of every lath.

And Sidney liked it—liked the simplicity, liked the freedom from neatness and order and display, liked and envied the old-bach quality of it all.

Uncle Rob, lying on the bed, had prepared for slumber by removing his shoes and outer clothing. He blinked at Sidney's amazing intrusion, but he said amiably enough, "Well, boy?"

"Uncle Rob, can't tell you how glad I am to be back at the old place!"

"H'm."

"Look, I—— Golly, I feel skittish as a young colt! Hardly know the old doc, my patients wouldn't! Rob, you got to help me. Mabelle don't want to stay here and farm it—maybe me and you partners, eh? But the kids and I are crazy to. How I hate that ole city! So do the kids."

"Yeh?"

"Sure they do. Didn't you hear how they said they wouldn't mind tramping to school and not having any movies?"

"Sid, maybe you'll understand kids when you get to be a granddad. Kids will always agree with anything that sounds exciting. Rob thinks it would be dandy to hoof it two miles through the snow to school. He won't! Not once he's done it!" Uncle Rob thrust his hands behind his skinny, bark-brown old neck on the maculate pillow. He was making perhaps the longest oration of his life. The light flickered, and a spider moved indignantly in its web in a corner. "No," said Uncle Rob, "he won't like it. I never did. And the schoolmaster used to lick me. I hated it, crawling through that snow and then get licked because you're late. And jiminy—haven't thought of it for thirty years, I guess, maybe forty, but I remember how some big fellow would dare you to put your tongue to your lunch pail, and it was maybe thirty below, and your tongue stuck to it and it took the hide right off! No, I never liked any of it, especially chores."

"Rob, listen! I'm serious! The kids will maybe kind of find it hard at first, but they'll get to like it, and they'll grow up real folks and not city saps. It'll be all right with them. I'll see to that. It's Mabelle. Listen, Rob, I've got a swell idea about her, and I want you to help me. You get hold of the ladies of the township—the Grange members and the Methodist ladies and like that. You tell 'em Mabelle is a swell city girl, and it would be dandy for the neighborhood if they could get her to stay here. She's grand, but she does kind of fall for flattery, and in the Bronx she ain't so important, and if these ladies came and told her they thought she was the cat's pajamas, maybe she'd fall for it, and then I guess maybe she might stay, if the ladies came——"

"They wouldn't!"

Uncle Rob had been rubbing his long and prickly chin and curling his toes in his gray socks.

"What do you mean?"

"Well, first place, the ladies round here would be onto your Mabelle. They ain't so backwoods as they was in your time. Take Mrs. Craig. Last three winters, her and her husband, Frank, have packed up the fliver and gone to Florida. But that ain't it. Fact is, Sid, I kind of sympathize with Mabelle."

"What do you mean?"

"Well, I never was strong for farming. Hard life, Sid. Always thought I'd like to keep store or something in the city. You forget how hard the work is here. You with your easy job, just filling a few teeth! No, I can't help you, Sid."

"I see. All right. Sorry for disturbing you."

As he crept downstairs in bewilderment, Sidney prayed—he who so rarely prayed—"O Lord, doesn't anybody but me love the land any more? What is going to happen to us? Why, all our life comes from the land!"

He knew that in the morning he would beg Mabelle to stay for a fortnight—and that she would not stay. It was his last night here. So all night long, slow and silent, he walked the country roads, looking at hemlock branches against the sky, solemnly shaking his head and wondering why he could never rid himself of this sinfulness of longing for the land; why he could never be grown-up and ambitious and worthy, like his father and Mabelle and Uncle Rob.

Young Man Axelbrod

The cottonwood is a tree of a slovenly and plebeian habit. Its woolly wisps turn gray the lawns and engender neighborhood hostilities about our town. Yet it is a mighty tree, a refuge and an inspiration; the sun flickers in its towering foliage, whence the tattoo of locusts enlivens our dusty summer afternoons. From the wheat country out to the sagebrush plains between the buttes and the Yellowstone it is the cottonwood that keeps a little grateful shade for sweating homesteaders.

In Joralemon we call Knute Axelbrod "Old Cottonwood." As a matter of fact, the name was derived not so much from the quality of the man as from the wide grove about his gaunt white house and red barn. He made a comely row of trees on each side of the country road, so that a humble, daily sort of a man, driving beneath them in his lumber wagon, might fancy himself lord of a private avenue.

And at sixty-five Knute was like one of his own cottonwoods, his roots deep in the soil, his trunk weathered by rain and blizzard and baking August noons, his crown spread to the wide horizon of day and the enormous sky of a prairie night.

This immigrant was an American even in speech. Save for a weakness about his j's and w's, he spoke

the twangy Yankee English of the land. He was the
more American because in his native Scandinavia he
had dreamed of America as a land of light. Always
through disillusion and weariness he beheld America
as the world's nursery for justice, for broad, fair towns,
and eager talk; and always he kept a young soul that
dared to desire beauty.

As a lad Knute Axelbrod had wished to be a famous
scholar, to learn the ease of foreign tongues, the romance of history, to unfold in the graciousness of wise
books. When he first came to America he worked in
a sawmill all day and studied all evening. He mastered
enough book-learning to teach district school for two
terms; then, when he was only eighteen, a great-
hearted pity for faded little Lena Wesselius moved
him to marry her. Gay enough, doubtless, was their
hike by prairie schooner to new farmlands, but Knute
was promptly caught in a net of poverty and family.
From eighteen to fifty-eight he was always snatching
children away from death or the farm away from
mortgages.

He had to be content—and generously content he
was—with the second-hand glory of his children's success and, for himself, with pilfered hours of reading—
that reading of big, thick, dismal volumes of history
and economics which the lone mature learner chooses.
Without ever losing his desire for strange cities and
the dignity of towers he stuck to his farm. He acquired
a half-section, free from debt, fertile, well-stocked,
adorned with a cement silo, a chicken-run, a new
windmill. He became comfortable, secure, and then he
was ready, it seemed, to die; for at sixty-three his work
was done, and he was unneeded and alone.

His wife was dead. His sons had scattered afar, one
a dentist in Fargo, another a farmer in the Golden
Valley. He had turned over his farm to his daughter
and son-in-law. They had begged him to live with
them, but Knute refused.

"No," he said, "you must learn to stand on your
own feet. I vill not give you the farm. You pay me

four hundred dollars a year rent, and I live on that and vatch you from my hill."

On a rise beside the lone cottonwood which he loved best of all his trees Knute built a tar-paper shack, and here he "bached it"; cooked his meals, made his bed, sometimes sat in the sun, read many books from the Joralemon library, and began to feel that he was free of the yoke of citizenship which he had borne all his life.

For hours at a time he sat on a backless kitchen chair before the shack, a wide-shouldered man, white-bearded, motionless; a seer despite his grotesquely baggy trousers, his collarless shirt. He looked across the miles of stubble to the steeple of the Jackrabbit Forks church and meditated upon the uses of life. At first he could not break the rigidity of habit. He rose at five, found work in cleaning his cabin and cultivating his garden, had dinner exactly at twelve, and went to bed by afterglow. But little by little he discovered that he could be irregular without being arrested. He stayed abed till seven or even eight. He got a large, deliberate, tortoise-shell cat, and played games with it, let it lap milk upon the table, called it the Princess, and confided to it that he had a "sneaking idee" that men were fools to work so hard. Around this coatless old man, his stained waistcoat flapping about a huge torso, in a shanty of rumpled bed and pine table covered with sheets of food-daubed newspaper, hovered all the passionate aspiration of youth and the dreams of ancient beauty.

He began to take long walks by night. In his necessitous life night had ever been a period of heavy slumber in close rooms. Now he discovered the mystery of the dark; saw the prairies wide-flung and misty beneath the moon, heard the voices of grass and cottonwoods and drowsy birds. He tramped for miles. His boots were dew-soaked, but he did not heed. He stopped upon hillocks, shyly threw wide his arms, and stood worshiping the naked, slumbering land.

These excursions he tried to keep secret, but they were bruited abroad. Neighbors, good, decent fellows with no sense about walking in the dew at night, when they were returning late from town, drunk, lashing their horses and flinging whisky bottles from racing democrat wagons, saw him, and they spread the tidings that Old Cottonwood was "getting nutty since he give up his farm to that son-in-law of his and retired. Seen the old codger wandering around at midnight. Wish I had his chance to sleep. Wouldn't catch me out in the night air."

Any rural community from Todd Center to Seringapatam is resentful of any person who varies from its standard, and is morbidly fascinated by any hint of madness. The countryside began to spy on Knute Axelbrod, to ask him questions, and to stare from the road at his shack. He was sensitively aware of it, and inclined to be surly to inquisitive acquaintances. Doubtless that was the beginning of his great pilgrimage.

As a part of the general wild license of his new life—really, he once roared at that startled cat, the Princess: "By gollies! I ain't going to brush my teeth tonight. All my life I've brushed 'em, and alvays wanted to skip a time vunce"—Knute took considerable pleasure in degenerating in his taste in scholarship. He wilfully declined to finish *The Conquest of Mexico,* and began to read light novels borrowed from the Joralemon library. So he rediscovered the lands of dancing and light wines, which all his life he had desired. Some economics and history he did read, but every evening he would stretch out in his buffalo-horn chair, his feet on the cot and the Princess in his lap, and invade Zenda or fall in love with Trilby.

Among the novels he chanced upon a highly optimistic story of Yale in which a worthy young man "earned his way through" college, stroked the crew, won Phi Beta Kappa, and had the most entertaining, yet moral, conversations on or adjacent to "the dear old fence."

As a result of this chronicle, at about three o'clock one morning, when Knute Axelbrod was sixty-four years of age, he decided that he would go to college. All his life he had wanted to. Why not do it?

When he awoke he was not so sure about it as when he had gone to sleep. He saw himself as ridiculous, a ponderous, oldish man among clean-limbed youths, like a dusty cottonwood among silver birches. But for months he wrestled and played with that idea of a great pilgrimage to the Mount of Muses; for he really supposed college to be that sort of place. He believed that all college students, except for the wealthy idlers, burned to acquire learning. He pictured Harvard and Yale and Princeton as ancient groves set with marble temples, before which large groups of Grecian youths talked gently about astronomy and good government. In his picture they never cut classes or ate.

With a longing for music and books and graciousness such as the most ambitious boy could never comprehend, this thick-faced farmer dedicated himself to beauty, and defied the unconquerable power of approaching old age. He sent for college catalogues and school books, and diligently began to prepare himself for college.

He found Latin irregular verbs and the whimsicalities of algebra fiendish. They had nothing to do with actual life as he had lived it. But he mastered them; he studied twelve hours a day, as once he had plodded through eighteen hours a day in the hayfield. With history and English literature he had comparatively little trouble; already he knew much of them from his recreative reading. From German neighbors he had picked up enough Platt-deutsch to make German easy. The trick of study began to come back to him from his small school teaching of forty-five years before. He began to believe that he could really put it through. He kept assuring himself that in college, with rare and sympathetic instructors to help him, there would not be this baffling search, this nervous strain.

But the unreality of the things he studied did disillusion him, and he tired of his new game. He kept it up chiefly because all his life he had kept up onerous labor without any taste for it. Toward the autumn of the second year of his eccentric life he no longer believed that he would ever go to college.

Then a busy little grocer stopped him on the street in Joralemon and quizzed him about his studies, to the delight of the informal club which always loafs at the corner of the hotel.

Knute was silent, but dangerously angry. He remembered just in time how he had once laid wrathful hands upon a hired man, and somehow the man's collar bone had been broken. He turned away and walked home, seven miles, still boiling. He picked up the Princess, and, with her mewing on his shoulder, tramped out again to enjoy the sunset.

He stopped at a reedy slough. He gazed at a hopping plover without seeing it. Suddenly he cried:

"I am going to college. It opens next veek. I t'ink that I can pass the examinations."

Two days later he had moved the Princess and his sticks of furniture to his son-in-law's house, had bought a new slouch hat, a celluloid collar and a solemn suit of black, had wrestled with God in prayer through all of a star-clad night, and had taken the train for Minneapolis, on the way to New Haven.

While he stared out of the car window Knute was warning himself that the millionaires' sons would make fun of him. Perhaps they would haze him. He bade himself avoid all these sons of Belial and cleave to his own people, those who "earned their way through."

At Chicago he was afraid with a great fear of the lightning flashes that the swift crowds made on his retina, the batteries of ranked motor cars that charged at him. He prayed, and ran for his train to New York. He came at last to New Haven.

Not with gibing rudeness, but with politely quizzical eyebrows, Yale received him, led him through entrance examinations, which, after sweaty plowing with

the pen, he barely passed, and found for him a roommate. The roommate was a large-browed soft white
grub named Ray Gribble, who had been teaching
school in New England and seemed chiefly to desire
college training so that he might make more money
as a teacher. Ray Gribble was a hustler; he instantly
got work tutoring the awkward son of a steel man,
and for board he waited on table.

He was Knute's chief acquaintance. Knute tried to
fool himself into thinking he liked the grub, but Ray
couldn't keep his damp hands off the old man's soul.
He had the skill of a professional exhorter of young
men in finding out Knute's motives, and when he discovered that Knute had a hidden desire to sip at gay,
polite literature, Ray said in a shocked way:

"Strikes me a man like you, that's getting old, ought
to be thinking more about saving your soul than about
all these frills. You leave this poetry and stuff to these
foreigners and artists, and you stick to Latin and math
and the Bible. I tell you, I've taught school, and I've
learned by experience."

With Ray Gribble, Knute lived grubbily, an existence of torn comforters and smelly lamp, of lexicons
and logarithm tables. No leisurely loafing by fireplaces
was theirs. They roomed in West Divinity, where
gather the theologues, the lesser sort of law students,
a whimsical genius or two, and a horde of unplaced
freshmen and "scrub seniors."

Knute was shockingly disappointed, but he stuck to
his room because outside of it he was afraid. He was a
grotesque figure, and he knew it, a white-polled giant
squeezed into a small seat in a classroom, listening to
instructors younger than his own sons. Once he tried
to sit on the fence. No one but "ringers" sat on the
fence any more, and at the sight of him trying to look
athletic and young, two upper-class men snickered,
and he sneaked away.

He came to hate Ray Gribble and his voluble companions of the submerged tenth of the class, the hew-
ers of tutorial wood. It is doubtless safer to mock the

flag than to question that best-established tradition of
our democracy—that those who "earn their way
through" college are necessarily stronger, braver, and
more assured of success than the weaklings who talk
by the fire. Every college story presents such a moral.
But tremblingly the historian submits that Knute discovered that waiting on table did not make lads more
heroic than did football or happy loafing. Fine fellows,
cheerful and fearless, were many of the boys who
"earned their way," and able to talk to richer classmates without fawning; but just as many of them assumed an abject respectability as the most convenient
pose. They were pickers up of unconsidered trifles;
they toadied to the classmates whom they tutored;
they wriggled before the faculty committee on scholar-
ships; they looked pious at Dwight Hall prayer-
meetings to make an impression on the serious
minded; and they drank one glass of beer at Jake's to
show the light minded that they meant nothing offen-
sive by their piety. In revenge for cringing to the inso-
lent athletes whom they tutored, they would, when
safe among their own kind, yammer about the "lack
of democracy of college today." Not that they were
so indiscreet as to do anything about it. They lacked
the stuff of really rebellious souls. Knute listened to
them and marveled. They sounded like young hired
men talking behind his barn at harvest time.

This submerged tenth hated the dilettantes of the
class even more than they hated the bloods. Against
one Gilbert Washburn, a rich esthete with more manner than any freshman ought to have, they raged righteously. They spoke of seriousness and industry till
Knute, who might once have desired to know lads
like Washburn, felt ashamed of himself as a wicked,
wasteful old man.

Humbly though he sought, he found no inspiration
and no comradeship. He was the freak of the class,
and aside from the submerged tenth, his classmates
were afraid of being "queered" by being seen with
him.

As he was still powerful, one who could take up a barrel of pork on his knees, he tried to find friendship among the athletes. He sat at Yale Field, watching the football tryouts, and tried to get acquainted with the candidates. They stared at him and answered his questions grudgingly—beefy youths who in their simple-hearted way showed that they considered him plain crazy.

The place itself began to lose the haze of magic through which he had first seen it. Earth is earth, whether one sees it in Camelot or Joralemon or on the Yale campus—or possibly even in the Harvard yard! The buildings ceased to be temples to Knute; they became structures of brick or stone, filled with young men who lounged at windows and watched him amusedly as he tried to slip by.

The Gargantuan hall of Commons became a tri-daily horror because at the table where he dined where two youths who, having uncommonly penetrating minds, discerned that Knute had a beard, and courageously told the world about it. One of them, named Atchison, was a superior person, very industrious and scholarly, glib in mathematics and manners. He despised Knute's lack of definite purpose in coming to college. The other was a play-boy, a wit and a stealer of street signs, who had a wonderful sense for a subtle jest; and his references to Knute's beard shook the table with jocund mirth three times a day. So these youths of gentle birth drove the shambling, wistful old man away from Commons, and thereafter he ate at the lunch counter at the Black Cat.

Lacking the stimulus of friendship, it was the harder for Knute to keep up the strain of studying the long assignments. What had been a week's pleasant reading in his shack was now thrown at him as a day's task. But he would not have minded the toil if he could have found one as young as himself. They were all so dreadfully old, the money-earners, the serious laborers at athletics, the instructors who worried over their life work of putting marks in class-record books.

Then, on a sore, bruised day, Knute did meet one
who was young.

Knute had heard that the professor who was the
idol of the college had berated the too-earnest lads in
his Browning class, and insisted that they read *Alice
in Wonderland*. Knute floundered dustily about in a
second-hand bookshop till he found an "Alice," and
he brought it home to read over his lunch of a hot-
dog sandwich. Something in the grave absurdity of the
book appealed to him, and he was chuckling over it
when Ray Gribble came into the room and glanced
at the reader.

"Huh!" said Mr. Gribble.

"That's a fine, funny book," said Knute.

"Huh! *Alice in Wonderland*! I've heard of it. Silly
nonsense. Why don't you read something really fine,
like Shakespeare or *Paradise Lost*?"

"Vell——" said Knute, all he could find to say.

With Ray Gribble's glassy eye on him, he could no
longer roll and roar with the book. He wondered if
indeed he ought not to be reading Milton's pompous
anthropological misconceptions. He went unhappily
out to an early history class, ably conducted by Blevins, Ph.D.

Knute admired Blevins, Ph.D. He was so tubbed
and eyeglassed and terribly right. But most of Blevins'
lambs did not like Blevins. They said he was a
"crank." They read newspapers in his class and covertly kicked one another.

In the smug, plastered classroom, his arm leaning
heavily on the broad tablet-arm of his chair, Knute
tried not to miss one of Blevins' sardonic proofs that
the correct date of the second marriage of Themis-
tocles was two years and seven days later than the
date assigned by that illiterate ass, Frutari of Padua.
Knute admired young Blevins' performance, and he
felt virtuous in application to these hard, unnonsensi-
cal facts.

He became aware that certain lewd fellows of the
lesser sort were playing poker just behind him. His

prairie-trained ear caught whispers of "Two to dole," and "Raise you two beans." Knute revolved, and frowned upon these mockers of sound learning. As he turned back he was aware that the offenders were chuckling, and continuing their game. He saw that Blevins, Ph.D., perceived that something was wrong; he frowned, but he said nothing. Knute sat in meditation. He saw Blevins as merely a boy. He was sorry for him. He would do the boy a good turn.

When class was over he hung about Blevins' desk till the other students had clattered out. He rumbled:

"Say, Professor, you're a fine fellow. I do something for you. If any of the boys make themselves a nuisance, you yust call on me, and I spank the son of a guns."

Blevins, Ph.D., spake in a manner of culture and nastiness:

"Thanks so much, Axelbrod, but I don't fancy that will ever be necessary. I am supposed to be a reasonably good disciplinarian. Good day. Oh, one moment. There's something I've been wishing to speak to you about. I do wish you wouldn't try quite so hard to show off whenever I call on you during quizzes. You answer at such needless length, and you smile as though there were something highly amusing about me. I'm quite willing to have you regard me as a humorous figure, privately, but there are certain classroom conventions, you know, certain little conventions."

"Why, Professor!" wailed Knute, "I never make fun of you! I didn't know I smile. If I do, I guess it's yust because I am so glad when my stupid old head gets the lesson good."

"Well, well, that's very gratifying, I'm sure. And if you will be a little more careful——"

Blevins, Ph.D., smiled a toothy, frozen smile, and trotted off to the Graduates' Club, to be witty about old Knute and his way of saying "yust," while in the deserted classroom Knute sat chill, an old man and doomed. Through the windows came the light of Indian summer; clean, boyish cries rose from the campus. But the lover of autumn smoothed his baggy sleeve, stared at the blackboard, and there saw only the gray of October stubble about his distant shack. As he pictured the college watching him, secretly making fun of him and his smile, he was now faint and ashamed, now bull-angry. He was lonely for his cat, his fine chair of buffalo horns, the sunny doorstep of his shack, and the understanding land. He had been in college for about one month.

Before he left the classroom he stepped behind the instructor's desk and looked at an imaginary class.

"I might have stood there as a prof if I could have come earlier," he said softly to himself.

Calmed by the liquid autumn gold that flowed through the streets, he walked out Whitney Avenue toward the butte-like hill of East Rock. He observed the caress of the light upon the scarped rock, heard the delicate music of leaves, breathed in air pregnant with tales of old New England. He exulted: "'Could write poetry now if I yust—if I yust could write poetry!"

He climbed to the top of East Rock, whence he could see the Yale buildings like the towers of Oxford, and see Long Island Sound, and the white glare of Long Island beyond the water. He marveled that Axelbrod of the cottonwood country was looking across an arm of the Atlantic to New York state. He noticed a freshman on a bench at the edge of the rock, and he became irritated. The freshman was Gilbert Washburn, the snob, the dilettante, of whom Ray Gribble had once said: "That guy is the disgrace of the class. He doesn't go out for anything, high stand or Dwight Hall or anything else. Thinks he's so doggone much better than the rest of the fellows that he doesn't associate with anybody. Thinks he's literary, they say, and yet he doesn't even heel the 'Lit,' like the regular literary fellows! Got no time for a loafing, mooning snob like that."

As Knute stared at the unaware Gil, whose profile was fine in outline against the sky, he was terrifically public-spirited and disapproving and that sort of moral thing. Though Gil was much too well dressed, he seemed moodily discontented.

"What he needs is to vork in a threshing crew and sleep in the hay," grumbled Knute almost in the virtuous manner of Gribble. "Then he vould know when he vas vell off, and not look like he had the earache. Pff!" Gil Washburn rose, trailed toward Knute, glanced at him, sat down on Knute's bench.

"Great view!" he said. His smile was eager.

That smile symbolized to Knute all the art of life he had come to college to find. He tumbled out of his moral attitude with ludicrous haste, and every wrinkle of his weathered face creased deep as he answered:

"Yes: I t'ink the Acropolis must be like this here."

"Say, look here, Axelbrod; I've been thinking about you."

"Yas?"

"We ought to know each other. We two are the class scandal. We came here to dream, and these busy little goats like Atchison and Giblets, or whatever your roommate's name is, think we're fools not to go out for marks. You may not agree with me, but I've decided that you and I are precisely alike."

"What makes you t'ink I come here to dream?" bristled Knute.

"Oh, I used to sit near you at Commons and hear you try to quell old Atchison whenever he got busy discussing the reasons for coming to college. That old, moth-eaten topic! I wonder if Cain and Abel didn't discuss it at the Eden Agricultural College. You know, Abel the mark-grabber, very pious and high stand, and Cain wanting to read poetry."

"Yes," said Knute, "and I guess Prof. Adam say, 'Cain, don't you read this poetry; it von't help you in algebry.'"

"Of course. Say, wonder if you'd like to look at this volume of Musset I was sentimental enough to lug up here today. Picked it up when I was abroad last year."

From his pocket Gil drew such a book as Knute

had never seen before, a slender volume, in a strange language, bound in hand-tooled crushed levant, an effeminate bibelot over which the prairie farmer gasped with luxurious pleasure. The book almost vanished in his big hands. With a timid forefinger he stroked the levant, ran through the leaves.

"I can't read it, but that's the kind of book I alvays t'ought there must be some like it," he sighed.

"Listen!" cried Gil. "Ysaye is playing up at Hartford tonight. Let's go hear him. We'll trolley up. Tried to get some of the fellows to come, but they thought I was a nut."

What an Ysaye was, Knute Axelbrod had no notion; but "Sure!" he boomed.

When they got to Hartford they found that between them they had just enough money to get dinner, hear Ysaye from gallery seats, and return only as far as Meriden. At Meriden Gil suggested:

"Let's walk back to New Haven, then. Can you make it?"

Knute had no knowledge as to whether it was four miles or forty back to the campus, but "Sure!" he said. For the last few months he had been noticing that, despite his bulk, he had to be careful, but tonight he could have flown.

In the music of Ysaye, the first real musician he had ever heard, Knute had found all the incredible things of which he had slowly been reading in William Morris and "Idylls of the King." Tall knights he had beheld, and slim princesses in white samite, the misty gates of forlorn towns, and the glory of the chivalry that never was.

They did walk, roaring down the road beneath the October moon, stopping to steal apples and to exclaim over silvered hills, taking a puerile and very natural joy in chasing a profane dog. It was Gil who talked, and Knute who listened, for the most part; but Knute was lured into tales of the pioneer days, of blizzards, of harvesting, and of the first flame of the green wheat. Regarding the Atchisons and Gribbles of the class both of them were youthfully bitter and supercilious. But they were not bitter long, for they were atavisms tonight. They were wandering minstrels, Gilbert the troubadour with his man-at-arms.

They reached the campus at about five in the morning. Fumbling for words that would express his feeling, Knute stammered:

"Vell, it vas fine. I go to bed now and I dream about——"

"Bed? Rats! Never believe in winding up a party when it's going strong. Too few good parties. Besides, it's only the shank of the evening. Besides, we're hungry. Besides—oh, besides! Wait here a second. I'm going up to my room to get some money, and we'll have some eats. Wait! Please do!"

Knute would have waited all night. He had lived almost seventy years and traveled fifteen hundred miles and endured Ray Gribble to find Gil Washburn.

Policemen wondered to see the celluloid-collared old man and the expensive-looking boy rolling arm in arm down Chapel Street in search of a restaurant suitable to poets. They were all closed.

"The Ghetto will be awake by now," said Gil. "We'll go buy some eats and take 'em up to my room. I've got some tea there."

Knute shouldered through dark streets beside him as naturally as though he had always been a nighthawk, with an aversion to anything as rustic as beds. Down on Oak Street, a place of low shops, smoky lights and alley mouths, they found the slum already astir. Gil contrived to purchase boxed biscuits, cream cheese, chicken-loaf, a bottle of cream. While Gil was chaffering, Knute stared out into the street milkily lighted by wavering gas and the first feebleness of coming day; he gazed upon Kosher signs and advertisements in Russian letters, shawled women and bearded rabbis; and as he looked he gathered contentment which he could never lose. He had traveled abroad tonight.

*   *   *

The room of Gil Washburn was all the useless, pleasant things Knute wanted it to be. There was more of Gil's Paris days in it than of his freshmanhood: Persian rugs, a silver tea service, etchings, and books. Knute Axelbrod of the tar-paper shack and piggy farmyards gazed in satisfaction. Vast bearded, sunk in an easy chair, he clucked amiably while Gil lighted a fire.

Over supper they spoke of great men and heroic ideals. It was good talk, and not unspiced with lively references to Gribble and Atchison and Blevins, all asleep now in their correct beds. Gil read snatches of Stevenson and Anatole France; then at last he read his own poetry.

It does not matter whether that poetry was good or bad. To Knute it was a miracle to find one who actually wrote it.

The talk grew slow, and they began to yawn. Knute was sensitive to the lowered key of their Indian-summer madness, and he hastily rose. As he said good-by he felt as though he had but to sleep a little while and return to this unending night of romance.

But he came out of the dormitory upon day. It was six-thirty of the morning, with a still, hard light upon red-brick walls.

"I can go to his room plenty times now; I find my friend," Knute said. He held tight the volume of Musset, which Gil had begged him to take.

As he started to walk the few steps to West Divinity Knute felt very tired. By daylight the adventure seemed more and more incredible.

As he entered the dormitory he sighed heavily:

"Age and youth, I guess they can't team together long." As he mounted the stairs he said: "If I saw the boy again, he vould get tired of me. I tell him all I got to say." And as he opened his door, he added: "This is what I come to college for—this one night. I go avay before I spoil it."

He wrote a note to Gil, and began to pack his telescope. He did not even wake Ray Gribble, sonorously sleeping in the stale air.

At five that afternoon, on the day coach of a west-bound train, an old man sat smiling. A lasting content was in his eyes, and in his hands a small book in French.

Go East, Young Man

The grandfather was Zebulun Dibble. He had a mustache like a horse's mane; he wore a boiled shirt with no collar, and he manufactured oatmeal, very wholesome and tasteless. He moved from New Hampshire out to the city of Zenith in 1875, and in 1880 became the proud but irritated father of T. Jefferson Dibble.

T. Jefferson turned the dusty oatmeal factory into a lyric steel-and-glass establishment for the manufacture of Oatees, Barlenated Rice and Puffy Wuffles, whereby he garnered a million dollars and became cultured, along about 1905. This was the beginning of the American fashion in culture which has expanded now into lectures by poetic Grand Dukes and Symphonies on the radio.

T. Jefferson belonged to the Opera Festival Committee and the Batik Exposition Conference, and he was the chairman of the Lecture Committee of the Phoenix Club. Not that all this enervating culture kept him from burning up the sales manager from nine-thirty a.m. to five p.m. He felt that he had been betrayed; he felt that his staff, Congress, and the labor unions had bitten the hand that fed them, if the sale of Rye Yeasties (Vitaminized) did not annually increase four per cent.

But away from the office, he announced at every

club and committee where he could wriggle into the
chairman's seat that America was the best country in
the world, by heavens, and Zenith the best city in
America, and how were we going to prove it? Not by
any vulgar boasting and boosting! No, sir! By showing
more culture than any other burg of equal size in the
world! Give him ten years! He'd see that Zenith had
more square feet of old masters, more fiddles in the
symphony orchestra, and more marble statues per
square mile than Munich!

T. Jefferson's only son, Whitney, appeared in 1906.
T. Jefferson winced every time the boys called him
"Whit." He winced pretty regularly. Whit showed
more vocation for swimming, ringing the doorbells of
timorous spinsters, and driving a flivver than for the
life of culture. But T. Jefferson was determined.

Just as he bellowed, "By golly, you'll sell Barley
Gems to the wholesalers or get out!" in the daytime,
so when he arrived at his neat slate-roofed English
Manor Style residence in Floral Heights, he bellowed
at Whit, "By golly, you'll learn to play the piano or
I'll lam the everlasting daylights out of you! Ain't you
ashamed! Wanting to go skating! The idea!"

Whitney was taught—at least theoretically he was
taught—the several arts of piano-playing, singing,
drawing, water-color painting, fencing, and French.
And through it all Whit remained ruddy, grinning, and
irretrievably given to money-making. For years, without T. Jefferson's ever discovering it, he conducted a
lucrative trade in transporting empty gin bottles in his
father's spare sedan from the Zenith Athletic Club to
the emporia of the bootleggers.

But he could draw. He sang like a crow, he fenced
like a sculptor, but he could draw, and when he was
sent to Yale he became the chief caricaturist of the
Yale Record.

For the first time his father was delighted. He had
Whit's original drawings framed in heavy gold, and
showed all of them to his friends and his committees
before they could escape. When Whit sold a small

sketch to *Life,* T. Jefferson sent him an autographed check for a hundred dollars, so that Whit, otherwise a decent youth, became a little vain about the world's need of his art. At Christmas, senior year, T. Jefferson (with the solemn expression of a Father about to Give Good Advice to his Son) lured him into the library, and flowered in language:

"Now, Whitney, the time has come, my boy, when you must take thought and decide what rôle in this world's—what rôle in the world—in fact, to what rôle you feel your talents are urging you, if you get what I mean."

"You mean what job I'll get after graduation?"

"No, no, no! The Dibbleses have had enough of jobs! I have money enough for all of us. I have had to toil and moil. But the Dibbleses are essentially an artistic family. Your grandfather loved to paint. It is true that circumstances were such that he was never able to paint anything but the barn, but he had a fine eye for color—he painted it blue and salmon-pink instead of red; and he was responsible for designing the old family mansion on Clay Street—I should never have given it up except that the bathrooms were antiquated—not a single colored tile in them.

"It was he who had the Moorish turret with the copper roof put on the mansion, when the architect wanted a square tower with a pagoda roof. And I myself, if I may say so, while I have not had the opportunity to develop my creative gifts, I was responsible for raising the fund of $267,800 to buy the Rembrandt for the Zenith Art Institute; and the fact that the Rembrandt later proved to be a fake, painted by a scoundrel named John J. Jones, was no fault of mine. So—in fact—if you understand me—how would you like to go to Paris, after graduation, and study art?"

"Paris!"

Whit had never been abroad. He pictured Paris as a series of bars, interspersed with sloe-eyed girls (he wasn't quite sure what sloe eyes were, but he was certain that the eyes of all Parisian cuties were sloe), palms blooming in January, and Bohemian studios where jolly artists and lively models lived on spaghetti, red wine, and a continuous singing of "*Auprès de Ma Blonde.*"

"Paris!" he said; and, "That would be elegant, sir!"

"My boy!" T. Jefferson put his puffy palm on Whit's shoulder in a marvelous impersonation of a Father about to Send His Son Forth into the Maelstrom of Life. "I am proud of you.

"I hope I shall live to see you one of the world's great pictorial artists, exhibiting in London, Rome, Zenith, and elsewhere, and whose pictures will carry a message of high ideals to all those who are dusty with striving, lifting their souls from the sordid struggle to the farther green places.

"That's what I often tell my sales manager, Mr. Mountgins—he ought to get away from mere thoughts of commerce and refresh himself at the Art Institute— and the stubborn jackass, he simply won't increase the sale of Korn Krumbles in southern Michigan! But as I was saying, I don't want you to approach Paris in any spirit of frivolity, but earnestly, as an opportunity of making a bigger and better—no, no, I mean a bigger and—a bigger—I mean a better world! I give you my blessings."

"Great! Watch me, Dad!"

When, after Christmas, Whit's classmates reveled in the great Senior Year pastime of wondering what they would do after graduation, Whit was offensively smug.

"I got an idea," said his classmate, Stuyvesant Wescott, who also came from Zenith. "Of course it's swell to go into law or bond selling—good for a hundred thou. a year—and a fellow oughtn't to waste his education and opportunities by going out for lower ideals. Think of that poor fish Ted Page, planning to teach in a prep school—associate with a lot of dirty kids and never make more'n five thou. a year! But the bond game is pretty well jammed. What do you think of getting in early on television? Millions in it!"

Mr. Whitney Dibble languidly rose, drew a six-inch scarlet cigarette holder from his pocket, lighted a ciga-

rette and flicked the ash off it with a disdainful forefinger. The cigarette holder, the languor, the disdain,
and the flicking habit were all strictly new to him, and
they were extremely disapproved of by his kind.

"I am not," he breathed, "at all interested in your
low-brow plans. I am going to Paris to study art. In
five years from now I shall be exhibiting in—in all
those galleries you exhibit in. I hope you have success
with your money-grubbing and your golf. Drop in to
see me at my *petit château* when you're abroad. I must
dot out now and do a bit of sketching."

Whitney Dibble, riding a Pullman to greatness, arrived in Paris on an October day of pearl and amber.
When he had dropped his baggage at his hotel, Whit
walked out exultantly. The Place de la Concorde
seemed to him a royal courtyard; Gabriel's twin buildings of the Marine Ministry were the residences of
emperors themselves. They seemed taller than the
most pushing skyscraper of New York, taller and nobler and more wise.

All Paris spoke to him of a life at once more vivid
and more demanding, less hospitable to intrusive
strangers, than any he had known. He felt young and
provincial, yet hotly ambitious.

Quivering with quiet exultation, he sat on a balcony
that evening, watching the lights fret the ancient Seine,
and next morning he scampered to the atelier of Monsieur Cyprien Schoelkopf, where he was immediately
to be recognized as a genius.

He was not disappointed. Monsieur Schoelkopf (he
was of the celebrated Breton family of Schoelkopf, he
explained) had a studio right out of fiction; very long,
very filthy, with a naked model on the throne. The
girls wore smocks baggy at the throat, and the men
wore corduroy jackets.

Monsieur Schoelkopf was delighted to accept Whit,
also his ten thousand francs in advance.

Whit longed to be seated at an easel, whanging immortal paint onto a taut canvas. He'd catch the mod-

el's very soul, make it speak through her eyes, with her mere body just indicated. . . . Great if his very first picture should be a salon piece!

But before leaping into grandeur he had to have a Bohemian background, and he went uneasily over the Left Bank looking for an apartment. (To live in comfort on the Right Bank would be bourgeois and even American.)

He rented an apartment 'way out on the Avenue Félix-Faure. It was quiet and light—and Whit was tired.

That evening he went to the famous Café Fanfaron, on the Boulevard Raspail, of which he had heard as the international (i.e., American) headquarters for everything that was newest and most shocking in painting, poetry, and devastating criticism in little magazines.

In front of the café the sidewalk was jammed with tables at which sat hundreds of young people, most of them laughing, most of them noticeable—girls in slinksy dresses; very low, young men with jaunty tweed jackets, curly hair and keen eyes; large men (and they seemed the most youthful of all) with huge beards that looked false.

Whit was waved to a table with a group of Americans. In half an hour he had made a date to go walking in the Bois de Boulogne with a large-eyed young lady named Isadora, he had been reassured that Paris was the one place in the world for a person with Creative Hormones, and he had been invited to a studio party by a lively man who was twenty-four as far up as the pouches beneath his eyes, and sixty-four above.

It was a good party.

They sat on the floor and drank cognac and shouted. The host, with no great urging, showed a few score of his paintings. In them, the houses staggered and the hills looked like garbage heaps, so Whit knew they were the genuine advanced things, and he was proud and happy.

From that night on, Whit was in a joyous turmoil of artistic adventure. He was the real thing—except, perhaps, during the hours at Monsieur Schoelkopf's, when he tried to paint.

Like most active young Americans, he discovered the extreme difficulty of going slow. During a fifty-minute class in Yale he had been able to draw twenty caricatures, all amusing, all vivid. That was the trouble with him! It was infinitely harder to spend fifty minutes on a square inch of painting.

Whit was reasonably honest. He snarled at himself that his pictures had about as much depth and significance as a *croquis* for a dressmakers' magazine.

And Monsieur Schoelkopf told him all about it. He stood tickling the back of Whit's neck with his beard, and observed "Huh!" And when Monsieur Schoelkopf said "Huh!" Whit wanted to go off and dig sewers.

So Whit fled from that morgue to the Café Fanfaron, and to Isadora, whom he had met his first night in Paris.

Isadora was not a painter. She wrote. She carried a brief case, of course. Once it snapped open, and in it Whit saw a bottle of vermouth, some blank paper, lovely pencils all red and blue and green and purple, a handkerchief and a pair of silk stockings. Yet he was not shocked when, later in the evening, Isadora announced that she was carrying in that brief case the manuscript of her novel.

Isadora came from Omaha, Nebraska, and she liked to be kissed.

They picnicked in the Forest of Fontainebleau, Isadora and he. Whit was certain that all his life he had longed for just this; to lunch on bread and cheese and cherries and Burgundy, then to lie under the fretwork of oak boughs, stripped by October, holding the hand of a girl who knew everything and who would certainly, in a year or two, drive Edith Wharton and Willa Cather off the map; to have with her a relationship as innocent as children, and, withal, romantic as the steeple-hatted princesses who had once hallooed to the hunt in this same royal forest.

"I think your water-color sketch of Notre Dame is wonderful!" said Isadora.

"I'm glad you like it," said Whitney.

"So original in concept!"

"Well, I tried to give it a new concept."

"That's the thing! The new! We must get away from the old-fashioned Cubists and Expressionists. It's so old-fashioned now to be crazy! We must have restraint."

"That's so. Austerity. That's the stuff. . . . Gee, doggone it, I wish there was some more of that wine left," said Whit.

"You're a darling!"

She leaned on her elbow to kiss him, she sprang up and fled through the woodland aisle. And he gamboled after her in a rapture which endured even through a bus ride back to the Fontainebleau station with a mess of tourists who admired all the wrong things.

The Fanfaron school of wisdom had a magnificent show window but not much on the shelves. It was a high-class evening's entertainment to listen to Miles O'Sullivan, the celebrated Irish critic from South Brooklyn, on the beauties of Proust. But when, for the fifth time, Whit had heard O'Sullivan gasp in a drowning voice, "I remember dear old Marcel saying to me, 'Miles, *mon petit,* you alone understand that exteriority can be expressed only by interiority,' " then Whit was stirred to taxi defiantly over to the Anglo-American Pharmacy and do the most American thing a man can do—buy a package of chewing gum.

Chewing gum was not the only American vice which was in low repute at the Fanfaron. In fact, the exiles agreed that with the possible exceptions of Poland, Guatemala, and mid–Victorian England, the United States was the dumbest country that had ever existed. They were equally strong about the inferiority of American skyscrapers, pork and beans, Chicago, hired girls, jazz, Reno, evening-jacket lapels, Tom Thumb golf courses, aviation records, tooth paste, bungalows, kitchenettes, dinettes, dishwashettes, eating tobacco, cafeterias, Booth Tarkington, corn flakes, flivvers, incinerators, corn on the cob, Coney Island, Rotarians, cement roads, trial marriages, Fundamentalism, preachers who talk on the radio, drugstore sandwiches, letters dictated but not read, noisy streets, noiseless typewriters, Mutt and Jeff, eye shades, mauve-and-crocus-yellow golf stockings, chile con carne, the Chrysler Building, Jimmy Walker, Hollywood, all the Ruths in Congress, Boy Scouts, Tourists-Welcome camps, hot dogs, Admiral Byrd, flagpole sitters, safety razors, the Chautauqua, and President Hoover.

The exiles unanimously declared that they were waiting to join the Foreign Legion of whatever country should first wipe out the United States in war.

For three months Whit was able to agree with all of this indictment, but a week after his picnic with Isadora he went suddenly democratic. Miles O'Sullivan had denounced the puerility of American fried chicken.

Now it was before dinner, and Miles was an excellent reporter. The more Whit listened, the more he longed for the crisp, crunching taste of fried chicken, with corn fritters and maple sirup, candied sweet potatoes, and all the other vulgarities loathed by the artistic American exiles who were brought up on them.

Whit sprang up, muttering "Urghhg," which Miles took as a tribute to his wit.

It wasn't.

Whit fled down the Boulevard Raspail. He had often noted, with low cultured sneers, a horribly American restaurant called "Cabin Mammy's Grill." He plunged into it now. In a voice of restrained hysteria he ordered fried chicken, candied sweets and corn fritters with sirup.

Now, to be fair on all sides—which is an impossibility— the chicken was dry, the corn fritters were soggy, the fried sweets were poisonous and the sirup had never seen Vermont. Yet Whit enjoyed that meal more than any of the superior food he had discovered in Paris.

The taste of it brought back everything that was native in him. . . . Return home for Christmas vacation in his freshman year; the good smell of the midwestern snow; the girls whom he had loved as a brat; the boys with whom he had played. A dinner down at Momauguin in senior year, and the kindly tragedy of parting.

They had been good days; cool and realistic and decent.

So Whit came out of Cabin Mammy's Grill thinking of snow on Chapel Street and the New Haven Green—and he was buffeted by the first snow of the Paris winter, and that wasn't so good.

Although he was a college graduate, Whitney had learned a little about geography, and he shouldn't have expected Paris to be tropical. Yet he had confusedly felt that this capital of the world could never conceivably be cold and grim. He turned up the collar of his light topcoat and started for—oh, for Nowhere.

After ten blocks, he was exhilarated by the snow and the blasty cold which had first dismayed him. From time to time he muttered something like a sketch for future thoughts:

"I can't paint! I'd be all right drawing machinery for a catalogue. That's about all! Paris! More beautiful than any town in America. But I'm not part of it. Have nothing to do with it. I've never met a real Frenchman, except my landlady, and that hired girl at the apartment and a few waiters and a few cops and the French literary gents that hang around the Fanfaron because we give 'em more of a hand than their own people would.

"Poor old T. Jefferson! He wants me to be a Genius! I guess you have to have a little genius to be a Genius. Gosh, I'd like to see Stuyvy Wescott tonight. With him, it would be fun to have a drink!"

Without being quite conscious of it, Whit drifted from the sacred Left Bank to the bourgeois Right. Instead of returning to the Fanfaron and Isadora, he took refuge at the Café de la Paix.

Just inside the door was a round-faced, spectacled American, perhaps fifty years old, looking wistfully about for company.

Whit could never have told by what long and involved process of thought he decided to pick up this

Babbitt. He flopped down at the stranger's table, and muttered, "Mind 'f I sit here?"

"No, son, tickled to death! American?"

"You bet."

"Well, say, it certainly is good to talk to a white man again! Living here?"

"I'm studying art."

"Well, well, is that a fact!"

"Sometimes I wonder if it is! I'm pretty bad."

"Well, what the deuce! You'll have a swell time here while you're a kid, and I guess prob'ly you'll learn a lot, and then you can go back to the States and start something. Easterner, ain't you?"

"No; I was born in Zenith."

"Well, is that a fact! Folks live there?"

"Yes. My father is T. Jefferson Dibble of the Small Grain Products Company."

"Well, I'm a son-of-à-gun! Why, say, I know your dad. My name's Titus—Buffalo Grain Forwarding Corp.—why, I've had a lot of dealings with your dad. Golly! Think of meeting somebody you know in *this* town! I'm leaving tomorrow, and this is the first time I've had a shot at any home-grown conversation. Say, son, I'd be honored if you'd come out and bust the town loose with me this evening."

They went to the Exhibit of the Two Hemispheres, which Miles O'Sullivan had recommended as the dirtiest show in Europe. Whit was shocked. He tried to enjoy it. He told himself that otherwise he would prove himself a provincial, a lowbrow—in fact, an American. But he was increasingly uncomfortable at the antics of the ladies at the Exhibit. He peeped at Mr. Titus, and discovered that he was nervously twirling a glass and clearing his throat.

"I don't care so much for this," muttered Whit.

"Neither do I, son! Let's beat it!"

They drove to the New Orleans bar and had a whisky-soda. They drove to the Kansas City bar and had a highball. They drove to the El Paso bar and had a rock and rye. They drove to the Virginia bar, and by now Mr. Titus was full of friendliness and manly joy.

Leaning against the bar, discoursing to a gentleman from South Dakota, Mr. Titus observed:

"I come from Buffalo. Name's Titus."

"I come from Yankton. Smith is my name."

"Well, well, so you're this fellow Smith I've heard so much about!"

"Ha, ha, ha, that's right."

"Know Buffalo?"

"Just passing through on the train."

"Well, now, I want to make you a bet that Buffalo will increase in pop'lation not less than twenty-seven per cent this decade."

"Have 'nother?"

"Have one on me."

"Well, let's toss for it."

"That's the idea. We'll toss for it. . . . Hey, Billy, got any galloping dominoes?"

When they had gambled for the drink, Mr. Titus bellowed, "Say, you haven't met my young friend Whinney Dibble."

"Glad meet you."

"He's an artist!"

"Zatta fact!"

"Yessir, great artist. Sells pictures everywhere. London and Fort Worth and Cop'nagen and everywhere. Thousands and thousands dollars. His dad's pal of mine. Wish I could see good old Dibble! Wish he were here tonight!"

And Mr. Titus wept, quietly, and Whit took him home.

Next morning, at a time when he should have been in the atelier of Monsieur Schoelkopf, Whit saw Mr. Titus off at the Gare St.-Lazare, and he was melancholy. There were so many pretty American girls taking the boat train; girls with whom he would have liked to play deck tennis.

So it chanced that Whit fell into the lowest vice any

American can show in Paris. He constantly picked up beefy and lonesome Americans and took them to precisely those places in Paris, like the Eiffel Tower, which were most taboo to the brave lads of the Fanfaron.

He tried frenziedly to paint one good picture at Monsieur Schoelkopf's; tried to rid himself of facility. He produced a decoration in purple and stony reds which he felt to be far from his neat photography.

And looking upon it, for once Monsieur Schoelkopf spoke: "You will be, some time, a good banker."

The day before Whit sailed for summer in Zenith, he took Isadora to the little glassed-in restaurant that from the shoulder of Montmartre looks over all Paris. She dropped her flowery airs. With both hands she held his, and besought him:

"Whit! Lover! You are going back to your poisonous Middle West. Your people will try to alienate you from Paris and all the freedom, all the impetus to creation, all the strange and lovely things that will exist here long after machines have been scrapped. Darling, don't let them get you, with their efficiency and their promise of millions!"

"Silly! Of course! I hate business. And next year I'll be back here with you!"

He had told the Fanfaron initiates not to see him off at the train. Feeling a little bleak, a little disregarded by this humming city of Paris, he went alone to the station, and he looked for no one as he wretchedly followed the porter to a seat in the boat train.

Suddenly he was overwhelmed by the shouts of a dozen familiars from the Fanfaron. It wasn't so important—though improbable—that they should have paid fifty centimes each for a *billet de quai*, for that they should have arisen before nine o'clock to see him off was astounding.

Isadora's kind arms were around him, and she was wailing, "You won't forget us; darling, you won't forget me!"

Miles O'Sullivan was wringing his hand and crying, "Whit, lad, don't let the dollars get you!"

All the rest were clamoring that they would feverishly await his return.

As the train banged out, he leaned out waving to
them, and he was conscious that whatever affectations
and egotism they had shown in their drool at the Fanfaron, all pretentiousness was wiped now from their
faces, and that he loved them.

He would come back to them.

All the way to Cherbourg he fretted over the things
he had not seen in Paris. He had been in the Louvre
only three times. He had never gone to Moret or to
the battlemented walls of Provins.

Whit ran into the living room at Floral Heights,
patted T. Jefferson on the shoulder, kissed his mother
and muttered:

"Gee, it certainly is grand to be back!"

"Oh, you can speak to us in French, if you want
to," said T. Jefferson Dibble, "we've been studying it
so we can return to Paris with you some time. *Avez
vous oo un temps charmant cette*—uh—year?"

"Oh, sure, *oui*. Say, you've redecorated the breakfast
room. That red-and-yellow tiling certainly is swell."

"Now *écoutez—écoute, moh fis*. It's not necessary
for you, Whitney, now that you have become a man
of the world, to spare our feelings. I know, and you
know, that that red-and-yellow tiling is vulgar. But to
return to pleasanter topics, I long for your impressions
of Paris. How many times did you go to the Louvre?"

"Oh. Oh, the Louvre! Well, a lot."

"I'm sure of it. By the way, a funny thing happened,
Whitney. A vulgarian by the name of Titus, from Buffalo, if I remember, wrote to me that he met you in
Paris. A shame that such a man, under pretense of
friendship with me, should have disturbed you."

"I thought he was a fine old coot, Dad."

"*Mon père!* No, my boy, you are again being conciliatory and trying to spare my feelings. This Titus is a
man for whom I have neither esteem nor—in fact, we
have nothing in common. Besides, the old hellion, he

did me out of eleven hundred and seventy dollars on a grain deal sixteen years ago! But as I say, your impressions of Paris! It must seem like a dream wreathed with the vapors of golden memory.

"Now, I believe, you intend to stay here for two months. I have been making plans. Even in this wretched midwestern town, I think that, with my aid, you will be able to avoid the banalities of the young men with whom you were reared. There is a splendid new Little Theater under process of organization, and perhaps you will wish to paint the scenery and act and even design the costumes.

"Then we are planning to raise a fund to get the E. Heez Flemming Finnish Grand Opera Company here for a week. That will help to occupy you. You'll be able to give these hicks your trained European view of Finnish Grand Opera. So, to start with this evening, I thought we might drop in on the lecture by Professor Gilfillan at the Walter Peter Club on 'Traces of Mechanistic Culture in the Coptic.' "

"That would be splendid, sir, but unfortunately— On the way I received a wire from Stuyv Wescott asking me to the dance at the country club this evening. I thought I'd dine with you and Mother, and then skip out there. Hate like the dickens to hurt their feelings."

"Of course, of course, my boy. A gentleman, especially when he is also a man of culture, must always think of *noblesse oblige*. I mean, you understand, of the duties of a gentleman. But don't let these vulgarians like Wescott impose on you. You see, my idea of it is like this . . ."

As he drove his father's smaller six to the country club, Whit was angry. He was thinking of what his friends—ex-friends—at the club would do in the way of boisterous "kidding." He could hear them—Stuyv Wescott, his roommate in Yale, Gilbert Scott, Tim Clark (Princeton '28) and all the rest—mocking:

"Why, it's our little Alphonse Gauguin!"

"Where's the corduroy pants?"

"I don't suppose you'd condescend to take a drink

with a poor dumb Babbitt that's been selling hardware while you've been associating with the counts and jukes and highbrows and highbrowesses!"

And, sniggering shamefacedly, "Say, how's the little midinettes and the *je ne sais quoi's* in Paris?"

He determined to tell them all to go to hell, to speak with quiet affection of Isadora and Miles O'Sullivan, and to hustle back to Paris as soon as possible. Stick in this provincial town, when there on Boulevard Raspail were inspiration and his friends?

Stay here? What an idea!

He came sulkily into the lounge of the country club, cleared now for dancing. Stuyvy Wescott, tangoing with a girl who glittered like a Christmas tree, saw him glowering at the door, chucked the girl into the ragbag, dashed over and grunted, "Whit, you old hound, I'm glad to see you! Let's duck the bunch and sneak down to the locker room. The trusty gin awaits!"

On the way, Stuyv nipped Gil Scott and Tim Clark out of the group.

Whit croaked—Youth, so self-conscious, so conservative, so little "flaming," so afraid of what it most desires and admires!—he croaked, "Well, let's get the razzing over! I s'pose you babies are ready to pan me good for being a loafer while you've been saving the country by discounting notes!"

The other three looked at him with mild, fond wonder.

Stuyv said meekly, "Why, what a low idea! Listen, Whit, we're tickled to death you've had a chance to do something besides keep the pot boiling. Must have been swell to have a chance at the real Europe and art. We've all done pretty well, but I guess any one of us would give his left leg to be able to sit down on the Champs Elysées and take time to figure out what it's all about."

Then Whit knew that these were his own people. He blurted, "Honestly, Stuyv, you mean to say you've envied me? Well, it's a grand town, Paris. And some great eggs there. And even some guys that can paint. But me, I'm no good!"

"Nonsense! Look, Whit, you have no idea what this money-grubbing is. Boy, you're lucky! And don't stay here! Don't let the dollars get you! Don't let all these babies with their promises of millions catch you! Beat it back to Paris. Culture, that's the new note!"

"Urghhg!" observed Whit.

"You bet," said Tim Clark.

Tim Clark had a sister, and the name of that sister was Betty.

Whit Dibble remembered her as a sub-flapper, always going off to be "finished" somewhere in the East. She was a Young Lady of twenty-odd now, and even to Whit's professionally artistic eye it seemed that her hair, sleek as a new-polished range, was interesting. They danced together, and looked at each other with a fury of traditional dislike.

Midmost of that dance Whit observed, "Betty. Darlingest!"

"Yeah?"

"Let's go out and sit on the lawn."

"Why?"

"I want to find out why you hate me."

"Hm. The lawn. I imagine it takes a training in Yale athletics and Paris artisticking to be so frank. Usually the kits start out with a suggestion of the club porch and the handsome modernist reed chairs and *then* they suggest the lawn and 'Oh, Greta, so charmé to meet you' afterwards!"

But during these intolerabilities Betty had swayed with him to the long high-pillared veranda, where they crouched together on a chintz-covered glider.

Whit tried to throw himself into what he conceived, largely from novels, to be Betty's youthful era. He murmured: "Kiddo, where have you been all my life?"

From Betty's end of the glider, a coolness like the long wet stretches of the golf course; a silence; then a very little voice:

"Whit, my child, you have been away too long! It's a year now, at least, since anyone—I mean anyone

you could know—has said, 'Where have you been all
my life?' Listen, dear! The worst thing about anybody's going artistic, like you, is that they're always
so ashamed of it. Jiminy! Your revered father and
the Onward and Upward Bookshop have grabbed off
Culture for keeps in this town. And yet——

"Dear, I think that somewhere there must be people
who do all these darn' arts without either being
ashamed of 'em—like you, you poor fish!—or thinking
they make the nice gilded cornice on the skyscraper,
like your dad. Dear, let's us be *us*. Cultured or hoboes,
or both. G'night!"

She had fled before he could spring up and be wise
in the manner of Isadora and Miles O'Sullivan, or the
more portentous manner of T. Jefferson Dibble.

Yet, irritably longing all the while for Betty Clark, he
had a tremendous time that night at the country club,
on the land where his grandfather had once grown corn.

What did they know, there in Paris? What did either
Isadora or Miles O'Sullivan know of those deep pro-
vincialisms, smelling always of the cornfields, which
were in him? For the first time since he had left Paris,
Whit felt that in himself might be some greatness.

He danced that night with many girls.

He saw Betty Clark only now and then, and from
afar. And the less he saw of her, the more important
it seemed to him that she should take him seriously.

There had been a time when Whit had each morning
heard the good, noisy, indignant call of T. Jefferson demanding, "Are you going to get up or ain't you going
to get up? Hey! Whit! If you don't wanna come down
for breakfast, you ain't gonna have any breakfast!"

Indeed it slightly disturbed him, when he awoke at
eleven of the morning, to find there had been no such
splendid, infuriating, decent uproar from T. Jefferson.

He crawled out of bed and descended the stairs. In
the lower hall he found his mother.

(It is unfortunate that in this earnest report of the

turning of males in the United States of America toward culture, it is not possible to give any great attention to Mrs. T. Jefferson Dibble. Aside from the fact that she was a woman, kindly and rather beautiful, she has no existence here except as the wife of T. Jefferson and the mother of Whitney.)

"Oh, Whit! Dear! I do hope your father won't be angry! He waited such a long while for you. But I am so glad, dearie, that he understands, at last, that possibly you may have just as much to do with all this Painting and Art and so on as he has! . . . But I mean to say: Your father is expecting you to join him at three this afternoon for the meeting of the Finnish Opera Furtherance Association. Oh, I guess it will be awfully interesting—it will be at the Thornleigh. Oh, Whit, dear, it's lovely to have you back!"

The meeting of the Finnish Opera Furtherance Association at the Hotel Thornleigh was interesting.

It was more than interesting.

Mrs. Montgomery Zeiss said that the Finns put it all over the Germans and Italians at giving a real modernistic version of opera.

Mr. T. Jefferson Dibble said that as his son, Whitney, had been so fortunate as to obtain a rather authoritative knowledge of European music, he (Whitney) would now explain everything to them.

After a lot of explanation about how artistic opera was, and how unquestionably artistic Zenith was, Whit muttered that he had to beat it. And while T. Jefferson stared at him with a sorrowful face, Whit fled the room.

At five o'clock Whit was sitting on the dock of Stuyv Wescott's bungalow on Lake Kennepoose, muttering, "Look, Stuyv, have you got a real job?"

"Yeah, I guess you'd call it a job."

"D'you mind telling me what you are making a year now?"

"About three thou. I guess I'll make six in a coupla years."

"Hm! I'd like to make some money. By the way—it just occurs to me, and I hope that I am not being too rude in asking—what *are* you doing?"

"I am an insurance agent," remarked Stuyv with a melancholy dignity.

"And you're already making three thousand dollars a year?"

"Yeah, something like that."

"I think I ought to be making some money. It's funny. In Europe it's the smart thing to live on money that somebody else made for you. I don't know whether it's good or bad, but fact is, somehow, most Americans feel lazy, feel useless, if they don't make their own money.

"Prob'ly the Europeans are right. Prob'ly it's because we're restless. But anyway, I'll be hanged if I'm going to live on the Old Man the rest of my life and pretend I'm a painter! The which I ain't! Listen, Stuyv! D'yuh think I'd make a good insurance man?"

"Terrible!"

"You're helpful. Everybody is helpful. Say! What's this new idea that it's disgraceful to make your own living?"

"Don't be a fool, Whit. Nobody thinks it's disgraceful, but you don't get this new current of thought in the Middle West that we gotta have art."

"Get it! Good heavens, I've got nothing else! I will say this for Paris—you can get away from people who believe in art just by going to the next café. Maybe I'll have to live there in order to be allowed to be an insurance agent!"

Stuyv Wescott was called to the telephone, and for three minutes Whit sat alone on the dock, looking across that clear, that candid, that sun-iced lake, round which hung silver birches and delicate willows and solid spruce. Here, Whit felt, was a place in which an American might find again, even in these days of eighty-story buildings and one-story manners, the courage of his forefathers.

A hell-diver, forever at his old game of pretending

to be a duck, bobbed out of the mirror of the lake, and Whitney Dibble at last knew that he was at home.

And not so unlike the hell-diver in her quickness and imperturbable complexity, Betty Clark ran down from the road behind the Wescott bungalow and profoundly remarked, "Oh! Hello!"

"I'm going to be an insurance man," remarked Whit.

"You're going to be an artist!"

"Sure I am. As an insurance man!"

"You make me sick."

"Betty, my child, you have been away too long! It's a year now, at least, since anyone—I mean anyone you could know—has said, 'You make me sick!'"

"Oh—oh! You make me sick!"

T. Jefferson was extremely angry when Whit appeared for dinner. He said that Whit had no idea how he had offended the Opera Committee that afternoon. Consequently, Whit had to go through the gruesome ordeal of accompanying his father to an artistic reception in the evening. It was not until eleven that he could escape for a poker game in an obscure suite of the Hotel Thornleigh.

There were present here not only such raw collegians as Stuyv Wescott, Gil Scott, and Tim Clark, but also a couple of older and more hardened vulgarians, whereof one was a Mr. Seidel, who had made a million dollars by developing the new University Heights district of Zenith.

When they had played for two hours, they stopped for hot dogs; and Room Service was again drastically ordered to "hustle up with the White Rock and ice."

Mr. Seidel, glass in hand, grumbled: "So you're an artist, Dibble? In Paris?"

"Yeah."

"And to think that a fella that could bluff me out of seven dollars on a pair of deuces should live over there, when he'd be an A-I real-estate salesman."

"Are you offering me a job?"

"Well, I hadn't thought about it. . . . Sure I am!"

"How much?"

"Twenty-five a week and commissions."

"It's done."

And the revolution was effected, save for the voice of Stuyv Wescott, wailing, "Don't do it, Whit! Don't let these babies get you with their promise of millions!"

Whit had never altogether lost his awe of T. Jefferson and he was unable to dig up the courage to tell his father of his treachery in becoming American again until eleven of the morning, when he called upon him at his office.

"Well, well, my boy, it's nice to see you!" said T. Jefferson. "I'm sorry that there is nothing really interesting for us to do today. But tomorrow noon we are going to a luncheon of the Bibliophile Club."

"That's what I came to see you about, Dad. I'm sorry, but I shan't be able to go tomorrow. I'll be working."

"Working?"

"Yes, sir. I've taken a job with the Seidel Development Company."

"Well, that may be interesting for this summer. When you return to Paris——"

"I'm not going back to Paris. I can't paint. I'm going to sell real estate."

The sound that T. Jefferson now made was rather like a carload of steers arriving at the Chicago stockyards. In this restricted space it is possible to give only a hundredth of his observations on Life and Culture, but among many other things he said:

"I might have known! I might have known it! I've always suspected that you were your mother's boy as much as mine. How sharper than a serpent's tooth! Serpent in a fella's own bosom!

"Here I've given up my life to manufacturing Puffy Wuffles, when all the time my longing was to be artistic, and now when I give you the chance—— Serpent's tooth! The old bard said it perfectly! Whit, my boy, I hope it isn't that you feel I can't afford it! In just a few days now, I'm going to start my schemes for extending the plant; going to get options on the five acres to the eastward. The production of Ritzy Rice will be doubled in the next year. And so, my boy . . . You'll either stick to your art or I'll disown you, sir! I mean, cut you off with a shilling! Yes, sir, a shilling! I'll by thunder make you artistic, if it's the last thing I do!"

On the same afternoon when he had, and very properly, been thrown out into the snowstorm with a shawl over his head, Whit borrowed five thousand from Stuyv Wescott's father, with it obtained options on the five acres upon which his father planned to build, with them reported to Mr. Seidel, from that low realtor received the five thousand dollars to repay Mr. Wescott, plus a five-thousand-dollar commission for himself and spent twenty-five dollars in flowers, and with them appeared at the house of Betty Clark at six-fifteen.

Betty came down, so lovely, so cool, so refreshing in skirts that clipped her ankles; and so coolly and refreshingly she said: "Hey, Whit, my dear! What can I do for you?"

"I don't think you can do anything besides help me spend the five thousand and twenty-five dollars I've made today. I spent the twenty-five for these flowers. They're very nice, aren't they?"

"They certainly are."

"But do you think they're worth twenty-five dollars?"

"Sure they are. Listen, darling! I'm so sorry that you wasted your time making five thousand dollars when you might have been painting. But of course an artist has to be an adventurer. I'm glad that you've tried it and that it's all over. We'll go back to Paris as soon as we're married, and have a jolly li'l' Bohemian flat there, and I'll try so hard to make all of your artistic friends welcome."

"Betty! Is your brother still here?"

"How should I know?"

"Would you mind finding out?"

"Why no. But why?"

"Dear Betty, you will understand what a scoundrel I am in a few minutes. Funny! I never meant to be a scoundrel. I never even meant to be a bad son. . . . Will you yell for Timmy, please?"

"Of course I will." She yelled, very competently.

Tim came downstairs, beaming. "I hope it's all over."

"That's the point," said Whit. "I am trying to persuade T. Jefferson that I don't want to be an artist. I'm trying—Lord knows what I'm trying!" With which childish statement Whit fled from the house.

He found a taxi and gave the driver the address of his boss, Mr. Seidel, at the Zenith Athletic Club.

In his room, sitting on the edge of his bed, Mr. Seidel was eating dinner. "Hello, boy, what's the trouble?" he said.

"Will you let me pay for a telephone call if I make it here?"

"Sure I will."

Whit remarked to the Athletic Club telephone girl, "I'd like to speak to Isadora at the Café Fanfaron, Paris."

The voice of that unknown beauty answered, "Which state, please?"

"France."

"France?"

"Yes, France."

"France, *Europe*?"

"Yes."

"And what was the name, please?"

"Isadora."

"What is the lady's last name?"

"I don't know. . . . Hey, get me Miles O'Sullivan, same address."

"Just a moment, please. I will get the supervisor."

A cool voice said, "To whom do you wish to speak, please?"

"I wish to speak, if I may, to Miles O'Sullivan at the Café Fanfaron. In Paris. . . . Right. Thank you very much. Will you call me as soon as you can?

"All right, thank you. . . . I am speaking from the Zenith Athletic Club and the bill is to be charged to Mr. Tiberius Seidel."

When the telephone rang, it was the voice of the head waiter of the Fanfaron, a Russian, that answered.

He said, *"Allo—allo!"*

"May I speak to Miles O'Sullivan?" demanded Whit.

"Je ne comprends pas."

"C'est Monsieur Dibble que parle—d'Amérique."

"D'Amérique?"

"Oui, et je desire to talk to Monsieur Miles O'Sullivan, right away, *tout suite."*

"Mais oui; je comprends. Vous-desirez parler avec Monsieur Miles O'Sullivang?"

"That's the idea. Make it snappy."

"Oui, right away."

Then O'Sullivan's voice on the phone.

While Mr. Seidel smiled and watched the second hand of his watch, Whit bellowed into the telephone, "Miles! Listen! I want to speak to Isadora."

That voice, coming across four thousand miles of rolling waves and laboring ships and darkness, mumbled, "Isadora *who*? Jones or Pater or Elgantine?"

"For heaven's sake, Miles, this is Whitney Dibble speaking from America! I want to speak to Isadora. *My* Isadora."

"Oh, you want to speak to Isadora? Well, I think she's out in front. Listen, laddie, I'll try to find her."

"Miles, this has already cost me more than a hundred dollars."

"And you have been caught by the people who think about dollars?"

"You're darned right I have! Will you please get Isadora quick?"

"You mean quickly, don't you?"

"Yeah, quick or quickly, but please get Isadora."

"Right you are, my lad."

It was after only $16.75 worth of conversation that Isadora was saying to him, "Hello, Whit darling, what is it?"

"Would you marry a real-estate man in Zenith, in the Middle West? Would you stand for my making ten thousand dollars a year?"

From four thousand miles away Isadora crowed, "Sure I will!"

"You may have to interrupt your creative work."

"Oh, my darling, my darling, I'll be so glad to quit four-flushing!"

Mr. Whitney Dibble looked at his chief and observed, "After I find out how much this long-distance call has cost, do you mind if I make a local call?"

Mr. Seidel observed, "Go as far as you like, but please give me a pension when you fire me out of the firm."

"Sure!"

Whit telephoned to the mansion of T. Jefferson Dibble.

T. Jefferson answered the telephone with a roar: "Yes, yes, yes, what do you want?"

"Dad, this is Whit. I tried to tell you this morning that I am engaged to a lovely intellectual author in Paris—Isadora."

"Isadora *what*?"

"Do you mean to tell me you don't know who Isadora is?"

"Oh, *Isadora*! The writer? Congratulations, my boy. I'm sorry I misunderstood you before."

"Yes. Just talked to her, long-distance, and she's promised to join me here."

"That's fine, boy! We'll certainly have an artistic center here in Zenith."

"Yeah, we certainly will."

Mr. Seidel remarked, "That local call will cost you just five cents besides the eighty-seven fifty."

"Fine, boss," said Whitney Dibble. "Say, can I interest you in a bungalow on Lake Kennepoose? It has two baths, a lovely living room, and—— Why do you waste your life in this stuffy club room, when you might have a real home?"

Moths in the Arc Light

Bates lay staring at the green-shaded light on his desk and disgustedly he realized that he must have been sleeping there for hours on the leather couch in his office. His eyes were peppery, his mouth dry. He rose, staggering with the burden of drowsiness, and glanced at his watch. It was three in the morning.

"Idiot!" he said.

He wreathed to the window, twelve stories above the New York pavements. The stupidity that lay over his senses like uncombed wool was blown away as he exulted in the beauty of the city night. It was as nearly quiet now as Manhattan ever becomes. Stilled were the trolleys and the whang of steel beams in the new building a block away. One taxicab bumbled on the dark pavement beneath. Bates looked across a swamp of roofs to East River, to a line of topaz lights arching over a bridge. The sky was not dark but of a luminous blue—a splendid, aspiring, naked blue, in which the stars hung golden.

"But why shouldn't I fall asleep here? I'll finish the night on the couch, and get after the New Bedford specifications before breakfast. I've never spent twenty-four hours in the office before. I'll do it!"

He said it with the pride of a successful man. But he ended, as he rambled back to the couch and removed his coat and shoes: "Still, I do wish there were somebody who cared a hang whether I came home or stayed away for a week!"

When the earliest stenographer arrived she found Bates at work. But often he was first at the office. No one knew of his discovery that before dawn the huckstering city is enchanted to blue and crocus yellow above shadowy roofs. He had no one who would ever encourage him to tell about it.

To Bates at thirty-five the world was composed of reenforced concrete; continents and striding seas were office partitions and inkwells, the latter for signing letters beginning "In reply to your valued query of seventh inst." Not for five years had he seen storm clouds across the hills or moths that flutter white over dusky meadows. To him the arc light was the dancing place for moths, and flowers grew not in pastures but in vases on restaurant tables. He was a city man and an office man. Papers, telephone calls, eight-thirty to six on the twelfth floor, were the natural features of life, and the glory and triumph of civilization was getting another traction company to introduce the Carstop Indicator.

But he belonged to the new generation of business men. He was not one of the race who boast that they have had "mighty little book learning," and who cannot be pictured without their derby hats, whether they are working, motoring, or in bed. Bates was slender, immaculate, polite as a well-bred woman, his mustache like a penciled eyebrow; yet in decision he was firm as a chunk of flint.

When he had come to New York from college Bates had believed that he was going to lead an existence of polite society and the opera. He had in fourteen years been to the opera six times. He dined regularly with acquaintances at the Yale Club, he knew two men in his bachelor apartment building by their first names, and he attended subscription dances and was agreeable to young women who had been out for three years. But New York is a thief of friends. Because in one night at a restaurant you may meet twenty new people, therefore in one day shall you also lose twenty older friends. You know a man and like him; he marries and moves to Great Neck; you see him once in two years. After thirty Bates was increasingly absorbed in the one thing that always wanted him, that appreciated his attention—the office.

He had gone from a motor company to the Carstop Indicator Company. He had spent a year in the Long Island City factory which manufactures the indicators for the Eastern trade. He had worked out an improvement in the automatic tripping device. At thirty-five he was a success. Yet he never failed when he was dining alone to wish that he was to call on a girl who was worth calling on.

After fourteen years of the candy-gobbling, cabaret-curious, nice-man-hunting daughters of New York, Bates had become unholily cautious. His attitude to the average débutante was that of an aviator to an anti-aircraft shell. And he was equally uncomfortable with older, more earnest women. They talked about economics. Bates had read a book all about economics shortly after graduation, but as he could never quite remember the title it didn't help him much in earnest conversations. He preferred to talk to his stenographer. He mentioned neither wine suppers nor her large black eyes. "Has the draftsman sent over the blue prints for Camden?" he said. Or: "Might hurry up the McGulden correspondence." That was real conversation. It got somewhere.

Then he began to talk to the girl in the building across the street.

That building was his scenery. He watched it as an old maid behind a lace curtain gapes at every passer-by on her village street. It had the charm of efficiency that is beginning to make American cities beautiful with a beauty that borrows nothing from French châteaux or English inns. The architect had supposed that he was planning neither a hotel nor a sparrow's paradise, but a place for offices. He had left off the limestone supporting caps that don't support anything, and the marble plaques which are touchingly believed to imitate armorial shields but which actually resemble enlarged shaving mugs. He had created a building as clean and straight and honest as the blade of a sword. It made Bates glad that he was a business man.

So much of the building opposite was of glass that the offices were as open to observation as the coops at a dog show. Bates knew by sight every man and woman in twenty rooms. From his desk he could not see the building, but when he was tired it was his habit to loaf by the window for a moment. He saw the men coming in at eight-thirty or nine, smoking and chatting before they got to work, settling at desks, getting up stiffly at lunch-time, and at closing hour, dulled to silence, snapping out the lights before they went home. When he worked late at night Bates was saved from loneliness by the consciousness of the one or two men who were sure to be centered under desk lights in offices across the way.

He sympathized with the office boy at whom the red-mustached boss was always snarling in the eleventh-floor office on the right, and was indignant at the boy he saw stealing stamps on the thirteenth. He laughed over a clerk on the eleventh changing into evening clothes at six—hopping on one leg to keep his trousers off the floor, and solemnly taking dress tie and collar from the top drawer of his desk. And it was a personal sorrow when tragedy came to his village; when the pretty, eager secretary of the manager in the twelfth-floor office exactly opposite was missing for several days, and one morning a funeral wreath was laid on her desk by the window.

The successor of the dead girl must have come immediately, but Bates did not notice her for a week. It was one of those weeks when he was snatched from Task A to Task B, and from B to hustle out C, when the salesman out on the road couldn't sell milk to a baby, when the telephone rang or a telegram came just as Bates thought he had a clear moment, when he copied again every night the list of things he ought to have done day before yesterday, and his idea of heaven was a steel vault without telephone connection. But at the end of the storm he had nothing to do except to try to look edifyingly busy, and to amble round and watch the stenographers stenograph and the office boy be officious.

He sat primly lounging in the big chair by the window, smoking a panetela and unconsciously gazing at the building across the street. He half observed that the manager in the office just opposite was dictating to a new secretary, a slim girl in blue taffeta with crisp white collar and cuffs. She did not slop over the desk tablet, yet she did not sit grimly, like the oldish stenographer in the office just above her. She seemed at the distance to be unusually businesslike. In all the hive that was laid open to Bates' observation she was distinguished by her erect, charming shoulders, her decisive step, as she was to be seen leaving the manager's desk, going through the partition—which to Bates' eye was an absurdly thin sheet of oak and glass—hastening to her typewriter, getting to work.

Bates forgot her; but at dusk, spring dusk, when he stood by his window, late at the office yet with nothing to do, enervated with soft melancholy because there was no place he wanted to go that evening, he noticed her again. Her chief and she were also staying late. Bates saw them talking; saw the chief sign a pile of correspondence, give it to her, nod, take his derby, yawn and plunge out into the general office, heading for the elevator. The secretary briskly carried away the correspondence. But she stopped at her desk beside a window. She pressed her eyes with her hand, passed it across them with the jerky motion of a medium coming out of a trance.

"Poor tired eyes!" Bates heard himself muttering.

No scent of blossoms nor any sound of eager birds reached the cement streets from the spring-flushed country, but there was restlessness in the eternal clatter, and as the darkening silhouette of the building opposite cut the reflected glow in the eastern sky his melancholy became a pain of emptiness. He yearned across to the keen-edged girl and imagined himself talking to her. In five minutes she was gone, but he remained at the window, then drooped slowly up to the Yale Club for dinner.

Doubtless Bates' life was making him selfish, but that evening while he was being incredibly bored at a musical comedy he did think of her, and for a second hoped that her eyes were rested.

He looked for her next morning as soon as he reached the office, and was displeased with the entire arrangement of the heavenly bodies because the light wasn't so good across there in the morning as in the afternoon.

Not till three o'clock was he certain that she was wearing what appeared to be a waist of corn-colored rough silk, and that for all her slight nervousness her throat was full and smooth. Last night he had believed her twenty-eight. He promoted her to twenty-three.

He sighed: "Capable-looking young woman. Wish my secretary were as interested in her work. She walks with—well, graceful. Now who can I get hold of for dinner tonight?"

II

He saw her coming in at nine o'clock; saw her unpin her hat and swiftly arrange her hair before her reflection in the ground glass of the partition. He saw her take morning dictation; bring customers in to the boss. He saw her slipping out to lunch, alone, at noon. He saw her quick, sure movements slacken as the afternoon became long and weary. He saw her preparing to go home at night, or staying late, even her straight shoulders hunched as she heavily picked out the last words on her typewriter. All through the day he followed her, and though he knew neither her name nor her origin, though he had never heard her voice, yet he understood this girl better than at marriage most men understand the women they marry.

The other people in her office treated her with respect. They bowed to her at morning, at night. They never teased her, as the fluffy telephone girl was teased. That interested Bates, but for many weeks she was no part of his life.

On an afternoon in early summer, when his hands were twitching and his eyeballs were hot coals from too-constant study of specifications, when everybody in the world seemed to be picking at his raw nerves and he longed for someone who would care for him, who would bathe his eyes and divert his mind from the rows of figures that danced blood-red against darkness as he closed his stinging lids, then he caught himself deliberately seeking the window, passionately needing a last glimpse of her as the one human being whom he really knew.

"Confound her, if she isn't over there I'll—well, I won't go home till she is!"

She was by the window, reading a letter. She looked up, caught him staring at her. It was a very dignified Mr. Bates who plumped on his hat and stalked away. Obviously he would never do anything so low as to spy on offices across the street! The word stuck in his mind, and scratched it. Certainly he had never spied, he declared in a high manner as he fumbled at a steak minute that was exactly like all the ten thousand steaks minute he had endured at restaurants. Well, he'd take care that no one ever came in and misunderstood his reflective resting by the window. He would never glance at that building again!

And so at nine o'clock next morning, with three telegrams and an overdue letter from Birmingham Power and Traction unopened on his desk, he was peering across the street and admiring a new hat, a Frenchy cornucopia with fold above fold of pale-blue straw, which the girl was removing from her sleek hair.

There are several ways of stopping smoking. You can hide your tobacco in a drawer in the next room, and lock the drawer, and hide the key. You can keep a schedule of the number of times you smoke. You can refuse to buy cigarettes, and smoke only those you can cadge from friends. These methods are all approved by the authorities, and there is only one trouble with them—not one of them makes you stop smoking.

There are also numerous ways of keeping from studying the architecture of buildings across the street. You can be scornful, or explain to yourself that you don't know anything about the employees of other offices, and you don't want to know anything. You can relax by sitting on the couch instead of standing by the window. The only trouble with these mental exercises is that you continue to find yourself gaping at the girl across and——

And you feel like a spy when you catch her in self-betrayals that pinch your heart. She marches out of the manager's office, cool, competent, strong, then droops by her desk and for a strained moment sits with thin fingers pressed to her pounding temples.

Every time she did that Bates forgot his coy games. His spirit sped across the cañon and hovered about her, roused from nagging worries about business and steaks minute and musical comedies which had come to be his most precious concerns. With agitating clearness he could feel his finger tips caressing her forehead, feel the sudden cold of evaporation on his hand as he bathed the tired, cramped back of her neck with alcohol.

He gave up his highly gentlemanly effort not to spy. He wondered if perhaps there wasn't something to all these metaphysical theories, if he wasn't sending currents of friendship across to cheer her frail, brave spirit in its fight to be businesslike. He forgot that he was as visible at his window as she at hers. So it happened that one evening when he was frankly staring at the girl she caught him, and turned her head away with a vexed jerk.

Bates was hurt because he had hurt her. He who had regarded life only from the standpoint of Bates, bachelor, found himself thinking through her, as though his mind had been absorbed in hers. With a shock of pain he could feel her lamenting that it was bad enough to be under the business strain all day, without being exposed to ogling in her house of glass. He wanted to protect her—from himself.

For a week he didn't once stand by the window, even to look down at the street, twelve stories below, which he had watched as from his mountain shack a quizzical hermit might con the life of the distant valley. He missed the view, and he was glad to miss it. He was actually giving up something for somebody. He felt human again.

Though he did not stand by the window it was surprising how many times a day he had to pass it, and how innocently he caught glimpses of the life across the way. More than once he saw her looking at him. Whenever she glanced up from work her eyes seemed drawn to his. But not flirtatiously, he believed. In the distance she seemed aloof as the small cold winter moon.

There was another day that was a whirl of craziness. Everybody wanted him at once. Telegrams crossed each other. The factory couldn't get materials. Two stenographers quarreled, and both of them quit, and the typewriter agency from which he got his girls had no one to send him just then save extremely alien enemies who confounded typewriters with washing machines. When the office was quiet and there was only about seven more hours of work on his desk, he collapsed. His lax arms fell beside him. He panted slowly. His spinning head drooped and his eyes were blurred.

"Oh, buck up!" he growled.

He lifted himself to his feet, slapped his arms, found himself at the window. Across there she was going home. Involuntarily—looking for a greeting from his one companion in work—he threw up his arm in a wave of farewell.

She saw it. She stood considering him, her two

hands up to her head as she pinned her hat. But she
left the window without a sign. Suddenly he was snapping: "I'll make you notice me! I'm not a noon-hour
window flirt! I won't stand your thinking I am!"

With a new energy of irritation he went back. Resting his eyes every quarter of an hour he sat studying
a legal claim, making notes. It was eight—nine—ten.
He was faint, yet not hungry. He rose. He was surprised to find himself happy. He hunted for the source
of the glow, and found it. He was going to draw that
frosty moon of a girl down to him.

In the morning when he came in he hastened to the
window and waited till she raised her head. He
waved—a quick, modest, amiable gesture. Every
morning and evening after that he sent across his
pleading signal. She never answered but she observed
him and—well, she never pulled down the window
shade.

His vacation was in July. Without quite knowing
why, he did not want to go to the formal seaside hotel
at which he usually spent three weeks in being polite
to aunts in their nieces' frocks, and in discovering that
as a golfer he was a good small-boat sailor. He found
himself heading for the Lebanon Valley, which is the
valley of peace; and he discovered that yellow cream
and wild blackberries and cowslips and the art of
walking without panting still exist. He wore soft shirts
and became tanned; he stopped worrying about the
insolvency of the Downstate Interurban Company,
and was even heard to laugh at the landlord's stories.

At least a tenth of his thoughts were devoted to
planning a vacation for the girl across. She should lie
with nervous fingers relaxed among the long-starred
grasses, and in the cornflower blue of the sky and
comic plump white clouds find healing. After arranging everything perfectly he always reminded himself
that she probably hadn't been with her firm long
enough to have earned more than a five-day vacation,
and with etched scorn he pointed out that he was a
fool to think about a girl of whom he knew only that:

She seemed to take dictation quickly.

She walked gracefully.

She appeared at a distance to have delicate oval cheeks.

She was between sixteen and forty.

She was not a man.

About Article Five, he was sure.

He was so strong-minded and practical with himself that by the end of his holidays the girl was cloudy in his mind. He was cured of sentimentalizing. He regarded with amusement his reenforced-concrete romance, his moth dance under the arc light's sterile glare. He would—oh, he'd call on Christine Parrish when he got back. Christine was the sister of a classmate of his; she danced well and said the right things about Park Avenue and the Washington Square Players.

He got back to town on Monday evening, just at closing time. He ran up to his office, to announce his return. He dashed into his private room—less dashingly to the window. The girl across was thumbing a book, probably finding a telephone number. She glanced up, raising a finger toward her lips. Then his hat was off, and he was bowing, waving. She sat with her half-raised hand suspended. Suddenly she threw it up in a flickering gesture of welcome.

Bates sat at his desk. The members of his staff as they came in to report—or just to be tactful and remind the chief of their valuable existence—had never seen him so cheerful. When they were gone he tried to remember what it was he had planned to do. Oh, yes; call up Christine Parrish. Let it go. He'd do it some other night. He went to the window. The girl was gone, but the pale ghost of her gesture seemed to glimmer in the darkening window.

He dined at the new Yale Club, and sat out on the roof after dinner with a couple of temporary widowers and Bunk Selby's kid brother, who had graduated in the spring. The city beneath them flared like burning grass. Broadway was a streak of tawny fire; across the East River a blast furnace stuttered flames; the Bilt-

more and Ritz and Manhattan, the Belmont and
Grand Central Station were palaces more mysterious
in their flashing first stories, their masses of shadow,
their splashes of white uplifted wall, than Venice on
carnival night. Bates loved the hot beauty of his city;
he was glad to be back; he didn't exactly know why,
but the coming fall and winter gave promise of endless
conquest and happiness. Not since he had first come
to the city had he looked forward so exultantly. Now,
as then, the future was not all neatly listed, but chaotic
and trembling with adventure.

All he said to the men smoking with him was
"Good vacation—fine loaf." Or, "Got any money on
copper?"

But they looked at him curiously.

"You sound as though you'd had a corking time.
What you been doing? Licking McLoughlin at tennis
or something?"

Bunk Selby's kid brother, not having been out of
college long enough to have become reliable and stupid, ventured: "Say, Bunk, I bet your young friend
Mr. Bates is in love!"

"Huh!" said Bunk with married fatness. "Batesy?
Never! He's the buds' best bunker."

III

At two minutes of nine the next morning Bates was
at the window. To him entered his stenographer, bearing mail.

"Oh, leave it on the desk," he complained.

At one minute past nine the girl across could be
seen in the general office, coming out of the dimness
to her window. He waved his arm. She sent back the
greeting. Then she turned her back on him. But he
went at his mail humming.

She always answered after that, and sometimes during the day she swiftly peered at him. It was only a
curt, quick recognition, but when he awoke he looked
forward to it. His rusty imagination creaking, he began

to make up stories about her. He was convinced that whatever she might be she was different from the good-natured, commonplace women in his own office. She was a mystery. She had a family. He presented her with a father of lean distinction, hawk nose, classical learning—and the most alarming inability to stick to the job, being in various versions a bishop, a college president, and a millionaire who had lost his money.

He decided that she was named Emily, because Emily meant all the things that typewriters and filing systems failed to mean. Emily connoted lavender-scented chests, old brocade, and twilit gardens brimmed with dewy, damask roses, spacious halls of white paneling, and books by the fire. Always it was Bates who restored her to the spacious halls, the brocade, and the arms of her bishop-professor-millionaire father.

There was one trouble with his fantasy: He didn't dare see her closer than across the street, didn't dare hear her voice, for fear the first sacred words of the lady of the damask roses might be: "Say, listen! Are you the fella that's been handing me the double O? Say, you got your nerve!"

Once when he was sailing out of the street entrance, breezy and prosperous, he realized that she was emerging across the way, and he ducked back into the hall. It was not hard to avoid her. The two buildings were great towns. There were two thousand people in Bates' building, perhaps three thousand in hers; and in the streams that tumbled through the doorways at night the individual people were as unrecognizable as in the mad passing of a retreating brigade.

It was late October when he first definitely made out her expression, first caught her smile across the chill and empty air that divided them. In these shortening days the electric lights were on before closing time, and in their radiance he could see her more clearly than by daylight.

In the last mail came a letter from the home office, informing him with generous praise that his salary was increased a thousand a year. All the world knows that vice presidents are not like office boys; they do not act ignorantly when they get a raise. But it is a fact that, after galloping to the door to see whether anybody was coming in, Bates did a foxtrot three times about his desk. He rushed to the window. Four times he had to visit it before she glanced up. He caught her attention by waving the letter. Her face was only half toward him, but he could make out her profile, gilded by the light over her desk. He held out the letter and with his forefinger traced each line, as though he were reading it to her. When he had finished he clapped his hands and whooped.

The delicate still lines of her face wrinkled; her lips parted; she was smiling, nodding, clapping her hands.

"She—she—she understands things!" crowed Bates.

He had noted that often instead of going out she ate a box lunch at her desk, meditatively looking down to the street as she munched a cake; that on Friday— either the office busy day or the day when her week's salary had almost run out—she always stayed in, and that she lunched at twelve. One Friday in early winter he had the housekeeper at his bachelor apartments prepare sandwiches, with coffee in a vacuum bottle. He knew that his subordinates, with their inevitable glad interest in any eccentricities of the chief, would wonder at his lunching in.

"None of their business, anyway!" he said feebly. But he observed to his stenographer: "What a rush! Guess I won't go out for lunch." He strolled past the desk of young Crackins, the bookkeeper, whom he suspected of being the office wit and of collecting breaks on the part of the boss as material for delicious scandal.

"Pretty busy, Crackins? Well, so am I. Fact, I don't think I'll go out to lunch. Just have a bite here."

Having provided dimmers for the fierce light that beats about a glass-topped desk he drew a straight chair to the window and spread his feast on the broad sill at a few minutes after twelve. Emily was gnawing a doughnut and drinking a glass of milk. He bowed, but he inoffensively nibbled half a sandwich before he got over his embarrassment and ventured to offer her a bite. She was motionless, the doughnut gravely suspended in air. She sprang up—left the window.

"Curse it, double curse it! Fool! Beast! Couldn't even let her eat lunch in peace! Intruding on her—spoiling her leisure."

Emily had returned to the window. She showed him a small water glass. She half filled it with milk from her own glass, and diffidently held it out. He rose and extended his hand for it. Across the windy space he took her gift and her greeting.

He laughed; he fancied that she was laughing back, though he could see her face only as a golden blur in the thin fall sunshine. They settled down, sharing lunches. He was insisting on her having another cup of coffee when he was conscious that the door to his private room had opened, that someone was entering.

Frantically he examined a number of imaginary specks on his cup. He didn't dare turn to see who the intruder was. He held up the cup, ran a finger round the edge and muttered "Dirty!" The intruder pattered beside him. Bates looked up at him innocently. It was Crackins, the office tease. And Crackins was grinning.

"Hair in the soup, Mr. Bates?"

"In the— Oh! Oh, yes. Hair in the soup. Yes. Dirty—dirty cup—have speak—speak housekeeper," Bates burbled.

"Do you mind my interrupting you? I wanted to ask you about the Farmers' Rail-line credit. They're three weeks behind in payment——"

Did Bates fancy it or was Crackins squinting through the window at Emily? With an effusiveness that was as appropriate to him as a mandolin to an Irish contractor, Bates bobbed up and led Crackin back to the main office. He couldn't get away for ten minutes. When he returned Emily was leaning against the window jamb and he saw her by a leaded casement in the bishop's mansion, dreaming on hollyhocks and sundial below.

She pantomimed the end of her picnic; turned her small black lunch box upside down and spread her hands with a plaintive gesture of "All gone!" He offered her coffee, sandwiches, a bar of chocolate; but she refused each with a shy, quick shake of her head. She pointed at her typewriter, waved once, and was back at work.

As Christmas approached, as New York grew so friendly that men nodded to people who hadn't had the flat next door for more than seven years, Bates wondered if Emily's Christmas would be solitary. He tried to think of a way to send her a remembrance. He couldn't. But on the day before he brought an enormous wreath to the office, and waited till he caught her eye. Not till four-thirty, when the lights were on, did he succeed. He hung the wreath at the window and bowed to her, one hand on his heart, the other out in salutation.

Snow flew through the cold void between them and among cliffs of concrete and steel ran the icy river of December air, but they stood together as a smile transfigured her face—face of a gold-wreathed miniature on warm old ivory, tired and a little sad, but tender with her Christmas smile.

IV

She was gone, and he needed her. She had been absent a week now, this evening of treacherous melancholy. Winter had grown old and tedious and hard to bear; the snow that had been jolly in December was a filthy smear in February. Had there ever been such a thing as summer—ever been a time when the corners had not been foul with slush and vexatious with pouncing wind? He was tired of shows and sick of dances, and with a warm personal hatred he hated all the people from out of town who had come to New York for the winter and crowded the New Yorkers out of their favorite dens in tea rooms and grills.

And Emily had disappeared. He didn't know

whether she had a new job or was lying sick in some worn-carpeted room, unattended, desperate. And he couldn't find out. He didn't know her name.

Partly because he dreaded what might happen to her, partly because he needed her, he was nervously somber as he looked across to her empty window tonight. The street below was a crazy tumult, a dance of madmen on a wet pavement purple from arc lights—frenzied bells of surface cars, impatient motors, ripping taxis, home-hungry people tumbling through the traffic or standing bewildered in the midst of it, expecting to be killed, shivering and stamping wet feet. A late-working pneumatic riveter punctured his nerves with its unresting r-r-r-r—the grinding machine of a gigantic dentist. The sky was wild, the jagged clouds rushing in panic, smeared with the dull red of afterglow. Only her light, across, was calm—and she was not there.

"I can't stand it! I've come to depend on her. I didn't know I could miss anybody like this. I wasn't living—then. Something has happened to me. I don't understand! I don't understand!" he said.

She was back next morning. He couldn't believe it. He kept returning to make sure, and she always waved, and he was surprised to see how humbly grateful he was for that recognition. She pantomimed coughing for him, and with a hand on her brow indicated that she had had fever. He inquiringly laid his cheek on his hand in the universal sign for going to bed. She nodded—yes, she had been abed with a cold.

As he left the window he knew that sooner or later he must meet her, even if she should prove to be the sort who would say "Listen, kiddo!" He couldn't risk losing her again. Only—well, there was no hurry. He wanted to be sure he wasn't ridiculous. Among the people he knew the greatest rule of life was never to be ridiculous.

He had retired from the window in absurd envy because the men and girls in the office across were shaking Emily's hand, welcoming her back. He began to think about them and about her office. He hadn't an idea what the business of the office was—whether they sold oil stock or carrier pigeons or did blackmail. It was too modern to have lettering on the windows. There were blue prints to be seen on the walls, but they might indicate architecture, machinery—anything.

He began to watch her office mates more closely, and took the most querulous likes and dislikes. Her boss— he was a decent chap; but that filing girl, whom he had caught giggling at Emily's aloof way, she was a back-alley cat, and Bates had a back-alley desire to slap her.

He was becoming a clumsy sort of mystic in his aching care for her. When he waved good-night he was sending her his deepest self to stand as an invisible power beside her all the dark night. When he watched the others in her office he was not a peering gossip; he was winning them over to affection for her.

But not too affectionate!

He disapproved of the new young man who went to work in the office opposite a week or two after Emily's return. The new young man went about in his shirt sleeves, but the shirt seemed to be of silk, and he wore large intelligentsia tortoise-shell spectacles, and smoked a college sort of pipe in a dear-old-dormitory way. He had trained his molasses-colored locks till each frightened hair knew its little place and meekly kept it all day long. He was a self-confident, airy new young man, and apparently he was at least assistant manager. He was to be beheld talking easily to Emily's chief, one foot up on a chair, puffing much gray smoke.

The new young man appeared to like Emily. He had his own stenographer in his coop 'way over at the left, but he was always hanging about Emily's desk, and she looked up at him brightly. He chatted with her at closing hour, and at such times her back was to the window; and across the street Bates discreditably neglected his work and stood muttering things about drowning puppies.

She still waved good-night to Bates, but he fancied that she was careless about it.

"Oh, I'm just the faithful old dog. Young chap comes along—I'm invited to the wedding! I bet I've been best man at more weddings than any other man in New York.

I know the Wedding March better than the organist of St. Thomas', and I can smell lost rings across the vestry. Of course. That's all they want me for," said Bates.

And he dictated a violent letter to the company which made the cards for the indicator, and bitterly asked the office boy if he could spare time from the movies to fill the inkwells during the next few months.

Once Emily and the new young man left the office together at closing time, and peering twelve stories down Bates saw them emerging, walking together down the street. The young man was bending over her, and as they were submerged in the crowd Emily glanced at him with a gay upward toss of her head.

The lonely man at the window above sighed. "Well—well, I wanted her to be happy. But that young pup—— Rats! He's probably very decent. Heavens and earth, I'm becoming a moral Peeping Tom! I hate myself! But—I'm going to meet her. I won't let him take her away! I won't!"

Easy to say, but like paralysis was Bates' training in doing what other nice people do—in never being ridiculous. He despised queer people, socialists and poets and chaps who let others know they were in love.

Still thinking about it a week later he noticed no one about him as he entered a near-by tea room for lunch, and sat at a tiny, white, fussy table, with a paranoiac carmine rabbit painted in one corner of the bare top. He vaguely stared at a menu of walnut sandwiches, cream-cheese sandwiches, and chicken hash.

He realized that over the top of the menu he was looking directly at Emily, alone, at another dinky white table across the room.

Suppose she should think that he had followed her? That he was a masher? Horrible!

He made himself small in his chair, and to the impatient waitress modestly murmured: "Chicken hash, please; cuppa coffee."

His fear melted as he made sure that Emily had not seen him. She was facing in the same direction as he, and farther down the room, so that her back was toward him, and her profile. She was reading a book while she neglectfully nibbled at a soft white roll, a nice-minded tea-room roll. He studied her hungrily.

She was older than he had thought, from her quick movements. She was twenty-seven, perhaps. Her smooth, pale cheeks, free of all padding or fat, all lax muscles of laziness, were silken. In everything she was fine; the product of breeding. She was, veritably, Emily!

He had never much noticed how women were dressed, but now he found himself valuing every detail: The good lines and simplicity of her blue frock with chiffon sleeves, her trim brown shoes, her unornamented small blue toque, cockily aside her head with military smartness. But somehow—— It was her overcoat, on the back of her chair, that got him—her plain brown overcoat with bands of imitation fur; rather a cheap coat, not very warm. The inside was turned back, so that he saw the tiny wrinkles in the lining where it lay over her shoulders—wrinkles as feminine as the faint scent of powder—and discovered that she had patched the armhole. He clenched his fists with a pity for her poverty that was not pity alone but a longing to do things for her.

Emily was stirring, closing her book, absently pawing for her check as she snatched the last sentences of the story before going back to work. He had, so far, only picked juicy little white pieces out of the chicken hash, and had ignobly put off the task of attacking the damp, decomposed toast. And he was hungry. But he didn't know what to do if in passing she recognized him.

He snatched his coat and hat and check, and galloped out, not looking back.

He went to a hotel and had a real lunch, alternately glowing because she really was the fine, fresh, shining girl he had fancied and cursing himself because he had not gone over and spoken to her. Wittily. Audaciously. Hadn't he been witty and audacious to the Binghamton traction directors?

And—now that he knew her he wasn't going to relinquish her to the windy young man with the owl spectacles!

At three-thirty-seven that afternoon without visible cause he leaped out of his chair, seized his hat, and hustled out through the office. He sedately entered the elevator. The elevator runner was a heavy, black-skirted amiable Irishwoman who remembered people. He wondered if he couldn't say to her, "I am about to go across the street and fall in love."

As for the first time in all his study of it he entered the building opposite, he was panting as though he had been smoking too much. His voice sounded thick as he said "Twelve out," in the elevator.

Usually, revolving business plans, he walked through buildings unseeing, but he was as aware of the twelfth-floor hall, of the marble footboards, the floor like fruit cake turned to stone, wire-glass lights, alabaster bowls of the indirect lighting, as though he were a country boy new to this strange indoor world where the roads were tunnels. He was afraid, and none too clear why he should be afraid, of one slim girl.

He had gone fifty feet from the elevator before it occurred to him that he hadn't the slightest idea where he was going.

He had lost his directions. There were two batteries of elevators, so that he could not get his bearings from them. He didn't know on which side her office was. Trying to look as though he really had business here he rambled till he found a window at the end of a corridor. He saw the *Times* tower, and was straight again. Her office would be on the right. But—where?

He had just realized that from the corridor he couldn't tell how many outside windows each office had. He had carefully counted from across the street and found that her window was the sixth from the right. But that might be in either the Floral Heights Development Company or the Alaska Belle Mining Corporation, S. Smith—it was not explained whether S. Smith was the Belle or the Corporation.

Bates stood still. A large, red, furry man exploded out of the Floral Heights office and stared at him. Bates haughtily retired to the window at the end of the corridor and glowered out. Another crushing thought had fallen on him. Suppose he did pick the right office? He would find himself in an enclosed waiting room. He couldn't very well say to an office boy: "Will you tell the young lady in the blue dress that the man across the street is here?"

That would be ridiculous.

But he didn't care a hang if he was ridiculous!

He bolted down the corridor, entered the door of the Alaska Belle Mining Corporation. He was in a mahogany and crushed-morocco boudoir of business. A girl with a black frock and a scarlet smile fawned, "Ye-es?" He wasn't sure, but he thought she was a flirtatious person whom he had noted as belonging in an office next to Emily's. He blundered: "C-could I see some of your literature?"

It was twenty minutes later when he escaped from a friendly young man—now gorgeous in a new checked suit, but positively known by Bates to have cleaned the lapels of his other suit with stuff out of a bottle two evenings before—who had tried to sell him stock in two gold mines and a ground-floor miracle in the copper line. Bates was made to feel as though he was betraying an old friend before he was permitted to go. He had to accept a library of choice views of lodes, smelters, river barges, and Alaskan scenery.

He decorously deposited the booklets one by one in the mail chute, and returned to his favorite corridor.

This time he entered the cream-and-blue waiting room of the Floral Heights Development Company. He had a wild, unformed plan of announcing himself as a building inspector and being taken through the office, unto the uttermost parts, which meant to Emily's desk. It was a romantic plan and adventurous—and he instantly abandoned it at the sight of the realistic office boy, who had red hair and knickers and the oldest, coldest eye in the world.

"You people deal in suburban realty, don't you?"

"Yep!"

"I'd like to see the manager." It would be Emily who would take him in!

"Whadyuhwannaseeimbout?"

"I may consider the purchase of a lot."

"Oh, I thought you was that collector from the towel company."

"Do I look it, my young friend?"

"You can't tell, these days—the way you fellows spend your money on clothes. Well, say, boss, the old man is out, but I'll chase Mr. Simmons out here."

Mr. Simmons was, it proved, the man whom Bates disliked more than any other person living. He was that tortoise-spectacled, honey-haired, airy young man who dared to lift his eyes to Emily. He entered with his cut-out open; he assumed that he was Bates' physician and confessor; he chanted that at Beautiful Floral Heights by the Hackensack, the hydrants gave champagne, all babies weighed fifteen pounds at birth, values doubled overnight, and cement garages grew on trees.

Bates escaped with another de-luxe library, which included a glossy postcard showing the remarkable greenness of Floral Heights grass and the redness and yellowness of "Bungalow erected for J. J. Keane." He took the postcard back to his office and addressed it to the one man in his class whom he detested.

V

For four days he ignored Emily. Oh, he waved good night; there was no reason for hurting her feelings by rudeness. But he did not watch her through the creeping office hours. And he called on Christine Parrish. He told himself that in Christine's atmosphere of leisure and the scent of white roses, in her chatter about the singles championship and Piping Rock and various men referred to as Bunk and Poodle and Georgie, he had come home to his own people. But when Christine on the davenport beside him looked demurely at him through the smoke of her cigarette he seemed to hear the frightful drum fire of the Wedding March, and he rushed to the protecting fireplace.

The next night when Emily, knife-clean Emily, waved good-by and exhaustedly snapped off her light Bates darted to the elevator and reached the street entrance before she appeared across the way. But he was still stiff with years of training in propriety. He stood watching her go down the street, turn the corner.

Crackins, the bookkeeper, blandly whistling as he left the building, was shocked to see Bates running out of the doorway, his arms revolving grotesquely, his unexercised legs stumbling as he dashed down a block and round the corner.

Bates reached her just as she entered the Subway kiosk and was absorbed in the swirl of pushing people. He put out his hand to touch her unconscious shoulder, then withdrew it shiveringly, like a cat whose paw has touched cold water.

She had gone two steps down. She did not know he was there.

"Emily!" he cried.

A dozen Subway hurriers glanced at him as they shoved past. Emily turned, half seeing. She hesitated, looked away from him again.

"Emily!"

He dashed down, stood beside her.

"Two lovers been quarreling," reflected an oldish woman as she plumped by them.

"I beg your pardon!" remonstrated Emily.

Her voice was clear, her tone sharp. These were the first words from his princess of the tower.

"I beg yours, but—I tried to catch your attention. I've been frightfully clumsy, but—— You see, hang it, I don't know your name, and when I—I happened to see you, I—I'd thought of you as 'Emily.' "

Her face was still, her eyes level. She was not indignant, but she waited, left it all to him.

He desperately lied: "Emily was my mother's name."

"Oh! Then I can't very well be angry, but——"

"You know who I am, don't you? The man across the street from——"

"Yes. Though I didn't know you at first. The man across is always so self-possessed!"

"I know. Don't rub it in. I'd always planned to be very superior and amusing and that sort of stuff when I met you, and make a tremendous impression."

Standing on the gritty steel-plated steps that led to the cavern of the Subway, jostled by hurtling people, he faltered on: "Things seem to have slipped, though. You see, I felt beastly lonely tonight. Aren't you, sometimes?"

"Always!"

"We'd become such good friends—you know, our lunches together, and all."

Her lips twitched, and she took pity on him with: "I know. Are you going up in the Subway? We can ride together, at least as far as Seventy-second."

This was before the days of shuttles and H's, when dozens of people knew their way about in the Subway, and one spoke confidently of arriving at a given station.

"No, I wasn't going. I wanted you to come to dinner with me! Do, please! If you haven't a date. I'm—I'm not really a masher. I've never asked a girl I didn't know, like this. I'm really—— Oh, hang it, I'm a solid citizen. Disgustingly so. My name is Bates. I'm g.m. of my office. If this weren't New York we'd have met months ago. Please! I'll take you right home after——"

Young women of the Upper West Side whose fathers were in Broad Street or in wholesale silk, young women with marquetry tables, with pictures in shadow boxes in their drawing rooms, and too many servants belowstairs, had been complimented when Bates took them to dinner. But this woman who worked, who had the tension wrinkle between her brows, listened and let him struggle.

"We can't talk here. Please walk up a block with me," he begged.

She came but she continued to inspect him. Once they were out of the hysteria of the Subway crowd, the ache of his embarrassment was relieved, and on a block of dead old brownstone houses embalmed among loft buildings he stopped and laughed aloud.

"I've been talking like an idiot. The crowd flustered me. And it was so different from the greeting I'd always planned. May I come and call on you sometimes, and present myself as a correct old bachelor, and ask you properly to go to dinner? Will you forgive me for having been so clumsy?"

She answered gravely: "No, you weren't. You were nice. You spoke as though you meant it. I was glad. No one in New York ever speaks to me as though he meant anything—except giving dictation."

He came close to saying: "What does the chump with the foolish spectacles mean?"

He saved himself by a flying mental leap as she went on: "And I like your laugh. I will go to dinner with you tonight if you wish."

"Thank you a lot. Where would you like to go? And shall we go to a movie or something to kill time before dinner?"

"You won't—— I'm not doing wrong, am I? I really feel as if I knew you. Do you despise me for tagging obediently along when I'm told to?"

"Oh! Despise—— You're saving a solitary man's life! Where——"

"Any place that isn't too much like a tea room. I go to tea rooms twice a day. I am ashamed every time I see a boiled egg, and I've estimated that if the strips of Japanese toweling I've dined over were placed end to end they would reach from Elkhart to Rajputana."

"I know. I wish we could go to a family dinner— not a smart one but an old-fashioned one, with mashed turnips, and Mother saying: 'Now eat your nice parsnips; little girls that can't eat parsnips can't eat mince pie.' "

"Oh, there aren't any families any more. You are nice!"

She was smiling directly at him, and he wanted to tuck her hand under his arm, but he didn't, and they went to a movie till seven. They did not talk during it. She was relaxed, her small tired hands curled together in her lap. He chose the balcony of the Firenze Room in the Grand Royal Hotel for dinner, because from its quiet leisure you can watch gay people and hear distant music. He ordered a dinner composed of such unnecessary things as hors d'oeuvres, which she wouldn't have in tea rooms. He did not order wine.

When the waiter was gone and they faced each other, with no walking, no movies, no stir of the streets to occupy them, they were silent. He was struggling enormously to find something to say, and finding nothing beyond the sound observation that winters are cold. She glanced over the balcony rail at a bouncing pink-and-silver girl dining below with three elephantishly skittish men in evening clothes. She seemed far easier than he. He couldn't get himself to be masterful. He examined the crest on a fork and carefully scratched three triangles on the cloth, and ran his watch chain between his fingers, and told himself not to fidget, and arranged two forks and a spoon in an unfeasible fortification of his water glass, and delicately scratched his ear and made a knot in his watch chain, and dropped a fork with an alarming clang, and burst out:

"Er-r-r—— Hang it, let's be conversational! I find myself lots dumber than an oyster. Or a fried scallop."

She laid her elbows on the table, smiled inquiringly, suggested: "Very well. But tell me who you are. And what does your office do? I've decided you dealt in Christmas mottoes. You have cardboard things round the walls."

He was eloquent about the Carstop Indicator. The device was, it seemed, everything from a city guide to a preventive of influenza. All traction magnates who failed to introduce it were——

"Now I shall sell you a lot at Floral Heights," she interrupted.

"Oh, you're right. I'm office mad. But it really is a good thing. I handle the Eastern territory. I'm a graduate—now I shall be autobiographical and intimate and get your sympathy for my past—I come from Shef.—Sheffield Scientific School of Yale University. My father was a chemical engineer, and I wrote one poem, at the age of eleven, and I have an uncle in Sing Sing for forgery. Now you know all about me. And I want to know if you really are Emily?"

"Meaning?"

"I didn't—er—exactly call you Emily because of my mother, but because the name means old gardens and a charming family. I have decided that your father was either a bishop or a Hartford banker."

She was exploring hors d'oeuvres. She laid down her fork and said evenly: "No. My father was a mill superintendent in Fall River. He was no good. He drank and gambled and died. My mother was quite nice. But there is nothing romantic about me. I did have three years in college, but I work because I have to. I have no future beyond possibly being manager of the girls in some big office. I am very competent but not very pleasant. I am horribly lonely in New York, but that may be my fault. One man likes me—a man in my office. But he laughs at my business ambitions. I am not happy, and I don't know what's ahead of me, and some day I may kill myself—and I definitely do not want sympathy. I've never been so frank as this to anyone, and I oughtn't to have been with you."

She stopped dead, looked at the trivial crowd below, and Bates felt as though he had pawed at her soul.

Awkwardly kind he ventured: "You live alone?"

"Yes."

"Can't you find some jolly girls to live with?"

"I've tried it. They got on my nerves. They were as hopeless as I was."

"Haven't you some livelier girl you can play with?"

"Only one. And she's pretty busy. She's a social worker. And where can we go? Concerts sometimes, and walks. Once we tried to go to a restaurant. You know—one of these Bohemian places. Three different drunken men tried to pick us up. This isn't a very gentle city."

"Emily—Emily—— I say, what is your name?"

"It's as unromantic as the rest of me: Sarah Pardee."

"Look here, Miss Pardee, I'm in touch with a good many different sorts of people in the city. Lived here a good while, and classmates. Will you let me do something for you? Introduce you to people I know; families and——"

She laid down her fork, carefully placed her hands flat on the table, side by side, palms down, examined them, fitted her thumbs closer together, and declared: "There is something you can do for me."

"Yes?" he thrilled.

"Get me a better job!"

He couldn't keep from grunting as though he had quite unexpectedly been hit by something.

"The Floral Heights people are nice to work for, but there's no future. Mr. Ransom can't see a woman as anything but a stenographer. I want to work up to office manager of some big concern or something."

He pleaded:

"B-but—— Of course I'll be glad to do that, but don't you want—— How about the human side? Don't you want to meet real New Yorkers?"

"No."

"Houses where you could drop in for tea on Sunday?"

"No."

"Girls of your own age, and dances, and——"

"No. I'm a business woman, nothing else. Shan't be anything else, I'm afraid. Not strong enough. I have to get to bed at ten. Spartan. It isn't much fun but it—oh, it keeps me going."

"Very well. I shall do as you wish. I'll telephone you by tomorrow noon."

He tried to make it sound politely disagreeable, but it is to be suspected that he was rather plaintive, for a glimmer of a smile touched her face as she said: "Thank you. If I could just find an opening. I don't know many employers here. I was in a Boston office for several years."

This ending, so like a lecture on auditing and costs, concluded Bates' quest for high romance.

He was horribly piqued and dignified, and he talked in an elevated manner of authors whom he felt he must have read, seeing that he had always intended to read them when he got time. Inside he felt rather sick. He informed himself that he had been a fool; that Emily—no, Miss Sarah Pardee!—was merely an enameled machine; and that he never wanted to see her again.

It was all of six minutes before he begged: "Did you like my waving good-night to you every evening?"

Dubiously: "Oh—yes."

"Did you make up foolish stories about me as I did about you?"

"No. I'll tell you." She spoke with faint, measured emphasis. "I have learned that I can get through a not very appealing life only by being heartless and unimaginative—except about my work. I was wildly imaginative as a girl; read Keats, and Kipling of course, and pretended that every man with a fine straight back was Strickland Sahib. Most stenographers keep up making believe. Poor tired things, they want to marry and have children, and file numbers and vocabularies merely bewilder them. But I—well, I want to succeed. So—work. And keep clear-brained, and exact. Know facts. I never allow fancies to bother me in office hours. I can tell you precisely the number of feet and inches of sewer pipe at Floral Heights, and I do not let myself gurgle over the pigeons that come up and coo on my window sill. I don't believe I shall ever be sentimental about anything again. Perhaps I've made a mistake. But—I'm not so sure. My father was full of the choicest sentiment, especially when he was drunk. Anyway, there I am. Not a woman, but a business woman."

"I'm sorry!"

He took her home. At her suggestion they walked up, through the late-winter clamminess. They passed a crying child on a doorstep beside a discouraged delicatessen. He noted that she looked at the child with an instant of mothering excitement, then hastened on.

"I'm not angry at her now. But even if I did want to see her again, I never would. She isn't human," he explained to himself.

At her door—door of a smug semiprivate rooming house on West Seventy-fourth Street—as he tried to think of a distinguished way of saying good-by he blurted: "Don't get too interested in the young man with spectacles. Make him wait till you study the genus New Yorker a little more. Your Mr. Simmons is amiable but shallow."

"How did you know I knew Mr. Simmons?" she marveled. "How did you know his name?"

It was the first time she had been off her guard, and he was able to retreat with a most satisfactory "One notices! Good night. You shall have your big job."

He peeped back from two houses away. She must have gone in without one glance toward him.

He told himself that he was glad their evening was over. But he swooped down on the Yale Club and asked five several men what they knew about jobs for a young woman, who, he asserted entirely without authorization, was a perfect typist, speedy at taking dictation, scientific at filing carbons—and able to find the carbons after she had scientifically filed them!—and so charming to clients that before they even saw one of the selling force they were longing to hand over their money.

He telephoned about it to a friend in a suburb, which necessitated his sitting in a smothering booth and shouting: "No, no, no! I want Pelham, not Chatham!" After he had gone to bed he had a thought so exciting and sleep-dispelling that he got up, closed the windows, shivered, hulked into his bathrobe and sat smoking a cigarette, with his feet inelegantly up on the radiator. Why not make a place for Emily in his own office?

He gave it up reluctantly. The office wasn't big enough to afford her a chance. And Emily—Miss Pardee—probably would refuse. He bitterly crushed out the light of the cigarette on the radiator, yanked the windows open and climbed back into bed. He furiously discovered that during his meditation the bed had become cold again. There were pockets of arctic iciness down in the lower corners.

"Urg!" snarled Bates.

He waved good morning to Emily next day, but brusquely, and she was casual in her answer. At eleven-seventeen, after the sixth telephone call, he had found the place. He telephoned to her.

"This is Mr. Bates, across the street."

He leaped up and by pulling the telephone out to the end of its green tether he could just reach the window and see her at the telephone by her window.

He smiled, but he went on sternly: "If you will go to the Technical and Home Syndicate—the new consolidation of trade publications—and ask for Mr. Hyden—H-y-d-e-n—in the advertising department, he will see that you get a chance. Really big office. Opportunities. Chance to manage a lot of stenographers, big commercial-research department, maybe a shot at advertising soliciting. Please refer to me. Er-r-r."

She looked across, saw him at the telephone, startled. Tenderness came over him in a hot wave.

But colorless was her voice as she answered, "That's very good of you."

He cut her off with a decisive "Good luck!" He stalked back to his desk. He was curiously gentle and hesitating with his subordinates all that day.

"Wonder if the old man had a pal die on him?" suggested Crackins, the bookkeeper, to the filing girl.

"He looks peaked. Pretty good scout, Batesy is, at that."

A week later Emily was gone from the office across. She had not telephoned good-by. In a month Bates encountered Hyden, of the Technical Syndicate office, who informed him: "That Miss Pardee you sent me is a crackajack. Right on the job, and intelligent. I've got her answering correspondence—dictating. She'll go quite a ways."

That was all. Bates was alone. Never from his twelfth-floor tower did he see her face or have the twilight benediction of farewell.

VI

He told himself that she was supercilious, that she was uninteresting, that he did not like her. He admitted that his office had lost its exciting daily promise of romance—that he was tired of all offices. But he insisted that she had nothing to do with that. He had surrounded her with a charm not her own.

However neatly he explained things to himself, it was still true that an empty pain like homesickness persisted whenever he looked out of his window—or didn't look out but sat at his desk and wanted to. When he worked late he often raised his head with a confused sense of missing something. The building across had become just a building across. All he could see in it was ordinary office drudges doing commonplace things. Even Mr. Simmons of the esthetic spectacles no longer roused interesting rage. As for Emily's successor, Bates hated her. She smirked, and her hair was a hurrah's nest.

March had come in; the streets were gritty with dust. Bates languidly got himself to call on Christine Parrish again. Amid the welcome narcissus bowls and vellum-backed seats and hand-tooled leather desk fittings of the Parrish library he was roused from the listlessness that like a black fog had been closing in on him. He reflected that Christine was sympathetic, and Emily merely a selfish imitation of a man. But Christine made him impatient. She was vague. She murmured: "Oh, it must be thrilling to see the street railways in all these funny towns." Funny towns! Huh! They made New York hustle. Christine's mind was flabby. Yes, and her soft shining arms would become flabby too. He wanted—oh, a girl that was compact, cold-bathed.

As he plodded home the shivering fog that lay over him hid the future. What had he ahead? Lonely bachelorhood—begging mere boys at the club to endure a game of poker with him?

He became irritable in the office. He tried to avoid it. He was neither surprised nor indignant when he overheard Crackins confide to his own stenographer: "The old man has an ingrowing grouch. We'll get him operated on. How much do you contribute, Countess? Ah, we thank you."

He was especially irritable on a watery, bleary April day when every idiot in New York and the outlying districts telephoned him. He thought ill of Alexander Graham Bell. The factory wanted to know whether they should rush the Bangor order. He hadn't explained that more than six times before. A purchasing agent from out of town called him up and wanted information about theater-ticket agencies and a tailor. The girl in the outside office let a wrong-number call get through to him, and a greasy voice bullied: "Is dis de Triumph Bottling Vorks? Vod? Get off de line! I don't vant you! Hang up!"

"Well, I most certainly don't want you!" snapped Bates. But it didn't relieve him at all.

"Tr-r-r-r!" snickered the telephone bell.

Bates ignored it.

"Tr-r-r-r-. R-r-r-r! Tr-r-r-r!"

"Yeah!" snarled Bates.

"Mr. Bates?"

"Yep!"

"Sarah Pardee speaking."

"Who?"

"Why—why, Emily! You sound busy, though. I won't——"

"Wait! W-w-wait! For heaven's sake! Is it really you? How are you? How are you? Terribly glad to hear your voice! How are you? We miss you——"

"We?"

"Well, I do! Nobody to say good-night. Heard from Hyden; doing fine. Awfully glad. What—er—what——"

"Mr. Bates, will you take me out to dinner some time this week; or next?"

"Will you come tonight?"

"You have no engagement?"

"No, no! Expected to dine alone. Please come. Will you meet me—— Shall we go up to the Belle Chic?"

"Please may we go to the Grand Royal again, and early, about six-thirty?"

"Of course. I'll meet you in the lobby. Six-thirty. Good-by."

He drew the words out lingeringly, but she cut him off with a crisp telephonic "G'-by."

Afterward he called up an acquaintance and broke the dinner engagement he had had for four days. He lied badly, and the man told him about it.

In his idiotic, beatific glow it wasn't for half an hour that the ugly thought crept grinning into his mind, but it persisted, squatting there, leering at him: "I wonder if she just wants me to get her another job?"

It served to quiet the intolerable excitement. In the Grand Royal lobby he greeted her with only a nod. . . . She was on time. Christine Parrish had a record minimum of twenty minutes late.

They descended the twisting stairs to the Firenze Room.

"Would you prefer the balcony or downstairs?" he said easily.

She turned.

She had seemed unchanged. Above the same brown fur-trimmed coat, which he knew better than any other garment in the world, was the same self-contained inspection of the world. Standing on the stairs she caught the lapel of her coat with a nervous hand, twisted it, dropped her eyes, looked up pleadingly.

"Would I be silly if I asked for the same table we had before? We—oh, it's good luck."

"Of course we'll have it."

"That's why I suggested dining early, so it wouldn't be taken. I have something rather serious to ask your advice about."

"Serious?"

"Oh, not—not tragic. But it puzzles me."

He was anxious as he followed her. Their table was untaken. He fussily took her coat, held her chair.

Her eyes became shrewdly clear again while he ordered dinner, and she said: "Will you please examine the crest on one of the forks?"

"Why?"

"Because you did last time. You were adorably absurd, and very nice, trying not to alarm the strange girl."

He had obediently picked up a fork, but he flung it down and commanded: "Look here, what is this that puzzles you?"

Her hand drooping over the balcony rail by their table was visibly trembling. She murmured: "I have discovered that I am a woman."

"I don't quite——"

"I've tried to keep from telling you, but I can't. I do—I do miss our good-nights and our lunches. I have done quite well at the Technical Syndicate, but I don't seem to care. I thought I had killed all sentimentality in me. I haven't. I'm sloppy-minded. No! I'm not! I don't care! I'm glad." A flush on her cheek like the rosy shadow of a wine glass on linen, she flung out: "I find I cared more for our silly games than I do for success. There's no one across the way now to smile at me. There's just a blank brick wall, with a horrible big garage sign, and I look at it before I go home nights. Oh, I'm a failure. I can't go on—fighting—alone—always alone!"

He had caught both her hands. He was unconscious of waiters and other guests. But she freed herself.

"No! Please! Just let me babble. I don't know whether I'm glad or sorry to find I haven't any brains. None! No courage! But all I want—— Will you dine with me once a month or so? Let me go Dutch——"

"Oh, my dear!"

"—and sometimes take me to the theater? Then I won't feel solitary. I can go on working, and make good, and perhaps get over—— Please! Don't think I'm a Bernard Shaw superwoman pursuing a man. It's just that—— You were the first person to make me welcome in New York. Will you forgive——"

"Emily, please don't be humble! I'd rather have you make me beg, as you used to." He stopped, gasped and added quietly: "Emily, will you marry me?"

"No."

"But you said——"

"I know. I miss you. But you're merely sorry for me. Honestly I'm not a clinger. I can stand alone—almost alone. It's sweet of you, and generous, but I didn't ask that. Just play with me sometimes."

"But I mean it. Dreadfully. I've thought of you every hour. Will you marry me? Now!"

"No."

"Some time?"

"How can I tell? A month ago I would have cut a girl who was so sloppy-minded that she would beg a man for friendship. I didn't know! I didn't know anything! But—— No! No!"

"See here, Emily. Are you free? Can I depend on you? Are you still interested in young Simmons?"

"He calls on me."

"Often?"

"Yes."

"You refused?"

"Yes. That was when I discovered I was a woman. But not—not his woman!"

"Mine, then! Mine! Think, dear—it's incredible, but the city didn't quite get us. We're still a man and a woman! What day is this? Oh, Wednesday. Listen. Thursday you go to the theater with me."

"Yes."

"Friday you find an excuse and have to see someone at the Floral Heights Company, and you wave to me from across the street, so that my office will be blessed again; and we meet afterward and go to supper with my friends the Parrishes."

"Yes-es."

"Saturday we lunch together, and walk clear through Van Cortlandt Park, and I become a masterful brute, and propose to you, and you accept me."

"Oh, yes, I suppose so. But that leaves Sunday. What do we do Sunday?"

Speed

At two in the morning, on Main Street of a Nebraska prairie town that ought to have been asleep since ten, a crowd was packed under a lone arc-light, chattering, laughing, and every moment peering down the dim street to westward.

Out in the road were two new automobile tires, and cans of gasoline, oil, water. The hose of a pressure air-pump stretched across the cement sidewalk, and beside it was an air-gauge in a new chamois case. Across the street a restaurant was glaring with unshaded electric lights; and a fluffy-haired, pert-nose girl alternately ran to the window and returned to look after the food she was keeping warm. The president of the local motor club, who was also owner of the chief garage, kept stuttering to a young man in brown union overalls, "Now be all ready—for land's sake, be ready. Remember, gotta change those casings in three minutes." They were awaiting a romantic event—the smashing of the cross-continent road-record by a Mallard car driven by J. T. Buffum.

Everyone there had seen pictures of Buffum in the sporting and automobile pages of the Lincoln and Kansas City papers; everyone knew that face, square, impassive, heavy-cheeked, kindly, with the unsmoked cigar between firm teeth, and the almost boyish bang

over a fine forehead. Two days ago he had been in
San Francisco, between the smeared gold of Chink
dens and the tumult of the Pacific. Two days from
now he would be in distant New York.

Miles away on the level prairie road a piercing jab
of light grew swiftly into two lights, while a distant
drum-roll turned into the burring roar of a huge un-
muffled engine. The devouring thing burst into town,
came fulminating down on them, stopped with a clash-
ing jerk. The crowd saw the leather-hooded man at
the mighty steering wheel nod to them, grinning,
human, companionable—the great Buffum.

"Hurray! Hurray!" came the cries, and the silence
changed to weaving gossip.

Already the garage youngster, with his boss and
three men from another garage, was yanking off two
worn casings, filling the gas tank, the oil well, the radiator. Buffum stiffly crawled from the car, stretched his
shoulders, his mighty arms and legs, in a leonine yawn.
"Jump out, Roy. Eats here," he muttered to the man
in the passenger seat. This man the spectators did not
heed. He was merely Buffum's mechanic and relay
driver, a poor thing who had never in his life driven
faster than ninety miles an hour.

The garage owner hustled Buffum across to the
lunchroom. The moment the car had stormed into
town the pretty waitress, jumping up and down with
impatience, had snatched the chicken from the warm-
ing oven, poured out the real coffee, proudly added
real cream. The lunch and the changing of casings
took three and a quarter minutes.

The clatter of the motor smote the quiet houses and
was gone. The town became drab and dull. The crowd
yawned and fumbled its way home.

Buffum planned to get in two hours of sleep after
leaving this Nebraska town. Roy Bender, the relay
driver, took the wheel. Buffum sat with his relaxed
body swaying to the leaping motion, while he drowsily
commented in a hoarse, slow shout that pushed

through the enveloping roar: "Look out for that hill, Roy. Going to be slippery."

"How can you tell?"

"I don't know. Maybe I smell it. But watch out, anyway. Good night, little playmate. Wake me up at four-fifteen."

That was all of the conversation for seventy-two miles.

It was dawn when Buffum drove again. He was silent; he was concentrated on keeping the speedometer just two miles higher than seemed safe. But for a mile or so, on straight stretches, he glanced with weary happiness at the morning meadows, at shimmering tapestry of grass and young wheat, and caught half a note of the song of a meadowlark. His mouth, so grimly tight in dangerous places, rose at the corners.

Toward noon, as Buffum was approaching the village of Apogee, Iowa, the smooth blaring of the motor was interrupted by a noise as though the engine was flying to pieces.

He yanked at the switch; before the car had quite halted, Roy and he had tumbled out at opposite sides, were running forward to lift the hood. The fan-guard, a heavy wire soldered on the radiator, had worked loose and bent a fan-blade, which had ripped out a handful of honeycomb. The inside of the radiator looked as though it had been hacked with a dull knife. The water was cascading out.

Buffum speculated: "Apogee next town. Can't get radiator there. None nearer 'n Clinton. Get this soldered. Here! You!"

The "Here! You!" was directed at the driver of an ancient roadster. "Got to hustle this boat into next town. Want you to haul me in."

Roy Bender had already snatched a tow-rope from the back of the racing car, was fastening it to the front axle of the Mallard, the rear of the roadster.

Buffum gave no time for disputes. "I'm J. T. Buffum. Racin' 'cross continent. Here's ten dollars. Want

your machine ten minutes. I'll drive." He had crowded
into the seat. Already, with Roy steering the Mallard,
they were headed for Apogee.

A shouting crowd ran out from house and store.
Buffum slowly looked them over. Of a man in corduroy trousers and khaki shirt, who had plumped out
of a garage, he demanded: "Who's the best solderer
in town?"

"I am. Good as anybody in Iowa."

"Now, wait! Know who I am?"

"Sure! You're Buffum."

"My radiator is shot to thunder. Got to be soldered.
I want six hours' work done in one hour, or less. How
about the hardware store? Isn't there a solderer there
that's even better than you?"

"Yes, I guess maybe old Frank Dieters is."

"Get him, and get the other good man, and get
busy. One of you work on each side. Roy Bender
here will boss you." Already Roy was taking down
the radiator. "One hour, remember. Hurry! Plenty of
money in it——"

"Oh, we don't care anything about the money!"

"Thanks, old man. Well, I might as well grab a little
sleep. Where'll I get a long-distance connection?" he
yawned.

"Across the street at Mrs. Rivers'. Be less noise
than in the garage, I guess."

Over the way was a house that was a large square
box with an octagonal cupola on the mansard roof. It
was set back in a yard of rough grass and old crab-
apple trees. At the gate were a smallish, severe
woman, in spectacles and apron, and a girl of twenty-
five or -six. Buffum looked at the girl twice, and tried
to make out what it was that distinguished her from
all the other women in the crowd that had come pushing and giggling to see the famous car.

She was sharply individualized. It was not that she
was tall and blazing. She was slight—and delicate as
a drypoint etching. Her chin was precise though soft;

she had a Roman nose, a feminized charming version of the Roman nose. The thing that made her distinctive, Buffum reflected, was her poise. The girl by the gate was as quietly aloof as the small cold moon of winter.

He plodded across the road. He hesitated before speaking.

"I hope there hasn't been an accident," she murmured to him.

"No, just a small repair."

"But, why does everyone seem so much concerned?"

"Why, it's—it's—I'm J. T. Buffum."

"Mr.—uh—Buffum?"

"I reckon you never heard of me."

"Why, uh—should I have?" Her eyes were serious, regretful at discourtesy.

"No. You shouldn't. I just mean—— Motor-fans usually have. I'm a racer. I'm driving from San Francisco to New York."

"Really? It will take you—ten days?"

"Four to five days."

"In two days you will be in the East? See the—the ocean? Oh!"

In her voice was wistfulness. Her eyes saw far-off things. But they came back to Apogee, Iowa, and to the big, dusty man in leather, with a penitent: "I'm ashamed not to have heard of you, but I—we haven't a car. I hope they will make your repair quickly. May Mother and I give you a glass of milk or something?"

"I'd be glad if you'd let me use your telephone. So noisy at——"

"Of course! Mother, this is Mr. Buffum, who is driving across the country. Oh—my name is Aurilla Rivers."

Buffum awkwardly tried to bow in two directions at once. Then he followed Aurilla Rivers' slender back. He noticed how smooth were her shoulder-blades. They were neither jagged nor wadded. It seemed to him that the blue silk of her waist took life from the warm and eager flesh beneath. In her studied serenity she had not lost her youth.

As he drew away from the prying crowd and the sound of hasty hammers and wrenches, he was conscious of clinging peace. The brick of the walk was worn to a soft rose, shaded by gently moving branches of lilac bushes. At the end was a wild-grape arbor and an ancient bench. The arbor was shadowy, and full of the feeling of long and tranquil years. In this land of new houses and new red barns and blazing miles of wheat, it seemed mysterious with antiquity.

And on the doorstep was the bleached vertebra of a whale. Buffum was confused. He traveled so much and so swiftly that he always had to stop to think whether he was East or West, and now—— Yes, this was Iowa. Of course. But that vertebra belonged to New England.

And to New England belonged the conch shell and the mahogany table in the wide hall with its strip of rag-carpet down which Miss Rivers led him to the telephone—an old-fashioned wall instrument. Buffum noticed that Miss Rivers conscientiously disappeared through the wide door at the end of the hall into a garden of pinks and pansies and sweet William.

"Please get me long distance."

"I'm long distance and short distance and——"

"All right. This is Buffum, the transcontinental racer. I want to talk to Detroit, Michigan—Mallard Motor Company—office of the president."

He waited ten minutes. He sat on the edge of a William and Mary chair, and felt obese, clumsy, extremely dirty. He ventured off his chair—disapproving of the thunder of his footsteps—and stood at the door of the parlor. The corner by the bow window seemed to be a shrine. Above a genuine antediluvian haircloth sofa were three pictures. In the center was a rather good painting of a man who was the very spirit of 1850 in New England—burnsides, grim white forehead, Roman nose, prim triangle of shirt front. On the right was a watercolor of a house, white doored, narrow eaved, small windowed, standing out against gray sand and blue water, with a moored motor-dory beyond. On the woodshed ell of the pictured house was nailed up the name-board of a ship—*Penninah Sparrow*.

On the left of the portrait was a fairly recent enlarged photograph of a man somewhat like the granther of 1850, so far as Romanness of nose went, but weaker and more pompous, a handsome old buck, with a pretentious broad eyeglass ribbon and hair that must have been silvery over a face that must have been deep-flushed.

By the sofa was a marble-topped stand on which were fresh sweet peas.

Then central called, and Buffum was talking to the president of the Mallard Motor Company, who for two days and nights had sat by the ticker, watching his flashing progress.

"Hello, chief. Buffum speaking. Held up for about an hour. Apogee, Iowa. Think I can make it up. But better move the schedule up through Illinois and Indiana. Huh? Radiator leak. 'By!"

He inquired the amount of toll, and rambled out to the garden. He had to hurry away, of course, and get some sleep, but it would be good for him to see Aurilla Rivers again, to take with him the memory of her cool resoluteness. She was coming toward him. He meekly followed her back through the hall, to the front steps. There he halted her. He would see quite enough of Roy Bender and the car before he reached New York.

"Please sit down here a moment, and tell me——"

"Yes?"

"Oh, about the country around here, and uh—— Oh! I owe you for the telephone call."

"Please! It's nothing."

"But it's something. It's two dollars and ninety-five cents."

"For a telephone call?"

He caught her hand and pressed the money into it.

She plumped down on the steps, and he discreetly lowered his bulk beside her. She turned on him, blazing:

"You infuriate me! You do things I've always wanted to—sweep across big distances, command men, have power. I suppose it's the old Yankee shipmasters coming out in me."

"Miss Rivers, I noticed a portrait in there. It seemed to me that the picture and the old sofa make a kind of shrine. And the fresh flowers." She stared a little before she said:

"Yes. It's a shrine. But you're the first one that ever guessed. How did you——"

"I don't know. I suppose it's because I went through some California missions a few days ago. Tell me about the people in the pictures."

"You wouldn't—— Oh, some day, perhaps."

"Some day! Now, you see here, child! Do you realize that in about forty minutes I'll be kiting out of here at seventy miles an hour? Imagine that I've met you a couple of times in the bank or the post office, and finally after about six months I've called here, and told your mother I like pansies. All right. All that is over. Now, who are you, Aurilla Rivers? Who and what and why and how and when?"

She smiled. She nodded. She told.

She was a school teacher now, but before her father had died—well, the enlarged photograph in there was her father, Bradley Rivers, pioneer lawyer of Apogee. He had come out from Cape Cod, as a boy. The sidewhiskered man of the central portrait was her grandfather, Captain Zenas Rivers, of West Harlepool, on the Cape. The house in the picture was the Rivers' mansion, birthplace of her father.

"Have you been on the Cape yourself?" Buffum queried. "I remember driving through Harlepool, but I don't recall anything but white houses and a meeting-house with a whale of a big steeple."

"The dream of my life has been to go to Harlepool. Once when Father had to go to Boston he did run

down there by himself. That's when he brought back
the portrait of Grandfather, and the painting of the
old house, and the furniture and all. He said it made
him so melancholy to see the changes in the town,
and he never would go again. Then—he died. I'm saving up money for a trip back East. I do believe in
democracy, but at the same time I feel that families
like the Riverses owe it to the world to set an example, and I want to find my own people again. My
own people!"

"Maybe you're right. I'm from the soil. Di-rect! But
somehow I can see it in you, same as I do in the
portrait of your grandfather. I wish I—— Well,
never mind."

"But you are an aristocrat. You do things that other
people don't dare to. While you were telephoning, I
saw our school principal, and he said you were a Vi-
king and all kinds of——"

"Here! Now! You! Quit! Stop! Wait! A lot of people, especially on newspapers, give me a lot of taffy
just because I can drive fast. What I need is someone
like you to make me realize what a roughneck I am."

She looked at him clear-eyed, and pondered: "I'm
afraid most of the Apogee boys think I'm rather
prim."

"They would! That's why they're stuck in Apogee."
Buffum searched her eyes and speculated: "I wonder
if we aren't alike in this way: Neither of us content to
plod. Most people never think of why they're living.
They reckon and guess and s'pose that maybe some
day they'll do better, and then—bing!—they're dead.
But you and I—I seem—I've known you a long time.
Will you remember me?"

"Oh, yes. There aren't so many seventy-an-hour
people in Apogee!"

From the gate Roy Bender was bellowing: "Ready
in two minutes, boss!"

Buffum was on his feet, drawing on his gauntlets
and leather coat. She looked at him gravely, while
he urged:

"Going on. Day from now, the strain will begin to kind of get me. Will you think about me then? Will you wireless me some good thoughts?"

"Yes!"—very quietly. He yanked off his big gauntlet. He felt her hand fragile in his. Then he was gone, marching down the walk, climbing into the car, demanding of Roy: "Look over oil and battery and ev'thing?"

"You bet. We did everything," said the garage man. "Get a little rest?"

"Yes. Had a chance to sit in the shade and loaf."

"Saw you talking to Aurilla Rivers——"

Roy interrupted: "All right, all right, boss. Shoot!"

Buffum heard the garage man out:

"Fine girl, Aurilla is. Smart 's a whip. She's a real swell. Born and brought up here, too."

"Who's this that Miss Rivers is engaged to?" Buffum risked.

"Well, I guess probably she'll marry Reverend Dawson. He's a dried-up old stick but he comes from the East. Some day she'll get tired of school teaching, and he'll grab her. Marry in haste and repent at Reno, like the fellow says."

"That's right. Fix up the bill, Roy? G'by."

Buffum was off. Five minutes later he was six and three-quarters miles away. In his mind was but one thought—to make up the lost time; in his eyes was no vision save speedometer and the road that rushed toward him.

A little after dark he rumbled at Roy: "Here. Take her. Going to get some sleep." He did sleep, for an hour, then struggling into full wakefulness he dug his knuckles into his eyes like a sleepy boy, glanced at the speedometer, laid a hand on the steering wheel and snapped at Roy: "All right. Move over."

At dawn nothing existed in the world save the compulsion to keep her at top speed. The earth was shut off from him by a wall of roar and speed. He did not rouse to human feeling even when he boomed into Columbus Circle, the breaker of the record.

He went instantly to bed: slept twenty-six and one-quarter hours, then attended a dinner given to himself, and made a speech that was unusually incoherent, because all through he remembered that he was due in San Francisco in eight days. He was to sail for Japan, and a road race round the shore of Hondo. Before he returned, Aurilla Rivers would undoubtedly have married the Reverend Mr. Dawson, have gone to Cape Cod on her wedding trip. She would think only with disgust of large men with grease on their faces.

He could take one day for the trip up and back. He could get to Cape Cod more quickly by motor than by train. He was going to have one more hour with Aurilla, on his way to San Francisco. He would be more interesting to her if he could gossip of her ancestral background. He could take pictures of the place to her, and perhaps an old chair from the mansion. As he drove down Front Street, in West Harlepool, he saw the house quite as it had appeared in Aurilla's picture with the name-board of a wrecked ship over the woodshed, the *Penninah Sparrow*.

Down the road was a one-room shop with the sign "Gaius Bearse, Gen'l Merchandise. Clam Forks, Windmills, and Souvenirs." Out on the porch poked a smallish man. Buffum ambled toward him and saw that the man was very old.

"Good morning. This Cap'n Bearse?" inquired Buffum.

"I be."

"Uh, uh! Say—uh, Cap'n, can you tell me who's living in the Rivers mansion now?"

"The which mansion?"

"Rivers. The house across there."

"Huh! That's the Kendrick house."

"But it was built by a Rivers."

"No, 'twa'n't. That house was built by Cap'n Cephas. Kendricks living in it ever since. Owned now by William Dean Kendrick. He's in the wool business, in Boston, but his folks comes down every summer. I ought to know. The Kendricks are kin of mine."

"B-but where did the Riverses live?"

"The Riverses? Oh, them! Come from the West, don't ye? Spend the summer here?"

"No. What makes you think I come from the West?"

"Rivers went out there. Bradley Rivers. He the one you're thinking of?"

"Yes."

"Friend of yours——"

"No. Just happened to hear about him."

"Well, I'll tell you. There never was any Rivers family."

"What?"

"The father of this here Bradley Rivers called himself Zenas Rivers. But land, Zenas' right name was Fernao Ribeiro. He was nothing but a Portygee deckhand. Fernao, or Zenas, became a wrecker. He was a good hand in a dory, but when he was drinking, he was a caution for snakes. He come straight from the Cape Verde Islands."

"I understand Bradley Rivers' ancestors were howling aristocrats, and came over on the *Mayflower*."

"Maybe so, maybe so. Aristocrats at drinking Jamaica rum, I guess. But they didn't come on no *Mayflower*. Zenas Rivers came over on the brig *Jennie B. Smith*!"

"I understand Zenas owned this—this Kendrick House?"

"Him? Why, boy, if Zenas or Brad either ever set foot across the threshold of that house, it was to fill the wood box, or maybe sell lobsters!"

"B-but—what kind of looking man was Zenas?"

"Thick-set, dark-complected fellow—real Portygee."

"Didn't he have a Roman nose?"

"Him? Huh! Had a nose like a herring."

"But Bradley had a Roman nose. Where'd he get it?"

"From his maw. She was a Yankee, but her folks wa'n't much account. So she married Zenas. Brad Riv-

ers always was an awful liar. He came back here about
seven-eight years ago, and he boasted he was the richest man in Kansas or maybe 'twas Milwaukee."

"Did he buy a picture of the Kendrick mansion
while he was here?"

"Believe he did. He got one of these artists to paint
a picture of the Kendrick house. And he bought a
couple of things of me—a horsehair sofy, and a picture
of old Cap'n Gould that May Gould left here."

"Did—did this Captain Gould in the portrait have
a Roman nose? And side whiskers? Stern looking?"

"That's him. What's Brad been telling you, boy?"

"Nothing!" sighed Buffum. "Then Rivers was just
a plain dub? Like me?"

"Plain? Brad Rivers? Well, Zenas sent Brad to
school to Taunton for a year or so, but just the same,
we always allowed he was so ordinary that there
wa'n't a dog belonging to a Kendrick or a Bearse or
a Doane that would bite him. Ask any of the old
codgers in town."

"I will, but—thanks."

He came down from the Apogee street, inconspicuously creeping through the dust, a large, amiable man
in a derby.

He had only fifty-one minutes before the return of
the Apogee branch train to the junction to connect
with the next express westward.

He rang; he pounded at the front door; he went
round to the back; and there he discovered Aurilla's
mother, washing napkins. She looked at him over her
spectacles, and she sniffed: "Yes?"

"Do you remember I came through here recently?
Racing car? I wanted to see Miss Rivers for a moment."

"You can't. She's at school, teaching."

"When will she be back? It's four now."

"Maybe right away, maybe not till six."

His train left at four-forty-nine. He waited on the
front steps. It was four-twenty-one when Aurilla Riv-

ers came along the walk. He rushed to her, his watch in his hand, and before she could speak, he was pouring out:

" 'Member me? Darn glad! Got less 'n twenty-eight minutes before have to catch train to San Francisco steamer Japan possibly India afterwards glad to see me please oh please don't be a Rivers be Aurilla just got twenty-seven 'n' half minutes glad?"

"Why—why—ye-es——"

"Thought about me?"

"Of course."

"Ever wish I might come shooting through again?"

"You're so egotistical!"

"No, just in a hurry. Only got twenty-seven minutes more! Ever wish I'd come back? Oh—please! Can't you hear the Japan steamer whistling—calling us?"

"Japan!"

"Like to see it?"

"Terribly."

"Will you come with me? I'll have a preacher meet us on the train. If you'll phone to Detroit, find out all about me. Come! Quick! Marry me! Just twenty-six and a half more."

She could only whisper in answer: "No. I mustn't think of it. It tempts me. But Mother would never consent."

"What has your mother to do——"

"Everything! With our people, the individual is nothing, the family's sacred. I must think of Bradley Rivers, and old Zenas, and hundreds of fine old Yankees, building up something so much bigger than just one individual happiness. It's, oh, noblesse oblige!" How could he, in face of her ancestor worship, tell the truth? He burst out:

"But you'd like to? Aurilla! Just twenty-five minutes now!" He chucked his watch in his pocket. "See here. I want to kiss you. I'm going seven thousand miles away, and I can't stand it, unless—— I'm going to kiss you, there under the grape arbor!" His fingers slipped under her elbow.

She came reluctantly, appealing, "No, no, please, no!" till he swept the words away with a kiss, and in the kiss she forgot all that she had said, and clung to him, begging: "Oh, don't go away. Don't leave me here in this dead village. Stay here—catch the next steamer! Persuade Mother——"

"I must catch this one. I'm due there—big race. Come!"

"With—without clothes?"

"Buy 'em on way—San Francisco!"

"No, I mustn't. And there are others to consider besides Mother."

"Mr. Dawson? Really care for him?"

"He's very gentle and considerate and really such a good scholar. Mother wants Mr. Dawson to get a pastorate on Cape Cod, and she thought that way I might pick up with the old threads, and be a real Rivers again. As Mrs. Dawson, I could find the old house and all——" She was interrupted by his two hands behind her shoulders, by his eyes searching hers with a bitter honesty.

"Don't you ever get tired of ancestors?" he cried.

"I do not! Whatever I may be—they were splendid. Once in a mutiny on the clipper that he was commanding, Zenas Rivers——"

"Dear, there wasn't any Zenas Rivers. He was a Portuguese immigrant named Ribeiro, Fernao Ribeiro. The picture there in the house is a Captain Gould."

She had slipped from his embrace. But he went steadily on, trying with eyes and voice to make her understand his tenderness:

"Old Zenas was a squat, dark chap, a wrecker, and not very nice. The first real aristocrat in your family is you."

"Wait! You mean that—that it wasn't any of it true? But the Rivers' mansion?"

"There isn't any. The house in the picture has always belonged to the Kendricks. I've just been on Cape Cod, and I found——"

"It isn't true? Not any of it, about the Rivers——"

"None of it. I didn't mean to tell you. If you don't believe me, you can write."

"Oh, don't! Wait!" She turned, looked to the right. He remembered that down the street to the right was a rise of ground with a straggly village cemetery. She murmured:

"Poor Dad! I loved him, oh, so much, but—I know Dad told fibs. But never to harm people. Just because he wanted us to be proud of him. Mr.—what is your name?"

"Buffum."

"Come."

He followed her swift steps into the house, into the room of the shrined portraits. She looked from "Zenas Rivers" to the sketch of the "Rivers' Mansion." She patted the glass over her father's photograph. She blew the dust from her fingers. She sighed: "It smells musty in here, so musty!" She ran to the mahogany chest of drawers and took out a sheet of parchment. On it, he saw, was a coat of arms. She picked up a pencil, turned over the parchment, and drew a flying motor car.

She turned and thrust the sketch at him, crying: "There's the coat of arms of the family to come, the crest of a new aristocracy that knows how to work!" With a solemnity that wasn't solemn at all, he intoned: "Miss Rivers, would you mind marrying me, somewhere between here and California?"

"Yes"—he kissed her—"if you can make"—she kissed him—"Mother understand. She has friends and a little money. She can get along without me. But she believes the aristocracy fable."

"May I lie to her?"

"Why, once might be desirable."

"I'll tell her my mother was a Kendrick of Harlepool, and I'll be terribly top-lofty, but in a hurry—especially the hurry! Just got thirteen minutes now!"

From the hall sounded Mrs. Rivers' petulant voice: "Aurilly!"

"Y-yes, Mother?"

"If you and that man are going to catch the train, you better be starting."

"W-w-why," Aurilla gasped; then, to Buffum: "I'll run right up and pack my bag."

"It's all 'tended to, Aurilly. Minute I saw that dratted man coming again, I knew he'd be in a hurry. But I do think you might let me know my son-in-law's name before you go. You only got eleven minutes. You better hurry—hurry—hurry!"

The Hack Driver

I dare say there's no man of large affairs, whether he is bank president or senator or dramatist, who hasn't a sneaking love for some old rum-hound in a frightful hat, living back in a shanty and making his living by ways you wouldn't care to examine too closely. (It was the Supreme Court Justice speaking. I do not pretend to guarantee his theories or his story.) He may be a Maine guide, or the old garageman who used to keep the livery stable, or a perfectly useless innkeeper who sneaks off to shoot ducks when he ought to be sweeping the floors, but your pompous big-city man will contrive to get back and see him every year, and loaf with him, and secretly prefer him to all the highfalutin leaders of the city.

There's that much truth, at least, to this Open Spaces stuff you read in advertisements of wild and woolly Western novels. I don't know the philosophy of it; perhaps it means that we retain a decent simplicity, no matter how much we are tied to Things, to houses and motors and expensive wives. Or again it may give away the whole game of civilization; may mean that the apparently civilized man is at heart nothing but a hobo who prefers flannel shirts and bristly cheeks and cussing and dirty tin plates to all the trim, hygienic, forward-looking life our women-folks make us put on for them.

When I graduated from law school I suppose I was about as artificial and idiotic and ambitious as most youngsters. I wanted to climb, socially and financially. I wanted to be famous and dine at large houses with men who shuddered at the Common People who don't dress for dinner. You see, I hadn't learned that the only thing duller than a polite dinner is the conversation afterward, when the victims are digesting the dinner and accumulating enough strength to be able to play bridge. Oh, I was a fine young calf! I even planned a rich marriage. Imagine then how I felt when, after taking honors and becoming fifteenth assistant clerk in the magnificent law firm of Hodgins, Hodgins, Berkman and Taupe, I was set not at preparing briefs but at serving summonses! Like a cheap private detective! Like a mangy sheriff's officer! They told me I had to begin that way and, holding my nose, I feebly went to work. I was kicked out of actresses' dressing rooms, and from time to time I was righteously beaten by large and indignant litigants. I came to know, and still more to hate, every dirty and shadowy corner of the city. I thought of fleeing to my home town, where I could at once become a full-fledged attorney-at-law. I rejoiced one day when they sent me out forty miles or so to a town called New Mullion, to serve a summons on one Oliver Lutkins. This Lutkins had worked in the Northern Woods, and he knew the facts about a certain timberland boundary agreement. We needed him as a witness, and he had dodged service.

When I got off the train at New Mullion, my sudden affection for sweet and simple villages was dashed by the look of the place, with its mud-gushing streets and its rows of shops either paintless or daubed with a sour brown. Though it must have numbered eight or nine thousand inhabitants, New Mullion was as littered as a mining camp. There was one agreeable-looking man at the station—the expressman. He was a person of perhaps forty, red-faced, cheerful, thick; he wore his overalls and denim jumper as though they belonged to him, he was quite dirty and very friendly and you knew at once he liked people and slapped them on the back out of pure easy affection.

"I want," I told him, "to find a fellow named Oliver Lutkins."

"Him? I saw him 'round here 'twan't an hour ago. Hard fellow to catch, though—always chasing around on some phony business or other. Probably trying to get up a poker game in the back of Fritz Beinke's harness shop. I'll tell you, boy—— Any hurry about locating Lutkins?"

"Yes. I want to catch the afternoon train back." I was as impressively secret as a stage detective.

"I'll tell you. I've got a hack. I'll get out the bone-shaker and we can drive around together and find Lutkins. I know most of the places he hangs out."

He was so frankly friendly, he so immediately took me into the circle of his affection, that I glowed with the warmth of it. I knew, of course, that he was drumming up business, but his kindness was real, and if I had to pay hack fare in order to find my man, I was glad that the money would go to this good fellow. I got him down to two dollars an hour; he brought from his cottage, a block away, an object like a black piano-box on wheels.

He didn't hold the door open, certainly he didn't say "Ready, sir." I think he would have died before calling anybody "sir." When he gets to Heaven's gate he'll call St. Peter "Pete," and I imagine the good saint will like it. He remarked, "Well, young fellow, here's the handsome equipage," and his grin—well, it made me feel that I had always been his neighbor. They're so ready to help a stranger, those villagers. He had already made it his own task to find Oliver Lutkins for me.

He said, and almost shyly: "I don't want to butt in on your private business, young fellow, but my guess is that you want to collect some money from Lutkins—he never pays anybody a cent; he still owes me six bits on a poker game I was fool enough to get

into. He ain't a bad sort of a Yahoo but he just naturally hates to loosen up on a coin of the realm. So if
you're trying to collect any money off him, we better
kind of you might say creep up on him and surround
him. If you go asking for him—anybody can tell you
come from the city, with that trick Fedora of yours—
he'll suspect something and take a sneak. If you want
me to, I'll go into Fritz Beinke's and ask for him, and
you can keep out of sight behind me."

I loved him for it. By myself I might never have
found Lutkins. Now, I was an army with reserves. In
a burst I told the hack driver that I wanted to serve
a summons on Lutkins; that the fellow had viciously
refused to testify in a suit where his knowledge of a
certain conversation would clear up everything. The
driver listened earnestly—and I was still young enough
to be grateful at being taken seriously by any man of
forty. At the end he pounded my shoulder (very pain-
fully) and chuckled: "Well, we'll spring a little surprise
on Brer Lutkins."

"Let's start, driver."

"Most folks around here call me Bill. Or Magnuson.
William Magnuson, fancy carting and hauling."

"All right, Bill. Shall we tackle this harness
shop—Beinke's?"

"Yes, jus' likely to be there as anywheres. Plays a
lot of poker and a great hand at bluffing—damn him!"
Bill seemed to admire Mr. Lutkins's ability as a scoundrel; I fancied that if he had been sheriff he would
have caught Lutkins with fervor and hanged him
with affection.

At the somewhat gloomy harness shop we descended and went in. The room was odorous with the
smell of dressed leather. A scanty sort of a man, presumably Mr. Beinke, was selling a horse collar to a
farmer.

"Seen Nolly Lutkins around today? Friend of his
looking for him," said Bill, with treacherous hearti-
ness.

Beinke looked past him at my shrinking alien self;

he hesitated and owned: "Yuh, he was in here a little while ago. Guess he's gone over to the Swede's to get a shave."

"Well, if he comes in, tell him I'm looking for him. Might get up a little game of poker. I've heard tell that Lutkins plays these here immoral games of chance."

"Yuh, I believe he's known to sit in on Authors," Beinke growled.

We sought the barber shop of "the Swede." Bill was again good enough to take the lead, while I lurked at the door. He asked not only the Swede but two customers if they had seen Lutkins. The Swede decidedly had not; he raged: "I ain't seen him, and I don't want to, but if you find him you can just collect the dollar thirty-five he owes me." One of the customers thought he had seen Lutkins "hiking down Main Street, this side of the hotel."

"Well, then," Bill concluded, as we labored up into the hack, "his credit at the Swede's being ausgewent, he's probably getting a scrape at Heinie Gray's. He's too darn lazy to shave himself."

At Gray's barber shop we missed Lutkins by only five minutes. He had just left—presumably for the poolroom. At the poolroom it appeared that he had merely bought a pack of cigarettes and gone on. Thus we pursued him, just behind him but never catching him, for an hour, till it was past one and I was hungry. Village born as I was, and in the city often lonely for good coarse country wit, I was so delighted by Bill's cynical opinions on the barbers and clergymen and doctors and draymen of New Mullion that I scarcely cared whether I found Lutkins or not.

"How about something to eat?" I suggested. "Let's go to a restaurant and I'll buy you a lunch."

"Well, ought to go home to the old woman. And I don't care much for these restaurants—ain't but four of 'em and they're all rotten. Tell you what we'll do. Like nice scenery? There's an elegant view from Wade's Hill. We'll get the old woman to put us up a lunch—she won't charge you but a half dollar, and it'd cost you that for a greasy feed at the café—and we'll go up there and have a Sunday-school picnic."

I knew that my friend Bill was not free from guile; I knew that his hospitality to the Young Fellow from the City was not altogether a matter of brotherly love. I was paying him for his time; in all I paid him for six hours (including the lunch hour) at what was then a terrific price. But he was no more dishonest than I, who charged the whole thing up to the Firm, and it would have been worth paying him myself to have his presence. His country serenity, his natural wisdom, was a refreshing bath to the city-twitching youngster. As we sat on the hilltop, looking across orchards and a creek which slipped among the willows, he talked of New Mullion, gave a whole gallery of portraits. He was cynical yet tender. Nothing had escaped him, yet there was nothing, no matter how ironically he laughed at it, which was beyond his understanding and forgiveness. In ruddy color he painted the rector's wife who when she was most in debt most loudly gave the responses at which he called the "Episcopalopian church." He commented on the boys who came home from college in "ice-cream pants," and on the lawyer who, after years of torrential argument with his wife, would put on either a linen collar or a necktie, but never both. He made them live. In that day I came to know New Mullion better than I did the city, and to love it better.

If Bill was ignorant of universities and of urban ways, yet much had he traveled in the realm of jobs. He had worked on railroad section gangs, in harvest fields and contractors' camps, and from his adventures he had brought back a philosophy of simplicity and laughter. He strengthened me. Nowadays, thinking of Bill, I know what people mean (though I abominate the simpering phrase) when they yearn over "real he-men."

We left that placid place of orchards and resumed the search for Oliver Lutkins. We could not find him. At last Bill cornered a friend of Lutkins and made him admit that "he guessed Oliver'd gone out to his ma's farm, three miles north."

We drove out there, mighty with strategy.

"I know Oliver's ma. She's a terror. She's a cyclone," Bill sighed. "I took a trunk out for her once, and she pretty near took my hide off because I didn't treat it like it was a crate of eggs. She's somewheres about nine feet tall and four feet thick and quick's a cat, and she sure manhandles the Queen's English. I'll bet Oliver has heard that somebody's on his trail and he's sneaked out there to hide behind his ma's skirts. Well, we'll try bawling her out. But you better let me do it, boy. You may be great at Latin and geography, but you ain't educated in cussing."

We drove into a poor farmyard; we were faced by an enormous and cheerful old woman. My guardian stockily stood before her and snarled, "Remember me? I'm Bill Magnuson, the expressman. I want to find your son Oliver. Friend of mine here from the city's got a present for him."

"I don't know anything about Oliver and I don't want to," she bellowed.

"Now you look here. We've stood for just about enough plenty nonsense. This young man is the attorney general's provost, and we got legal right to search any and all premises for the person of one Oliver Lutkins."

Bill made it seem terrific, and the Amazon seemed impressed. She retired into the kitchen and we followed. From the low old range, turned by years of heat into a dark silvery gray, she snatched a sadiron, and she marched on us, clamoring, "You just search all you want to—providin' you don't mind getting burnt to a cinder!" She bellowed, she swelled, she laughed at our nervous retreat.

"Let's get out of this. She'll murder us," Bill groaned and, outside: "Did you see her grin? She was making fun of us. Can you beat that for nerve?"

I agreed that it was lese majesty.

We did, however, make adequate search. The cot-

tage had but one story. Bill went round it, peeking in
at all the windows. We explored the barn and the
stable; we were reasonably certain that Lutkins was
not there. It was nearly time for me to catch the afternoon train, and Bill drove me to the station. On the
way to the city I worried very little over my failure to
find Lutkins. I was too absorbed in the thought of
Bill Magnuson. Really, I considered returning to New
Mullion to practice law. If I had found Bill so deeply
and richly human might I not come to love the yet
uncharted Fritz Beinke and the Swede barber and a
hundred other slow-spoken, simple, wise neighbors? I
saw a candid and happy life beyond the neat learnings
of universities' law firms. I was excited, as one who
has found a treasure.

But if I did not think much about Lutkins, the office
did. I found them in a state next morning; the suit
was ready to come to trial; they had to have Lutkins;
I was a disgrace and a fool. That morning my eminent
career almost came to an end. The Chief did everything but commit mayhem; he somewhat more than
hinted that I would do well at ditch-digging. I was
ordered back to New Mullion, and with me they sent
an ex-lumber-camp clerk who knew Lutkins. I was
rather sorry, because it would prevent my loafing
again in the gorgeous indolence of Bill Magnuson.

When the train drew in at New Mullion, Bill was
on the station platform, near his dray. What was curious was that the old dragon, Lutkins's mother, was
there talking to him, and they were not quarreling
but laughing.

From the car steps I pointed them out to the
lumber-camp clerk, and in young hero-worship I murmured: "There's a fine fellow, a real man."

"Meet him here yesterday?" asked the clerk.

"I spent the day with him."

"He help you hunt for Oliver Lutkins?"

"Yes, he helped me a lot."

"He must have! He's Lutkins himself!"

But what really hurt was that when I served the

summons Lutkins and his mother laughed at me as though I were a bright boy of seven, and with loving solicitude they begged me to go to a neighbor's house and take a cup of coffee.

"I told 'em about you, and they're dying to have a look at you," said Lutkins joyfully. "They're about the only folks in town that missed seeing you yesterday."

He Had a Brother

It was the familiar morning guilt, the old-fashioned evangelical American sense of guilt, which oppressed Haddon even more than the anguish beating in his temples, the rancid taste in his mouth, the dryness of his hands. He could not escape; he had to admit that on the evening before he had again played the fool. But as long as possible he protected his aching mind from reviewing the especial sorts of idiocy he had committed, while he tried to protect his body—curious racked body that once had lived so peacefully and sweetly with him—from the tortures of every light-ray, every yammer of the street.

He smoothed his pillow; he beat it as though it were an enemy. In his temporary insanity of a hang-over he sat up and banged it with his fists. Then he collapsed against its cool smoothness and tried to find surcease from the agony of going on living.

He could not hide, even in the pillow's tolerance from last evening's folly—along with a few recollections of other evenings the past week. Was it possible that he, this decent, well-meaning Charles Haddon lying here, had got into a brawl with that filthy little bounder, Jalmers, had offered to fight him, had wept and gone on demanding a fight, while the other guests laughed at him and sneered?

Slowly, but inescapably as fire creeping into the cotton-wool that was his brain, he remembered standing in the butler's pantry of his host, offering to help mix another cocktail and having his help contemptuously refused; trying to fish an olive from a bottle, dropping the bottle and hearing it smash; hearing the hostess say, "Oh, it doesn't *matter*!" in a way which indicated that it did matter; and all the time weeping, "Jalmers insulted my bes' frien'. I'm going smash 'is face."

And who was it that had snapped, "Oh, do shut up"?

He felt cold to remember how many people had made that suggestion last evening. It seemed thousands.

Right now, at serene and sober breakfast tables, they were probably talking about him and saying, "Drinking himself to death."

Thank heaven, Micky McShea had taken him away from——

Now where the deuce had all this been, this party where he had rowed with Jalmers? Oh, yes, at Mrs. Oscala's. He remembered—his body motionless, his head still motionless in the depths of the pillow but his brain whirling like a propeller—that Micky and he had gone up to Mrs. Oscala's for a drink after the theater.

Neither of them had been too sober. There had been such a convenient drug store next door to the theater, a drug store that dealt in sodas, magazines, gin, and cannibal sandwiches, and possibly even in drugs. (For it is not true that there are no New York drug stores which handle drugs. I know several.)

And they had panhandled a drink from a friend's flask between acts.

He groaned. He, the highly respectable Mr. Charles Haddon, attorney, of the eminent New York firm of Arnault, Vexler and Haddon, had at forty-two become as much a panhandler as any hobo on the road. He had almost begged that fellow for a drink. And he was rather sure, now, that Micky and he had intruded upon Mrs. Oscala's party—that he would never again be invited to her gold-scarlet-purple-onyx-black-glass apartment.

How dry his mouth was!

And after Mrs. Oscala's, just where had they gone?

He realized that he did not know. The last he remembered was lacrimously shaking hands with little Jalmers, and being forgiven. Well! He was, for five seconds, almost proud. After all this, he had taken hold of himself and got himself home, had somehow performed the drunk's familiar miracle of mountain-climbing up into a taxi, giving the driver an address, paying him, getting himself through the lobby of his hotel and into the elevator, undressing himself and decently going to bed.

It was just then that Charles Haddon realized that—no hope!—he could not go back to sleep, however much his dizzy brain and shaky body wailed for it. He must face the new day's judicial realization of his idiocy.

And he realized that he had not, after all, undressed himself quite so neatly as he had believed. His trembly hand crept out and discovered that he was clad not in pajamas but in his undergarments, his socks and his dress trousers—he knew they were dress trousers as his fingers crept down the double braid at the trousers-seam.

He sat bolt up. He was perplexed to see that he had not gone to bed in his bedroom but in the living-room of his suite at the Hotel Shropshire—the hotel where he had made a pretense of making a home ever since his wife had divorced him with an amiable and excoriating Paris divorce. Hm! He must have been even drunker than he had thought, to have fallen asleep here. He must——

And then Mr. Charles Haddon, of Arnault, Vexler and Haddon, attorneys at law, discovered that he was in a strange room, in an absolutely strange flat, partly undressed, lying on a couch, with a silken coverlet thrown over him. He hadn't the filmiest notion where he was, how he had got there. Had he passed out at Mrs. Oscala's? Was he still there? No. Her drawing-room was all "modernistic," galloping triangles and hysterical brass, while this room was serene with white paneling and old Chippendale.

He threw his legs over the side of the couch, gripping his forehead to keep it from bursting with sudden agony, and wrapped the coverlet around his silly undershirted shoulders. There was no one to be seen, no sound anywhere from whatever unknown rooms might stretch beyond. Was it night or day?

The damask curtains were drawn at the tall windows at the end of the long room, but a gap let in a pallid light like that of early morning. Haddon groped for his watch, in the evening waistcoat which lay in a messy heap with his dress shirt, his coat and collar and tie and one shoe, in a disdainful wing-chair beside the couch. It was only seven. Thank the Lord! He could escape before his unknown host came in.

He would have given a great sum for a long cold glass of water, for the chance to wash his stinging eyes, but he dared not prowl. Why! The owner of the apartment might not even know he was here! In his drunken somnambulism he might have come here after the owner had gone to bed. Staggering, groaning a little, he huddled into his wrinkled dress shirt, with a red wine stain across it, and, puffing, sat down to draw on his shoes.

He did not know how to find his way out of the apartment. There were three doors to the room. He decided on the door at the other end from the windows, but he stood before it uneasily for half a minute. Suppose it should open on a bedroom and a startled host—a frightened host reaching for a revolver—a screaming woman?

He edged the door open with hands nervous as snakes. Cheers! It led to a corridor and what must be the outer door. Creeping past closed doors behind which he imagined scores of enemies, he bolted into the vestibule and, as the elevator came to his ringing, he felt safe.

But, glancing into the elevator mirror, he almost snarled at his image—Charles Haddon, the immaculate, in wrinkled dress coat, streaked shirt-front, at seven of a June morning. And the elevator-runner seemed doubtful; the hallman in the pretentious Moorish-Gothic-Chinese lobby below almost stopped him. With a feeling of being reprieved from execution, Haddon scrambled through the bronze-proud doors, and into a taxi.

Then he faced his thoughts.

He told himself—no Salvation Army brigadier could have done it better—exactly how many kinds of a blasted fool he had been. But he had done that before, a good many times. Now there was a new agitation in him. If he had, he warned himself, actually so passed out that he had gone, or had been taken, to a strange apartment in his stupor, what else might he not have done? Why! He might have awakened this morning in a police cell, charged with murder; might have killed with no memory of it.

He shuddered. Then: "I've been saying I ought to go on the water wagon. No 'going to go on it' now! I'm *on* it, right this minute! Scared not to be. No tapering off! Quit cold! Not another drink, not one, for——"

All the way to his hotel he argued it out: whether to be dry for a week, for a month, or forever. With a gloating feeling of having accomplished vast victories, he fixed on three months.

It was much easier to be firm in his mind about the three months than about this same morning. All through his edifying resolves he was aching, "I wish I had a drink right now!" It was hard to keep from feeling for his pocket-flask to see if that useful object, empty before nine last evening, hadn't perhaps miraculously filled itself. But in a glow, ignoring the way in which the servants in the Hotel Shropshire lobby tried to ignore the spectacle of a guest arriving in soiled evening clothes at seven-thirty in the morning, he went up to his apartment and crawled righteously under a cold shower.

It hurt.

Feeling better, he tramped to the ice-box in his kitchenette and inaugurated his new life of temperance by having two stiff whisky-and-sodas, shuddering as they brought him to life again, changed him from an abject Mr. Hyde to a complacent Dr. Jekyll. He managed to keep from hearing his own scornful remarks to himself, and he was able to drink a cup of coffee and eat half of a fried egg without feeling sick—not very sick.

He was even able, after reading the newspaper, including the want ads and the summer-resort advertisements, to dress and go to the office and arrive there only an hour late.

By twelve, when he had had two more drinks—sneaking them down in the wash-room of the office—he was radiant enough to explain that he really wasn't a dirty dog and a traitor to himself and to his honor to take these drinks. He pointed out, as though he were judge, jury, and attorney for the defense all in one, that of course he had never for a second, in "going on the water wagon," meant to include today. Naturally, he couldn't! Not feeling the way he did after last night! But starting tomorrow—absolutely, and for three straight months!

And at twelve o'clock he convinced himself again that it was entirely due to Prohibition and to having been divorced by his wife that he, the Charles Haddon who ten years ago had never been drunk in his life, had taken to hiding himself from the boredom of living in the pink clouds of alcohol.

And at twelve he telephoned to Micky McShea, his companion of the disastrous evening before.

They were curious friends, Haddon and Micky, and very good ones. Neither they nor anyone else understood why. Haddon was reticent, smartly dressed, grave, given to learned books, rather a snob, not very popular, an excellent corporation lawyer, and a hater of any sport more vigorous than motoring.

Micky McShea, otherwise Mr. Vincent Carruthers Van Valkenberg McShea, Princeton 1906, polo star and tennis champion till he had grown too fat and short-winded, inheritor and president of the exalted Rio and Eastern Importing Company, was the darling of any not-too-high-brow gathering. He knew all the off-color stories that had ever been told. His laugh was like subway blasting, and the liquor that was a lust, a longing and a torment to Charles Haddon was apparently only an agreeable tickler to Mick McShea.

About the only things that they had in common were their clubs, their mild wealth and the fact that both had been divorced by their wives with Whisky named as correspondent.

Haddon and Micky were not uncommonly agreeable to each other. At bridge, their remarks on overbidding would have caused a shooting, in the more correct days of Cripple Creek. Yet they were together almost every evening, and the only time when Micky became more violent than in his abuse of Haddon was when someone else dared to hint that he didn't like Haddon's vocabulary or his wrist watch. (Haddon wore a wrist watch. Micky didn't. But then, Micky had been only a major of artillery on the Western Front in the war, whereas Haddon had talked strongly about going into the intelligence department, if the war lasted till 1920 or so.)

When the psychologists have finally explained why men go to war, why men rave over one feminine nose and abhor another of precisely the same dimensions and pinkiness, why certain men are willing to endure the horrible limelight-soaked lack of privacy involved in being President of the United States, then they might turn to something really difficult, and explain why friends like each other.

Certainly there was nothing particularly amiable in

the address of Mr. Charles Haddon to Mr. Micky McShea on the telephone:

"Say, where did you get to last night, anyway?"

And Micky sounded as though he were addressing a debtor:

"Yuh, and a fine guy you were! Oh, Lord, what a hang-over I had this morning!"

"Say, where did we go after—— Uh, doing anything for lunch?"

"Certainly not!" growled Micky. "Suppose anybody that's decent would be seen with me when they know I run around with you? Meet you at the Bond Club at one-fifteen. Try to stay sober till then!"

At one-twenty, when Haddon arrived at the club, he had a private snifter in the wash-room.

At one-twenty-five, when Micky arrived, he invited Haddon to have a drink, and Haddon, after being peculiarly snooty about "drinking so early in the day," accepted the invitation—twice. Then they looked happy and slightly vague.

They lunched beside the half-block of windows in their peculiarly American sort of club, more American than sugar-corn or Will Rogers: the twenty-second story of a skyscraper looking down on North River, with tugs streaking across the harbor and freighters for Singapore and Saloniki trudging out to sea.

"Say, just where did we go after Mrs. Oscala's last night, Micky? To tell you the truth, I'm a little hazy."

Micky looked at him pityingly. For so plump and ruddy-faced and glossily bald a man, with his hectic striped scarf and his too-well-cut waistcoat, Micky sounded almost tender. "You poor kid, you did get it bad! Don't you remember at all?"

"Of course I do!" testily. "But there's some details——"

"Don't you remember that Grout, the admiralty lawyer, was at Mother Oscala's, and he and Mrs. Grout were going home same time we were, and you insisted on their taking us up to their place on Park Avenue and giving us another drink? They didn't cotton to the idea much, but they took us along, and you said that if Grout had his rights, he'd be Chief Justice of the Supreme Court, and then you said his gin was rotten—as it was!—and then you tried to make love to Mrs. Grout, and you said you were a little tired and wanted to lie down for just a second, and you passed out, blam!

"When we tried to get you up, you wanted to fight the whole bunch of us. You said Grout was a 'dirty little ambulance-chasing shyster.' We finally had to let you stay there on the couch, and me—oh, golly, I wasn't any too sober, myself!—I came home.

"Now listen, kid. The Grouts were awful nice about it. They knew you were drunk and not responsible. But same time— Mind you, I guess I've drunk as much hard liquor as most people in this town, and from *temps* to *temps*, as we say in Paris, I've tried to lick taxi-drivers. But same time, old boy, you've got to stop——"

Haddon did not hear Micky's temperance lecture. He was still with horror and self-hatred. Judge Grout, though not at all a teetotaler, was a dignified, restrained, rather irritable pundit who belonged to the Century Club and St. Thomas' Church; he was precisely the kind whose murmurs could turn Charles Haddon from a respectable and responsible attorney into a gutter-rat—into such a gutter-rat as he had felt himself to be at seven that morning.

All that afternoon he did not have a drink—oh, except the one or two that his twitchy nerves demanded before he could talk to weighty clients.

At five-thirty he bravely decided not to go to the cocktail party given by Judge Rigadon (the one who gave those dreadfully stiff sentences to bootleggers). In fact, he went home and lonely though he found that brocaded barrenness of a hotel apartment, he endured it for several minutes, and so he did not arrive at Judge Rigadon's cocktail party till almost six-thirty.

There he met a lawyer friend, Dick Souter, who was giving a party at the Vraie Vivienne night club, and——

Next morning, at ten o'clock, Charles Haddon awoke to discover that he was lying in dinner clothes across his bed—his own, this time—and to recall, between gripes of nausea and pangs of headache, that the night before he had tried to fight a waiter at the night club, that Dick Souter had said to him, "For heaven's sake, will you shut up, Haddon?" and that in a state of hurt and noble dignity he had wavered through the miles and leagues, the forests and hills and wide-flung steppes of the night club, and gone home.

But this time Haddon made no good resolutions. Neither did he try to go to the office. "I'm licked. I've got to do something," he muttered.

He made, now, no pretense of being lightly able to "go on the water wagon." He was frightened. He had a bromide, a high-ball, not as things he wanted but as horrible drugs for a sick man.

"Licked! Got to have someone to help me!"

It was June, and business at the firm was light. It was June, and in his boyhood town, Glen Western, there were meadows to quiet sick nerves. And in Glen Western was his brother, Ed Haddon.

He had not seen Ed for three years.

Ed was not, like Charles Haddon, a "success." He was the village druggist, and he had married Mildred Brown—you know Mildred Brown, the daughter of the conductor on the Ragusa and Alfalalfa branch of the N.Y.C.? But Ed, Charles suddenly remembered, was the steadiest, honestest, soberest man living. Dirty shame he hadn't had Ed come down to New York for so long now!

With a not quite sane haste, his hand twitching, Haddon gave a long-distance call for Glen Western and for Mr. Ed Haddon. While awaiting it, he called his office, announced to the chief that he felt a little sick, that he was going away for a week, and that there was nothing on the cards that couldn't be handled by young Rufus Early.

With hot cheeks he imagined how the chief, old

Arnault, would worry, and how that young beast Early would snicker about Haddon's "sickness." But——

Oh, hang 'em all! Better to be a little ridiculous than to be dead, as he would be, soon, if this kept up! And he was not coming back in a week. Perhaps never! Perhaps a year from now he would be a country attorney in Glen Western, a plodding, dusty fellow, but sane again and decent and kind.

Then on the telephone was Mildred, his sister-in-law, saying, "Why, that would be real nice if you could come. Oh, yes, sure, you bet, lots of room. Ed's off today, fishing at Purgis Lake. Yes, we'll be real glad to have you. I'll meet you with the car at the seven-sixteen."

He had the whole picture of the village street, the peace of maples, the friendliness of little stores and white houses with comfortable lawns, the smell of lake-breezes, the companionship of home-town boys who called him not Mr. Haddon or Charles or Charlie, but Chuck.

He was disappointed that Ed and Mildred no longer lived in the Grampa Haddon house, with the old "natural wood" rockers on the broad porch and the patchy lawn with a twine hammock between two box-elders. Their new house was a stuccoed bungalow, smelling of varnish and mail-order rugs, and instead of the slovenly, good-natured old porch, it had a perky little stoop with red-tiled flooring and four stiff wicker chairs.

As they drove up to the bungalow, Mildred said smugly, "You see, even poor *we* haven't done so *badly,* after *all!*"

Though he had been hysterically glad to see her dependable round face at the station, he disliked her then, and he disliked heartily the guest-room with its mean air of a hospital.

But in the June evening, after a supper of fresh fried pike and tea biscuits and scalloped potatoes and floating island, which tickled him with its memory of boyhood, as they sat out on the stoop there was a smell of unlaundered grass, a rustle of water from neighborhood hoses, a soft whir of motor tires on the dirt road and the immemorial village sound of dogs idly barking. It was utter peace. It was his boyhood. It was the revival of the boy, Charles Haddon, who had been so ambitious and studious and untempted . . . And he definitely did not want a drink!

Then he heard New York.

In town, he had been too habituated to it to hear it. Now, in its absence, his ears suddenly caught the whole bedlam that for years had assailed him— elevated, clacking feet, river horns, insane riveters, voices indignant or boisterous or whining, and the harsh *grrrrrr* sound which motor tires made on hard pavements all day, all night, dawn and noon, noon and twilight. And he was safe from it! He was here!

They had been talking as becomes Home Folks.

"Say, what ever became of that Bill Tyler that used to be the implement dealer?" and, "Do you ever hear from Cousin Myron?" and, "I guess Old Man Warman must be pretty well fixed by now." These dronings had protected the kindred strangers one from another.

Now, as the village silence suddenly roared at Charles, he cried, "You don't know how nice it is to be here with you! New York has, uh—— Well, it's kind of got on my nerves. You know. Overwork, and hard to sleep nights with all the racket and—— But here I feel like a new human being, already."

With no defiance but with an infinite sisterly kindness, Mildred patted his arm. Ed, lounging against the stuccoed wall, stalked over to pat his shoulder.

Mildred murmured, "You poor darling! It must be terrible to fight the city all the time. Well, we want you to rest. We can't give you much in the amusement line, but we'll be awful glad if you find you can rest in our little home and—and you needn't get up till half past eight! If the girl is too busy, I'll fry you an egg for breakfast."

Then they talked almost as frankly as though they were not related.

Mostly it was Charles Haddon who talked. He had been longing for a father confessor. He had been ashamed to tell his troubles to that Micky McShea who went nightly through as arduous campaigns in the crusade for pleasure as himself, but came out of them with a Turkish-bath pinkiness and glow.

The ears of Ed and Mildred almost creaked with intentness as he bewailed the strain of city life: office politics, the demands of clients, the competition, the horrible expensiveness. He had very little to say about drinking and exactly nothing to say about finding himself in strange gutters at awakening, but it was clear enough, even to the innocence of Glen Western, that he had—oh, just now and then—found relief in a stray cocktail when the stress had been too great.

With the delight of the godly in the presence of sin, they snapped at this agreeable hint of scandal.

"Guess you people in the city do quite a lot of boozing, sometimes, don't you?" Ed urged.

He lost all caution and poured out. "Too cursed much altogether!" He might have been warned by their soft gurgles of delight at discovering the clay feet of their bronze brother, but recklessly he burned on:

"Of course I'm temperate. Take mighty good care not to drink too much. But same time—— Oh, you can scarcely realize the tempo of the city. It *gets* you! And there's evenings when you've worked so hard all day that you haven't one ounce of strength left, when you're shaky with tiredness, and yet you have a frightfully important date for the evening. You'd give your left leg to be able to go to bed. And then, of course, a few cocktails keep you going."

"A few?" Ed groaned happily. "Do folks ever take more than one cocktail? Golly! Wouldn't want to tamper with *my* health that way!"

Just then the first neighbor arrived, to inspect the returned prodigal and look for the signs of husks in his hair. Charles was relieved to have the talk rescued from peril and turned into such familiar security as, "Well, Chuck, guess it feels pretty good to be back in a real town again, hey?" and, "Say, remember the time when Hal Evans licked you and you went home crying?"

Actually, Charles Haddon had not recalled that amiable incident for twenty-five years. Now he blushed and felt irritated—felt inferior to the Glen Western against which he had rebelled as a passionate, nervous child. But these smarting recollections were safer than the confession to which, he felt, he had almost been betrayed.

They talked on, the Haddons and intermittent neighbors, till a very late hour, almost till the bawdy hour of eleven, a full hour later than Ed Haddon's decent normal bedtime; talked on the porch, with the serene lights of village homes among lilac bushes and the maples. In the morning Charles slept till nine. He had awakened only to the sounds of cock-crow, of a train whistle far off in the gap of the hills, and these pleasant murmurs had been but assurances of regained security, of the miracle of turning from a nerve-tortured wreck into an eager boy again.

He tramped, he fished, he slept under trees. If there was no particular spice in the conversation at Ed Haddon's table, there was no jabbing worry. Now, when Mildred, as she would put it, "took little digs at him," he was amused.

He won another fortnight's leave from the office. He dropped, as though New York were but a myth and a passing dream, into the old relations with such of his boyhood friends as had not gone off to Buffalo, Schenectady, to the corn lands of the West. And so it chanced that after a week when he had drunk nothing save rare, secret, shamed nips from the one quart of Scotch which he had brought from New York and which he had concealed behind the radiator in his room, he fell into Glen Western's version of a High Whoopee.

The same Hal Evans who had once sent him home bawling was now become Mr. H. Everett Evans, attorney surveyor and agent for the Bristol and Buenos Aires

Assurance Co., Inc. But Hal had remained the village terror. "People say he drinks!" the village whispered.

Hal was, in fact, in his one lone bald self, the Monte Carlo, the Montmartre, the Broadway, of Glen Western. He had to work hard, in a village so sinless and so interested in sin, but he had by some magnificence kept up his position of Satan in Paradise, and he was proud of it, and they were proud of him for it.

When Charles Haddon arrived, this village terror of an Evans was away. The populace credited him with being occupied with purple orgies in the Roman splendors of Buffalo, though actually he was trying to persuade the farmers of Cattaraugus County to take out lightning insurance.

But when H. Everett returned, he bustled to Charles and he whispered, "Saaaaaay, boy, it's good to have a live one in this burg again! Say, I'll bet the I-Knew-Him-When Club have been calling you 'Chuck'! Well, say, you certainly are 'Charlie' to me, and no mean cracks about it, either! And tonight we throw a party!"

They did, and after this wise was the party.

It was composed of Mr. H. Everett Evans, Mr. Charles Haddon of New York, Mr. Hap Macbeth, undertaker and dealer in Fine Furniture, Mr. Pete Gallup, dealer in Shoes, Hats and Gents' Furnishings, and Mr. Mort Wheeler, motor agent and part proprietor of Ye Olde Glen Western Inn. First, as was proper, they bought two prescriptions from Doc Engel for two dollars apiece. In the interests of conviviality the doc knocked off fifty cents on each prescription, and he hinted that if his Aunt Emmy from Gowanda weren't staying with them, he cer'nly would be glad to come along and show Old Chuck a Good Time.

Since to cash in these golden prescriptions at Ed Haddon's, here in town, would be to betray their honor guest, they drove in Mr. Wheeler's second-hand sedan to the town of Melanchthon, ten miles away.

It was true that Melanchthon couldn't, as H. Everett so well said, "touch a candle to Glen Western for pep and looks." Glen Western had cement pavement on three streets, whereas Melanchthon was paved only on Main Street. And Melanchthon hadn't even a Carnegie Library, while Glen Western—as H. Everett understood it, though he himself hadn't much time to waste with books—had one of the best libraries in that part of the country.

But one thing Melanchthon did have: a drug store whose proprietor was a "real guy." He did not split his prescription rye and, unlike that holier-than-thou Ed Haddon, he was pleased to have a drink with the boys after they had procured their remedy for 'flu.

With the two pints of rye from this haven, the party drove back to Glen Western and up to the side road by the I.O.O.F. Cemetery, which was the one safe refuge for merry fellows. There they passed the two pint bottles from lip to lip, and each of them, except Charles Haddon, told again all the dirty stories he knew. And it was during this orgy that Charles was completely won to virtue.

He drank what would, in New York, have been one-tenth of an evening's ration. He told no stories, and he was not greatly diverted by those he heard. When the mad merry-andrews dropped him at the residence of Ed Haddon, he sat by himself on the porch, rejoicing that he was free of his letch for drunkenness and quarreling, equally rejoicing that Ed and Mildred would never know of this, his one last evening of debauchery.

He went to bed at a quarter after eleven—Ed and Mildred had been snoring now for an hour. He awoke at seven, glad of his clear head and the end of his madness.

Now it is fabled by travelers that the inhabitants of India, Africa, and other heathen lands without bath-tubs, luncheon clubs devoted to Service, theories of relativity and all the other blessings which we here daily enjoy, have mysterious ways of spreading news, probably by telepathy, so that five minutes after General the Honorable Sir John Spoggins, the esteemed explorer, has changed his shirt, in the jungle in N'Goynga, the incident is perfectly known in Prgzka, thirty-seven kilometers away. But it must be insisted, for the fair fame of these United States, that no jungle magic of telepathy can touch a Gopher Prairie or a Glen Western.

The party had been held in the distant reaches beside the Odd Fellows' Cemetery, from a quarter to ten to a quarter to eleven at night. And presumably there had been no great number of Pinkertons or newspaper reporters hiding there. Yet when Charles came down to breakfast at sixteen minutes after seven the next morning, Mildred looked at him with a curious, excited intentness which indicated to him that she knew all about it. She said nothing, and she said it noisily.

At eight, Charles started for the drug store, with the confiding intention of buying a pack of cigarettes. Now, from the residence of Mr. Ed Haddon to his drug store was no great distance; it was, in fact, three blocks, and in Glen Western the blocks are short and quiet. But in that small journey, old Mr. White cackled, "Guess you boys had quite a time last night"; old Mrs. Ebberle whinnied, "Well, I'm surprised to see you up so early after what happened last night"; and the Reverend Mr. Jonas, with the grass-stains on his knees, held Charles' hand in the most uncomfortable manner and lamented, "Mr. Haddon, of course I'm practically a newcomer to Glen Western. Ain't been here but two years. So I ain't one of your older friends. But brother, do you feel that you're giving the Younger Generation the Example that a City Lawyer like you had oughta?"

At the drug store, Brother Ed, after carefully ringing up the fifteen cents for the cigarettes, grunted, "Say, Charlie, I want to see you in the back room!"

Far more uncomfortable than he had ever been in arguing a case before the Supreme Court, Charles followed him into that strange den of carboys and strawboard boxes and litters of excelsior.

"Now you look here, Charlie. I ain't one to criticize anybody. 'Live and let live' is my motto. But same time, if you're going to stay with Mildred and me, you gotta act nice!"

In the hundredth of a hundredth of a second, Charles Haddon went through rather an elaborate mental picture. He saw himself telling Ed what he thought. He saw himself—but so politely!—thanking Mildred for her hospitality and catching the nine-seventeen for New York. He saw himself back in New York—and he knew that he could not go back yet, even with the protection of Micky McShea.

With no apparent hesitation he said, "Do you mean our party last night, Ed?"

"You know what I mean, all right!"

"I'm sorry, Ed. There won't be another."

If Charles Haddon had nightly indulged in Babylonian orgies, he could not have been more closely watched. He did have the sense to hasten home and get rid of his now empty bottle of Scotch. He hid it on a beam over the furnace in the cellar. He knew, in the next two days, that Ed and Mildred were searching his room.

His notes on the Sancho case had been disturbed; his shirts, placed with his usual fussiness in the top drawer of the bureau, had been turned over. At mid-day dinner and evening supper he was sure, from the bright insect-like way in which they were watching, that Ed and Mildred were hoping to find him drunk.

And so it came to pass that because they so righteously suggested drunkenness, he wanted to be drunken.

In the illusion of returning to his boyhood, he had for certain days escaped that strain of New York and of losing his wife which had expressed itself in alcoholic insanity. He had really believed that maple trees and lilac bushes could save him from the suicide which had inarticulately been behind his every thought. But now the leering, peering expectation of Ed and Mildred brought back to him hourly the alcohol which he had tried to forget.

They were convinced that he was somehow getting those several daily cocktails of which he had indiscreetly told, and so, it must regretfully be stated, here in the propriety of Glen Western he went to the devil.

He had no great admiration for H. Everett Evans, but H. Everett was sympathetic, as only fellow sinners can be. H. Everett steered him to the county bootlegger, an immensely fat farmer who had a still behind his corn-crib. In the farmhouse kitchen, Charles sat between the pump and the rusty stove, every afternoon. It was a happy refuge.

The bootlegger, chuckling through each cell of his thick body, told of the time when his weighty wife had kept three officers at bay while he smashed every bottle in the house; he told merrily of his term in the penitentiary and how chummy he had become with the warden, and how he had made wine for the warden out of the grapes on the wall.

It was a peaceful place, and kindly. Yet every moment there, Charles Haddon felt guilty. And every moment that he was back in the righteous household of Ed and Mildred Haddon, he longed to return. Daily, either Mildred or Ed managed to remark, "Well, I guess you find it pretty slow here, but maybe if you'd try to lead a nice, decent life for a little while, it wouldn't be so bad for you, even if it ain't quite so gay as New York!"

Charles was conscious that every time he returned from the farmer-bootlegger's they were sniffing at his breath. And now a curious thing happened. He started for New York, for its peace and anonymity—he did not merely start; he fled—yet that flight took him a week.

All that had been the highly reputable and responsible Mr. Charles Haddon of New York dripped from him. He was again little Charlie Haddon, young Chuck; he was again afraid of the power and magic of his big brother Ed.

It was simple, in the end. He used one of the oldest and stalest devices in the world. He borrowed H. Everett's car, drove to Melanchthon, telephoned to his office in New York and had them telegraph to him that the office simply could not carry on without him.

He hoped, in a little-boy way, that Ed and Mildred would be impressed by the telegram with its suggestion that the entire court-system of New York State was held up for his return.

They were not.

He said good-by to them at the station with all the proper drama. He waved and shouted. He pretended to listen while they said, "Now be sure and write!" And when the dusty and acrid day-coach had rattled away, Charles Haddon fell suddenly into an abysm of terror. This for him was death. He had gone to the only refuge he knew, and it had failed him. Was he now returning to nights of idiocy and mornings of horror?

The train arrived in New York at four of the afternoon, and Charles went directly to the office of Micky McShea. He was a most respectable-looking person as he came into the brown-leather decorum of the Rio and Eastern Importing Company; a rather slight, fragile man, with a curiously high forehead; a man most correct as to boots and tie.

He waited quietly till Mr. McShea should have finished his conversation with Don Antonio Lopez of Brazil; most quietly he entered Micky's private office; most quietly he sat down in an enormous leather chair. And, still quietly, he said, "Micky, I guess I'm through. I got to drinking just about as bad, up in Glen Western. Shall I croak myself? No! I mean it! I can't go on."

And whatever quietness he displayed, it was noisy beside the stillness with which Micky McShea answered:

"Charles, I'm sorry to hear you say that. If you want to pop off, by all means do so. I could scarcely blame you, naturally! Because I've been planning to do so myself!"

"What?"

"Just that. My doc has given me six months to live if
I— Oh, you know! And I don't want to wait in the
death-house! He says I could live for maybe another
twenty years if I quit drinking, but I don't see——"
Micky's voice rose in hysteria. "I can't, Charles! I'm
gone! I might as well quit right now. I'm finished. I
might as well get it over. Nobody cares a hang. I'm——"

Charles Haddon rose, and there was nothing now
of neatness in him. His fists closed while Micky raved:

"Oh, whatzit matter? Let's go out with a bang!
Come on, Haddon, let's have li'l drink!"

From the upper left drawer of his desk, Micky produced a bottle of Scotch and flourished it wildly. Haddon snatched the bottle and coldly poured the
contents down the wash-bowl.

"Now, that's a nice thing to do!" protested Micky
feebly. "But what the deuce! I got 'nother bottle!
Don't you want drink, 'self?"

The truth was that Charles Haddon very much
wanted a drink. He had thought about it all the way
from that station.

But he said, and he almost believed it, "I do not
want a drink! I've cut it out. I told you I was drinking
up home but I decided to quit. Now come on. We're
going to get out of this."

He persuaded the protesting, almost maniacal
Micky to come with him for a taxi ride to the coolness
of Long Beach. He became more and more testy as
Micky suggested roadhouses at which they might stop.
He took Micky back to Micky's Louis Quinze au
Moins apartment, fed him crackers and milk, and put
him to bed.

When Micky was asleep, it came to Charles that he
still wanted a drink. He knew all about Micky's adequate booze cupboard. But he couldn't play a dirty
trick like that! He was going to save Micky, if it cost
him his own life.

For a fortnight, the first fortnight in five years,
Charles Haddon drank no alcohol whatever, though

he felt that he needed it in the stress of caring for Micky McShea. Micky took every advantage of being an invalid. He became insanely cunning, he sneaked, he tried to get a drink when Charles was napping, so Charles finally had to pour out every drop of that admirable cellar.

And, to be able to manhandle Micky should he really become wild, he took exercise daily, he breathed deeply, he forgot his worries about his law-practice and about his divorced wife, and devoted himself to the care of Micky.

Charles was, fortunately, not quite alone in his care for Micky. The moment he had taken Micky home from the office, he had called for the doctor. Micky's doctor, Bill Cady, M.D., was a sophisticated person who understood that a man could take a drink or let it alone, and in all probability would take it. He was a smiling, tired, jolly, exhausted man—the country doctor in New York, the man on whom all the specialists and costly surgeons battened. He had a small mustache and a steady hand.

He sat with Charles hour on hour after they had coaxed Micky into bed. Apparently he never slept, and when Micky awoke clamoring at five in the morning, Charles was able to get Doctor Cady to come around in half an hour.

With the help of the doctor, Charles had Micky in such beaming health in two weeks that he was able to forget his responsibility and to begin to think again for himself.

They sat, those two men, Charles and Doctor Cady, in Micky's apartment on an evening of early July.

"Well, I think we've got the old boy into pretty good shape now," said Charles. "In a few days I'll drive him up to New England or some place and complete the cure. And I certainly need it myself! I've been giving him my nights and days now for two weeks."

"Yeah," said the doctor.

"So have you, of course. But then, I guess that's just part of your job."

"Yeah, I guess it is," said the doctor.

"But me, of course, I'm not used to it. Well, we pulled it off! And now I'd rather like a drink myself! You see, I had to quit, in order not to show Micky a bad example. I even got rid of all his booze here. But now—I say! I could have my bootlegger here in ten minutes. Don't you think you'd like a drink? I looked in a moment ago, and Micky is sound asleep, so he won't know about it."

Doctor Cady rose from the wing-chair. He was young, and his mustache was rather unimportant, but he had the manner of one who deals with the sanctities of life and death. And said Doctor Cady, "Oh, the devil!"

"Eh?" said Charles Haddon.

"You blithering fool!" said Doctor Cady. "Haddon, I don't think I can stand it any longer," he continued. "Micky has a lot of endurance as an actor, but I haven't. Man, haven't you ever guessed—do you mean to say you've never guessed—that Micky hasn't needed me for one second, all this fortnight? That he's played at being shot to pieces so you would quit drinking yourself? That we're all of us sick and tired of trying to care for you? That the next time you call me at five in the morning, I'll kill you? Tumble to yourself, man, and quit being a blithering baby!"

Charles Haddon did four things. He managed to swallow such humiliation as he had never known. He shook hands with Micky and said only "Thanks." He went home to face his own soul, nor did he blink the smallness thereof. And he desired to take, and did not take, a drink.

He had found a brother, and for a brother one would do anything.

A Letter from the Queen

Doctor Selig was an adventurer. He did not look it, certainly. He was an amiable young bachelor with thin hair. He was instructor in history and economics in Erasmus College, and he had to sit on a foolish little platform and try to coax some fifty young men and women, who were interested only in cuddling and four-door sedans, to become hysterical about the law of diminishing returns.

But at night, in his decorous boarding house, he sometimes smoked a pipe, which was viewed as obscene in the religious shades of Erasmus, and he was boldly writing a book which was to make him famous.

Of course everyone is writing a book. But Selig's was different. It was profound. How good it was can be seen from the fact that with only three quarters of it done, it already had fifteen hundred footnotes—such lively comments as "*Vid.* J.A.S.H.S. VIII, 234 *et seq*." A real book, nothing flippant or commercialized.

It was called *The Influence of American Diplomacy on the Internal Policies of Paneuropa*.

"Paneuropa," Selig felt, "was a nice and scholarly way of saying "Europe.""

It would really have been an interesting book if Doctor Selig had not believed that all literature is excellent in proportion as it is hard to read. He had touched a world romantic and little known. Hidden in old documents, like discovering in a desert an oasis where girls laugh and fountains chatter and the market place is noisy, he found the story of Franklin, who in his mousy fur cap was the Don Juan of Paris, of Adams fighting the British Government to prevent their recognizing the Confederacy, of Benjamin Thompson, the Massachusetts Yankee who in 1791 was chief counselor of Bavaria, with the title of Count Rumford.

Selig was moved by these men who made the young America more admired than she is today. And he was moved and, in a most unscholarly way, he became a little angry as he reviewed the story of Senator Ryder.

He knew, of course, that Lafayette Ryder had prevented war between England and America in the first reign of Grover Cleveland; he knew that Ryder had been Secretary of State, and Ambassador to France, courted by Paris for his wisdom, his manners, his wit; that as Senator he had fathered (and mothered and wet-nursed) the Ryder-Hanklin Bill, which had saved our wheat markets; and that his two books, *Possibilities of Disarmament* and *The Anglo-American Empire,* were not merely glib propaganda for peace, but such inspired documents as would have prevented the Boer War, the Spanish-American War, the Great War, if there had been in his Victorian world a dozen men with minds like his. This Selig knew, but he could not remember when Ryder had died.

Then he discovered with aghast astonishment that Senator Ryder was not dead, but still alive at ninety-two, forgotten by the country he had helped to build.

Yes, Selig felt bitterly, we honor our great men in America—sometimes for as much as two months after the particular act of greatness that tickles us. But this is a democracy. We mustn't let anyone suppose that because we have given him an (undesired) parade up Broadway and a (furiously resented) soaking of publicity on March first, he may expect to be taken seriously on May second.

The Admiral Dewey whom the press for a week labeled as a combination of Nelson, Napoleon, and Chevalier Bayard, they later nagged to his grave. If a dramatist has a success one season, then may the gods help him, because for the rest of his life everyone will attend his plays only in the hope that he will fail.

But sometimes the great glad-hearted hordes of boosters do not drag down the idol in the hope of finding clay feet, but just forget him with the vast, contemptuous, heavy indifference of a hundred and twenty million people.

So felt Doctor Selig, angrily, and he planned for the end of his book a passionate resurrection of Senator Ryder. He had a shy hope that his book would appear before the Senator's death, to make him happy.

Reading the Senator's speeches, studying his pictures in magazine files, he felt that he knew him intimately. He could see, as though the Senator were in the room, that tall ease, the contrast of long thin nose, gay eyes, and vast globular brow that made Ryder seem a combination of Puritan, clown, and benevolent scholar.

Selig longed to write to him and ask—oh, a thousand things that only he could explain; the proposals of Lionel Sackville-West regarding Colombia; what Queen Victoria really had said in that famous but unpublished letter to President Harrison about the New-foundland fisheries. Why couldn't he write to him?

No! The man was ninety-two, and Selig had too much reverence to disturb him, along with a wholesome suspicion that his letter would be kicked out by the man who had once told Gladstone to go to the devil.

So forgotten was the Senator that Selig could not, at first, find where he lived. Who's Who gave no address. Selig's superior, Professor Munk, who was believed to know everything in the world except the whereabouts of his last-season's straw hat, bleated, "My dear chap, Ryder is dwelling in some cemetery! He passed beyond, if I remember, in 1901."

The mild Doctor Selig almost did homicide upon a venerable midwestern historian.

At last, in a bulletin issued by the Anti-Prohibition League, Selig found among the list of directors: "Lafayette Ryder (form. U.S. Sen., Sec'y State), West Wickley, Vermont." Though the Senator's residence could make no difference to him, that night Selig was so excited that he smoked an extra pipe of tobacco.

He was planning his coming summer vacation, during which he hoped to finish his book. The presence of the Senator drew him toward Vermont, and in an educational magazine he found the advertisement: "Sky Peaks, near Wickley, Vt., woodland nook with peace and a library—congenial and intellectual company and writers—tennis, handball, riding—nightly Sing round Old-time Bonfire—fur. bung. low rates."

That was what he wanted: a nook and a library and lots of low rates, along with nearness to his idol. He booked a fur. bung. for the summer, and he carried his suitcase to the station on the beautiful day when the young fiends who through the year had tormented him with unanswerable questions streaked off to all parts of the world and for three tremendous months permitted him to be a private human being.

When he reached Vermont, Selig found Sky Peaks an old farm, redecorated in a distressingly tea-roomy fashion. His single bungalow, formerly an honest corn-crib, was now painted robin's-egg blue with yellow trimmings and christened "Shelley." But the camp was on an upland, and air sweet from hayfield and spruce grove healed his lungs, spotted with classroom dust.

At his first dinner at Sky Peaks, he demanded of the host, one Mr. Iddle, "Doesn't Senator Ryder live somewhere near here?"

"Oh, yes, up on the mountain, about four miles south."

"Hope I catch a glimpse of him some day."

"I'll run you over to see him any time you'd like."

"Oh, I couldn't do that! Couldn't intrude!"

"Nonsense! Of course he's old, but he takes quite

an interest in the countryside. Fact, I bought this place
from him and—— Don't forget the Sing tonight."

At eight that evening Iddle came to drag Selig from
the security of his corncrib just as he was getting the
relations of the Locarno Pact and the Versailles Treaty
beautifully coördinated.

It was that kind of Sing. "The Long, Long Trail,"
and "All God's Chillun Got Shoes." (God's Chillun
also possessed coats, pants, vests, flivvers, and water-
melons interminably.) Beside Selig at the campfire sat
a young woman with eyes, a nose, a sweater, and an
athletic skirt, none of them very good or particularly
bad. He would not have noticed her, but she picked
on him:

"They tell me you're in Erasmus, Doctor Selig."

"Um."

"Real attention to character. And after all, what
benefit is there in developing the intellect if the character isn't developed to keep pace with it? You see,
I'm in educational work myself—oh, of course nothing
like being on a college faculty, but I teach history in
the Lincoln High School at Schenectady—my name is
Selma Swanson. We must have some good talks about
teaching history, mustn't we!"

"Um!" said Selig, and escaped, though it was not
till he was safely in his corncrib that he said aloud,
"We must *not!*"

For three months he was not going to be a teacher,
or heed the horrors of character-building. He was
going to be a great scholar. Even Senator Ryder might
be excited to know how powerful an intellect was
soothing itself to sleep in a corncrib four miles away!

He was grinding hard next afternoon when his host,
Iddle, stormed in with: "I've got to run in to Wickley
Center. Go right near old Ryder's. Come on. I'll intro-
duce you to him."

"Oh, no, honestly!"

"Don't be silly: I imagine he's lonely. Come on!"

Before Selig could make up his mind to get out of
Iddle's tempestuous flivver and walk back, they were

driving up a mountain road and past marble gateposts
into an estate. Through a damp grove of birches and
maples they came out on meadows dominated by an
old brick house with a huge porch facing the check-
ered valley. They stopped with a dash at the porch,
and on it Selig saw an old man sunk in a canvas deck
chair and covered with a shawl. In the shadow the
light seemed to concentrate on his bald head, like a
sphere of polished vellum, and on long bloodless
hands lying as in death on shawl-draped knees. In his
eyes there was no life nor desire for it.

Iddle leaped out, bellowing, "Afternoon, Senator!
Lovely day, isn't it? I've brought a man to call on you.
This is Mr. Selig of—uh—one of our colleges. I'll be
back in an hour."

He seized Selig's arm—he was abominably strong—
and almost pulled him out of the car. Selig's mind was
one wretched puddle of confusion. Before he could
dredge any definite thought out of it, Iddle had rattled
away, and Selig stood below the porch, hypnotized by
the stare of Senator Ryder—too old for hate or anger,
but not too old for slow contempt.

Not one word Ryder said.

Selig cried, like a schoolboy unjustly accused:

"Honestly, Senator, the last thing I wanted to do
was to intrude on you. I thought Iddle would just introduce us and take me away. I suppose he meant
well. And perhaps subconsciously I did want to intrude! I know your *Possibilities of Disarmament* and
Anglo-American Empire so well——"

The Senator stirred like an antediluvian owl awakening at twilight. His eyes came to life. One expected
him to croak, like a cynical old bird, but his still voice
was fastidious:

"I didn't suppose anyone had looked into my books
since 1910." Painful yet gracious was the gesture with
which he waved Selig to a chair. "You are a teacher?"

"Instructor in a small Ohio college. Economics and
history. I'm writing a monograph on our diplomacy,

and naturally—— There are so many things that only you could explain!"

"Because I'm so old?"

"No! Because you've had so much knowledge and courage—perhaps they're the same thing! Every day, literally, in working on my book I've wished I could consult you. For instance—— Tell me, sir, didn't Secretary of State Olney really want war with England over Venezuela? Wasn't he trying to be a tin hero?"

"No!" The old man threw off his shawl. It was somehow a little shocking to find him not in an ancient robe laced with gold, but in a crisp linen summer suit with a smart bow tie. He sat up, alert, his voice harsher. "No! He was a patriot. Sturdy. Honest. Willing to be conciliatory but not flinching. Miss Tully!"

At the Senator's cry, out of the wide fanlighted door of the house slid a trained nurse. Her uniform was so starched that it almost clattered, but she was a peony sort of young woman, the sort who would insist on brightly mothering any male, of any age, whether or not he desired to be mothered. She glared at the intruding Selig; she shook her finger at Senator Ryder, and simpered:

"Now I do hope you aren't tiring yourself, else I shall have to be ever so stern and make you go to bed. The doctor said——"

"Damn the doctor! Tell Mrs. Tinkham to bring me down the file of letters from Richard Olney, Washington, for 1895—O-l-n-e-y—and hustle it!"

Miss Tully gone, the Senator growled, "Got no more use for a nurse than a cat for two tails! It's that mutton-headed doctor, the old fool! He's seventy-five years old, and he hasn't had a thought since 1888. Doctors!"

He delivered an address on the art of medicine with such vigorous blasphemy that Selig shrank in horrified admiration. And the Senator didn't abate the blazing crimson of his oration at the entrance of his secretary, Mrs. Tinkham, a small, narrow, bleached, virginal widow.

Selig expected her to leap off the porch and commit suicide in terror. She didn't. She waited, she yawned gently, she handed the Senator a manila envelope, and gently she vanished.

The Senator grinned. "She'll pray at me tonight! She daren't while you're here. There! I feel better. Good cussing is a therapeutic agent that has been forgotten in these degenerate days. I could teach you more about cussing than about diplomacy—to which cussing is a most valuable aid. Now here is a letter that Secretary Olney wrote me about the significance of his correspondence with England."

It was a page of history. Selig handled it with more reverence than he had given to any material object in his life.

He exclaimed, "Oh, yes, you used—of course I've never seen the rest of this letter, and I can't tell you, sir, how excited I am to see it. But didn't you use this first paragraph—it must be about on page 276 of your *Anglo-American Empire*?"

"I believe I did. It's not my favorite reading!"

"You know, of course, that it was reprinted from your book in the *Journal of the American Society of Historical Sources* last year?"

"Was it?" The old man seemed vastly pleased. He beamed at Selig as at a young but tested friend. He chuckled, "Well, I suppose I appreciate now how King Tut felt when they remembered him and dug him up. . . . Miss Tully! Hey! Miss Tully, will you be so good as to tell Martens to bring us whisky and soda, with two glasses? Eh? Now you look here, young woman; we'll fight out the whole question of my senile viciousness after our guest has gone. Two glasses, I said! . . . Now about Secretary Olney. The fact of the case was . . ."

Two hours later, Senator Ryder was still talking and in that two hours he had given Selig such unrecorded information as the researcher could not have found in two years of study.

Selig had for two hours walked with presidents and

ambassadors; he had the dinner conversation of foreign ministers, conversations so private, so world-affecting, that they never had been set down, even in letters. The Senator had revealed his friendship with King Edward, and the predictions about the future World War the King had made over a glass of mineral water.

The mild college instructor, who till this afternoon had never spoken to anyone more important than the president of a prairie college, was exalted with a feeling that he had become the confidant of kings and field marshals, of Anatole France and Lord Haldane, of Sarah Bernhardt and George Meredith.

He had always known but till now he had never understood that in private these great personages were plain human beings, like Doctor Wilbur Selig of Erasmus. It made him feel close to King Edward to hear (though the Senator may have exaggerated) that the King could not pronounce his own name without a German accent; it made him feel a man of the world to learn the details of a certain not very elevating party at which an English duke and a German prince and a Portuguese king, accompanied by questionable ladies, had in bibulous intimacy sung to Senator Ryder's leadership the lyric, "How Dry I Am."

During that two hours, there had been ten minutes when he had been entirely off in a Conan Doyle spirit world. His notion of prodigious alcoholic dissipation was a bottle of home-brewed beer once a month. He had tried to mix himself a light whisky and soda—he noted, with some anxiety about the proper drinking-manners in diplomatic society, that he took approximately one third as much whisky as the Senator.

But while the old man rolled his drink in his mouth and shook his bald head rapturously and showed no effect, Selig was suddenly lifted six million miles above the earth, through pink-gray clouds shot with lightning, and at that altitude he floated dizzily while below him the Senator discoursed on the relations of Cuban sugar to Colorado beets.

And once Iddle blatted into sight, in his dirty flivver, suggested taking him away, and was blessedly dismissed by the Senator's curt, "Doctor Selig is staying here for dinner. I'll send him back in my car."

Dinner . . . Selig, though he rarely read fiction, had read in some novel about "candle-flames, stilled in the twilight and reflected in the long stretch of waxed mahogany as in a clouded mirror—candles and roses and old silver." He had read, too, about stag horns and heraldic shields and the swords of old warriors.

Now, actually, the Senator's dining room had neither stag horn nor heraldic shield nor sword, and if there were still candle-flames, there was no mahogany to reflect them, but instead a silver stretch of damask. It was a long room, simple, with old portraits against white panels. Yet Selig felt that he was transported into all the romance he had ever read.

The dinner was countrylike. By now, Selig expected peacocks' tongues and caviar; he got steak and cantaloupe and corn pudding. But there were four glasses at each plate, and along with water, which was the familiar drink at Erasmus, he had, and timidly, tasted sherry, Burgundy, and champagne.

If Wilbur Selig of Iowa and Erasmus had known anything, it was that champagne was peculiarly wicked, associated with light ladies, lewd talk, and losses at roulette invariably terminating in suicide. Yet it was just as he was nibbling at his very first glass of champagne that Senator Ryder began to talk of his delight in the rise of Anglo-Catholicism.

No. It was none of it real.

If he was exhilarated that he had been kept for dinner, he was ecstatic when the Senator said, "Would you care to come for dinner again day after tomorrow? Good. I'll send Martens for you at seven-thirty. Don't dress."

In a dream phantasmagoria he started home, driven by Martens, the Senator's chauffeur-butler, with unnumbered things that had puzzled him in writing his book made clear.

When he arrived at the Sky Peaks camp, the guests were still sitting about the dull campfire.

"My!" said Miss Selma Swanson, teacher of history. "Mr. Iddle says you've spent the whole evening with Senator Ryder. Mr. Iddle says he's a grand person—used to be a great politician."

"Oh, he was kind enough to help me about some confused problems," murmured Selig.

But as he went to bed—in a reformed corncrib—he exulted, "I bet I could become quite a good friend of the Senator! Wouldn't that be wonderful!"

Lafayette Ryder, when his visitor—a man named Selig or Selim—was gone, sat at the long dining table with a cigarette and a distressingly empty cognac glass. He was meditating, "Nice eager young chap. Provincial. But mannerly. I wonder if there really are a few people who know that Lafe Ryder once existed?"

He rang, and the crisply coy Miss Tully, the nurse, waltzed into the dining room, bubbling, "So we're all ready to go to bed now, Senator!"

"We are not! I didn't ring for you; I rang for Martens."

"He's driving your guest."

"Humph! Send in cook. I want some more brandy."

"Oh, now, Daddy Ryder! You aren't going to be naughty, are you?"

"I am! And who the deuce ever told you to call me 'Daddy'? Daddy!"

"You did. Last year."

"I don't—this year. Bring me the brandy bottle."

"If I do, will you go to bed then?"

"I will not!"

"But the doctor——"

"The doctor is a misbegotten hound with a face like a fish. And other things. I feel cheerful tonight. I shall sit up late. Till All Hours."

They compromised on eleven-thirty instead of All Hours, and one glass of brandy instead of the bottle. But, vexed at having thus compromised—as so often, in ninety-odd years, he had been vexed at having compromised with Empires—the Senator was (said Miss Tully) very naughty in his bath.

"I swear," said Miss Tully afterward, to Mrs. Tinkham, the secretary, "if he didn't pay so well, I'd leave that horrid old man tomorrow. Just because he was a politician or something, once, to think he can sass a trained nurse!"

"You would not!" said Mrs. Tinkham. "But he *is* naughty."

And they did not know that, supposedly safe in his four-poster bed, the old man was lying awake, smoking a cigarette and reflecting:

"The gods have always been much better to me than I have deserved. Just when I thought I was submerged in a flood of women and doctors, along comes a man for companion, a young man who seems to be a potential scholar, and who might preserve for the world what I tried to do. Oh, stop pitying yourself, Lafe Ryder! . . . I wish I could sleep."

Senator Ryder reflected, the next morning, that he had probably counted too much on young Selig. But when Selig came again for dinner, the Senator was gratified to see how quickly he was already fitting into a house probably more elaborate than any he had known. And quite easily he told of what the Senator accounted his uncivilized farm boyhood, his life in a state university.

"So much the better that he is naïve, not one of these third-secretary cubs who think they're cosmopolitan because they went to Groton," considered the Senator. "I must do something for him."

Again he lay awake that night, and suddenly he had what seemed to him an inspired idea.

"I'll give young Selig a lift. All this money and no one but hang-jawed relatives to give it to! Give him a year of freedom. Pay him—he probably earns twenty-five hundred a year; pay him five thousand and expenses to arrange my files. If he makes good, I'd let him publish my papers after I pass out. The letters from John Hay, from Blaine, from Choate! No set of unpublished documents like it in America! It would *make* the boy!"

Mrs. Tinkham would object. Be jealous. She might quit. Splendid! Lafe, you arrant old coward, you've been trying to get rid of that woman without hurting her feelings for three years! At that, she'll probably marry you on your dying bed!"

He chuckled, a wicked, low, delighted sound, the old man alone in darkness.

"Yes, and if he shows the quality I think he has, leave him a little money to carry on with while he edits the letters. Leave him—let's see."

It was supposed among Senator Ryder's lip-licking relatives and necessitous hangers-on that he had left of the Ryder fortune perhaps two hundred thousand dollars. Only his broker and he knew that he had by secret investment increased it to a million, these ten years of dark, invalid life.

He lay planning a new will. The present one left half his fortune to his university, a quarter to the town of Wickley for a community center, the rest to nephews and nieces, with ten thousand each for the Tully, the Tinkham, Martens, and the much-badgered doctor, with a grave proviso that the doctor should never again dictate to any patient how much he should smoke.

Now to Doctor Selig, asleep and not even dream-warned in his absurd corncrib, was presented the sum of twenty-five thousand dollars, the blessings of an old man, and a store of historical documents which could not be priced in coin.

In the morning, with a headache, and very strong with Miss Tully about the taste of the aspirin—he suggested that she had dipped it in arsenic—the Senator reduced Selig to five thousand, but that night it went back to twenty-five.

How pleased the young man would be.

*   *   *

Doctor Wilbur Selig, on the first night when he had unexpectedly been bidden to stay for dinner with Senator Ryder, was as stirred as by—— What *would* most stir Doctor Wilbur Selig? A great play? A raise in salary? An Erasmus football victory?

At the second dinner, with the house and the hero less novel to him, he was calmly happy, and zealous about getting information. The third dinner, a week after, was agreeable enough, but he paid rather more attention to the squab in casserole than to the Senator's revelations about the Baring panic, and he was a little annoyed that the Senator insisted (so selfishly) on his staying till midnight, instead of going home to bed at a reasonable hour like ten—with, perhaps, before retiring, a few minutes of chat with that awfully nice bright girl, Miss Selma Swanson.

And through that third dinner he found himself reluctantly critical of the Senator's morals.

Hang it, here was a man of good family, who had had a chance to see all that was noblest and best in the world, and why did he feel he had to use such bad language, why did he drink so much? Selig wasn't (he proudly reminded himself) the least bit narrow-minded. But an old man like this ought to be thinking of making his peace; ought to be ashamed of cursing like a stableboy.

He reproved himself next morning, "He's been mighty nice to me. He's a good old coot—at heart. And of course a great statesman."

But he snapped back to irritation when he had a telephone call from Martens, the chauffeur: "Senator Ryder would like you to come over for tea this afternoon. He has something to show you."

"All right, I'll be over."

Selig was curt about it, and he raged, "Now, by thunder, of all the thoughtless, selfish old codgers! As if I didn't have anything to do but dance attendance on him and amuse him! And here I'd planned to finish a chapter this afternoon! 'Course he does give me some inside information, but still—as if I needed all the tittle-tattle of embassies for my book! Got all the stuff I need now. And how am I to get over there? The selfish old hound never thinks of that! Does he suppose I can afford a car to go over? I'll have to walk! Got half a mind not to go!"

The sulkiness with which he came to tea softened when the Senator began to talk about the Queen Victoria letter.

Historians knew that during the presidency of Benjamin Harrison, when there was hostility between America and Britain over the seizure by both sides of fishing boats, Queen Victoria had written in her own hand to President Harrison. It was believed that she deplored her royal inability to appeal directly to Parliament, and suggested his first taking the difficulty up with Congress. But precisely what was in this unofficial letter, apparently no one knew.

This afternoon Senator Ryder said placidly, "I happen to have the original of the letter in my possession."

"What?"

"Perhaps some day I'll give you a glimpse of it. I think I have the right to let you quote it."

Selig was electrified. It would be a sensation—he would be a sensation! He could see his book, and himself, on the front pages. But the Senator passed on to a trivial, quite improper anecdote about a certain Brazilian ambassador and a Washington milliner, and Selig was irritable again. Darn it, it was indecent for a man of over ninety to think of such things! And why the deuce was he so skittish and secretive about his old letter? If he was going to show it, why not do it?

So perhaps Doctor Selig of Erasmus was not quite so gracious as a Doctor Selig of Erasmus should have been when, at parting, the old man drew from under his shawl a worn blue-gray pamphlet, and piped:

"I'm going to give you this, if you'd like it. There's only six copies left in the world, I believe. It's the third one of my books—privately printed and not ordinarily listed with the others. It has, I imagine, a few things in it the historians don't know; the real story of the Paris commune."

"Oh, thanks," Selig said brusquely and, to himself, in the Senator's car, he pointed out that it showed what an egotistic old codger Ryder was to suppose that just because he'd written something, it must be a blooming treasure!

He glanced into the book. It seemed to have information. But he wasn't stirred, for it was out of line with what he had decided were the subjects of value to Doctor Selig and, therefore, of general interest.

After tea, now, it was too late for work before dinner, and he had Ryder's chauffeur set him down at Tredwell's General Store, which had become for members of the Sky Peaks camp a combination of department store, post office and café, where they drank wild toasts in lemon pop.

Miss Selma Swanson was there, and Selig laughingly treated her to chewing gum, Attaboy Peanut Candy Rolls, and seven fishhooks. They had such a lively time discussing that funny Miss Elkington up at the camp.

When he started off, with Miss Swanson, he left the Senator's book behind him in the store. He did not miss it till he had gone to bed.

Two days afterward, the Senator's chauffeur again telephoned an invitation to tea for that afternoon, but this time Selig snapped, "Sorry! Tell the Senator I unfortunately shan't be able to come!"

"Just a moment, please," said the chauffeur. "The Senator wishes to know if you care to come to dinner tomorrow evening—eight—he'll send for you."

"Well—— Yes, tell him I'll be glad to come."

After all, dinner here at Sky Peaks was pretty bad, and he'd get away early in the evening.

He rejoiced in having his afternoon free for work. But the confounded insistence of the Senator had so bothered him that he banged a book on his table and strolled outside.

The members of the camp were playing One Old Cat, with Selma Swanson, very jolly in knickerbockers, as cheer leader. They yelped at Selig to join them and, after a stately refusal or two, he did. He had a good time. Afterward he pretended to wrestle with Miss Swanson—she had the supplest waist and, seen close up, the moistest eyes. So he was glad that he had not wasted his afternoon listening to that old bore.

The next afternoon, at six, a splendid chapter done, he went off for a climb up Mount Poverty with Miss Swanson. The late sun was so rich on pasture, pine clumps, and distant meadows, and Miss Swanson was so lively in tweed skirt and brogues—but the stockings were silk—that he regretted having promised to be at the Senator's at eight.

"But of course I always keep my promises," he reflected proudly.

They sat on a flat rock perched above the valley, and he observed in rather a classroom tone, "How remarkable that light is—the way it picks out that farmhouse roof, and then the shadow of those maples on the grass. Did you ever realize that it's less the shape of things than the light that gives a landscape beauty?"

"No, I don't think I ever did. That's so. It's the light! My, how observant you are!"

"Oh, no, I'm not. I'm afraid I'm just a bookworm."

"Oh, you are not! Of course you're tremendously scholarly—my, I've learned so much about study from you—but then, you're so active—you were just a circus playing One Old Cat yesterday. I do admire an all-round man."

At seven-thirty, holding her firm hand, he was saying, "But really, there's so much that I lack that—— But you do think I'm right about it's being so much manlier not to drink like that old man? By the way, we must start back."

At a quarter to eight, after he had kissed her and apologized and kissed her, he remarked, "Still, he can wait a while—won't make any difference."

At eight: "Golly, it's so late! Had no idea. Well, I better not go at all now. I'll just phone him this evening and say I got balled up on the date. Look! Let's go down to the lake and dine on the wharf at the boathouse, just you and I."

"Oh, that would be grand!" said Miss Selma Swanson.

Lafayette Ryder sat on the porch that, along with his dining room and bedroom, had become his entire world, and waited for the kind young friend who was giving back to him the world he had once known. His lawyer was coming from New York in three days, and there was the matter of the codicil to his will. But— the Senator stirred impatiently—this money matter was grubby; he had for Selig something rarer than money—a gift for a scholar.

He looked at it and smiled. It was a double sheet of thick bond, with "Windsor Castle" engraved at the top. Above this address was written in a thin hand: "To my friend L. Ryder, to use if he ever sees fit. Benj. Harrison."

The letter began, "To His Excellency, the President," and it was signed, "Victoria R." In a few lines between inscription and signature there was a new history of the great Victoria and of the Nineteenth Century. . . . Dynamite does not come in large packages.

The old man tucked the letter into a pocket down beneath the rosy shawl that reached up to his gray face.

Miss Tully rustled out, to beg, "Daddy, you won't take more than one cocktail tonight? The doctor says it's so bad for you!"

"Heh! Maybe I will and maybe I won't! What time is it?"

"A quarter to eight."

"Doctor Selig will be here at eight. If Martens doesn't have the cocktails out on the porch three minutes after he gets back, I'll skin him. And you needn't go looking for the cigarettes in my room, either! I've hidden them in a brand-new place, and I'll probably sit up and smoke till dawn. Fact, doubt if I shall go to bed at all. Doubt if I'll take my bath."

He chuckled as Miss Tully wailed, "You're so naughty!"

The Senator need not have asked the time. He had groped down under the shawl and looked at his watch every five minutes since seven. He inwardly glared at himself for his foolishness in anticipating his young friend, but—all the old ones were gone.

That was the devilishness of living so many years. Gone, so long. People wrote idiotic letters to him, still, begging for his autograph, for money, but who save this fine young Selig had come to him? . . . So long now!

At eight, he stirred, not this time like a drowsy old owl, but like an eagle, its lean head thrusting forth from its pile of hunched feathers, ready to soar. He listened for the car.

At ten minutes past, he swore, competently. Confound that Martens!

At twenty past, the car swept up the driveway. Out of it stepped only Martens, touching his cap, murmuring, "Very sorry, sir. Mr. Selig was not at the camp."

"Then why the devil didn't you wait?"

"I did, sir, as long as I dared."

"Poor fellow! He may have been lost on the mountain. We must start a search!"

"Very sorry, sir, but if I may say so, as I was driving back past the foot of the Mount Poverty trail, I saw Mr. Selig with a young woman, sir, and they were talking and laughing and going away from the camp, sir. I'm afraid——"

"Very well. That will do."

"I'll serve dinner at once, sir. Do you wish your cocktail out here?"

"I won't have one. Send Miss Tully."

When the nurse had fluttered to him, she cried out with alarm. Senator Ryder was sunk down into his shawl. She bent over him to hear his whisper:

"If it doesn't keep you from your dinner, my dear,

I think I'd like to be helped up to bed. I don't care for anything to eat. I feel tired."

While she was anxiously stripping the shawl from him, he looked long, as one seeing it for the last time, at the darkening valley. But as she helped him up, he suddenly became active. He snatched from his pocket a stiff double sheet of paper and tore it into fragments which he fiercely scattered over the porch with one sweep of his long arm.

Then he collapsed over her shoulder.

I'm a Stranger Here Myself

Travel broadens the mind. It also quickens the sympathies and bestows on one a ready fund of knowledge. And it is useful to talk about when you get back home.

The Johnsons have now been broadened and quickened. The signature "J. Johnson & Wife," followed by "Northernapolis, G.C.," appears in hotel registers from Florida to Maine. "G.C.," of course, stands for their state, the state with the highest bank-deposits and moral standards of any in the Union—the grand old state of God's Country. Let me tell *you*, sir, whenever you meet a man from God's Country, he's willing to tell you so. And does.

J. Johnson & Wife had raised their children and their mortgage, and had bought a small car and a large fireless cooker, when the catastrophe happened. Mrs. Johnson was defeated for the presidency of the Wednesday and Chautauqua Reading Circle by a designing woman who had talked herself into office on the strength of having spent a winter at Pasadena, California, observing the West. Mrs. Johnson went home with her hat-brim low and her lips tight together, and announced to Mr. Johnson that they would travel, and be broadened and quickened.

Mr. Johnson meekly observed that it would be nice to explore the Florida Everglades, and to study business conditions in New York. So, in December, they left their eldest son in charge of the business, and started on an eight-months' tour of the Picturesque Resorts of Our Own Land. In fact, they were going to have an itinerary. Mrs. Johnson's second cousin, Bessie, had suggested the itinerary. Cousin Bessie had spent two weeks in Florida. She said it was all non-sense to go to places like Palm Beach and St. Augustine—just because rich snobs from New York went there was no reason why independent folks from God's Country, that did their own thinking, should waste their good money. So, with Cousin Bessie's help, Mrs. Johnson made out the following schedule of the beauty-spots of Florida:

Jacksonville, East Palatka, South Daytona, North Tampa, West Miami, Sulphur Water, Jigger Mounds, Diamond Back Ridge, Flatwoods, New Iowa, New Dublin, New Cincinnati, and New New York.

It takes a lot of high-minded heroism to stick faithfully to an itinerary, what with having to catch trains at midnight and all, but with the negligible assistance of Mr. Johnson, Mrs. Johnson stuck to it, though they often had to do two towns in one day. And oh! the rewards in culture! It is true they didn't have time to stop and look for orange-groves or Seminoles or millionaires, but they often felt as though they could smell the odor of oranges wafted to them on the gay breezes, though that may perhaps have been due to fellow-tourists eating oranges and peanuts. Certainly they saw plenty of palms, and at Jacksonville, in the Boston Museum of Curiosities, Including the Biggest Fish Ever Killed, in Fierce Marine Battle, by Capt. Pedro O'Toole, the Johnsons beheld a real live alligator.

After the trials and weariness of their explorations, Mrs. Johnson permitted them to settle down for a six-weeks' rest at the Pennsylvania House, in New Chicago, the City Beautiful of the Southland.

New Chicago may not be as old as St. Augustine and these towns that make such claims about antiquity, and heaven only knows if Ponce de Leon really did find any Fountain of Youth at all, and New Chicago may not be filled with a lot of millionaires chasing around in these wheel-chairs and drinking brandy and horse's necks, but New Chicago is neighborly, that's what it is, neighborly. And homey. It was founded by Northern capital, just for tourists. If a gentleman wishes to wear comfy old clothes, he doesn't find some snob in white pants looking askance at him. And New Chicago is so beautiful, and all modern conveniences—none of these rattletrap houses that you find in some Southern cities. It has forty miles of pavement, and nineteen churches, and is in general as spick and span as Detroit or Minneapolis. Why, when you go along the streets, with the cozy boarding-houses, and the well-built private houses of frame, or of ornamental brick with fancy porches and bay-windows and colored glass over the front door, and these nice new two-story concrete bungalows, you can scarcely tell you aren't in a suburb of New York or Chicago, it's all so wide-awake and nicely fixed up and full of Northern hustle. And there's very little danger of being thrown into contact with these lazy, shiftless, native Florida crackers, just fishermen and farmers and common, uninteresting people that have never heard about economics or osteopathy or New Thought or any modern movements. Not but what New Chicago is very Southern and resorty, you understand, with its palms and poinsettias and all sorts of exotic plants and beauty in general.

There isn't any liquor or dancing to tempt the men-folks, and there is an educational Chautauqua every January, with the very best entertainers, and finally New Chicago has, by actual measurement, more lineal miles of rocking chairs and nice women gossiping and knitting than Ormond and Daytona put together.

At first Mr. Johnson made signs of objecting to the fact that nobody at New Chicago seemed to go fishing. But the hotel and Board of Trade literature convinced him that there was the best fishing in the South within easy reach, and so he settled down and got a good deal of pleasure out of planning to go fishing some day; in fact, went so far as to buy some hooks at the drugstore. He found some men from God's Country who were in the same line of business as himself, and they used to gather in the park and pitch quoits and talk about business conditions back home and have a perfectly hilarious time swapping jokes about Ford cars, and Mike and Pat, and Jakey and Ikey.

Mrs. Johnson also made many acquaintances, such nice, chatty, comfy people, who just took her in and told her about their grandchildren, and made her feel welcome right away.

You see, the minute you arrive at New Chicago, you go and register your name and address at the Board of Trade Building, and all the people from your state look you up immediately, and you have Wisconsin picnics, or Ohio card-parties, or New Hampshire parades, or Middle-West I.O.O.F. suppers. Almost every evening there is some jolly little state gathering in the parlor of one of the hotels, with recitations and songs—Gospel and humorous—and speeches about the state, if there are any lawyers present. Everybody has to do a stunt. Mrs. Johnson made such an impression at the God's Country Rustic Skule Party, when she got up and blushed and said, "I didn't know I was going to be called on for a piece, and I hadn't thought of anything to say, and after hearing all the nice speeches I guess I'll just say 'ditto'!" Mr. Johnson told her afterward that her stunt made the hit of the evening.

New Chicago was no less desirable from a standpoint of economy. For thirty-two dollars a week the Johnsons had three meals a day, nice, wholesome homey meals, with no French sauces and fancy fixin's, and a dainty room such as would, to quote the hotel prospectus, "Appeal to the finest lady of the land, or most hardened tourist, with handsome Michigan Chippendale bureau, two chairs in each room, and bed to lull you to happy dreams, after day spent in the jolly sports of New Chicago, strictly under new management, new linen of fine quality to appeal to heart of most fastidious, bathroom on each floor, ice water cheerfully brought by neat and obliging attendants."

If you were one of these nervous, strenuous folks who felt that you had to have a lot of young people, why, there were several nice young people in town, though it is true that there was quite a large proportion of older people who had reached the point where they were able to get away from business in the winter-time. Still there were some girls who played the piano, and knew pencil and paper games, and they were the life of the knitting circle with their gay young chatter, especially Miss Nellie Slavens, the well-known Iowa professional reader, who scarcely looked a day over thirty, and was a college graduate, the South Dakota Dairy College. Then there was the clerk of Ocean Villa, right next door, such a sociable young man from Trenton, always in demand for parties, and looked so well in his West Palm Beach suit.

And if you wanted sports there were athletic exercises a-plenty, though there wasn't this crowd that show off their silk bathing-suits on the beach, and pay twenty-five dollars for an aeroplane ride, as they do at Palm Beach. Any bright day you could see eight or ten people in bathing at Rocky Shore. Almost every boarding house had a croquet ground, and three of them had tennis courts. The Mayberry sisters, Kittie and Jane, nice sensible girls of thirty or so, were often to be seen playing. And you could always get up a crowd and charter Dominick Segui's launch, when the engine was in repair, and have a trip down to the shell mound. So, you see, there was any amount of rational sport, and no need for anyone to go to these sporty places.

In short, the Johnsons found every day at New Chicago just one round of innocent pleasures. After a good, wholesome, hearty breakfast of oatmeal, steak, eggs, buckwheats, sausage, and coffee—none of these grits and cornbread that they have the nerve to offer

you for breakfast some places in the South—the Johnsons read the *Northernapolis Herald,* which they got
from a live, hustling newsdealer from Minneapolis,
and had so much enjoyment out of learning about the
deaths and sicknesses and all back home, though it
did hurt Mrs. Johnson to see how the new president
of the Wednesday Reading Circle was letting it run
down. Then they went over to the drugstore, run by
a live, hustling Toledo man, and Mr. Johnson bought
three Flor de Wheeling cigars, while Mrs. Johnson had
a chocolate ice-cream soda and some souvenir post-
cards. Then for the rest of the day they were free to
walk, or talk, or just sit and be comfy on the porch
of their hotel. And there was always such an interesting group of broad-gauged, conservative, liberal, wide-
awake, homey, well-traveled folks on the porch to
talk to.

For you who may not have been broadened and
quickened, or had opportunities for elevating and in-
formative talk, I will give an example of such a conversation as might have been heard on the porch of the
Pennsylvania House at any time between seven-thirty
a.m. and nine-thirty p.m., and I assure you it isn't a
bit above the average run in New Chicago:

"Well, I see there's some new God's Country people come to town, Mr. Johnson—Willis M. Beaver and
wife, from Monroe County. Staying at the Chateau
Nebraska."

"Well, well! Why, I've met his brother at the state
convention of Order of Peaweevils. Funny, him being
here, way off in the Sunny South, and me knowing
his brother. World's pretty small, after all. But still, it
certainly is a liberal education to travel."

"Oh, Mrs. Johnson, don't you want to come to our
basket-weaving club? We make baskets out of these
long pine needles, with raffia——"

Before Mrs. Johnson can answer her husband says,
quick as a flash, with that ready wit of his, "Say, uh,
Mrs. Bezuzus, I'm glad those pine needles are good
for something anyway!"

"Ha, ha!" asserts Mr. Smith. "You said something there! Why, I'd rather have a West Virginia oak in my yard than all the pines and palms in Florida. Same with these early strawberries they talk so much about, not but what it's nice to write home to the folks that you're having strawberries this time of year, but I swear, we wouldn't feed 'em to hogs, up where I come from."

"You hit it right, Brother Smith." It is Dr. Bjones of Kansas speaking, and after Mrs. Bezuzus has suitably commented on the manners, garments, and social standing of some passing newlyweds, Dr. Bjones goes on in his forcible scientific manner: "Same with these Southern fish, not but what I like fresh sea-food and crabs, but I tell you these bass and whitings can't hold a candle to the fresh-water pickerel you get up North. Then these Floridians talk so much about how poisonous their darned old rattlesnakes are. Why, we got rattlers in Kansas that are just as bad any day!"

"But what gets me is the natives, Doc. Shiftless. What this country needs is some Northern hustle."

"That's so, Brother Snuck. Shiftless. And besides that——"

"Oh, Mrs. Smith, I want to show you the sweater I'm knitting."

"——besides being shiftless, look at how they sting us. Simply make all the money they can out of us tourists. Oranges two for a nickel! Why, I can buy jus' good oranges at home for that!"

"And the land! They can talk all they want to about rocky hill soil, but I wouldn't give one of my Berkshire Hill holdings for all the land south of Baltimore. I can sell you——"

"Pretty warm today."

"Yes, I was writing to Jessie, guess she wished she was down here. She wrote me it was snowing and ten below——"

Mrs. Johnson was always afire for accurate botanical information, and of the scientific Dr. Bjones she inquired, "What are these palmettoes good for?"

"Well, you know, I'm kind of a stranger in Florida, too, but I believe the natives eat the nuts from them."

"Oh, can anybody tell me what connections I make for Ciudad Dinero?"

"Why, you take the 9:16, Mrs. Bezuzus, and change at Lemon Grove——"

"No, you change at Avocado and take the jitney—"

"Is there a good hotel at Ciudad?"

"Well, I've heard the Blubb House is a first-class place; three-dollar-a-day house. Oh, how did you like the Royal Miasma at——"

"Oh, I suppose it's awful famous, and it's very dressy, everybody changed their clothes for supper, but I prefer Cape Cod Court, not an expensive place, you understand, but so homey——"

"Yes, but for table give me Dr. Gunk's Health Cottage, and the beds there——"

"Well, we started in on the West Coast and went to St. Petersburg and Tampa and Fort Myers, and then back to Ocala and Silver Springs, and took the Ocklawaha trip and all, and we stopped a day at Palatka——"

"Oh, Mrs. Bjones, how do you do that stitch?"

Often the crowd on the porch ceased these lighter divertissements and spoke seriously of real highbrow topics, like Bryan and Villa and defense and T. R. and self-starters and Billy Sunday and Harold Bell Wright. The Johnsons certainly had come to the right shop for being broadened and quickened, and Mrs. Johnson often told her husband that she would take back to the Wednesday Reading Circle such a fund of ready information and ideas as a Certain Person couldn't have gotten in California if she'd stayed there a hundred years!

So went the Johnsons' hours of gaieties manycolored and tropical, and when the long, happy day was over, New Chicago afforded them a succulent supper or a dainty repast, and then ho! for the movies, and no city has better movies than New Chicago, scenes from the whole wide world spread before you there on the screen, scenes from Paris and Pekin and Peoria, made by the best Los Angeles companies. At least once a week the Johnsons were able to see their favorite film hero, Effingham Fish, in a convulsing comedy.

How wondrous 'tis to travel in unfamiliar climes!

Spring was on its way, and at last the Johnsons were ready to bid farewell to New Chicago, the land of mystery and languor, adventure and dolce far niente.

Their trunk was packed. Mr. Johnson's slippers had been run to earth, or at least to dust, under their bed, and his razor-strop had been recovered from behind the bureau, when Mrs. Johnson suddenly exclaimed, "Oh! Why, we haven't studied the flora and fauna of Florida yet, and I don't know but what we ought to, for club-papers."

"Well, you haven't got all the time in the world left for it," said Mr. Johnson, who had a pretty wit.

"Well, we're all packed, and we have three hours before the train goes."

She dragged him out and they hired a surrey driven by a bright, hustling Northern negro—not one of these ignorant Southern darkies—and they galloped out to Dr. Bible's orange-grove, admission ten cents, one of the show-places in the suburbs of New Chicago.

There it was, trees and fruit and—and everything; a sight to broaden and quicken one.

The Johnsons solemnly gazed at it. "Yes," said Mrs. Johnson, "that's an orange-grove! Just think! And grapefruit. . . . It's very pretty. . . . I wonder if they sell postcard views of it."

"Yes," said Mr. Johnson, "that's an orange-grove. Well, well! . . . Well, I guess we better drive on."

They next studied the shell mound. There's something very elevating about the sight of such a relic of long-past ages—shows how past ages lived, you know—gives you a broader sympathy with history and all that. There she was, all in layers, millions of shells, just where the Indians had thrown them. Ages and ages ago. The Johnsons must have gazed at the mound for five or ten minutes. Mr. Johnson was so interested that he asked the driver, "Do they ever find tommy-hawks in these mounds?"

"Don't know, sir," said the driver thoughtfully. "I'm a stranger in New Chicago."

"Yes," said Mr. Johnson, "I shouldn't wonder if they found relics there. Very, very ancient, I should say. When you think of how filling just one oyster-fry is, and then all these shells— Well, mama, I guess that's about all we wanted to see, isn't it?"

"Well, we might drive back by Mr. Capo's estate; they tell me he has some fine Florida shrubbery there."

They passed the Capo estate, but there wasn't much to see—just trees with kind of white berries, and tall shrubs with stalks curiously like the bamboo fish-poles that boys use, back home. Mrs. Johnson's eagle glance darted to the one object of interest, and she wanted to know something:

"Stop, driver. John, I wonder what that plant is there, like a little palm, with that thing like a cabbage in the center. I wonder if it isn't a pineapple plant."

We, having the unfair position of author, know that it was really a sago palm—not that we wish to boast of our knowledge of floras, and so, if you will pardon our interruption:

"Well," said Mr. Johnson helpfully.

"I understand they grow farther south. But even so this might be an exotic pineapple, just grown here in gardens."

"Well, maybe. There's a couple of people coming. Why don't you ask them?"

They let the first of the two approaching men pass them—he was only a common, ignorant native. But the second was a fine, keen, hustling fellow on a bicycle, and Mrs. Johnson hailed him: "Can you tell me what that plant is?"

"That, madam——"

The Johnsons listened attentively, alert as ever in acquiring knowledge.

"—that plant? Well, I don't just exactly know. I'm a stranger here myself."

The Johnsons had to hurry back for their train, but they interestedly discussed all the flora and fauna on the way, including pines, buzzards, and pickaninnies. "Isn't it nice," said Mrs. Johnson, "to plunge right out and explore like this! I just bet that cat, with her winter in California, never stirred out of her own dooryard. Well, Florida certainly has been a novel experience, and improved our minds so much. Driver, is that a mocking-bird, on that skinny dead tree?"

"Yassum, that's a mocking-bird. . . . Or maybe it's a robin."

II

Adding experiences in Georgia and Virginia and the Carolinas to their knowledge of Florida, the Johnsons saw and drank deep of Savannah, Charleston, Asheville, Richmond, and Newport News. They were able to do all five cities in six days, while the Bezuzuses had taken eight for them. In Charleston they saw Calhoun's grave and learned all about the aristocratic society. They were so pleasantly entertained there, by a very prominent and successful business acquaintance of Mr. Johnson's, a Mr. Max Rosenfleisch of New York, who had bought a fine old Southern mansion in Charleston and thus, of course, was right in with all the old families socially. Mr. Rosenfleisch said he liked the aristocrats, but was going to change a lot of their old-fashioned social ways, and show them how to have a real swell time, with cabarets and theater parties, instead of these slow dances, and teach them to dine at seven instead of three or four. The Johnsons were quite thrilled at witnessing the start of this social revolution—I tell you, it's when you travel that you have such unusual adventures. They themselves would actually have met some of the inner social set of Charleston, but Mr. Rosenfleisch was having the den redecorated before giving any more of his smart, exclusive parties, and meantime the Johnsons had to be getting on—to a tourist, time is valuable.

At the beginning of spring, when the narcissi and the excursionists are out, the Johnsons arrived at Washington, where every good citizen should go, to show the lawmakers that we uphold their hands, and to give them our ideas about enlarging the army. The Johnsons found the nicest sightseeing car, with such a bright young man from Denver for barker, and he told how high the Washington Monument was, how much the Patent Office had cost to build, how long it had taken to decorate the Congressional Library in the Spanish Omelet style, how far the guns in the Navy Yard would shoot, where Joe Cannon lived, and numerous other broadening and quickening facts which filled them with pride in being citizens of the greatest country in the world.

The Johnsons' congressman received them with flattering attentions which would have turned heads less level than theirs; he rushed over and shook hands with them the minute they came into his private office, and while just for the moment he couldn't remember their name, he had it right on the tip of his tongue, and said, "Why, of course, of course," when Mr. Johnson refreshed his memory. He recalled perfectly having shaken hands with them once at Northernapolis. He was so sorry that he was expecting the Ways and Means Committee to meet in his office, right away, for he did so want to have them stay there and chat with him about the folks back home. As an indication of his pleasure in seeing them, he honored them with a special card which enabled them to hear the epoch-making debates in Congress, from a gallery reserved just for distinguished visitors and friends of congressmen. As they listened to a vigorous oration on the duty on terrapin, Mrs. Johnson said triumphantly: "John, I guess that cat never heard anything like that in her Pasadena that she's always talking about at the Reading Circle!"

Travelers have to be of heroic mold to endure the dangers and disasters of exploration; and the Johnsons showed the quiet dignity of noblesse oblige during a most disagreeable incident at Washington. . . . Mrs. Johnson wished to find the house in which Commodore Decatur had lived, as an ancestor of hers had been a very near and dear friend of one of the Commodore's gunswabbers. She asked quite a number of apparently well-informed tourists, but, with a pathetic lack of sound information, they all murmured that they didn't know, being themselves strangers in Washington. Then she had the original idea of asking the clerk at their hotel.

"Decatur House?" he said. "I know where the Ebbitt House is, and the White House, and Colonel House, but I pass up the Decatur House. Sorry . . . Here, boy, shoot this package up to 427."

"Why, I mean the historic old mansion of Commodore Decatur."

"Madam, I can tell you where to get your Kodak films developed, and where to find the largest oysters in town, and where to pay your bill, and what time the 5:43 train goes, but that's all I know. I come from Chicago, and if God is good to me, I'm going back there, where there's no congressmen, and they keep the tourists inside the Loop."

"Well, can't you tell us where we can find out?"

"Madam, you will find a guide-book at the news-stand."

From the news-stand they overheard the clerk saying to a fellow menial:

"—yes, I know, I oughtn't to be a grouch, but she wouldn't take 'no' for an answer. And ten minutes ago some other female wanted to know where Lincoln was buried, and just before that an old boy was sore because I couldn't tell him what is the sum total of all the pensions the Government is paying, and before that somebody wanted to know how much the dome of the Capitol weighs. These tin-can paper-bag tourists drive me wild. I ain't just an information bureau—I'm a whole bedroom suite, installment plan."

Mr. Johnson said to his wife with that quiet force

which all his associates in Northernapolis know and
admire, "If he means us by 'tin-can paper-bag tourists,' I'm going to chastise him, I am, no matter what
it costs! In fact, I'll speak to the manager!"

"Now, John," his wife urged, "he simply is beneath
your contempt."

"Well, perhaps that's right."

The Johnsons decided not to waste a quarter on a
guide-book, and strolled out to ask a policeman where
the Decatur House was.

Although they found that Washington was like Florida in needing Western hustle, what with the service
so slow that they didn't finish dinner before twelve-
thirty, some noons, yet the Johnsons discovered a
news-stand where they could buy the *Northernapolis
Herald,* and there was the nicest big drugstore run by
a live, hustling Milwaukee man, where Mr. Johnson
could get his favorite Flor de Wheeling cigars, while
Mrs. Johnson had a chocolate ice-cream soda and
some post-cards. And a movie-theater featuring Effingham Fish in comedies. So, altogether, in their
Washington sojourn they had much homey pleasure
as well as broadening insight into how public affairs
are conducted. And the nicest souvenirs.

Again they took their staves and wardrobe-scrip and
continued their pilgrimage to the ancient and historic
spots of our own land. They were able to do Baltimore
and Philadelphia thoroughly in two days, and would
have finished up Atlantic City in another day, except
that they found it was so much cheaper to get rates
by the week. Then off for New York.

Mrs. Johnson was willing to sacrifice, to wear herself
to the bone, studying the deeper esthetic, psychologi-
cal and economic problems of New York, that she
might bring home new ideas to the Wednesday Reading Circle. But New York wouldn't let itself be studied. It was perfectly crazy. Everybody in New York,
they found, spent all his time in cafés, tea-rooms, cabarets, or Bohemian restaurants where women smoke.
The only homey, comfortable place they found was a

nice quiet drugstore where Mr. Johnson got his Flor de Wheeling cigars. And the prices—! They were glad to pass on to New Haven, to Hartford, the Berkshires, and Boston—where they saw several headquarters of Washington, and the most interesting graves, Emerson and Hawthorne and all sorts of people, and such nice artistic post-cards. Then to Maine, and, in mid-summer, down to Cape Cod, and Provincetown.

The Johnsons didn't plan to spend more than one day at Provincetown. They felt that Northernapolis was beginning to need them, and they had really seen everything there was to see in the East and South. But at Provincetown they had such a pleasant surprise that they stayed two whole weeks—they ran into Dr. and Mrs. Bjones of Wichita, with whom they had had the jolly times at New Chicago. With the Bjoneses the Johnsons picnicked on the dunes, and even went swimming once, and sat on the porch of Mrs. Ebenezer's boarding house, discussing various hotels and the Bjoneses' interesting itinerary. They didn't want to be mean, but they couldn't help crowing a little when they found that they had seen six graves of famous men which the Bjoneses had missed entirely!

The Johnsons didn't really like Provincetown. Of course the Bjoneses were interesting, and after a time they met some nice comfy people from Indianapolis and Omaha, and Mr. Johnson was able to get his Flor de Wheeling cigars. But Provincetown was filled with fishermen, acting as though they owned the place, and smelling it all up with their dories and schooners and nets and heaven knows what all, dirty, common Portuguese and Yankee fishermen, slopping along the street in nasty old oilskins covered with fish-scales, and not caring if they brushed right up against you. And the old wharves, all smelly. Mr. and Mrs. Johnson were the first to be interested in any new phenomenon and once they went right out on a wharf and asked all about the fishing industry and whaling. But still—as Mr. Johnson said with that ready satire which made him so popular a speaker at the dinners of the Northernapolis Chamber of Commerce—they didn't care to associate with dead fish all their lives, even if they did like Effingham Fish in the movies!

When the Bjoneses left there was nothing more to study, nothing to observe.

Said Mrs. Johnson, "We've seen every inch of the South and East, now, and no one can say we haven't been unprejudiced and open-minded—the way we've gone into the flora and fauna, and among industries and all—but I must say we haven't seen a single place that begins to come up to Northernapolis."

"You never said a better thing in your life, mama, and what's more, we'll start for Northernapolis tomorrow!"

They were due to arrive in Northernapolis at two p.m. Mrs. Johnson was making notes for Wednesday Reading Circle papers about the Fruit of the Tropics, the Negro Problem, Fishing on Cape Cod, and How the Government Is Conducted at Washington.

"Guess that hen won't talk so much about Pasadena after this," Mr. Johnson chuckled. "Say, we'll have time to say 'howdy' to the folks and go to the movies to-night, to celebrate our return. And I'll be able to get a decent cigar again—can't buy a Flor de Wheeling on a single one of these trains. Well, mama, it'll be pretty good to get back where we know every inch, and won't have to ask questions and feel like outsiders, eh?"

Such a surprise as it would be for the children! The Johnsons hadn't wired them they were coming.

Northernapolis! The fine, big, dirty factories— evidences of Northernapolis's hustling spirit! The good old-fashioned homy station! The Central House 'bus!

They stood out on Main Street, excitedly hailing a street car. Then——

You see, as a matter of fact this isn't a satire, but a rather tragic story about two pathetic, good-hearted, friendly yearners, as you should already have perceived——

Then Mr. Johnson dropped his suit-case and stood amazed. A block down from the station was a whole new row of two-story brick stores. "Why," he exclaimed, "I never read about that row going up!" He was bewildered, lost. He turned to a man who was also waiting for the car and inquired, "What's those new buildings?"

"Dunno," said the man. "I'm a stranger here myself."

Ring Around a Rosy

T. Eliot Hopkins was a nice young man at forty-two, and he had done nicely all the nice things—Williams College, a New York brokerage office, his first million, his first Phyfe table, careful polo at Del Monte, the discovery that it was smart to enjoy the opera and the discovery that it was much smarter to ridicule it. In fact, by the time he had a penthouse on Park Avenue, Eliot understood the theory of relativity as applied to the world of fashion—that a man is distinguished not by what he likes but by what he is witty enough to loathe.

As for Eleanor, his wife, she came from Chicago, so naturally she had a cousin married to a French count and another cousin who would have married an Italian marquis if it had not been discovered that he was already married and not a marquis. Still, he really was Italian.

Their first year in the penthouse was ecstatic. Thirty stories up, atop 9999 Park Avenue, looking to east and north and south, it had a terrace exclamatory with scarlet wicker chairs, Pompeian marble benches, and a genuine rose garden attended by a real gardener—at three dollars an hour, from the florist's. On the terrace opened the duplex living room, fifty feet long, its Caen stone walls and twenty-foot windows soaring

up to a raftered ceiling of English oak. But to a nosey
and domestic mind, to one who had known Eleanor
when she lived in a six-room bungalow in Wilmette,
these glories of city-dominating terrace and castle hall
were less impressive than the little perfections of the
apartment: The kitchen which was a little like a chem-
ist's laboratory and more like the cabin of an electric
locomotive; the bathrooms of plate glass and purple
tile, and the master's bathroom with an open fireplace.
Through this domain Eleanor bustled for a year, slipping out to look across the East River to the farthest
hills and gas houses of Long Island, dashing inside to
turn on the automatic pipe organ, plumping down at
her most Art Moderne desk of silver, aluminum and
black glass to write dinner invitations. And they entertained. Vastly. These gigantic rooms demanded people, and sometimes there were forty guests at the
unique diamond-shaped dinner table, with five old
family retainers sneaked in from the caterer's. With
such a turnover of guests, there weren't always enough
bank vice presidents and English authors and baronets
and other really worthwhile people on the market, and
Eleanor had to fall back on persons who were nothing
but old friends, which was pretty hard on a girl. So
she was not altogether contented, even before things
happened.

They were important things. Eliot sold short before
the stock-market depression. His first million was
joined by two others, and he immediately took up
reading, art criticism and refined manners. He also
bought new jodhpurs. I am not quite sure what jodhpurs are, but then T. Eliot hadn't known, either, six
years before. They have to do with polo, though
whether they are something you ride or wear or hit
the ball with, I have not been informed. But I do
know that Eliot's jodhpurs were singularly well spoken
of at Meadowbrook, and whatever else they may have
been, they were not cursed by being American. They
were as soundly English as cold toast.

Now, selling short at a time when everyone else is

dismally long is likely to have a large effect on nice people, and Eleanor agreed with Eliot that it was shocking—it was worse than shocking, it was a bore— that they should have to go on slaving their lives away among commercial lowbrows, when in England, say, people of Their Class led lives composed entirely of beauty, graciousness, leisure and servants who didn't jiggle the tea tray.

The penthouse seemed to her a little gaudy, a little difficult. With the stupidity of servants, it took her hours a day to prepare for even the simplest dinner party. It was like poor Eliot's having to dash out and be in his office in the dawn, at ten o'clock, and often give up his afternoons of golf because his clerks were · so idiotically dumb that he couldn't trust them.

When they had taken the penthouse, a friend of Eleanor's had been so conservative as to buy a quiet little house in Turtle Bay and furnish it with English antiques. Mahogany. White fireplaces. Just a shack. But now Eleanor found the shack restful. The drawing-room did not seem empty with but two of them for tea, and the little befrilled maid was not too humble, as she would have been in the vastnesses of the penthouse.

All the way home Eleanor looked wistfully out of the limousine. She wished that there weren't a law against her walking, this warm June evening. But she wanted to be walking, not on an avenue but in a real certificated English lane—rosy cottages, old women curtsying, nightingales rising from the hedges, or whatever nightingales do rise from; witty chatter at the gate with their neighbor, General Wimbledom, former C. in C. in India; not one of these horrid New Yorkers who talk about bond issues.

When Eliot dragged home, hot, his eyes blurred with weariness, he groaned at Eleanor, "I'm glad we're not going out tonight! Let's dine on the terrace."

"But we are going out, my pet! I'm restless. I can't stand this private Grand Central. I feel like a redcap.

Let's go to that nice little French speak-easy on Forty-ninth and try to make ourselves believe we've had sense enough to go to Europe."

"All right. I wish we had gone. If nothing begins to happen in the market—— Maybe we'll be abroad before the summer's over."

The Chez Edouard has, like all distinguished French restaurants, a Swiss manager, Czech waiters, a Bavarian cook, a Greek coat checker, and scenes from Venice painted on the walls of a decayed drawing-room, and, unlike most of them, it has German wine. Eleanor crooned over the thought of onion soup, chicken cutlet Pojarski, crêpes suzette, and Oppenheimer Kreuz Spätlese.

"America—New York—isn't so bad after all, if you belong, if you know where to go," exulted Eleanor.

Then the waiter wouldn't wait.

Eleanor raised a gracious finger, Eleanor raised an irritated hand, Eliot sank so low as to snap his fingers, and the waiter merely leered at them and did not come. He was attending a noisy group of six business men, who were beginning a sound meal with six cocktails apiece—tip after each round.

"It's absolutely dreadful what America does even to good foreign servants!" Eleanor raged. "They become so impertinent and inefficient! It's something in the air of this awful country. They're so selfish and inconsiderate—and yet so nice as long as they stay abroad. I wish we were there—in Europe—where we could lead a civilized life."

"Yes," said Eliot. "Little inns. Nice."

When they were finally served with chicken cutlets Pojarski, and Eleanor had come to believe that after all she would live through it, she encountered the most terrible affliction of all. One of the so noisy interlopers wambled across and addressed her: "Sister, I just noticed we're taking more of the waiter's time than we ought to. You had to bawl him out before he brought your chicken croquettes. Excuse us! If you and the gentleman would come over and join us in a little libation—— Excuse the liberty, but we've got some pretty decent, old-fashioned, house-broken rye, and if we could have the pleasure——"

During this shocking affront Eleanor had gaped at Eliot in terror. He rescued her in a brave and high-toned manner; he said dryly to the intruder, "Very kind of you, but we have quite enough to drink here, thank you, and we must be going immediately."

"Imagine a dreadful thing like that happening in any other country! England, for instance!" Eleanor murmured afterward. "Simply no privacy anywhere in America. Dreadful! Let's get out of this dreadful restaurant."

Nor was she any the more pleased when the checking girl, whisking her white flannel topcoat across the counter, gurgled, "Here you are, dearie."

"And no respect for their betters! Just Bolshiviks!" pronounced Eleanor.

They had sent away the car. Eleanor—as a girl she had often walked six miles on a picnic—suggested to Eliot, "It would be awfully jolly and adventurous to walk home!"

They came on the new Titanic Talkie Theater—Cooled Air—Capacity 4000. Eliot yawned, "Ever been in one of these super-movie palaces? I never have. Let's see what it's like."

"You know what it will be like. Dreadful. Vulgar. But let's see."

The lobby was a replica, but somewhat reduced, of Seville Cathedral. A bowing doorman, in gold lace, scarlet tunic and a busby with a purple plume, admitted them through gilded bronze doors to an inner lobby, walled with silk tapestry, floored with the largest Oriental rug in the world, and dotted with solid silver statues of negligent ladies, parakeets in golden cages on pedestals of Chinese lacquer, a fountain whose stream was illuminated with revolving lights, lemon-colored and green and crimson, and vast red club chairs beside which, for ash receivers, were Florentine wine jars.

"Oh! This hurts!" wailed Eleanor.

A line of ushers, young men in the uniforms of West Point cadets, stood at attention. One of them galloped forward and, bending from the waist, held out a white-gloved hand for their tickets.

"I'm paralyzed! This is like an opium eater's dream of a mid-Victorian royal palace. Must we go in?" fretted Eleanor.

"No! Let's go home. Think how nice a cool Tom Collins would be on the terrace," said Eliot, and to the usher: "Thanks, I think we've seen enough."

The stateliness, the choiceness and aristocracy of their exit were a little crumpled by the military usher's blatting behind them, "Well, can you lay that! The Prince of Wales and Tex Guinan—that's who they are!" And at the door they heard from a comfortable woman enthroned in a tall Spanish chair, addressing her lady friend, "I always did like a good artistic talkie with Doug Fairbanks and some old antique castles, and like that. I can't stand this lowdown sex stuff. Gotta have art or nothing."

Eleanor had lived in New York so long that she rarely saw it. She did tonight, with liveliness and hatred.

Broadway was turned into a county fair, with orange-juice stands, pineapple-juice stands, show windows with nuts arranged in circles and diamonds, radio shops blaring, shops jammed with clothing models draped in aching brown suits with green shirts, green ties, green-bordered handkerchiefs. The people on Broadway Eleanor lumped as "impossible"—hoarse newsboys, Hungarians and Sicilians and Polish Jews guffawing on corners, tight-mouthed men with gray derbies concealing their eyes, standing in snarling conferences, silk-stockinged girls laughing like grackles.

"Dreadful!" she observed.

They looked east to a skyscraper like a gigantic arm threatening the sky with the silver mace that was its tower.

"Our buildings are so big and pretentious! Nothing

kindly, nothing civilized about them. So—oh, so new!"
complained Eleanor.

"Um—yes," said Eliot.

At home, from their terrace, they looked across the
East River, then south and west to the wriggling electricity of Broadway, where tawdry signs, high on hotels, turned crimson and gold and aching white with
hysterical quickness. A searchlight wounded the star-
less dark. And the noises scratched her nerves. Once
she had felt that together they made a symphony; now
she distinguished and hated them. Tugboats brayed
and howled on the river. Trains on the three elevated
railways clanked like monstrous shaken chains, and
street cars bumped with infuriating dullness. A million
motors snarled, four million motor tires together
joined in a vast hissing, like torn silk, and through all
the uproar smashed the gong of an ambulance.

"Let's get out of it! Let's have a house in England!"
cried Eleanor. "Peace! Civilized society! Perfect servants! Old tradition! Let's go!"

In the offices of Messrs. Trottingham, Strusby and
Beal, Estate Agents, London, Eliot and Eleanor, once
they had convinced a severe lady reception clerk that,
though they were Americans, they really did want to
lease a house, were shown a portfolio of houses with
such ivy-dripping Tudor walls, such rose gardens, such
sunny slopes of lawn between oaks ancient as Robin
Hood, that they wriggled like children in a candy shop.
They had been well trained by reading fiction and the
comic papers; they knew enough not to laugh when
they read "16 bd., 2 bthrms., usual offices, choice fern-
ery, stbling., 12, garge., 1 car." So they were taken
into favor, and young Mr. Claude Beal himself drove
them down to Tiberius Hall, in Sussex.

"The Hall," he said, "belongs to Sir Horace and
Lady Mingo. You will remember that Sir Horace was
formerly solicitor-general."

"Oh, yes," said Eliot.

"Quite," said Eleanor.

"Sir Horace wishes to rent only because his health is not good. He is no longer a young man. He requires a hotter climate. He is thinking of Italy. Naturally Lady Mingo and he hate to leave so charming a place, you will understand."

"I see," said Eliot.

"Hush," said Eleanor.

"But if they find really reliable tenants, they might— you see? But you understand that I'm not trying to do a bit of selling, as you Yankees say."

"I see. Yes," said Eliot.

They passed through the gateway of Tiberius Hall— the stone gateposts were worn by three centuries—and saw the gatekeeper's lodge. On the shoulder of the stone chimney were gargoyles that had looked on the passing Queen Elizabeth, and before the latticed windows, with crocus-yellow curtains, were boxes of red geraniums.

Laburnums edged the quarter mile of driveway and shut off most of the estate, but they saw a glade with deer feeding in a mistiness of tender sunlight. "Not," mused Eleanor, "like our dreadful, glaring, raw sunlight at home." They came suddenly on the Hall. It was of Tudor, pure, the stone mellow. The chimneys were fantastically twisted; the red-tiled roof was soft with mosses; the tall windows of the ground floor gave on a terrace of ancient flagging. But what grasped at her, caressed her, more than the house itself was the lawn at one side where, under the shadow of oaks, half a dozen people sat in basket chairs at tea, attended by a butler whose cheeks were venerable pouches of respectability, and by a maid fresh as a mint drop in her cap and apron.

"We're going to take it," Eleanor whispered.

"We certainly are!"

"Here, we'll really live!"

"Yes! Tea, with servants like that! Polo and golf with gentlemen, not with money grubbers! Neighbors who've actually read a book! Nell, we've come home!"

*   *   *

"This country," said Sir Horace Mingo, "has gone utterly to the dogs."

"It has indeed," said Lady Mingo. "No competent servants since the war. Not one. The wages they demand, and their incredible stupidity—impossible to find a cook who can do a gooseberry trifle properly—and their impertinence! Did I tell you how pertly Bindger answered me when I spoke to her about staying out till ten?"

"You did, beloved. *In extenso,* if you will permit me to say so, I agree with you. My man—and to think of paying him twenty-two bob a week; when I was a youngster the fellow would have been delighted to have ten—he cannot press trousers so that they won't resemble bags. 'Higgs,' I often say to him, 'I don't quite understand why it is that when you have given your loving attention to my trousers they always resemble bags'; and as to his awakening me when I tell him to, he never fails to be either five minutes late or, what is essentially more annoying, ten minutes early, or when your confounded Bindger brings my tea in the morning it is invariably cold, and if I speak to her about it she merely sniffs and tosses her head and—but——"

While Sir Horace is catching his breath it must be interjected that this conversation of the Mingos, before the James II fireplace at Tiberius Hall, had been patriotically enjoyed three months before Eliot and Eleanor Hopkins, on their penthouse terrace, had decided to flee from the land of electricity and clamor.

"But," rumbled Sir Horace, in that port-and-Stilton voice which had made him the pursuing fiend to the sinful when he had been solicitor-general, "the fact that in the entire length and breadth of England today, and I dare say Scotland as well, it is utterly impossible, at any absurd wage, to find a servant who is not lazy, ignorant, dirty, thieving—and many of them dare to be impertinent, even to me!—this indisputable decay in English service is no more alarming than the fact that in our own class, good manners, sound learning and simple decency appear to have vanished. Young men up at Oxford who waste their time on Socialism and chemistry—chemistry! for a gentleman!—instead of acquiring a respectable knowledge of the classics! Young women who smoke, curse, go about exhibiting their backs——"

"Horace!"

"Well, they do! I'm scarcely to blame, am I? Have I ever gone about exhibiting my back? Have I caused whole restaurants to be shocked by the spectacle of my back? And that is not all. Everywhere! The pictures instead of Shakespeare! Motors making our lanes a horror and a slaughter! Shops that have electric lights and enormous windows and everything save honest wares and shop attendants with respectful manners! Shopkeepers setting themselves up to be better and certainly richer than the best county families! In fact, the whole blasted country becoming Americanized. . . . And cocktails! Cocktails! My word, if anybody had ever offered my old father a cocktail, I should think he would have knocked him down!

"England has always had a bad climate. But there was a day when the manners of the gentry and the charms of domestic life made up for it. But now I can see no reason why we should remain here. Why can't we go to Italy? That fellow Mussolini, he may not be English, but he has taught the masses discipline. You don't find impertinent servants and obscene gentlewomen there, I'll wager!"

"Yes. Why don't we go, Horace?"

"How can we? With this expensive place on our hands? If I were some petrol johnny, or a City bloke, or someone who had made his money selling spurious remedies, we might be able to afford it. But having been merely a servant of His Majesty all my life, merely devoting such legal knowledge and discernment as I might chance to have to the cause of Justice and——"

"But we might rent the place, Horace. Oh! Think of a jolly little villa at San Remo or on Lake Maggiore, with the lovely sunshine and mountains and those too sweet Italian servants who retain some sense of the dignity and joy of service!"

"Rent it to whom—whom? Our class are all impoverished."

"But there's the Argentines and Americans and Armenians. You know. All those curious A races where everyone is a millionaire. How they would appreciate a place with lawns! I'm told there isn't a single pretty lawn in America. How could there be? They would be so glad——"

"Though I couldn't imagine any American being trusted with our Lord Penzance sweetbriers!"

"But, Horace, a sweet little peasant villa at Baveno; just ten or twelve rooms."

"Well—— After all, Victoria, why should people of some breeding, as I flatter myself we do possess, be shut up in this shocking country, when we might be in the sun of Italy—and Doctor Immens-Bourne says it would be so much better for my rheumatism. Shall we speak to an estate agent? If there are any honest and mannerly estate johnnys left in this atrocious country!"

On the terrace of crumbling pink and yellow tiles, sufficiently shaded by the little orange trees in pots, Sir Horace and Lady Mingo sat looking across Lake Maggiore to the bulk of Sasso del Ferro, along whose mountain trails perched stone villages. A small steamer swaggered up the lake; after its puffing there was no sound save goat bells and a clattering cart.

"Oh, the peace of it! Oh, the wise old peace of Italy!" sighed Lady Mingo, and the wrinkles in her vellumlike cheeks seemed smoother, her pale old eyes less weary.

"Yes!" said Sir Horace. He was not so pontifical as he had been at Tiberius Hall. "Peace. No jazz! No noisy English servants yelping music-hall songs and banging things about!"

From the kitchen, a floor below the terrace, a sound

of the cook banging his copper pots, and a maid yelping a few bars of *Traviata*.

"Yes! The sweet Italian servants! So gay and yet so polite! Smiling! And the lovely sun all day! Why we ever stayed—— Oh, Horace, I do hope I shan't be punished for saying such things. Of course England is the greatest country in the world, and when I think of people like my father and the dean, of course no other country could ever produce great gentlemen like them, but at the same time, I really don't care if we never leave Italy again! And those sweet ruins at Fiesole! And the trains always quite absolutely on time since Mussolini came! And—— Oh, Horace, it's really quite too simply perfect!"

"Rather! Quite! You know, I'd thought I should worry about Tiberius Hall. But that's a very decent chap—that Hoffman Eliot—Hopkins—Eliot Hopkins—what is the chap's absurd name?—quite gentlemanly, for an American. I was astonished. None of these strange clothes Americans wear. I really quite took him for an English gentleman, until he opened his mouth. Astonishing! He hadn't a red sweater or a great, huge felt hat or a velvet dinner jacket, or any of these odd things that Americans ordinarily wear. And now we must dress, my dear. Professor Pulciano will be here at half after seven. So decent of him to rent us this—this paradise!"

He was youngish and rather rich, but Carlo Pulciano had not remained in the Italian army after the war, though his brother was commanding general of one of the departments, nor would he listen to his sister-in-law's insistence that he blossom in the salons of Rome.

He had previously scandalized them by teaching economics in the University of Pisa, by sitting over buckram-bound books full of tedious figures, and when the Black Shirts had marched on Rome and taken over the country, when it was not wise to speculate too much about economics, Pulciano had the more offended his people by buying this largish villa on the Pallanza peninsula at Lake Maggiore and retiring to his books and bees.

But in that still paradise he became restless and a little confused. All through the morning he would, in discussions none the less mad because they were entirely within his head, be completely pro-Fascist, admiring the Fascist discipline, the ideal of planned industry, the rousing of youngsters from sun loafing into drilling. Then, all afternoon, he would be Communistic or Social Democratic.

But whatever he was, here he was forever nothing. He had no one with whom to talk. It was not safe. And to Carl Pulciano talking was life; talking late at night, feverishly, over cigarettes and Lacrima Cristi; talking on dusty walks; talking through elegant dinners so ardently that he did not notice whether he was eating veal stew or *zabaglione*. Forever talking!

He would not have minded turning Fascist complete, provided he might have lived in a place where everyone hated Fascismo, so that furiously, all night, he might have defended it. He admitted, with one of the few grins this earnest young man ever put on, that he didn't so much want any particular social system as the freedom to discuss, in any way, at any time, over any kind of liquor, all social systems.

He longed for Germany, where he had studied economics as a young man. Germany! There was the land where he could talk unendingly! There was the land where, though the *Politzei* might harry you off the grass, you could say precisely what you thought or, greater luxury yet, say what you didn't think at all, just for the pleasure of it.

Pulciano cursed the fact that he had sunk most of his money in this villa and could not afford to go live in Germany. He had loved Italy; for it he had been wounded on the Piave. He had loved this villa and the peace of its blue lake waters. He had come to hate them both.

He hated the servants—so ready to promise everything and so unlikely to do anything; so smiling of the

eye and so angry in their hearts. He hated the climate.
"It would be in Italy that we have the chilliest and
wettest winters in Christendom, yet the mush-headed
people insist it's always sunny and will not put in even
fireplaces." He hated the food. "I'd give all the confounded pastes and fruits in the world for a decent
Mass of dark beer and a pig's knuckle at Munich!"
He hated funeral processions, policemen with cocks'
plumes on their hats, plaster shrines, the silly wicker
on wine bottles, wax matches that burned his fingers,
and even—so far was he gone in treason against
Italy—cigars with straws in them. But he did nothing
about it. He was too busy hating to do much of
anything.

He was delighted when the manager of the Grand
Hotel d'Isola Bella came inquiring whether he might
not care to lease his villa to a crazy English nobleman
named Sir Mingo. Yes, for a year.

A week later, with many bundles and straw suitcases, Carlo Pulciano was on the train for Berlin and
free talk, free thinking—long free thoughts over long
cheap beers.

The doctrine of most American and British carica-
turists, and all French ones, is that every German is
fat, tow-headed, and given to vast beers, while every
German woman is still fatter, and clad invariably in a
chip hat and the chintz covering for a wing chair.

Baron Helmuth von Mittenbach, Silesian Junker
and passionate mechanical engineer, had ruddy hair
and blue eyes filled with light. He was slender, and
looked rather more English than the Prince of Wales.
The Baroness, Hilda, was slim as an icicle and as
smooth, and she liked dancing in the night clubs off
the Kurfürstendamm, in Berlin, till four of the morning. Neither of them liked beer, nor had ever drunk
it since school days.

During the war, which ended when he was thirty,
Helmuth had tried to join the flying circus of his friend
Von Richthofen. He would have enjoyed swooping,

possibly even being swooped upon. But he was too good a designer, and headquarters kept him improving the tank, and the one time when he sneaked off to try out his own tank at the front, they strafed him so that he stayed back of the line after that, fuming in a room verminous with steel shavings.

He was, therefore, more excited after the war than during it. Now he could take a real part! Now engineers were to be not assistants and yes men, like quartermasters or photographers or royal princes, but the real lords, shaping a new Germany.

He believed that the struggle to rebuild German glory would be a crusade holy and united. Now that the republic had come, with so little blood spilling, the political parties would join; the politicians would give up that ultimate selfishness of insisting on the superiority of their own ideals.

He was certain that the salvation of Germany was in industrial efficiency. They hadn't the man power and raw stuffs of America or Russia, nor the army of France, nor the ships and empire of Great Britain. They must make things more swiftly, better and more economically than any other land. They must no longer grudgingly adopt machinery when they had to admit that a machine could do the work of a hundred men, but take machinery as a religion.

Helmuth took it so. It is definitely not true that Helmuth and the youngish men who worked with him in those driving days thought mostly, or even much at all, about the profits they and their bosses might make out of machinery and rationalization. It was not true that they saw machinery as the oppressor of ordinary men. Rather, they saw it as the extension of man's force and dignity.

Here you had an ordinary human, with an ordinary, clumsy fist. Put a lever or an electric switch into it, and it had the power of a thousand elephants. Man that walked wearily, swam like a puppy, and flew not at all, man that had been weakest and most despicable of all the major mammals, was with motor and subma-

rine and plane, with dynamo and linotype, suddenly
to be not mammal at all but like the angels. So
dreamed Baron Mittenbach, while he grunted and
hunched his shoulders over his drawing board, while
in the best parade-ground manner he called a careless
foreman an accursed-swine-hound-thunder-weather-
once-again-for-the-sake-of-Heaven.

He had gone as chief engineer to the great
A.A.G.—the so-called Universal Automobile Trust.
His hobbies were light, cheap tractors for small farms,
and light, cheap cars. He planned sedans which would
sell, when exchange was normal again, for what, in
American, would be a hundred and fifty dollars. By
night, at home, he planned other devices, some idiotic,
some blandly practical—eighteen-thousand-ton liners
to leave out the swimming pools and marble pillars
streaked like oxtail soup and to cross the Atlantic in
three days; floating aviation fields, a string of fifteen
of them across the ocean, so that a fallen plane would
never be more than an hour from rescue; a parachute
to ease down an entire plane, should the motor die or
a wing drop off. Crazy as any other poet, and as excited. But happier.

He had reason at first for his excitement and his
happiness. Though the Germans gabbled of every
known political scheme, from union with Russia to
union with England, they jumped into the deification
of modern industry, as schoolboys into a summer lake.
They worked ten hours a day, twelve, fourteen, not
wearily but with a zest in believing that their sweat
was cementing a greater Germany. They ruthlessly
stripped factories and at whatever cost put in rows of
chemical retorts a quarter mile long, conveyor belts,
automatic oil furnaces, high-speed steel.

Helmuth was fortunate in being able to have a
decent and restful house not too far from his factory,
for though he drove at a speed which caused the police to look pained, he could not, he told himself, take
all morning getting to work. There were too many
exciting things to do. The factory was in the Spandau

district of Berlin, and reasonably near, among the placid villas and linden rows of Grunewald, Hilda and Helmuth took a brick-and-stucco house with a mosaic eagle shining over the tile balcony.

The attic floor had been a private gaming room. Snorting at these signs of idleness and pride, Helmuth stripped out the card tables, roulette wheel, billiard table, dumped them in the basement, and set up a lathe, a work-bench, a drawing board, an electric furnace.

Here all evening, while Hilda restlessly studied Russian or yawned over cross-word puzzles, this grandson of a field marshal, in a workman's jumper and atrocious felt slippers, experimented with aluminum alloys or drew plans of a monorail which would do the six hundred and sixty miles from Berlin to Paris in six hours, with carriages like drawing-rooms, glass walled, twenty feet wide.

It was a good time—for a year. The destruction of the currency did not worry Helmuth; he was convinced that man should be saved by gasoline alone. But after two years, or three, he roused from his dream to see that the German recovery was not altogether a pure, naïve crusade; that the politicians would not forget their petty little differences. There were not two or three parties, as in Britain and America, but eight, ten, a dozen; and these parties clamorously advocated almost everything save total immersion. They advocated the return of the Kaiser, or immediate Communism; they advocated a cautious state Socialism, or wider power for the industrialists; they advocated combining with Austria, or the independence of Bavaria.

Outside the political parties, there were some thousands of noisy and highly admired prophets who had no interest in Helmuth's turret lathes and r.p.m.'s, but who shouted in little halls and little blurry magazines that the world was to be saved by vegetarianism, or going naked, or abolishing armies, or integrating spoken plays with the movie film, or growing carrots instead of wheat, or colonizing Brazil, or attending spiritualist seances, or mountain climbing, or speaking Esperanto.

In his worship of clean, driving, unsentimental steel, Helmuth despised equally all cult mongers and all politicians, however famous. They talked; they chewed over old straw; they pushed themselves into personal notoriety. He didn't, just now, care a hang whether he lived under a democracy or a monarchy or a Soviet, so long as they would let him make more tractors.

The more eloquent the politicians were, in their bright oratory in the Reichstag or the jolly conferences at Lausanne and Geneva, the more he hated them. His gods were Duisberg and Citroen and Ford and Edison and the Wright brothers, and since most of the pantheon were Americans, he came to worship that country as his Olympus.

The German politicians talked—all the Germans talked, he snarled. They were so proud of having mental freedom. Yes, snorted Helmuth, and the Irish were so proud of having fairies! Freedom for what—for escape from discipline into loquacious idleness, or for the zest of hard work? He hated peculiarly—doubtless unjustly—the intellectuals whom he had known in the university, who gabbled that there was something inescapably evil about machines; that because the transition from handicrafts to machinery had certainly produced unemployment, this unemployment must always continue; who whimpered that we must all go back to the country and live perfectly simple old-fashioned lives—with, however, telephones and open plumbing and typewriters and automobiles and electric lights and quick mail and newspapers.

"Yah! My picture of those gentry," Helmuth grumbled to Hilda, "is that they sit in machine-made modernistic metal chairs, telephoning to one another that they want us to stop manufacturing telephones and just beautifully write them! Good night. Tomorrow I must be up early and write a carburetor and sculp a grease gun."

Thus irritated, he looked daily more toward

America. There, he believed, everybody was united in
the one common purpose of solving economic injus-
tices, not by turning every capitalist into a starved pro-
letarian but by making all competent proletarians into
capitalists. The more he read American magazines and
yearned for American vitality and ingenuity, the more
he grumbled about Germany. And his Hilda, who was
most of the time happily ignorant of everything he
was saying, here joined him.

In America, she had heard, there was no need of
servants, because everything was done, and perfectly,
by machinery. And she was so sick, she confided, of
German servants since the war. What had got into
them? Regular Communists! They no longer had respect for the better classes, and the government was
supporting them in their demands. What with compul-
sory insurance and the law that you couldn't, without
notice, kick out even the most impertinent maid, there
was no running a house. She longed for electric dish-
washers and washing machines, but their landlord was
old-fashioned; he would not put them in.

America!

Just when Helmuth and Hilda were keenest about
it, he met McPherson Jones, of the Engel & Jones
High Speed Tractor Company of Long Island City,
who was scouting about Europe looking for new effi-
ciencies. Helmuth spoke a photographic English.
Jones and he went to Essen, to the Ruhr, and argued
about beer and about torque in aviation. Jones offered
him a place high on the staff of Engel & Jones, with
a breath-taking salary; and a month later Helmuth and
Hilda were on the high seas—to the miserable Hilda
it was evident why they were called high.

Helmuth had sublet his house to an Italian, a Prof.
Carlo Pulciano, who was going to study something or
other at the university. Helmuth did not leave Berlin
till a fortnight after he had turned the house over to
Pulciano. He called to say good-by, and Pulciano
proudly showed him the changes he had made. On
the top floor Helmuth did a little youthful suffering.

Pulciano had ripped out the lathe, the work-bench, the drawing board, and fitted up the room in imitation of an old Bavarian inn, with heavy wooden tables, stone beer mugs, a barrel of beer, and painted mottoes announcing that men who gave earnest attention to anything save drinking, kissing, singing and snoring were invariably jackasses.

"I tell you," cried Pulciano, "here I shall have again the good free talk of my German student days! I am in your Germany so happy! You Germans realize that the purpose of life is not just doing, but thinking, and setting thoughts in jeweled words—and again I get decent red cabbage!"

"*Ja?*" said Helmuth. It can sound extraordinarily like "Yeah?"

He groaned to himself, "Just the old, thick-necked, beer-steaming Germany we have been trying to kill! I want a race stark and lean and clear and cold bathed and unafraid of the song of flywheels!"

With Hilda seasick, Helmuth found solace in the smoking room of the steamer. By the end of three days he knew a dozen Americans—a banker, the superintendent of a steel plant, two automobile-foreign-sales men, a doctor who had been studying gross pathology in Vienna.

He expected them to resent his coming to America in rivalry with their earnings; he expected them to smile at his English. But they welcomed him to the tournament. "Come on! If you can get anything away from us in America, it just makes the game better," they said; and: "Your English? Listen, baron. The only trouble with you is, you went to a school where they let the teams weaken themselves by looking at books between the halves. By the way, will you happen to be in Detroit, time of the Michigan-Notre Dame game? Wish you'd come stay with us and I'll drive you down. Like to have you meet the wife and show her up—she thinks she can parley Deutsch."

"They are," Helmuth glowed to Hilda, "the kindest

and politest people I have ever known. But just the same, *ich sage Dir bestimmt,* that Mr. Tolson is all wrong about the front-wheel drive. . . . I wonder about the market for speed boats in Norway?"

He had accepted invitations to Bar Harbor, Seattle, Moose Jaw, Gramercy Square, Franconia Notch, and Social Circle, Georgia, before he saw the skyscrapers from New York Harbor.

"They are my friends! I have never had so many friends—not in my life!" he rejoiced, and with a feeling that the towers of New York were his own, he pointed them out to a slightly shaky Hilda beside him.

"They are very pretty. They are not all worn, like cathedral spires," he said. "I wonder what the wind pressure per square meter is with a sixty-kilometer wind? I wonder if electric welding costs more than riveting? I wonder whether the marble here comes from Italy or Vermont? Yes, it is exciting; I am very thrilled. . . . I wonder what is the tensile strength of the steel in these buildings?"

But his friend, Doctor Moore, the Omaha surgeon, could not answer any of these obvious questions, though he was a real American.

A week after their arrival, Baron and Baroness Mittenbach leased a penthouse atop the apartment house at 9999 Park Avenue. It belonged to some people named Hopkins, now living in the South of England.

They took possession on an autumn afternoon. Hilda raced through the great living room ecstatically. "I say to you, Helmuth, so a beautiful room have I never seen! Stone walls! And the rafters! Windows like a cathedral! And the organ, quite gold! It is no larger than the great Hall in my father's *Schloss,* but so much more wonderful. Always I hated those tattered tapestries and the moldy stag horns! But this room is indeed something noble!"

Squealing, with Helmuth beside her and not much less childish, she explored the wonders of the kitchen and butler's pantry—electric dishwasher and coffee urn and toaster and vacuum cleaner and clock and egg cooker. She couldn't quite make out the electric waffle iron; she wasn't sure whether it was for cooking or pleating. But on the automatic refrigerator they both fell with shouts. This was a possession they had envied their richer friends in Berlin. They cautiously pulled out an ice tray and gazed with fatuous admiration on the beautiful cubes of ice.

"Much better than diamonds," said Helmuth.

Refrigerator, gas stove, small electric range, luxurious enameled sink and kitchen cabinet were all finished in white and canary yellow; the kitchen was gayer than any boudoir.

"Already I am a—how is it called?—hunnerd-procent American," observed Helmuth in what he believed to be English. "The old system, it was to make beautiful the salon and the chapel, and make hateful the kitchen, the heart of the house. Yes, I am a modern! We do something, we engineers. We do not believe that the more a room is used, the less *gemütlich* it should be. Modern, yes, and very old. We go back to medieval days, when men were not ashamed to eat and love, and when kitchens were more important than reception rooms, and when——"

"Here," said Hilda, "I would be happy if we had no servants at all, and I did all the work. I shall cook the dinner—tomorrow. Tonight let us find that lovely spikizzy—is right?—of which the doctor has spoken on the steamer."

When, on the wine list of the Chez Edouard, they found an Oppenheimer Kreuz Spätlese, they asked each other why anyone should go to Europe. Their only trouble was that the waiter was a bit slow. But they understood, for he was much engaged with a jolly group of six men at the next table.

One of the six noticed the plight of the Von Mittenbachs and, coming to their table, said, "Sorry we're grabbing off so much of the waiter's time. Afraid we're holding up your dinner. So, meanwhile—if you'll excuse the liberty—won't you folks come have a drink with us?"

"That would be very nice," said Helmuth.

He was, after all, a shy young man, and he was grateful for the way in which these strangers took him in. They were all, it seemed, in motor manufacturing. When they learned that he had just come from Germany to join them, instantly a card was out of every pocket, an address was scribbled, and each had insisted that when he went to South Bend, or Toledo, or Detroit, he must dine with them—"and I hope the missus will be along with you."

In a glow that burned out of him all the loneliness he had felt that afternoon in the cold shadow of the monstrous skyscrapers, Helmuth returned with Hilda to their table and dinner.

"So kind to a foreigner, a poor unknown engineer," said Helmuth. "No wonder no American ever wants to go abroad for more than a visit of a month!"

From the terrace before their penthouse they stared across the East River, then south and west to the wriggling electricity of Broadway. They were thirty stories up; they seemed to be looking on the whole world, but a world transformed into exultant light.

"It is as though we were in a castle on a huge sheer cliff, a castle on the Matterhorn himself, and yet in the midst of Berlin and London and Paris joined into one," said Helmuth. "This is perhaps—not true, Hilda?—the greatest spectacle of the world! Why speak they of the Acropolis, the Colosseum, the Rhineland, when they have this magic?"

Tugboats shouted cheerily on the East River; liners roared gallantly from the North River; the elevated trains, streaks of golden light, chanted on their three tracks; and the million motor horns spoke of the beautiful and exciting places to which the cars were going.

"And it's ours now! We've found our home! We shall know all this city, all those people in the lovely motors down there! I think we stay here the rest of our lives!" said Helmuth.

Hilda pondered, "Yes, except—except neither Germany nor America has any mystery. I want us some day to go to China, Japan. There it gives mystery. And I hear the servants are divine, and so cheap. Don't you think we might go live in China—soon?''

Selected Bibliography

Works by Sinclair Lewis

Hike and the Aeroplane (1912, writing
  as Tom Graham)
Our Mr. Wrenn (1914)
The Trail of the Hawk (1915)
The Job (1917)
The Innocents (1917)
Free Air (1919)
Main Street (1920)
Babbitt (1922)
Arrowsmith (1925)
Mantrap (1926)
Elmer Gantry (1927)
The Man Who Knew Coolidge (1928)
Dodsworth (1929)
Ann Vickers (1933)
Work of Art (1934)
It Can't Happen Here (1935)
The Prodigal Parents (1938)
Bethel Merriday (1940)
Gideon Planish (1943)
Cass Timberlane (1945)
Kingsblood Royal (1947)
The God-Seeker (1949)
World So Wide (1951, posthumously)

Biography and Criticism

Anderson, Carl L. *The Swedish Acceptance of American Literature*. Philadelphia: University of Pennsylvania Press, 1957.

Bucco, Martin, ed. *Critical Essays on Sinclair Lewis*. Boston: G. K. Hall, 1986.

Dupree, Ellen. " 'Snoway talkcher father': Nativism and the Modern Family in *Babbitt*." *Midwestern Miscellany* 28 (2000): pp. 41–49.

Eby, Clare Virgina " 'Extremely Married': Marriage as Experience and Institution in *The Job, Main Street*, and *Babbitt*." *Sinclair Lewis: New Essays in Criticism*. Ed. James M. Hutchisson. Troy, NY: Whitston, 1997, pp. 38–51.

Forseth, Roger. "Sinclair Lewis, Drink, and the Literary Imagination." *Sinclair Lewis at 100: Papers Presented at a Centennial Conference*. Ed. Michael Connaughton. St. Cloud, MN: St. Cloud State University, 1985, pp. 11–26.

Gross, Barry. " 'Yours Sincerely, Sinclair Levy': Lewis and the Jews." *Sinclair Lewis at 100: Papers Presented at a Centennial Conference*. Ed. Michael Connaughton. St. Cloud, MN: St. Cloud State University, 1985, pp. 1–9.

Hapke, Laura. *Tales of the Working Girl: Wage-Earning Women in American Literature, 1890–1925*. Boston: Twayne-Macmillan, 1992.

Hutchisson, James M. *The Rise of Sinclair Lewis, 1920–1930*. University Park: Pennsylvania State University Press, 1996.

Karfeldt, Erik Axel. "Why Sinclair Lewis Got the Nobel Prize." *Why Sinclair Lewis Got the Nobel Prize and Address by Sinclair Lewis Before the Swedish Academy*. Trans. Naboth Hedin. New York: Harcourt

Brace, 1930. Rpt. in *Twentieth Century Interpretations of* Arrowsmith: *A Collection of Critical Essays*. Ed. Robert J. Griffin. Englewood Cliffs, NJ: Prentice-Hall, 1968, pp. 77–82.

Lingeman, Richard. *Sinclair Lewis: Rebel from Main Street*. New York: Random House, 2002.

Love, Glen A. Babbitt: *An American Life*. New York: Twayne, 1993.

Moodie, Clara Lee R. "The Book That Has Never Been Published." *Sinclair Lewis at 100: Papers Presented at a Centennial Conference*. Ed. Michael Connaughton. St. Cloud, MN: St. Cloud State University, 1985, pp. 201–12.

Parry, Sally E. "The Changing Fictional Faces of Sinclair Lewis' Wives." *Studies in American Fiction* 17.1 (1989): pp. 65–79.

Schorer, Mark. *Sinclair Lewis: An American Life*. New York: McGraw-Hill, 1961.

Updike, John. "Exile on Main Street." *New Yorker* (17 May 1993): pp. 91–97.

Vidal, Gore. "The Romance of Sinclair Lewis." *New York Review of Books* 39 (8 October 1992): pp. 14, 16–20.

Watts, Emily Stipes. *The Businessman in American Literature*. Athens: University of Georgia Press, 1982.

READ THE TOP 25 SIGNET CLASSICS

WWW.SIGNETCLASSICS.COM